# RIP TIDE

# RIP TIDE

SARAH WHITNEY

Rip Tide
by Sarah Whitney

Copyright 2026 by Sarah Whitney

This book is a work of fiction. Names, characters, businesses, organizations, places and events and incidents are either the product of the author's imagination or are used fictitiously. Any resemblance to actual persons, living or dead, events, or locales is entirely coincidental.

Contact info:
riptidenovel@gmail.com

Cover and Interior Design By: Ashley Santoro
Front, Back, and Interior Photos: Sarah Whitney
Front and Back Cloud Photos: Stock Photos
Shell Art: Sarah Whitney

Genre: Romantasy

Library of Congress Catalog Card Number

ISBN:
979-8-9935461-0-0 (Hardcover)
979-8-9935461-1-7 (Paperback)
979-8-9935461-2-4 (Ebook)
979-8-9935461-3-1 (B&N Paperback)
979-8-9935461-4-8 (B&N Hardcover)

Do everything with so much love in your heart
that you could not bear to do it any other way.


-Yogi Desai

To the Ocean...


… and to David and Amelia, for being my everything <3

# THE WHALE'S ORACLE:

Neglect, Poison, Pilfer, Waste, Refuse, Acid, Heat:
Seven cuts by Brother,
Blind, with no memory of kin.
Relinquished symbiosis with Earth,
He has forgotten his indebtedness.
His destruction spreads to the mother of life, the Ocean,
All life wasted.

One Hope remains.
Fates intertwined, and pulled by one.
The Merikoi, Land Brother, and the Goddess of the Sea.
If she dies a Sister, she will be forever gone.
If heart memory is rekindled, unity forged, guise shattered:
Power resurrected-
Hope reigns.
Beware a lover's vigil, a play at Fate's perilous game, a careful line:
Consummation before love, or recognition before consummation
decimates Hope, power forever lost.
Can you help her find her way back to love?

# CHAPTER 1

28 YEARS AGO

POI

My ears pop as the shadows turn inside out. I'm shown a dark cove filled with centuries of human trash. Shipwrecks, bent bicycles, lost lobster traps, glass bottles, plastic caps, and rusted engine parts. Whales float belly up, red stains trailing. Amidst the gore, I see Thalassa's heart-shaped face, distorted with pain. Darkness compounds again, and I return to my body.

My heart collapses around blood. Fingers fumbling, I fasten my spear against my back. Before me, a cloud of jellyfish float upwards through the black seas, light circuiting like the filaments of early lightbulbs. Levi launches his spear, cutting through three flickering forms which bulge together. The jellyfish corral becomes a staccato of light as the hunting troupe descends.

Where was that? Thalassa told me she was going to the corals. We hide nothing from one another. Why would she be somewhere else? I whistle through the water to signify it's time to head out.

Levi whips his head around, confusion scrunched onto his tan face. "What? We just got here!"

His jellyfish wilt into darkness. The hunting troupe of twenty draws around me. Treading water with shadowy tails, their reflective eyes dart around as if trying to spot an oncoming threat. Their spears hold only a couple of gelatinous masses-nowhere near what we came here for. Jellyfish are what sustain us in these dying seas. The hunters should stay.

"I'm leaving for the Ridge." I call out as I cut through darkness towards the fortress. The water gets heavier as I speed up, like pushing through a wall. I'll need someone to tell me exactly where she went. It's so strange that I don't know, and it makes me more uneasy.

Leagues of darkness leave room for my mind to consider the worst. I hold out hope that Thalassa's pain was only pain. Maybe pain from emotional loss and not from any physical injury. How could she be caught up in a mass whale killing? She couldn't have made it to Japan's waters since this morning. And the old shipwrecks were European, not Asian. The trash looked American. A good thing. America's coastline is closest.

The moonlit outline of the Ridge's submerged peaks and hills rushes into view. Gracelessly throwing myself towards the seam between ocean and air-filled fortress, the entrance wobbles madly, and spills water across the black slate as I steady my feet.

I quickly yank my cloak off the wall, and wrap it around myself as I run down the narrow passageway, feet slapping loudly against rock. There's time. There has to be time.

I'll pass our bedroom on the way to the dining hall. There's a chance she's there. Torchlights erupt into life as I approach, blowing out as I pass. They're only alight for the snap of a finger. I pass our old door. There's no time to check.

As if in a vacuum, nameless weight crushes me from all sides, squeezing me forward. Tight black stone corridors blur past me. I skip steps up a winding staircase, hands out and propelling myself off the walls towards the dining hall.

Several groups of Mer are gathered around silver driftwood tables, playing cards and drinking wine. Laude sees me first. She stands. Her ghostly skin tone is nearly translucent over her tall, athletic frame. Her protuberant red eyes miss nothing. She reads my alarmed and frantic state. She strides two steps closer and lowers her voice, speaking with clipped urgency, "Poi. What's going—"

"Where's Thalassa?" I strain to keep the panic out of my voice.

Her platinum brows knit. "She went to the Red Fern Corals, I believe, but she should be back by now…"

"She's not there. Do you have any idea of where else she could be?" My words are rushed. There isn't time.

She's stiff. "Why? Why wouldn't she be at the corals?"

I bite back harsh demands. "Because I saw her somewhere else, I just don't know where yet. She's in danger. What do you know Laude?"

She glances down at the floor with a furrowed brow before looking back at me and staring hard. "She's gone to the Coast of Maine once or twice now."

I double take. "Why? And where, specifically?"

"I don't know where."

I don't miss her omission, and humans flash to my mind. Dread compounds. Humans always spell disaster. "What's she doing near humans?"

Laude's lips tighten, "I don't know. Possibly tracking the marine deaths."

"Why don't I know about this?" Hornets swarm in my chest, and a warped clock ticks at the back of my head. "I'm going to find her."

I pace out of the hall, and run all the way back towards the great entrance. I throw my cape unceremoniously at the wall, missing the peg. I launch myself through the barrier and into the icy grip of the ocean. I twist and shift into Mer, my long tail feeling the current like feathered wings in the wind.

"Poi…" My brother's voice is in my ears, calling to me from the black sea.

I swim towards his faint form. His sage irises glow like fireflies in the night, moonlight dabbles his ebony skin, and his tail glitters mutely in the gray waters. His regal features are contorted as if he has been stung by a ray.

His fingers find my shoulders and grip tightly. His eyes are deep as the ocean, puffy and red-rimmed, one eye squeezing more tightly than the other. His deep voice whispers, "She died."

Like an explosion, my heart beats once. All the parts of myself seem to shatter into dust. It can't be true. It just can't. I swing back and away from him, yanking out of his grasp, heart drenching in suffocating tar. I roar with madness, "Where is she? Just tell me where she is and I will fix this. She will be fine!"

His voice continues to be uncharacteristically gentle, "She won't— she's gone—"

I glower at him, repeating angrily, "Just tell me where she is!"

"Cuttle Cove—but she's not there anymore… Poi—the US Navy was doing a missiles test while she was in the harbor— she, and the humpbacks, died nearly immediately."

White hot anger sears through my veins. This can't be real. "WHAT? How do you know this!? Why were you there? Why are you not dead too?"

"I heard the blast from a hundred miles off, but I knew she was closer to shore—I wanted to check on her—when I went to investigate…" His face constricts with pain again, voice a moan, "I saw her being pulled into a boat…"

But I can't listen to his slow speech, I can't handle his grief. This isn't real. I shove him aside, swearing and yelling "STOP IT! SHE'S FINE—"

I shoot forward, tearing through the inky water. I can ask questions later.

"She died as a human." His voice is close, he's followed me, and I drop at his words, heart sinking like lead.

"No…" rasps from deep in my gut, and tears through my throat. Heat burns at my eyes. I turn to face my brother, gripping his shoulders fiercely. "You're lying! Tell me you're lying!"

He shakes his head, eyes filled with anguish, "I saw the lobstermen pull her bloody human body into their boat. She died there, Poi, she's not going to return to us. Her spirit is gone."

Rage rips through my every cell. How could he lie like this? I want to punch him, I want him to feel the pain. I shove him away from me. "You're a fucking liar. MOVE. I'm going to fix this."

His vise-like fingers grip my biceps from behind, stopping my forward motion, his voice is strained in my ear- pitching and growling as if he's crying. "Please, grip reality. The humans took her. She died a human. She's gone— forever."

Wildfire sears through my chest cavity, burning a black hole which sucks everything in faster than light. I ball my fists and twist out of his grip, roaring.

I torpedo myself into the blackness, pain ripping at every cell of my being as if the ocean is made of jagged fishing hooks. She's not dead. She's not.

Pain ripples through me as my brother's words ricochet and knot in my head. I shift into my fastest form, a swordfish. I spear through the water, one goal in mind. Find her.

I block out all other thought, all feeling. Find her.

I slow at the hazy forms of ghostly shipwrecks, the same as in the vision. The groans of a naval ship leaving the harbor grate at my flesh. I shift into Mer, and the sea is metallic with blood, and putrid with the stench of gore. Bloated whale carcasses float like aimless dirigibles in the receding tide. Their dark eyes blank, jutting jaws open and swallowing seawater. She is not among them. I comb the muddy bottom, strewn with human trash. No sign of her. Heart racing, I zig-zag again across the beer cans, gnarled plastic, and scrap metal- she's not here.

Chest threatening to implode, I swim around the shrinking seawater perimeter of the large cove, scanning land for her- my eyes darting between barnacled log-pillar docks, stacks of yellow lobster traps, wild rosebushes, and imposing restaurants stacked on granite squares. Nothing. I pull myself up into each moored lobstering boat, each luxury speed boat, nude, and not caring about the occasional flash of headlights into the harbor as they round the road beside the shops and restaurants. I search the unlocked tiny cabins and around weather-worn, rusted, and foam-oozing seats. In the last boat, farthest from the harbor, with the stench of dead whale guts and excrement clinging to my skin, I collapse into a white leather seat.

From deep in my gut, I unleash a hard, insane, howling scream. It does nothing to release the crippling pain. We just lost our eternity together. Gasping for air, I realize I never even though that was possible. My lungs can't pull in air, despite my heaving chest, but my mind jars me with reality like a hailstorm: She'll never reincarnate to Mer again. As a human, she'll lose her memory. How could I ever find her? She'll reincarnate once- maybe twice- and then she'll be gone forever- each realization shatters a part of my soul. Despite our millennia together, it still wasn't enough. I need her forever. I need her here- and she needs me- her soul is lost...

Darkness bites into my soul and rips me apart until I'm only a carcass. I yell into the whipping wind, ripping my hair in my fingertips, pulling at my skull, wishing for a different reality. Shaking overtakes my body. I puke over the side of the speedboat.

I sit on the rain-soaked carpeted floor. I shake, eyes hot and face wet. I rock, and unseeing, chant, "She's not gone. She'll be human. She's not gone—I will find her."

# CHAPTER 2

STELLA

The seal stares at me with the black eyes of a puppy. So strikingly familiar. I walk around her outdoor glass enclosure, filled with seawater and another full-grown seal. Their wild bodies are strewn with silver speckles, reminding me of dappled light through waves. Their rotund bodies bob for air. The nearest seal flares her nostrils like a dog snout as she kisses and smears the glass with white whiskers sprouting outwards like cactus spines.

Through the smudged plexiglass, I hold her gaze, wondering why I feel such a connection between us. I grew up on an island in Maine, surrounded by harbor seals, and have this freaky sense that they know some secret about me. Or maybe they just know a lot more than most people give them credit for.

Their enclosure is no larger than a walk-in closet. Dozens of people stream towards the main exhibits in the Aquarium of Boston. A few people have stopped to take photos, and stare smiling at the little seal captured on their screens before giddily speeding on.

I stare back at the puppy-eyed seal. She pleadingly holds my gaze rather than divulging any secrets. There's not a doubt in my mind that she knows exactly how trapped she is. She watches me as if she knows I'm the only human who might give them a hope, as if I might understand those eyes. And, undeniably, I do understand her. I feel trapped too.

It's been... everything. From the mind-numbing uselessness of my desk job, to things just being very weird with Jonas- my boyfriend of four years. When it all tallies up, I feel like I've been treading water, not making any real progress towards who I really am. I can't look at the size of the tank, without thinking about what my life is now. And just like the seals, I don't know how to get out towards open sea.

I inspect the tank. How do the trainers feed these creatures? Strolling around to the far side of the tank, I see a padlock on the black metal lid. Aha. I glance around. Young children excitedly pull parents towards the entrance. Couples stroll, and gaggles of loud teenagers meander, but no one seems to take notice of my shifty gaze. My palms are sweating. Suddenly, I fully realize where my mind is going. With every fiber of my being, I want to shatter this glass and release these seals.

I have never gotten more than a speeding ticket in all my 26 years of life. Sure, underage drinking happened, but this would technically be vandalism and burglary...

And who am I kidding? I'm 125 pounds, and although I'm athletically built, there's no way I could single-handedly smuggle a seal out of here. The idea of me hefting a slippery seal onto my back makes me smirk. Quickly, it sours into a grimace.

The delicate black snout of the seal is pressed up against the glass of the tiny enclosure, just above the water line, fogging the glass as she attempts to breathe. This simple act seems a struggle. My chest burns with anger- at the aquarium, and at myself for doing nothing. With an apologetic look towards the seal, I turn, and retrace my steps the mile back to the office.

Staring down at my desk, my legs are cranky at the prospect of sitting again. An encumbering sales goal report is waiting behind that black screen. I glance up at the glaring florescent lights, thinking this is really not what I wanted my life to amount to. The coworker behind our partition leans around and glances at me impatiently. Sighing quietly, I sit.

I feel shrunken and small in this swivelly chair. The screen of the black monitor reflects me like a ghost: sandy blonde hair darkened, freckles dulled, colorless green eyes peering over high cheekbones. I look tired. I am trying so hard to make life work. And still, this life just isn't me. My work clothes feel like a costume. I mean, I'm wearing a freaking pants suit...

As a kid, I lived with my face glued to novels by night, reading about magical worlds and adventures, and by day I was at the water, jumping over rocks and finding crabs and periwinkles. I always had a feeling that magic was real, that the world is more than what we see. But looking around, this is as far from magic as it gets. It's just- where else is there to go?

I console myself with the fact that at this job, I have plenty of time to surreptitiously research whatever I want online. Everybody does it. It's an open secret. As long as I get enough done each week, I fly under the radar.

Opening the browser, I tap in "Harbor Seal Range." Grinding my teeth, I read: "Harbor Seals travel about 30 miles for food and breeding, and have been recorded to dive 1600 feet deep into the water." My mind flashes to the closet-sized seal enclosure. My heart clenches. I'm not doing what I want here, but I have no idea of how to get out. Frustrated, avoiding my sales number report, I open a PowerPoint presentation, and start adjusting it for a team sales pitch.

Moments later, I re-open the browser. Google stares at me. I search "how to break aquarium glass." There are barely any results. YouTube, is far more successful. I watch sketchy videos of people throwing spark plug bits at car windows. The glass shatters.

Ringing phone lines, pattering keyboards, and terse conversations are the theme song to my quickly unravelling sanity. It would be crazy to actually try to break the seals out. I would just end up getting arrested and fined.

I google where to buy spark plugs. Embarrassed, I see auto shops crowd the results que. They're pretty cheap. I recognize one of the shops is just a block away from my apartment.

I shut the browser and return to the pitch.

Avoiding plastic waste, I refused the plastic bag at the auto shop. Spark plug in hand, I drop my keys on the counter and slip out of my spring windbreaker. The part is heavy in my palm, and looks like a combination between a bolt, a screw, and a…ceramic white thing? I am so unfamiliar with car parts that it's cliché.

Nervously, I open the white doors of our pantry and tip toe to reach our toolbox. J.G. is written in white sharpie along the black hammer shaft, Jonah's initials. I just want to see if I can break off the ceramic bits.

I walk through our living room and the marred, dingy coffee-colored walls painted and neglected by the landlord feel more oppressive than usual. The faux leather couches Jonas and I struggled to agree on are oriented in an awkward adjacent tilt, due to the strange positioning of the open-dining area and off-limits fireplace in which a tiny brown sparrow nested in over the winter. The wide black screen of the television dominates the room. Beside it, I slide open the patio door.

Laying the spark plug on the cement, I unceremoniously crack the hammer onto it, and it coheres by crumbling into sharp shards. Each little fleck of white taunts me from the mottled cement, asking me if I'll break in as many ways as it could. Will I save the seals at the expense of the normal life I've conformed to build?

I pinch the pieces between my thumb and forefinger, collecting, and the experiment is over. I really realize what I am thinking about. I pull out my phone and google the fine for theft in Massachusetts: $25,000. Maybe two years in prison. Yikes.

This idea would bankrupt me, take two years of my life, and ruin my resume… yet disturbingly, I am still gripped by the concept of freeing the puppy-eyed seals. I don't want to give up on them. They're intelligent creatures, and they're meant to be wild. They shouldn't be living in a shoebox. I must be going insane, because not releasing the seals is starting to be a more painful surrendering of who I am, than that of destroying my own material identity.

I think of Jonas. He would think I was absolutely bat-shit crazy for even considering saving the seals. If I got caught, or if he ever found out, I'm certain it would ruin our relationship. Maybe, instead, I can help the seals in a safer way. Like write a petition or organize a protest.

Sighing at the tiny shards, I cover my fingers over my palm, and prepare to dump them in the trash. The inside lights are on and the TV is already flashing as I open the screen door.

"What's with the hammer?" Jonas addresses me critically from the couch. He's lounging in his gym shorts and Nike shirt. His pale blonde hair is darkened with sweat, and the red blotchiness from his workout is fading from his fair skin. His sweaty socks are peeled off and discarded with a week's more of his sock garden, sewn beneath the coffee table.

I attempt to block the broken spark plug in my small hand as I walk quickly towards the kitchen trash bin. I call back at him, "Oh… just working on an art project…"

"With a spark plug?"

I jump with his voice in my ear and quickly brush the shards off my palm and into the bin. "Yeah, failed art project."

He squints his pale blue eyes at me, "You know, people use broken spark plugs to break windows…"

Damn. He is such an avid technology user, he's always on his phone, always looking things up, that he seems to know more random shit than is really healthy for anyone to know.

His face shifts to extreme concern, and his pale arms block the entry, "Why are you thinking about breaking windows? Stella, that's really weird…"

I'm cornered. I sigh, "I was just thinking about something, I wasn't actually going to do it…" But the words are hard to say.

He looks at me like I'm a drowned fish, his voice like a stern parent's, "What's wrong with you? Why are you thinking about breaking a window?"

Whatever. I throw caution to the wind. "I went to the aquarium today, and did you know, they have two harbor seals in a cage that is literally smaller than our closet? They need a thirty-mile range!!"

He shakes his head, assessing me with critical eyes, "Not this again. You know you shouldn't go there, it always just makes you upset."

I glare at him, he's just being controlling, saying I shouldn't go places because it might make me mad… maybe I should be mad. Maybe more people should get mad, and then we wouldn't have torture houses like aquariums.

I shrug, silent, wishing he hadn't caught me with the sparkplug experiment. He glances at the trash bin.

"So you were going to throw a spark plug at the aquarium glass, fail to actually break it, and get fined thousands of dollars and probably get arrested?"

I resist rolling my eyes and point to the trash bin instead.

He's not derailed. His baby blue eyes hold vehement judgement and scrutiny, and his voice is thick with disgust, "Stella, you're getting way too extreme. Your opinions are making you crazy."

His words cut me down. He wasn't always like this. He used to be intrigued by my wild ideas- or at least pretend to be… I guess. Either way, I glare at him, seething, but keep my voice level, "My opinions… are my mind. They make up who I am."

His eyes shift to the side, "Yeah… maybe we should sit down."

Nervously, I follow him to the couch, expecting a more in-depth lecture on my apparently skewed judgement. I sit next to him, but I don't try to rest my legs across his. Something feels very weird. My stomach starts to twist.

He looks hesitant, his voice uneasy. "Look, I want to break up."

"What?" Blurts from my mouth. My head is whirling. For the first time in my life, I might puke with fear. I never, ever expected to hear those words come out of his mouth. We have never talked about breaking up. I hold the blanket close to me, trying to steady my shaking.

"I'm sorry. It's just—" he begins, but I don't hear a word he's saying.

I run to the bathroom, and return with a racing heart. In a very bad way, my body feels like it might float.

"This just doesn't make sense." I try to stay composed. This is a conversation. Just talk him around. "You said you loved me forever."

He grimaces. "I thought I would."

I fall into a deep, deep well of emotion. The world crashes in on me and I'm sobbing uncontrollably. I have committed so much energy to loving this man for four years. I can't speak for shock.

He continues "I think I said I loved you too soon. Love can be more than this. I've just been… kind of going along with it for a few years… because it was easy."

Disbelieving, I try to listen for why it's not working, why he doesn't love me anymore.

"I just started to think, do I want to be in this relationship in ten years? In the future? And I realized I don't. We're just too different. We fight too much—"

"We don't fight too much." I interrupt, then shut my mouth, realizing I'm arguing. But really, I don't think of us as a couple that's constantly fighting… that can't be it.

He gives me a stern look, "You're just too opinionated."

I feel small.

"I just don't want this anymore." His face is full of regret. "I'm sorry."

My world is spinning, unravelling, gone. He's moved out, and I'm moving back home. Home is the only place that feels like a thread of myself worth holding. I feel an inexplicable itch to console myself by the ocean. When everything else fades away in my life- the death of my grandmother, and of my parents long ago- the ocean is the only thing that holds me together.

Numbly, I think of how maybe he and I were like those two seals, cramped together, not really able to breathe, expand, and be ourselves. I'm not sure if I'm just consoling myself or if it's true. Maybe I can't be loved for being me, if I'm not actually being me. So, I'm freeing myself. I quit my soul-sucking desk job. I'm going to figure out what being me means again.

The three-hour drive makes me think more than I want. The news radio has already repeated all its stories, and each song I hear grates at me, so silence is all I can take. Out of all the things Jonas told me, "too opinionated" rings in my mind. I grit my teeth. Too opinionated. My opinions are my mind... did he really go all this time without caring about what was really in my head? Four years of him just "putting up" with me? I look down and realize I'm going eighty. I ease my foot off the pedal. I try to just focus on the green highway signs and trees, not think about what's peeling away layers of my heart and making me feel sore.

Dresden, I've never noticed that town before, hmm.

As the town signs pass, a secret part of my heart knows, not everything was right. I have an urge to see the stars at night, to hike mountains, to breathe in fresh air. And he was perfectly happy watching endless TV each day. I breathe in, and allow myself to think these thoughts. I let myself wonder, what it would be like to find someone to have adventures with? Someone who likes my mind just as much as the rest of me? I told myself Jonas was as good as it gets. Maybe he wasn't.

As I cross the bridge onto Spear Island, I roll down the windows and drink in the briny ocean air. Winding through the narrow island roads, I feel a hug of familiarity. Home. The long island is littered with lobster traps, unseaworthy boats, and weathered buoys. I spot the weathered wooden panels of 38 Meadow Cove, settled into overgrowth, surrounded by with wildflowers and spindly spruce trees. Returning home is harder, without Jonah at my side. It was good to have company here.

Unlocking the heavy door, I open the dusty blinds, and head to the basement to turn on the water. I haven't been back for a few months. My grandmother's favorite books still line the bookshelves, untouched. She's been gone for five years now, but I have always wanted to have this home to come back to. It's my only semblance of family, aside from an aunt I don't really talk to.

My grandmother always kept a framed picture of my parents on the sideboard near our dining table. I sometimes glance at the photo, but aside from Grandma's stories, they're strangers to me. In the picture, they're both long-haired and happy, holding each other on the muddy grounds of a music festival. They had me when they were young, raging alcoholics who dabbled in the heroine which lead to their deaths. My grandmother raised me from when I was almost two, and I know I was a very lucky kid to have had her. She was the best example of a human this earth can make.

After heaving my bags up to my second-floor room, I look out the darkened window. In the light, I would see a grassy hill, blue horizon just barely peaking over. But through the darkness, the distant hush of waves crashing calls like a rugged demand.

I creak down the stairs, unlock the back door, and it slams as I walk down the back porch the steps. I crunch across the gravel road towards the public access and follow the grassy path along the high rock ledges. I walk gingerly out onto the uneven open rocks, and pause to watch the half-moon reflecting a pathway of light across the black sea.

I had been spending too much time under florescent-lit ceilings and succumbing to my ex's favorite TV shows. The shimmering silver light dancing in the darkness stirs something mysterious and wild in me. The waves slosh gently against the rocks, a warm breeze floats around me. Something in me prowls anxiously, like a dormant bear awoken in Spring. Was this the part of me I was compromising? The deepest part of my core, a beast I was trying to tame?

I let her out- a furry, wild thing that loves the sound of crickets and crashing waves, that just needs the smell of brine in her lungs. A deep sadness looms in me, to think I could have suppressed this longer. To think I told myself I didn't need this for so long… My pathetic, traitorous soul, willing to give up who I really am, for a love that didn't want me. I promise myself to never do it again.

The stars are splayed out like glitter in the sky, their distance incomprehensible to my eyes. I slowly make my way closer to the breathing sea. I sit down on a rock, and allow myself to cry.

# CHAPTER 3

PRESENT TIME

POI

The sticky varnish on the wooden table catches the plastic cup as I attempt to raise it and drink. Familiar with this by now, I gently twist the cup and lift the water to my lips. I gaze out to the harbor as I think. I always manage to get a seat by the window, and I believe the waitresses are always a little too hopeful at my sitting alone here once a month. However, I think the elderly owner has warned them against me, as I have appeared to remain twenty-eight for twenty-seven years. Beth is her name. We used to appear the same age. I can feel her wrinkle-rimmed gaze on me now, and every time I sit for a meal here. Her suspicion has been quieted by my generosity.

I know it's slightly reckless, coming here amongst the same humans for so many years. Especially at a time when human technology makes them even more dangerous. But Thalassa might show up. I have a hunch that she's reincarnated somewhere near where she died- so I'm hoping against hope that someday she might just stroll into this dark little tavern called McGreggories. I've dreamed about what I would do so many times. The fantasy has changed drastically now that I know she's an adult. I think that if I had seen her as a child, I would have just kept tabs until she was fully grown, and then tried to woo her. But now that she's an adult- I just can't risk her moving to some random part of the world- hell, she already may be in some random part of the world. But I can't think that. I have to believe she at least has roots here. Maybe a human family to return to. I don't know human family culture as well as I know their politics and technology, but I picture her having a dog. One of those dogs with the yellow fur. I can't picture her having siblings.

I have darker imaginings as well. I've tortured myself so many times by thinking of her death. I'm haunted by the whale carcasses- their injuries a record of their painful deaths. Her death wasn't fast or painless. Her eardrums and organs likely imploded with the pressure of the missile test. It grinds at my core and increases my struggle not to hate humans.

Instead, I try to refocus on her incredible ability to shift into human form while experiencing a disorienting level of pain. True to her great leadership until the end, she refused to give up the existence of our kind. She sacrificed her eternal life for the continuation of the peaceful secrecy of our race.

A bleached blonde human slowly lowers a plate before me, lingering in my space. Her synthetic perfume catches unpleasantly in my nostrils. She leans in and dominantly places lacquered hand on the table. Her cleavage isn't subtle, and I look away, embarrassed- not for her show of skin, but for her clear desperation of being wanted.

"Do you need anything else?" Her voice is high and girly, and I can't help but pick up on the forced nature of her presentation.

"I'm all set, thank you." I risk a glance at her face again, not wanting to be rude.

She purses her lips together, and unabashedly looks me up and down, before turning to leave.

I inwardly sigh. Returning to the surface is hard for many reasons. Human women are another. They have a harder time taking the hint that I'm not interested. At least with the Mer, they understand my deep connection and devotion to Thalassa. They know I could never love another woman. I know that bedding another woman would be a sick, painful reminder of what I am missing.

I open the white lips of a clamshell, steaming with heat, and quickly strip the cooked belly from its encasement. I dip the muddy form into a warm water, and skip the butter before popping it in my mouth.

The tavern door opens, and frames Laude. A clam belly catches in my throat, and I swallow it down roughly. Her tall, thin frame looks strange in human clothes- loose jeans and a black spaghetti strap top. Black ink snakes around her left arm in the form of hammerhead sharks which halt along her back and beneath her collarbone. Sunglasses shade her wild red irises. Her platinum pixie hair sticks out all around her head. Some Mer are practiced at blending into human culture- Laude is not one of them.

She stalks over to me not with the grace of a ballerina, as her build would suggest to human eyes, but with the force of an army general. Which, equating to our hunting troupe, she is. She has the most strategizing mind out of all the Mer- at times to a chilling degree. The grizzled, older men around the dark tavern twist their bulging beer guts and their stubble-strewn saggy hide necks, and ogle her ivory skin.

She pulls out the chair across from me, and sits without speaking. It's hard to read her expression on a good day, but sunglasses render her implacable. I'm also off my game. This is where I let my hopes of seeing Thalassa, crowd out all fears of never finding her. My walls are down. And finally, I've never told anyone that I come here. So I'm not only shocked, but impressed that she's found me.

"This isn't working." She finally says tersely.

I look away, and out the window at the orange light glimmering and circumnavigating the lobstering boats bobbing on the choppy surf.

"Per your orders, scouts are now scouring New England." She pauses, voice low. "But this—" She cuts herself off.

My peripheral vision catches the waitress approaching. "Here's a water for you." She sets a plastic cup down in front of Laude, who smiles without revealing her sharp rows of teeth.

"How are you liking the steamers?" The waitress leans in too close again, clearly unperturbed by Laude sitting across from me.

I thank her and order Laude the same, the waitress leaves, and I look out across the bay for a few silent moments.

I can feel Laude's stare, but when I turn towards her, the black panels of Laude's shades only reflect my image. I don't know how humans can communicate wearing these all the time. It's strange not seeing her eyes, and stranger still to see little images of myself reflected back. My dark hair is unruly as usual, my brows are knit over dark eyes, and my mouth reveals concern. My expression is brimming with the maelstrom I'm constantly attempting to conceal. I don't like how transparently I can see a tinge of fear mixed in with my barely masked grief. I had an easier time believing I could find her in the earlier years- now that she's an adult- she could be anywhere… but I can't let the fear take hold. I will find her.

"You have scouts that will find her." Her voice is gruff. "I understand your wish to find her yourself. But as your head Survival Strategist, the human threats are mounting, and we really can't afford for you to be waiting for Thalassa in a place that she will never come."

It stings. Logically, I recognize that she's right. My wandering around this town has never come up with any leads towards finding her. The human threats are increasingly oppressive, and I'm lucky to get a full night's sleep these days. However, not coming here, would feel like giving up on her. This town and this dingy tavern are the only threads I have to her human life.

"I have some new ideas on how we can locate her. Hire a human private detective, increase her search party size," Her head nods slightly to the side as she ticks off her ideas from her mental list, "…enlist humans in the search, use some sort of online face recognition with social media…"

"We don't have a picture of her to match. And what information could we really give to a private detective?" I can't help finding a way to argue with her brilliant ideas, despite wanting to use them, because I see it's her way of getting me to give up this ritual.

She clicks her tongue impatiently. "I know you don't want to give this up, but the waste problem keeps piling up, among others, and it's getting to the point where I don't feel comfortable making these decisions when you're gone."

A bubbly voice announces, "Here you are!" The waitress places the steamers down before Laude. She checks in with us again, hopeful glint in her eyes dwindling, and leaves.

"Look—" I start, attempting to conceal the incredible grief weighing me down at the idea of giving this place up- of giving up my end of the search, of my vigil. But I can't let my strategists doubt me. It could be a terrible ripple effect throughout the kingdom. We need to stay as strong and united as possible. In this moment, I so thoroughly despise being found out. At some point, I will need to figure out how she solved that mystery. For now, I need to regain control of this situation. My voice is firm, "You're right. You have great ideas. I think we should attempt to implement each of them except enlisting humans in the search, aside from a detective. However, my attempts to find Thalassa are not just the grievances of a widow, but Mer survival tactics. If nothing else, the Whale's Prophesy should illustrate that. We cannot survive without her. She is our One Hope." I can't help feeling my heart clench painfully around her name.

"Poi," Laude's voice is abrasive, "there's no way she's going to come into this sticky, beer smelling, pervert infested old tavern." Her glare permeates through the thick black panels.

I sigh. "This area holds a trace of her energy. It's where she died. Some part of her may be compelled to return."

"Fine." She snaps. "We'll set someone up here. But you need to be at the Ridge."

I slowly raise an eyebrow. I appreciate her counsel, her loyalty, her tough love, but I've never been bossed around by her, and it's not going to start now. My voice is stern, "Laude. I determine where I need to be. I appreciate your advice, but despite my grief, I am still able to aptly rule our people. I need you to respect my rule. I have other reasons as to why I return here, of which I will not divulge. You can afford to make decisions for the Mer three days out of a month."

"A week." She growls.

I sigh. "Fine. I'll make it four days."

She grimaces, and starts expertly peeling clam stomachs out of shells with her spidery fingers.

My other reason for returning here, is my wild hope. Maybe just me- my soul itself, could be enough for her soul to gravitate towards. And how could that ever work if I was always in the ocean?

## STELLA

Seasons pass and as my heart continues to heal, I return to the sea like the rhythm of waves. Easing back from high tide, the sea is a flat expanse of calm, and settle on rocks near enough to touch it. The breeze off the horizon is constant, but gentle. I breathe in deep, inhaling brine and sunshine and the secret ingredients of freshness.

Buoys bob taughtly in the high waters. Clear visibility reveals the adjacent peninsula and smattering of four islands, rising out of the sea on bald gray rock worn with storm lines and topped with dense pines. Tattered lobstering boats wind out of the harbor with motors rumbling like rheumatoid coughs.

Forty feet out, a figure pops out of the current- a cormorant? I squint. It's the blocky black head of a seal, slick and reflective in the bright light. My heart leaps and my teeth are cold with the wind as I smile. He sniffs the air in several directions, black whiskers following. This is where he belongs.

Stunned by the realization that my walls are gone too, I am taken with the urge to swim. I could do and be whatever I want. And for some reason, I get the feeling that freedom and an unnamable something I need very badly are in the cold, wild sea. It grips my heart with dangerous ferocity. I gaze longingly at the submerged seaweed dancing lazily- carelessly swept and stretched to and fro by the loving caress of the crystalline green sea.

I don't swim. The current is too strong here. It's too cold in April- what am I thinking? The snow just barely melted, and it might be replaced by more. These strong urges I get to be in a deadly sea are thoroughly disturbing.

The dark seal slips into the sapphire silken sea, and I look into her world below. Green and murky, I can only see the blurry forms of hairy green rocks riddled with bald patches of white barnacles.

A second seal pops up- her head silvery gray and bobbing like a buoy. I watch her breathe between worlds. Her slick silver body rolls forward, exposing light silver sides and black freckles along her spine. She slips back into the blue, and despite all reason, I lust for that world.

The creak of the rocking chair on the back porch mingles with the rising whistling tunes of the recent arrival of spring birds. They're late this year, but they're here. Just in the past few days, bright green sprigs of spiny and twisting baby leaves peeled out of the barren deciduous trees and mangy wild brambles of wild roses which join the conifers to line the overgrown backyard.

Spooning bland porridge and rocking, I churn over my recent dedication to researching ocean threats. It's been just under two months, and I've felt more passionate reading about environmental issues than I ever felt about Jonas. I even sealed the deal by signing up to go to an environmental action group.

After a considerable amount of time mulling over the faults of my last relationship, I walk down to the shore. Reaching my favorite outlook, I stand high above the glacier-strewn rocks. The sun and sea soak into my soul. I feel lighter as the brine clears out the grief in my lungs. The sky is brilliant blue, the ocean a flat expanse out into wild open seas. The wintery wind whips abrasively at my cheeks, thwarting the month of May. The waves surge into gray layered rock, popping and belching and sucking.

A young couple sits far below, leaning towards the sea with an arm outstretched as their rectangular phone screen reflects the sun. Just feet away from the violent and hungry incoming tide, they could be swept out by one hiccup of the sea.

Impulsively, I call over to them, "Hi, um, that isn't very safe—are you from here?"

The twiggy guy wearing a baggy hoody seems about twenty, and shakes his head.

I call above the whistling wind, "Yeah, you'll want to sit where the rocks are still dry- the tide is coming in, and sometimes there are rouge waves that could pull you out to sea." I don't want to be melodramatic, so I don't mention how there have been equally naïve people who have died here.

The cherub-faced girl purses her lips into uncomfortable smile which feels like a middle-finger even from thirty feet away. Her boyfriend starts to stand, but she holds him against her side and aims her phone. Her hair whips across her face in a non-romantic way, and the white froth of the waves spits across their chests. Selfie accomplished, they slowly scramble over the slick boulders to higher ground.

As much as I love the ocean, I do not want to be a victim to it. The vigorous waves here inspire a healthy fear in my heart. I respect the ocean for its utterly untamable power, and refusal to be anything but honest expression of its essence. I study its rugged wild beauty. I don't need to literally escape into the sea, that isn't even possible. Instead, I can just attempt to embody its inspiring elements.

Restlessness builds in me like a coming storm. My dreams are filled with an urgency so intense I can barely sleep. I'm barreled with waves of fear for the ocean's survival, and gripped by a longing for real life, whatever that is. Further, this morning I dreamt that I was underwater and seals were actually speaking to me.

As much as I loved that, I realize it's time for a little more human interaction. The Save the Seas meeting is today, and the address turns out to be a weathered white house along Highway 9. It's a home and an auto-body shop in one. A strange metalwork sculpture, at once resembling a T-Rex and a chicken, beckons cars from the road. The gravel drive is packed with cars with bumper stickers that say: "Yes Farms, Yes Food," "Sasquatch is my Spirit Animal," and "Radical Love."

These are my people. I get a trill of nerves as I make my way up the back stairs. The dusty unfinished indoor stairwell leads up to an attic space lined with yellow pine rafters and lofted ceilings. In the center of legions of boxes and broken trinkets, a floral couch and metal folding chairs war to create a meeting space. There are about fifteen people chatting, and a few look up and wave briefly as I perch on an unobtrusive metal chair.

"Yes, I can't imagine the money New England Gas is spending on this campaign." A man is saying to a few of the others. He has a scruffy chestnut beard and a tailored brown leather vest. From the way he holds himself, I decide he must be the Save the Seas President.

I look around the room of what appears to be artists, farmers, and local business owners. The woman across from me stands out. She appears to be about forty, but her striking feature is the bright lilac hair braided delicately around her head. Her swanky black top reveals an intricate tribal tattoo winding up her arm, and I squint at it. Hammerhead sharks. How strange. She seems to feel my gaze on her, and her eyes flick to mine. Then widen. Her pale purple eyes match her hair exactly. It's an extremely impressive contact lens and hair dye match.

Without removing her gaze from mine, she aggressively grips the man's jacket beside her, and tugs at him until he looks over. He gasps audibly, his wide electric green eyes bulging. His pale hair is thinning and wild, like he just received an electric shock.

As if I've transformed into a triceratops, they keep staring. My heart starts beating nervously. Maybe they think they recognize me for some reason. I look away uncomfortably, giving them the chance to give up on their rude, inexplicable ogling of me. They'll give up and look away, if I just keep ignoring them.

I can't hear the group conversation. Their gaze burns into me like an empty skillet left on the burner for too long. Not able to withstand it any longer, I look over again. They're being freaks. They're both just staring at me, unencumbered, not even listening to the guy in the tailored vest. Their lips are moving quickly as they speak in hushed tones.

Flabbergasted, I wonder what I did to cause this. I narrow my eyes at them, but they are not deterred. I breathe angrily and focus my attention towards the guy in the vest, just wanting this meeting to start. I fold my legs, and perch my elbow awkwardly, so I can rest my hand to hide my face from their stares.

A few more people have joined the group, and the scruffy-bearded, vested man greets the group. And it turns out he is the President, and his name is Will. We go around the circle introducing ourselves, and then he begins:

"Welcome folks! I'm glad you all made it!" He clasps his hands over his crossed knee as his closely set brown eyes gaze slowly around the circle, acknowledging each person. It's a little intimidating. "Each meeting is a bit different, as the regulars know, but basically, our current focus is to bar construction of a new gas pipeline. New England Gas wants to create coastal gas ports which will cut across hundreds of acres of pristine wetlands and protected habitats, threatening endangered species. In addition to this, investment in fossil fuel infrastructure just doesn't make sense in a world where climate change is getting more dangerous every day."

As he continues, I discretely part my fingers and risk a side-glance at the lilac lunatic. She's not looking at me. I begin to relax. Maybe the worst of the weirdness is over.

About halfway through the meeting, as we are firing off ideas and brainstorming action, the strange duo quietly stand and leave, waving apologetically. Will nods at them, his eyes creasing with his smile.

As they disappear down the stairwell, I deflate with relief. This whole time I had been holding my breath like hardening cement. My mind wanders to reflecting on how strange that interaction had been, attempting to understand what could have merited such an extreme reaction to my appearance.

Moments later, I am jarred by a faux groggy-voiced woman, "He wasn't the one, you know? I realized that, and thought, thank gawd, because I don't want to waste my time, you know?"

She has wavy blonde hair messily tied up into a pony tail, wearing overalls covered with paint splotches, and her beauty is unrepressed by her large nose.

"Yes. I am so glad you're realizing this." To my left, a girl with crop cut hair nods emphatically.

Apparently, the main meeting has fizzled out, and these two are picking up on a well-worn conversation. Clearly not minding my glances, her lips bough around her large teeth as she addresses her friend again, "You just know when it's right, you know? And he never made you think 'yes, it's you.'" She speaks in a lower-key, knowing tone, "He clearly wasn't your soul mate. Soul mates don't do the crap he did to you."

Pony tail nods emphatically at her friends' wisdom, "Right. Totally. I am holding out for my soul mate this time."

Every time they casually drop the phrase "soul mates," I stiffen a little. I don't think I believe in that. Soul mates? It just feels unrealistic. Despite wanting to, I'm afraid to believe in fairy tales.

The brunette winks at me and glances back at her friend as she speaks. "There are guys out there, for us. That will love us for who we are, not what they want us to be."

Okay, that's a romantic idea. It's tempting to believe in. I smile back at the brunette, but feel a tightness in my chest. Suddenly, I realize my eyes are a tad watery. Horrified, I swallow down the emotions, I gather my things, wave, and stumble down the stairs.

My car grips our gravel drive, and my headlights shine on the cedar wood-paneled gray house, small and unassuming, reflecting light in the two antique windows beside the front door. The narrow front porch holds window planters filled only with dirt and dead weeds reaching to the peeling paint by the worn welcome mat. Grandma's house is dark and empty, and my solitude in this world hits me at full force.

I open the fridge, pull out cold stir fry in the white carton, grab a fork, and head up the squeaking stairs. I don't look towards Grandma's old room, I walk into mine. I turn on my phone and watch a television show for the first time since watching TV with Jonas. It distracts me, but when the left-overs are gone, and the show is off, I only feel empty.

Knowing tomorrow will be better, I turn off the lights, and close my eyes. The dark lack of stimulus, makes my thoughts louder, and it's as if someone turned up the dial on my loneliness. Of course I can't sleep. My mind is wound up on the question of soul mates. I could not be more vulnerable than now, to the idea of a soul that always loves you and is somehow meant to find you, even across the chasm of death and reincarnation.

I wish there was some way of knowing for sure if it's real or fake. My mind keeps whirring and whirring. I know Jonas wasn't my soul mate. But there were moments when I told myself he was. I really, really wanted him to be. What if he is, and I just messed it up? But you can't mess up soul mates by being yourself. And being myself is what drove him away. He's not the one. And I knew this, maybe the whole time, deep down.

Gripped by an urge to see the stars, I throw on a jacket and quietly walk out beneath the night sky. Putting my knit hat under my head, I lay back on the uneven cold rock. Waves hush against the earth. The bright orbs of light that scatter the sky feel so far away. It makes the universe feel impossibly huge. I wonder if I would ever be able to find him. If I have a soul mate. I wonder if I will ever know. I decide I want to believe in soul mates. Maybe from some angle, he's orbiting beneath the same stars.

# CHAPTER 4

POI

Water streams around my bullet-shaped body. Shafts of condensed light pull through the surface, angling towards me as I speed forward. I breach, rounding my back into the warm sun, exhale, breathe, and weave with the rest of the pod as we propel ourselves into the crystalline blue.

Leagues of ocean are visible below us, and the warping clear blue sky is endless above. There is every reason to let my heart open to the beauty. I'm surrounded by the complex melodic speak uttered by dozens of wild dolphins. But no matter what form I shift into, I can't get free, and I can't escape the truth.

She hasn't come back. I've failed to find her.

Here, below the sunshine and waves, the truth is clear. It's been twenty-seven years. That's nearly half of a human lifetime. She could be dead by now. She could be gone forever.

Silver bodies speed past me, and I realize I have stilled. Something in me feels so heavy that I can't move. I slowly drop.

Six dolphins and a baby turn, thick tails high above their heads, performing gliding headstands as they approach, balancing with flippers splayed like penguin's feet, they watch me curiously. Through their long beaks and tiny white teeth, they ask if I'm okay.

I nod, thanking them in their pod's dialect, and ensuring them they can leave. I attempt this a few times, certain of my precise pronunciation of their pod's exaggerated popping clicks and abbreviated crackles, but they don't leave. They come closer. The rest of the pod halts their forward motion. Suddenly the current of hundreds of dolphins speeding past has slowed. Instead they flit a few hundred yards ahead, playing between and below the waves. Nearly eight hundred dolphins are temporarily surrendering their hunting path. For me. My chest feels tighter.

Kailili, the Matriarch of the Tieyierro- one of the largest pods in the Atlantic, chitters at the five hovering dolphins, causing them to disperse and join the play. She draws nearer, her white belly reflecting light blue, silver fins spanning out like fans, her baby practically suctioned to her side. Her wide, wisened black eyes track me.

I'm always astounded by her focused presence, her grace, her radiant beauty. Her small rounded chin elegantly rests against her upper beak, drawing a v-like smile. Light circular scars dot the left side of her snout, and just beyond her wide eyes, scratches trail along the sides of her belly. Light swirls of gray draw up her beak and towards her blowhole. Her dorsal fin points up from her oval form like a delicate pinky finger. Her appearance is sweet and unassuming, yet she is one of the most powerful beings in the Atlantic- a highly respected leader, and a healer graced by the Great Ocean Spirit.

Kailili slides across my path, hovering in the sea, her marble-sized black eye staring into both of mine in turns. "We know you're hurting."

I freeze. She's picking up my emotions like they're something she can hear. Being around the most empathetic beings in the world, is maybe the worst attempt at escaping pain that I could make. It's impossible to hide emotions with dolphins. Especially with Kailili.

Her tiny baby, Chiri, slips beneath my chest, twittering, "Be happy."

"He can't, Chiri." Kailili gently reprimands.

Her baby returns to her, nuzzling beneath her fin.

Kailili hovers before me, divining truths I have not divulged. Her silver beak as long as the bill of a baseball cap, her light gray skin glistens in the sunlight. "He has to give into the pain first," Her eye narrows, "If he wants to get through it."

Sadness is a sticky, achy ball in me.

The matriarch waits.

I choke out, "I can't let her go."

Her long jaw drops, revealing her curling pink tongue as she speaks. "The pain is your last remnant of her, I understand. Your struggle with it is how you keep her close."

Something in me is cracking. I don't want it to. Trying to stop the chasm from widening, I tense against the feelings, attempting to restrain them.

Her chittering calls are soft between us, "If you stop fighting the pain, if you let it wash over you, there will be release on the other side."

"I can't—" I croak.

"The part of her you hold will not leave—it will only transform."

I hesitate, fearful of allowing myself to be enveloped by the full force of loss. It wouldn't end. It wouldn't work. I wouldn't make it out the other side. And I don't want to get over my soul mate.

She darts forward and bops my beak upwards with hers- like a slap on the wrist. She backs up again, floating a foot before me, head cocked to the side, her eye locked on me.

She continues, "You are stronger than this situation, than this pain. You are more than all of it. We can feel that she still lives. But if you don't become hopeful in your soul, if you can't find peace and faith with her energy in you, you will never find her." She angles one black eye towards mine, rounded beak open, "This is a test, Poseidon."

I watch the flames from her favorite seat in her favorite room. She's in my lap again, cuddled up and as weightless as the ghost of her memory. Her honey blonde hair curling out across my arms, head gently nestled against my chest, as she reads the book propped on her knees. She smells as sweet as a harp's song.

Orange flames lick around the bone white driftwood, crackling to fill the gaping silence. Heavy ledgers line the shelves beside the stone fireplace, and behind me, rows of books are packed into the inlaid bookshelves, freestanding shelves create aisles, and many more armchairs and desks are scattered around the room.

Over the past twenty-eight years, the emptiness hasn't stopped aching. If anything, it's a festering wound that can't seem to heal. But at Kailili's words, a bubble of hope was injected into the overwhelming darkness of my mind. Thalassa is still alive.

I cracked to the pain a week after Kailili's lesson. My first attempts to access my emotions rigidly failed like the rusted cogs of two-hundred-year old industrial mills. The inner parts of myself were encrusted very deep, and I couldn't get through. Desperate to make progress, I sought out and stayed with Kailili and her pod for a full transition of the moon. With words, whistles, and energy, Kailili coaxed my emotions forward. When the pain finally broke through, it pummeled my insides with the force of tsunami-height Polynesian waves. I went through phases of not being able to see straight, raging against the pain, and only seeing bright colorful lights. Now I can feel my heart again, and it hurts. Badly.

I need to find Thalassa now more than ever, and I didn't think that was possible. Similar to as I suspected but never spoke, Kailili explained that I can find my soul mate through connecting with the bit of Thalassa's soul that will always be tied to mine. Previously, I visited places on land thinking that simply my presence would cause our physical energies to be drawn together like magnets.

Kailili grips a strand of kelp in her sharp beak, ripping it free from the embankment, and tosses it my way. "Like roots of a plant searching for nourishment that's invisible to our eyes, your coming together must happen in a spiritual, metaphysical way, before the physical can be manifested."

"Poseidon, you must stop your search in order to find her. Nothing you can physically do will ever bring you closer to her. Instead, shift the energy. Know that everything happens first on a spiritual level. Focus on spirit. Harmonize peacefully with her spiritual energy in order to cause energy to shift and draw you together, physically."

Kailili released me from my mania. Before, to stop searching for Thalassa was to accept defeat. Now I see that the search was like trying to play chess with flies. The real way for us to find each other is through spirit first. Once I was able to slow down, I could recognize my previous experiences with the spirit world, reincarnation, and Shifting. In the deeper reality from where all things flow, there is no space or time. In a way, Thalassa and I are already together, and I just need to access it. This is a test of my faith.

I marvel at Kailili's ability to transform the soul- she practically brought me back from the dead, and I will be forever grateful. Strangely, I feel a raw sort of almost-peace. I can breathe again. I feel like my muscles had been frozen for decades, and now are limber enough to allow blood to coarse through. I can see the world's beauty again.

I stare into the flames, continuing to imagine Thalassa, just the same, but human, in my arms. I have followed Kailili's guidance the best that I can. This is the third day of spending most of my time just peacefully imagining her presence returning, as a human, as she is now.

The door whines open, and I jolt. Thalassa's ghost is gone. Books cram into the bookcases, leather chairs and tables litter the floor, but the room is barren.

"Poi!" Naido's words echo off the cavern walls. He slides into view on slippery feet, trailing a river of water. His long black hair is loose and dripping around his shoulders, and his navy cloak sticks to his willowy frame.

Liquidly, I stand to greet him.

His momentum brings him just before me- his square face red with exertion, a thin-lipped, toothy, hysterical smile splitting his face. His hands reach up and viciously grip my shoulders, bright black eyes darting between mine.

His voice uncharacteristically serious, "I have news."

My heart squeezes with hope. But with so many pressures from humans, news could come in many forms. No matter what, I know that his visions are solid- he's not the most prolific oracle I've ever worked with, but he's the most accurate.

My throat tightens as I speak, "Alright. What did you dream?"

With brows peaked, and bright, watery eyes, he squeaks, "She's coming back."

Thudding in my chest. I resist the wild hope erupting in me. I stay perfectly still, staring down into his black eyes.

"She will return." He reinforces, his goofy smile widening further.

I pause with shock. "You're sure?"

"Our Queen, your Thalassa, will return. Fate hasn't made it easy, but if you play your cards right, she could regain her memory and her immortality."

Hysterical laughs overtake me. I look up at the arching ceiling, the strange sounds leaping out of my lungs and refracting back to me. Naido's laughter joins in mine. The pure unbelievable tilting of reality shocks me to my core. Kailili was right.

The sun infiltrates every corner of the hall, like the glaring bright hope running like lightning beneath my skin. I've gathered the entire Mer community that is currently at the Ridge, and watch my people fidget amongst the driftwood tables, about to hear of the trifling twisted rules of Fate's new game. If I can just get her by my side again, I'm sure we can weather this. The idea of her by my side again sends my adrenaline-worn body into another round of electric loops.

My throat constricts and I stare ahead and above the crowd as Naido's recites the prophesy, and the words crash around me again. My emotions are a slosh of hope and anguish which burn in my chest like crackling fire. My true love, and the Queen Guardian of the Sea, will return as a human, without a memory of us, with no memory of me. She will be in perilous danger of dying in human form and never reincarnating again- forever and permanently lost.

But Fate has left a slim chance that we could get her back. The rules are already engraved into my mind: no one can utter a word of her true identity, she can't find out who she is, and the only thing that can bring her back is her falling in love with me again, and finally binding that with an act of love. However, if we consummate our attraction before her love is true- she will remain a human, and her soul will be lost forever.

I have no fear of my ability to abstain. Just the idea of seeing her again overwhelms me, is more than I could have hoped for two moons ago. I stop thinking of her and blink back the water rebelliously playing around my eyelids. I bring myself back to the moment.

Naido's final words linger, and a hush louder than sirens fills the hall. My chest heaves as I pray my skin holds me together.

Kiara and Laude watch me with wide, shocked eyes.

There are no smiles. It's as if everyone else has been so traumatized by losing her, that they too are cautious of optimism.

I speak over the hush, my voice a low rumble compared to Naido's tenor, "To clarify, when she returns, it will be everyone's responsibility to keep her from the truth. Go out of your way to ensure that she believes she is an ineffectual human, here only for her perspective on human society." I gaze around, and my eyes land on the beguiling face of my pesky brother, Hades. His perfectly symmetrical features and clear sage-green eyes hide the true tumult beneath. After Persephone left him, his eyes always seemed to linger on Thalassa. If my observations are correct, he has very little to lose by exposing the truth to Thalassa, and everything to gain. He could lend any human an artifice of eternal life in the Underworld.

With a forceful friction in my voice, I aim my next statement at him, "If anyone even *accidentally* hints of her true identity, they will be marooned on land, never to be a Mer again. Brother, if you step just a *little* too close to disclosure, I swear I will seal over all vaults to the Underworld and ensure that you die as a human."

I am never this harsh. But the situation begs it. I let my eyes swing out to the rest of the Mer packed tightly and sitting uncharacteristically still. "No one is to imply previous relationships she has had to you, or to anyone else, and especially not to myself. To ensure this, keep your distance from her. Do not answer any questions that her incurably curious mind will have. Finally, if we really are blessed to have her back here again, please do not stare at her. Please do not do anything that would set off a red flag in her clever brain, because she will search out answers like a relentless orca targets a seal. We need to keep her secret to save her future, to save all of—"

A clattering of slapping bare feet utters from the hallway, and all the heads in the hall turn towards the entrance. A torrent of whispering erupts, as we were believed to be the only Mer in the Ridge.

Leyra grips the entrance, and motions for me to come. Knowing she must have just returned from land, my heart lurches again. Human clothes cling to her drenched form, her wet hair a hue of eggplant, angular face glistening and red. Gasping, Marc appears behind her, broad shoulders bent over, his hands over his knees as he catches his breath and drips water onto the rock.

Staring down at the whispering hall, I quickly announce, "Please wait for my return."

I quickly cross towards the worn-out pair. I feel the weight of all eyes tracking me as I approach. I address them formally, implying that they should not blurt whatever they are bursting to say.

"Leyra, Marc. Let's find a private space for your news."

As we walk down the hallway towards an empty lounge, hope pushes against me like gust of wind. These are my land scouts- looking for hints of Thalassa's whereabouts.

With a shaking hand, I hold the door open for them, and they filter into the hammock-filled room before I lock the door. I can't risk anyone overhearing- I can't risk anyone impeding this chance to save her.

Condensed lines of light wobble around the room. Two manta rays glide past the wide window which runs the length of the narrow lounge. The green sea is clear as the sky above. It implies joy and beauty with each twinkle of light. But I have seen many of these days in Thalassa's absence, and I have trained myself not to create hope based on the weather.

Leyra and Marc ignore the sagging rope hammocks, and stand before me anxiously. Leyra's small lilac eyes are lighter than her damp hair. Her small frame is tanned, yet more worn from living on land. Small wrinkles line her eyes, and creases wear across her forehead. Marc's wild hair has thinned, exposing peaks of his broad skull above his ears. His wandering eye has strayed further since we last met. Their human-like frailty is the scar of sacrifice for their absent Queen, and for the entire Guardianship of the Sea.

"We've found her," Leyra blurts.

My heart jabs quickly.

I look between them, both with the appearance of highly caffeinated humans, jacked up and on alert.

Marc nods. "It's her."

My heart wrenches towards the door. Suddenly I don't want to know all the details. All that can wait. Time is crucial, anything could have happened to her by now. I can't risk any more time passing. I just want to get to her. "Lead the way."

## STELLA

I walk as far out on the rocky point as is safe from the barreling waves. The long cracks in the jagged rocks run like the bark of a gnarled old tree. Churning waves nip at the surrounding islands and peninsula. On the horizon, a tiny lighthouse is barely visible. The ocean is the perfect shade of blueberry as it roils beneath the pale clear sky. The chilly air bites my cheeks, and dries my eyes.

Cross-currents smack the outcropping, making the waves unpredictable. I watch ducks bravely bobbing in rough surf, only diving down to escape the larger waves at the last comprehensible instant. The water swirls turquoise with bubbles. The ducks pop out from behind the wave, pearls of water rolling off their black and white feathers. Suddenly, a black head emerges just ten feet beyond the breaking waves. I gasp with the unusual closeness of the encounter. Normally seals are exceedingly suspicious of humans, and keep a healthy distance.

This seal peeks out of the shimmering blue, large black eyes gazing directly at me. He seems to be unperturbed by my proximity. The black nostrils along his puppy snout flare as he breathes the fresh air. His arching whiskers bristle in the breeze.

I gaze at him, transfixed with his boldness he disappears back into the haze of turbulent air pockets. Maybe the seals are getting used to me. I stare out at the flat horizon with sense of hope swelling in my chest, all senses of black loneliness turned to ash.

An unusual quiet over comes the sea, like a pause, that makes me feel edgy. A large wave builds- twice as far out as the previous sets. I stand up nervously, ready to walk a little higher up to gain safety. A rushing sound fills my ears as the ocean peels back, exposing a landscape of long, barnacle-covered earth and bundles of backward-strewn seaweed. The wave rolls like a wind-up toy, picking up power, then gushes forward, pouring transparently over the rocks below. It heaves up and swells over the dry land, not yet breaking. I swear and start skipping over rocks to higher ground, glancing back to see that the water has engulfed the thirty feet of previously dry outcropping behind me. My mind races with disbelief.

A mass of rapid white-water rips past my knees and knocks me down, an electric shock of cold. I'm swimming in the torrent of icy cold as the wave continues to gush up onto higher land. The wave lifts me high, and crashes just feet in front of me. Suddenly, I'm caught by a rip current, and I barely have time to catch my breath as an invisible force jerks me under.

I'm a good swimmer. I hold my breath against the manic, pummeling waves, yet somehow don't hit rock. I try swimming to what I think is sideways- out of the rip current. Dizzy and nauseous with spinning in the surf, my lungs demand air. No. I can do this. I open my eyes to the burning salt water and see dim light above, and attempt to navigate upwards instead.

I see a shadowy form pass above me, and involuntarily scream. Breaking the seal, my lungs needily drink in salt water.

Wheezing in ocean and coughing out air, I notice the dizzying current has disappeared. Convulsing with suffocation and terror, I force my eyes open to locate the animal. Please don't be a shark.

Swimming towards me quickly, and veiled in shadowy murk, the figure approaches. And my muscles relax gratefully. Someone is saving me. Everything turns to nothing.

# CHAPTER 5

STELLA

I wake up to the strange sensation of sucking from my lungs. My mouth shuts, and opens. Air funnels into my lungs faster than I could breathe it in. My heart starts to thump again, and I begin panicking again as air expands my lungs. Groggily, I realize my whole body is numb with cold, but I feel something warm against my mouth, the sides of my head, and a warming sensation expelling from my lungs. Something is not right. I still feel the pressure of water on all sides, but I am breathing.

I open my eyes to see a face leaned to the side and pressed against mine. I scream into his mouth which is clamped to mine. Panic heightening, I keep screaming and start swatting at the evil sea-demon attached to my face, sucking the life from me.

Unflinchingly, his hands grip my face tighter, and with his warm lips still pressed hard against mine, he stops pushing air into my lungs. He leans back slightly so that our noses touch and faces align.

Whoah, he's handsome. My heart skips and gut tugs. His eyes are dark burning suns. There's something familiar in his gaze, and I become quiet. I can't place it. His gaze is willing me to calm, and I study what I can see of his face. His dark brows, thick hair, and olive skin suggest Greek decent. His nose isn't greasy against mine, but smooth and clear. Blushing, I realize his lips have now been simply resting against mine for a long moment. His hands soften their grip on the sides of my head.

The gurgle of churning waves crashing against rock, alerts me to the fact that I'm breathing in the ocean. Somehow, my lungs are calmly expanding without new air. Maybe some sort of magic, but more likely a dreaming stage of oxygen-deprived drowning.

He closes his lips, causing mine to mirror his. He raises his dark eyebrows and meaningfully looks to my lips, then to my eyes. I am guessing this means: "don't drink ocean." He slowly takes his warm lips from mine, and I can see his whole face. My throat constricts with nerves and I'm grateful I can't talk, because I'm sure it would be nonsense. He's staring at me with a searching gaze, holding my head gently, and looking between my eyes with some emotion I can't place.

I look at him more closely too. His dark wavy hair is floating lazily around the elegant planes of his face which is otherworldly in its beauty. His high cheekbones and cut lines of his square face are angelic. His seductively sculpted lips look like they hold secrets, and his long-lashed dark kaleidoscope eyes yank at something deep within me. Then I notice how tan and muscular his shoulders and arms are, and my eyes trail down his chiseled midline, and is he nak—oh my god— *tail*!

Below his rippling abdomen, flesh meets scales, and my eyes rake along his long dark tail disappearing into the green murk below. I flinch and twist, pointing to the tail, and staring at him incredulously. Merman?

His broad shoulders lift in a heavy sigh, and my eyes catch on a silvery flash along his torso, where small scaled flaps lift. Transfixed, I stare at the neatly tucked gills along the sides of his ribcage, delicately pushing out each breath. Curiously, I meet his gaze.

His dark brows are knit, and his mouth is tight at the edges. The expression doesn't even come near to marring his beauty, but such a bereft state doesn't make sense for such an enchantingly perfect Merman. And then I wonder again if I've actually drowned, or am still in the process, and just hallucinating. Yes. That is definitely what's happening. But it's an entrancingly sexy neuron misfire. My deprived brain is really pulling out all the stops. Go me.

Slowly, as if trying not to scare a wild animal, he drops his hands from my face. My cheeks chill. His large hand pulls my arm, turning me in the water so that I am against his hard chest. My heart hiccups and breathing staggers as he binds his arms tightly around my middle. But instead of going up towards the air and land, he dives. We plunge deeper into the murky depths of the sea. Interesting twist, brain. You'd think I would at least want to dream of surviving. Apparently, my last wish is for a mermaid fantasy, not breathing air again.

The green shallow cliffs give way to a blur of dark midnight. Icy ocean pulls at my skin until I am numb. I figure I must be getting towards the final stages of hallucination, before death. I keep having the sensation of waking up, only seeing darkness, and falling asleep again. Like a comforting mirage, I feel warm masculine muscles against my back, and strong arms around my waist. I am very happy with my imagination. It's nice to feel wanted again. Thank you, dying brain.

Another vision shines bright in my mind, and I am utterly shocked with the extra stores of oxygen in my body. I wonder if, although it feels like many hours are passing, if it has only been maybe one minute, and even my concept of time is being warped as I decline towards death. For some reason, dying doesn't scare me anymore. I focus on the hazy orange light coming into view. It begins to sparkle. The light separates into the twinkle of thousands of tiny orange lights, spanning out like a horizon. It reminds me of seeing a city by plane at night. It's very pretty.

As we draw nearer, I see the lights are shining through windows, and we are approaching an underwater mountain range. We're speeding towards a glistening window arching to the size of a cathedral door. Just before the lit room, he pauses, and swings me forward. Out of the ocean, I splash sideways into air.

Gravity grips me, and I fall hard onto the slate floor, banging my knees and pooling seawater. I gasp in musty oxygen, dragging it into my confused lungs. My eyes water and sting with salt. Freaking realistic dream. Could do without this part.

I don't even hear him cross, but suddenly he's at my side, crouching in a midnight blue silken robe. I stare up in disbelief, "Now you're human?" I rasp.

He raises his eyebrows matter-of-factly with a sheepish grin, spreading his hands, "I am."

His knees are bent outwards against his long cloak, his ankles are covered with hair, and he has very clean feet. Pushing myself up to rest on my arms behind me, I rasp a sigh of delirious satisfaction.

"This is a really cool dream."

He twitches a smile. "It's… not a dream." He seems to speak hesitantly.

I cock my head, watching his perfect balance on his heels, and shake my head. "Well it's not real. So…"

He reaches out and squeezes my big toe. And I don't feel it at all. "Nope. Don't feel it. See? Not real."

He flicks up his eyes with a hint of a smirk. "Okay, your toes are numb. Try biting your tongue."

I glare, but try it. Stab of pain. Interesting. I look at him strangely, "But… how could I have survived… what could this possibly be…" I splutter.

He reaches a long-fingered hand out, "C'mon. You're exhausted."

I take his hand, which engulfs mine, and he pulls me up. I sway uncertainly. "I'm really cold." I realize.

"Yes you are," he nods. "I'll take care of that."

I try to walk forward, but my knees give out. I feel his arms under me, scooping me up, and suddenly I'm against his chest. My face is pressed against his hot collarbone. My eyes involuntarily flutter shut, and I faintly notice he smells amazing.

I wake up as he's lowering me to a stone floor that is warm under my feet. I stand uncertainly, legs stiff. A grotto pool lays before us, and ghostly white steam curls towards the low cavern ceilings. Torch light flickers on the mysteriously rippling black water. The circular cave walls are rough as if naturally formed, and the whole room gives a sense of being in a warm cocoon.

"This will warm you up." He gestures, then heads towards the only entrance, an open arch. "I'll leave you in privacy. Try not to fall asleep."

"Thanks," I manage, blinking against my drooping eyelids.

After watching him leave, I peel off my soaking wet clothes, grunting with the effort as exhaustion weighs down on me like a wooly mammoth. I collapse onto the floor and pull hard to unstick my skinny jeans.

Approaching the white steam curling above black rippling water, I hesitate at the edge, hoping it's not too hot. It scalds my toes. I realize my body is too cold to submerge, so I sit at the edge, wafting warm steam towards my goosebumpy pale skin. My toes and feet are splotchy bone white and entirely numb. I bite my lip fearfully, and remind myself that frostbite doesn't matter if it's a dream. Groggily, I chastise myself. I need to get better at controlling my dreams.

Eventually, I ease my legs into the water, shivering. I slowly manage to drop my whole body into the comforting warmth. I find an underwater ledge to sit on, and watch the water bend and pull the yellow torch lights. I lean my head back on the rock, and close my eyes, and think, how ironic, that water is what soothes me after nearly drowning in it. Just as I'm trying to decide if I'm having an after-death experience, or still hallucinating, I drift off to sleep.

## POI

I can't blink. Heart pounding, I'm compelled to stride up and down the dim passageways near her, dragging my hand along the wall so I can feel the rough rock and remember this is real. She's here. This isn't a dream, this isn't a hallucination. Our love has become manifest. Thalassa is here.

My chest is swelling so dangerously that it's painful. I wipe wetness from my cheeks. I relish in my ability to breathe air deep into my lungs again. I stop at a filmy window, separating air from sea. Not wanting to put too much distance between myself and Thalassa, I simply stand before the barrier. Threading my right hand through the vertical water's surface, I paint a circle that glows neon green. The circle of sea essence swirls into an orb which swells past the film of air and hovers between both worlds.

I speak, and the glowing orb quivers as it swallows my words, "Great Ocean Spirit, thank you..." I struggle to find the right words, "Thank you for bringing us together again. Please protect her- don't let her find out the truth. Let her become her full self again. The whole Ocean needs her. I need her. Please help us."

At the finality of my words, the orb shudders. It slips fully into the sea, and disperses like a glittering, twinkling firework.

I freeze up my legs against returning to Thalassa. Every fiber of my being wants to convince her to fall in love with me right now- to utilize all that I know about her to expedite the process- so we can just be us again. Having my hands on her the whole trip back to the Ridge... it spiked a yearning to wrap her around me again, to just hug her again. But that would certainly cause suspicion. And I don't want to creep her out, or force her away. I want her to choose to stay here.

That aside, for as much as I loved seeing her face again, it hurt that she didn't recognize me. Thalassa being right here- but without any of her memory- without the ease between us- just spikes another torrent of loss. I must suppress and hide this pain, and I must restrain from using what I already know of her to bring us closer. Her gift is that of Communication, and can spot any tactics from a mile away. If she suspects I know more about her than I should, that will be another red flag that could set her off investigating. And I don't want to manipulate her. I realize a lonely, rusty part of me wants so badly for her to choose me again.

I pace again, for something to do as I think. How am I even going to do this? I will certainly need to be sure to- oh shit. I asked the whole community to stay at yesterday's prophesy announcement... I wonder how long it took them to figure out I wasn't returning... I will need to hold another gathering tonight- so no one is surprised at her presence and accidentally gives everything away...

I turn again, my strides gliding me down the darkened hall and past dancing torchlights. I think of how we first fell in love- in the fourth dimension of the gods, before we came to Earth, before Earth had life. Ions of happily coexisting has not prepared me for wooing her again. I'm not sure I even remember how. More than anything- I don't want to spook her. She has a human memory, and likely believes herself to be trapped here. The last thing I want is for her to also feel sexually harassed.

Sighing, I realize I not only don't know how to date, I don't even know how to flirt. This is going to be a mess.

Easily an hour has passed, and she has not reemerged from the grotto hot spring. An hour is certainly enough time to warm up again. I don't want to intrude on her privacy, but it's very late, and she needs good sleep.

Holding my breath, I risk a peek into the torch-lit grotto. Her head is leaned back along the edge, and she's softly snoring. I can't help a wide grin. I begin to walk into the room, and then stop myself at the sight of her clothes. If she had her memory, my presence here would be no problem. However, in her current human state, she might flip out. I have no idea how being human, and her twenty-six years on land have changed her, but I'm going to venture a guess that being seen in the nude by a stranger would not pass as okay.

I turn and re-enter the hallway, weighing my options. Selfishly. I could wake Laude or Kiara, and either of them could gather her up and take her to a bedroom. But I don't want to pass her off- I want to be with her.

A little snorting snore whispers into the hallway, and I smirk again. She is so thoroughly unconscious, that there's no way she'll even remember how she got into a bed. I realize I could wake her up, have her dress herself, and she'd be able to easily fall asleep again. Great. New option.

I grab an extra cloak, and approach her snoring form. Her wide, full lips are open, revealing two straight rows of teeth, and her tiny pink tongue. Her thin eyebrows are seemingly raised in an expression of interest of her dreamscape as her eyes skitter under her light eyelids. She looks exactly the same as she always has, except that her freckles across her high cheekbones and the bridge of her small nose are so faded they're nearly nonexistent. Her dark blonde hair is pulled into a pony tail, dried now, but wickedly knotted.

The black water kisses her tiny shoulders, and I divert my gaze from looking lower. Yes, she's my soul mate, but she doesn't know that. I squat beside her, and clear my throat to say her name, but then inwardly curse myself as I realize I nearly just destroyed every hope we have. Already. Damnit. I am going to have to be extremely careful. This is harder than I thought.

I clear my throat again, but she doesn't stir. I gently stroke her cheek under my thumb. Her eyelids flutter, and her wide emerald eyes, glassy with sleep, look around without really seeing. Her eyelids close again. She's in deep sleep mode. I recognize this, and I thrill at being able to recognize parts of her existence again. Even her sleep. I stare down at her, my heart purring dangerously, loving this closeness.

I can't help but stroke her silken cheek in my attempt to wake her. "Darling," I falter, I need to be far more careful than that. What am I doing? I can't use endearing terms. I lift my hand and, still crouching, edge distance between us.

"Sleepy one… you can't stay here…" I whisper to her gently, and her eyes open again, this time she's able to look over and focus on me, but I can tell she remains in the limbo between waking and sleeping. I murmur, "Climb out and put this on. I'll wait at the door."

Miraculously, I hear the water splash as she gets out, and in a short moment she's by my side. My heart melts at seeing her again, but she's swaying with exhaustion, her ponytail akimbo, her eyelids heavy. The journey across the Atlantic has exhausted her. Suddenly, I worry about her human health. Maybe that was too much for a human. I try to swallow my panic. Without asking, I lean down and pull her into my arms again. She leans her head against my aching chest, and immediately her eyes flutter shut.

I'll have to thank Kailili in a big way. I can't believe this is real… For three days I imagined Thalassa in my arms, and now she is here, lightly drooling against my cloak. I can't help grinning, and my heart is leaping wildly, summersaulting in my chest. I barely notice the stone passageways as I carry her through them. I hungrily study the sleepy lines of my love's face, and the feel of her against my chest, realizing this is the closest I will be to her for a while.

I bring her to the cottage on the sea, the lone island along all of the Ridge which stays safely above the high tide line. Maybe being exposed to the sun and in the beautiful view of the surrounding sea, will help Thalassa adjust from her human life and into Mer life. I imagine that the caves, grottos and passageways of the mountainous submerged Ridge below, could by human perception, feel damp and dark.

The thick oaken door whines open and the cottage offers reprieve from the chilly night winds. Sensing our presence, the torchlights flicker on, and the fireplace erupts in purple flames. There are indeed some benefits to staying on good terms with my brother- who harnesses and programs fire to his will.

The large mahogany king bed dominates the room, flashing me with many memories of nights spent in it with Thalassa. We would spend our summers in this room, and returning to it now, with her in my arms, is like opening an old journal entry. Instinctively, I look down at her sleeping body, how her thin silken cloak drapes against her perky chest, her thin waist, how her toned legs peek out of the cloak at her thighs…

Aching for her, wanting to climb on top of her, I whip back the covers, place her on the bed gently, and quickly cover her with the blankets. Better. I back up and watch her from a distance. Her chin drops, and she resumes breathing through her mouth. I cannot believe that she is right there, right here, with me. Thank the Ocean Spirit itself, the Dolphin Spirit, and Kailili for her wisdom. Fate, I'm coming for you.

# CHAPTER 6

STELLA

Dreaming doesn't feel so much like sleep as it does a reel of underwater experiences. My mind created a dreamscape of brilliant corals and exotic fish. I can still hear waves crashing roughly on rock. It's very realistic. Then I shift and realize I am in bed, and every inch of me is aching. I open my eyes with a gasp and sit up quickly. What the hell? Am I actually alive?

I gape out at the square of pale blue ocean. It's framed by an open door, and a room made of iron gray rock, which I am in. My mind is reeling. What *happened*?

I squeeze my mind, willing it to remember. I certainly don't remember being brought here. The last thing I remember was a warm bath…and drowning, and hallucinating I was saved… by a… merman? Have I lost my mind?

I look around the room, taking it in slowly. I am in a luxurious four-poster mahogany king-sized bed with fluffy white comforters. A massive armoire sits in the right corner near the door. A desk with a single chair beneath the window to my left, and a small bedside table to my right. A large stone fireplace looms unlit beside the wardrobe. Wrought iron torches decorate the walls. Two adjacent, circular windows bring light into the room, and looking out, I see a slit of ocean and the white sky.

Sitting up with a groan, I breathe into my ragged, raw lungs. I am definitely alive. Painfully alive. I exhale like I just finished a massive exam. So clearly, someone saved me, and I just hallucinated the whole time, which explains why I have no idea where I am. Okay. I can figure this out. I just need to get a look around, get my bearings.

Shivering, I don't see my clothes anywhere. Instead, I'm wearing a deep plum colored silk cloak with flowing sleeves. The fabric is beautiful, warmly catching and holding the light, but the style is like that of a witch Halloween costume. Who the heck would dress me in this? It's got to be some sort of practical joke. But who would do that? Certainly not old high school friends— they don't still live on Spear Island.

Curiously, I slip out of the bed, muscles surprisingly worn and achy. I open the armoire to see a wardrobe of exotic silken fabrics with shells sewn across. I pluck through them with awe, wondering who's closet I am looking through, and where she could possibly be wearing these clothes to. Curiouser and curiouser.

None of the items came cheap. They're all very skimpy yet elaborate. I notice a few long gowns, and inhale with admiration. "Wow…" I can't help but whisper. One number is a strapless midnight blue, splaying out widely at the bottom, and covered with what looks like sapphires. Those can *not* be real.

With a metallic squeak, I open the other side, and am jolted by my frazzled appearance in the peeling old mirror on the door. Through the tarnished metal age spots of the frame, I see my hair is a knot of blonde mess, my green eyes are popping against their red agitation from saltwater, and my full lips look somewhat battered. I look away, shaken. Maybe not everything was a hallucination. But what parts could possibly be real? The mouth-to-mouth must have been on land. Through the panic and insanity, there's no way I was a reliable witness to my own life.

Looking back towards the wardrobe, I focus on simply finding a more normal outfit to wear. Then I can figure out where I am. This side of the cabinet holds more practical items. Stacks of plain t-shirts and shorts, as well as boxes of silky bras, bandeaus and underwear. "Thank god!" I whisper, whipping on fresh undergarments and normal clothes.

Closing the wardrobe, I look around the room again, rubbing my exposed arms and shivering. Sighing, I slip on the witch cloak again for warmth. If anyone is about to take a photo of me I will just own it. Act like I wanted to look like an overgrown trick-or-treater in May.

I walk out through the door, and my mind goes quiet. Bright white light cascades through a blanket of cottony clouds. The ocean is breathing quietly as if asleep. My eyes scan the horizon, and from this vantage point, there is no other land in sight. I walk around to the other side of the cottage. Hazy white meets periwinkle blue, all around. Uninterrupted. A pinch of fear twists inside me. Where the hell am I.

I sit down on the jagged black rocks, exhausted already. If someone had to bring me out here... maybe I got pulled out by a riptide. Maybe a fisherman picked me up in a boat... but why would he leave me here?

"Hi." Comes a male voice.

I turn and freeze with shock. The man, (merman??) from my hallucinations, standing tall with two bare feet. Gorgeous as ever. His smooth olive skin glows in the sunlight. High cheekbones hollow above his sensual burgundy lips. A small cleft knits beneath his chin, interrupting the hint of black stubble across his chin and jaw line. His nose is straight and strong, nostrils curling delicately at the sides. His wavy jet-black hair is thick and almost wiry as it falls around his ears, pulled by the light breeze. He's looking at me with dark-lashed amber eyes so serious that something below my navel pulls. Wow. He is hottttt.

He crosses his tanned, muscled arms as if he doesn't know what to do with them. This guy must be addicted to the gym, because his chest muscles mold his v-neck shirt. His broad shoulders round against the wind coming from behind him. His ripped jean shorts reveal more muscles, and nearly furry legs.

His stare is unnerving. His voice is somehow both light and rumbling, "So... you still think this is a dream?"

I reassess. The leg hair somehow proves he is not a merman... But I did dream that exactly this handsome apparition saved me from the ocean. In merman form.

Did I miraculously have a paranormal premonition of this man, or did my panicked mind skew reality?

"I'm not sure now," I squint my eyes... He could be a fisherman. He's certainly tan and muscled enough. But his face isn't weather-worn, and looks far too J-Crew for that. "I'm sorry, I think I was hallucinating. Did you save me?" I want to say: I dreamed you were a merman, but I hold my tongue.

He squints like he just tasted a lemon, and looks off towards the horizon. "Save... is a funny word..."

Why do I recognize him then? "So... it wasn't you... but you helped." I nod certainly, then can't hold back my questions any longer, "Where's the fisherman that saved me? Where's the boat? And...why haven't you brought me back to the mainland yet?" I look around uncertainly but I already know there's no boat.

He hasn't answered a single question. I look back towards him. He starts, with one eyebrow raised and opens his firm mouth, "This is not going to make any sense to you."

I cock my head at him.

"I..." He seems to be formulating how he wants to break bad news, he raises both eyebrows expressively, "I brought you here... to..."

I blink, confused. "Brought?" I repeat.

He nods once, staring at me flatly. "I did."

I think back, "So... after that freak wave, you're saying you could have brought me back to land, but instead you brought me...here?" I look around, confused. There is no other land in sight, where is here, if it's not nowhere?

He looks away for a moment, and pulls his hand through his thick wavy hair. When he looks back at me, his jaw is set. "I created that freak wave. Then I brought you here."

I make a face. "Ha. No. You're messing with me. Thanks very much for saving me. But please, can we get on with the truth now?" I smile at him like I've caught him in his game.

He looks at me seriously, and I stare back.

"Fine." He breaks his gaze from me, and lifts his jacked right arm to the side. He pulls his hand back just slightly, then flicks his hand forward.

I raise an eyebrow, snorting with a laugh. "What does your dance move have to do with anything?"

Deadpan, he says, "Watch the water."

Curiously, I do. It's sloshing lazily against the rock.

"Keep watching it." He calmly directs.

I patiently watch the lethargic waves, glancing at his hand move again, and wondering if I have merely been kidnapped by an insane lifeguard.

As he pulls his hand backwards, I hear the ocean gurgling and sucking across the earth as it retreats. I turn to watch as five feet before me, an unusually forceful, monster wave smacks violently against the rocks and rockets thirty feet into the air. Freaking out, I jump backwards.

The drops splatter back across the rock as the ocean returns to its previously tepid state. My mind sobers. Somehow, that freak wave, was his doing. I round on him slowly.

He is standing tall at easily above six foot, with his cut jaw lifted, surveying me regally. His demeanor seems like a wall he has put up to protect himself from my inescapable reaction…

Hot fury broils in me like lava, as my voice strains, "You STOLE ME?" My hands fly out in disbelief.

He stands rooted to the spot, unmoving. "For good reason."

"HA!" I bark. "And what the hell could that be? What the hell could you need from me that is more important than my life?" I rest my gesturing arms on my hips.

He sighs. And takes a few cautionary steps forward, so that we are nearly an arm's length away from one another. He looks about twenty-eight, but his voice sounds aged, "I'm deeply sorry. I just hope, that with time, you will come to understand." His dark eyes fixate on me. "I know you will understand." He pauses, and I wait for something to make sense. It doesn't. He continues in a distractingly velvety voice, "For now, you will have meager explanations that may not seem like enough."

His being this close to me makes my anger simmer down, to be replaced by several other heated emotions. But I need at least hear his lamest explanations, so I ask, "And those are…?"

He breathes in slowly, and appears more poised. "I have brought you here to help our kind. The Merikoi."

My eyebrows crunch in confusion, and I put out a hand to stop him continuing, "Waitwait. The what?" Surprising myself, my hand lands to grab hold of his wrist. He looks down at my hand, and I quickly remove it.

He must think I am very slow, but he appears to be trying to hold his composure. He speaks clearly, "You saw me yesterday- humans call us mermaids."

I shake my head, not understanding. "But that was a hallucination. A dream… Wait. How do you know what I hallucinated?"

He raises an eyebrow with humor.

Comprehension should dawn on me, but it can't. I scrunch my nose, "Sorry. I just don't believe you."

The outer edges of his brows raise, "That's fine. You will eventually. As I was saying, we brought you here to aid the Mer, with your knowledge of humans."

I rub my face, "Okay, say mermaids are real, and this isn't some giant prank…" I look around, but we really do seem to be stranded on an island together.

"Merikoi." He corrects smoothly.

I take a breath, "Okay, Merikoi. Say they are real."

He nods with a tiny smirk and a hint of a glimmer in his eye.

"Then why would you pick me," I touch my collarbone, "Of all people? I mean…I'm not an important scientist or politician or something."

He shrugs and glances away, "Low profile."

I squint at him, "Isn't that kind of risky?"

He pauses, "Maybe."

I stare at him, disbelieving everything.

His body language shifts, and he jerks his head back to the cottage, "C'mon, I'll show you around."

I stay rooted to the spot, deciding. I still don't believe any of this, but I do want to know what's next. And how could I not follow him?

As I trail behind, I feel my wild beast stir again- pacing around and sniffing the air, excited with the prospect of chaos and the unknown. It purrs adventure.

The weatherworn cobbled stone cottage, is clearly centuries old, but I wonder how many. Nothing but heathery grasses and wildflowers separate it from the dark rocks and the sea. It's perfectly aligned to face the four directions, the old oaken door faces North, and the greater length of the small outcropping.

The Mer heads past the wall of rounded rock of the cottage, feet padding between breaths of tiny white flowers. He leaps between the uneven rocks, and climbs down a rock face with elegance and speed. "C'mon," he calls as his thick arms flex and he lowers himself down a small cliff and drops out of sight.

I grew up by the shore, so I keep up fairly well. But I stumble at the cliff, not having expected an eight-foot drop. I turn to climb down a different way, edging along the uneven shelves, and meeting him among flat boulders shimmering silver in the clear morning light.

He glances at me, and then walks straight through that same, eight-foot or higher, shining rock face.

My eyes bulge. Just as I had started to think maybe I wasn't hallucinating…

I walk up towards the wall uncertainly. Reaching my fingers out, I wonder if my depth perception was disturbed by my recent water-logging. My fingertips don't touch rough rock as I expect, but only the empty air. I tentatively step closer, reaching. My hand disappears into cold air, but it looks like my hand has been cemented into the rock. I step closer, and watch as my arm slips easily into the rock. Legs buzzing, I tentatively stick one foot across, it vanishes into solid rock. I step down onto cooler air, and the ball of my foot meets chilly stone. Adrenaline runs up my foot, through the top of my spine, connecting the spaces. Holding my breath, I watch the sunny stone barrier come so close that it looks like a topographic map.

Chilly air swirls at my face, and I open my eyes to see filtered light shining on the smooth charcoal gray of a narrow cave wall. Below, the Mer watches me from a spiral staircase, casually leaning against the wall with one knee out.

I glance around at the curtain-like barrier, I can barely fixate my eyes on it, and beyond, translucent blue skies shine innocently on the seemingly innocuous craggy island.

I look back at him, "That's amazing."

A smile hints at his lips, "It's helpful."

We wind down a staircase carved into earth, my hand trailing along to feel the cool, sandpaper texture of the wall. As we wind deeper beneath the surface, damp cold clings around my skin. Wrought-iron torches flicker on, shining an eerie green hue as we approach, dimming as we pass- shadowy darkness looming just before and behind us.

A haze of warm light greets us at the bottom of the staircase, and we walk in step down a long hallway large enough to fit a train. This hall is too straight to be naturally-occurring, the Mer must have carved it out themselves. I wonder just how large this underwater fortress could be.

We pass silvery wafting bubbles that seal doorways, shivering slightly as we pass. Lining the passageway, watery rooms glow with green light. Reflections from the torches around us warp and mystify the contents of each room. We pass one oak doorway, and I wonder if there is a room full of air behind it. I realize that most of this fortress must be filled with the ocean. It's a little daunting, and I wonder at the strength of those magical wobbling barriers.

As we continue, delicate filigree carves into the onyx walls, tracing doorways and filling out into ornate ocean scenes. I want to just stand and stare at the delicate lines, the sprawling, cursive-like text, and the sketches of sea creatures and mermaids. I wonder if the walls tell stories like their rudimentary sister, cave paintings.

Suddenly we are approaching an ornate door frame, entirely gilt in gold, imprinted with molds of exotic shells, and covered with what might be Mer writing. The gold spills out and stains the nearby carvings with light. As we walk through, a cacophony of voices fills my ears- a strange hybrid between the lilting tunes of an arboretum and the throaty, slower sounds of human speech. The smell of baked fish makes my stomach ache and shift with hunger. The ceilings are lofted magnificently high above, where not rock, but a massive film of air wobbles with the pressure of the seas. Green light filters down, creating a strangely calm ambiance. Four-story white marble pillars surround the hall, reminiscent of Greek temple. Adjoined to the impressive pillars, three levels of balconies rim the hall, with many doors on the North and South ends. The black stone floor is scattered with white driftwood tables, and people, very like humans, are milling around and eating breakfast.

The people are like a cross-section of Boston- if everyone were wearing skimpy silken clothing, some witch-like robes, and insanely fit. Sitting around the long tables, just like humans would, they're chatting over breakfast. It seems the fashion to have tattoos of sea creatures on their arms or across their back or chest. Examining closer, I see most everyone is between twenty and forty. I gasp as I notice a man with a ridge of sharp fins along his outer forearm, and see several more as I glance around. My eyes catch that some have filmy webbing between their fingers, or massively orb-like, inhuman eyes and too-wide fish-like smiles. They're all quite frightening, in the most intriguing way.

As we walk deeper into the room, the Mer notice us like a set of dominoes falling. Within seconds, the room is hushed as they stare at me, unabashed. I guess I probably am the only human here. I try to be polite and not stare back, but immediately fail. Like a kid with no self-control, I can't help but gawk at their alien-like features. My guide-of-sorts notices the staring match I'm holding with the room, puts a hand on the small of my back, and leads me to a queue. Static tingles spread out from where he touches.

As we edge towards breakfast, varieties of shrunken and strange skeletal fish sneer and ogle me with dead eyes. Gratefully, I notice a chowder and collections seaweed as well. But cooked food? Seems odd. "Why do you guys eat cooked food? And why in a room full of air?"

He squints a smirk, "Good question… we eat raw all the time. But sometimes cooked tastes more interesting, we can add seasoning. And the air?" He looks around, and standing close, my body hums with his proximity. "It is way harder to eat with your breakfast floating around you."

I feel my lips curl up, "I guess that does make sense."

I realize that despite his reserved nature, he's kind of easy to talk to.

With seafood chowder cupped in large clamshells, he guides me to a quiet alcove, with a private table. There are staghorn corals adorning the walls, topped with white candles, unlit but melted artfully. Abutting the wall, the end of the table is a scattered collection of gorgeous shells and rounded quartz rocks.

He assesses me without touching his breakfast. His amber eyes appear darker in the muted light. I feel a tug in my chest. I get the nagging sensation that I know him. Or maybe it's just me wanting to know him very badly.

"I guess it's about time I asked for your name." He muses.

I blink, how did I forget to ask his? Then I notice his face. Oh, right. "Stella."

He blinks slowly, "Interesting."

I knit my eyebrows and squint at him, "Why is that interesting?"

He draws up straighter, shrugging. "It's an uncommon name."

Suddenly, three people are shoving towards our table. Rather, two women walking towards us at a normal pace, and a tall ebony man is shoving through them to get to us first. They both nearly drop their shells of soup, and glare at him reprovingly while shouting unrecognizable words at him.

His slightly angular face is handsome, with pronounced cheekbones, and features of exquisite elegance. His muscled arms and broad shoulders stretch his white linen shirt. He reaches us first, smiling winningly, his striking mint green eyes shining. "Who's your friend Poi?"

Aha. His name. I like it.

"Stella, this is my brother, Hades."

I wonder at the name. Same name as the fabled Ruler of the Underworld. Hades slides in next to Poi, and it's strange to think they could be actually be brothers, but maybe it's different with the Mer.

The two women catch up, both sitting on either side of me.

"Stella, this is Laude- a good friend and my top strategy advisor."

On my left sits a tall, moon-pale woman with a short platinum hair. Her severely angular bone structure and long, diamond-shaped nose are made strikingly beautiful with her protuberant blood-red eyes. Charcoal black hammerhead shark tattoos sift across her long bony arms, adding to her militaristic appearance. Joltingly, they remind me of the lilac haired woman with the same tattoos… were they Mer? My brain scrabbles for understanding and suspicion bubbles up in me.

Laude smiles to reveal a set of tiny, piranha-like teeth which cause me to flinch, but her extremely composed manner off-sets the alarming effect of her inhuman features.

"And this is Kiara," Poi continues, "Old friend. She's our top clothing designer, organizes music performances here, and is fantastic on the xylophone."

She looks the opposite of Laude- her heavy-jawed triangle-shaped face has small, sweet features and a tiny upturned nose. Her midnight black eyes have shocking purple flecks. Her clothing is more artistic than the others- decorated with an array of tiny shells which accent her warm mocha skin, voluptuous curves, and athletic build. Golden tattoos of turtles climb her forearms all the way up to her shoulders. Her woven hair is in a tight braid which winds around her head. She smiles warmly, "Hey Stella. Nice to meet you."

She's so genuine, I impulsively smile back.

"So, Poi. What does she know?" Hades is grinning broadly at me, as if I'm already a good friend.

Poi's eyes dart to him dangerously, and Hade's smile falters. Poi's voice is tight, "That Merikoi exist."

"Oh that's nothing…" Hades gazes across at me, sage eyes sweet, "Little one, there's so much to talk about…"

Poi narrows his dark eyes at his brother, and looks downright dangerous. He whispers low, "I won't hesitate on my promise to you, brother."

Hades stares back at his brother, their looming forms in quiet communication. Poi's jaw is flexing, and I am getting the feeling they don't get along so well.

Hades blows out air from his mouth and rolls his eyes until they meet mine. "Has he at least told you that he's Poseidon?"

I smile demurely while rolling my eyes. Clearly, Hades is all about messing with the new person. "No, he hasn't mentioned that…"

Hades' eyebrows nearly reach his hairline as he rounds on Poi. His fingers firmly grasp Poi's thick shoulder, "Well this is going to be entertaining. Entertaining and fun!" Hades beams madly between us.

Poi subtly shakes his head and grumbles, "You are intolerable."

Hades folds his hands on the table, smiling happily, seemingly watching the two of us. I watch him back- his behavior is so strange. He raises his eyebrows at Poi, "She doesn't believe it."

"I know." Poi picks up an antique silver fork and prods his breakfast, ignoring us now.

Knitting my eyebrows, I look at Poi. I'm trying to decide whether he's also playing the game of "mess with the newcomer," or just placating Hades' game, when Laude chimes in.

Her voice is clear and brisk as she addresses Poi, "The hunters are all set for this evening."

"Thank gawd..." Hades mouth hangs open, "I am so sick of eating farmed oysters and clams... it's all they've got around here." He gripes, looking to me for sympathy, which I feel the opposite of.

"Um, what's wrong with that?" I ask. Being from Maine, I have a weak spot for steamers.

He stares at me like I'm stupid. "Umm... only because a little variety would be nice."

"We have a large variety of seaweeds..." Poi smiles at him helpfully.

Hades glares at his brother. "And snails. I'm sick of snails."

"Don't forget all the bottom feeders." Poi inserts.

Hades shivers. "You mean those freaky see-through glowy guys? Yuck."

"I'm a little sick of it too..." Kiara meekly glances between Poi and Hades.

"Well, this is survival guys." Laude cuts in. "The humans haven't left us a lot to fish for, and we can't allow the entire system to collapse."

"Laude," Kiara leans over the table, and between them, I lean back a bit. "We don't have a massive population to feed."

"I would say two hundred thousand of us —in the Atlantic alone—is sizable." Her thin eyebrows have shot up to her platinum hairline.

Kiara breathes in a deep breath, gearing up for rebuttal.

Poi interjects, "Let's change the topic before we depress our guest." He smiles at me apologetically.

I bite my lip. "I actually like it..." I try to explain, "We have a lot of the same issues on land—with food systems collapsing, but at least you guys are dealing with it. It's refreshing."

Poi's cat-like eyes rake over me, thoughtful.

"She's full of surprises." Hades squints at me like I'm a lab specimen he's inspecting.

I prickle. It reminds me of how Jonas used to treat my opinions, as if a woman shouldn't have so many.

Even in this underwater fortress, hundreds of miles away from human existence, the same prejudices against women exist. I sigh and look between the strikingly handsome men. I shouldn't have gotten my hopes up.

# CHAPTER 7

STELLA

Laude and Kiara have spent their day giving me the tour of the fortress built into this submerged mountain range. They explained that we're currently in the Mid-Atlantic Ridge – the longest mountain range on Earth, which lays a seam down the Atlantic Ocean. Once, the Mer were spread out along the coasts, living in corals and underwater caves. Thanks to humanity's new technology and further encroachment on the sea, now all the Mer in the Atlantic live along this underwater mountain range, many in separate colonies, separated by hundreds and thousands of miles. But this part of the Ridge is the largest, and most central community.

We must have walked no less than ten miles of corridors and stairs. My legs are burning, and my mind is reeling with images of dark passageways winding up and down through the damp stone earth, passing rooms of air, but also several that were open to the ocean. They showed me the gardens from an expansive large window overlooking the mountain side. The beautiful rolling hills were dappled with striped, roaming and stretching, wave-filtered light. The hills looked wild, but Laude explained to me that it was actually a complex ecosystem the Mer had built and fostered. All across the mountain range grows a large variety of edible vegetation, as well as oysters and starfish and all the other life those plants attract.

Leg muscles protesting, we reach the Armory just in time to watch the Hunt depart. The ceilings are low rock, and the walls are crowded with collections of ridiculously long, twisting spears and short daggers. Yet it's dusty, and reminds me of a dark library.

Lean and muscular Mer stride around, exchanging weapons and fastening them to their bodies with tightly woven seaweed ropes. The women wear tightly braided hair and tight strappy bandeaus above ripped abs that would shame any Pilates teacher. As I glance around at the bare-chested men, muscled like professional athletes minus the steroids, I try not to let my jaw literally drop. All of them are littered with beautiful tattoos stretching from their arms, tracing around their muscles, and crawling across their chests or backs. Loud and quick foreign language echoes around the room, interrupted only by laughter and the clang of spears being unhitched from the walls.

Laude strides over to the wall of lethal, metal and stone-tipped spears. The thin spear shafts seem to be coated in a gleaming, pitch-like residue which protects them from rotting. Laude spins a few before taking one down which towers over her height. She grabs a halter, slips it over her head, and expertly reaches around and secures the spear before heading back for two daggers.

Kiara follows my gaze, "Yeah, Laude is in heaven. She probably won't even remember to say 'bye.'"

I smirk, and watch as Laude winds through the crowd of weapon-clad Mer. They do look a bit disturbing- the ancient weaponry paired with several sets of sharp teeth, blood-red eyes, and too-wide mouths.

I can't help glancing around for Poi, but I can't see past the swarming wall of tall and bulky hunters. I try to squelch my disappointment. I am not getting sucked in to a crush. No.

A green light burns bright in the middle of the group, and they all back into a crowded, layered circle. Each gaze is transfixed upon the perfect burning globe of green light which floats like a sun between them, wicking moisture from the air.

Suddenly the deep timbres of Poi's voice are the only sound in the room. "Great Ocean Spirit, we offer up this miriga to you…" The chiseled lines of his face are lit peridot in the relative darkness, as if he's telling a spooky ghost story. Ropes hitch across his carved chest, binding two lethal, three-pronged spears to his back. My eyes widen- tridents? He's far too sexy to be the mythical, white-bearded Poseidon. Forget it, his choice of weaponry has got to be a coincidence.

He stands between the circle and the strange hazy orb, the light flickers against his toned body as his hands nearly cradle the light- as if creating it. I glance around for a projector or some kind of source, catch myself, and feel silly. Obviously, the Mer don't have electricity or anything comparable. Poi must be the source of this floating light. Yet again I'm floored by how far reality actually stretches. The glowing orb is brightening by the second, and is almost hard to look at. I blink to clear my vision.

All the hunters are looking to Poi, and he is addressing the bright orb, his eyes intense and unblinking, reflecting burning white light. "We ask that you protect your Guardians as we hunt. Please protect us from human discovery. Please provide us sustenance, nothing more. We thank you."

The orb twitches like an eyeball, and lightening-like, rockets over heads and splashes across the filmy barrier into the sea. It sparkles and explodes, dispersing into nothing. The crowd closes around Poi again, corralling to follow the orb.

Poi stands by the window-like, magical film which holds back the force of the ocean. He motions for certain groups to come forward, and others to wait. He seems to be in charge. Hades' joke crawls back into my mind, claiming Poi is "Poseidon," the Greek God of the Sea.

But it's just insane to me. Apparently, I can believe in mermaids, but Gods that look like men and women? That's a leap. God might be real, but there's no way it's gendered or human in any way. I just can't believe that.

I mean… Poi doesn't even act like a God or a king— he doesn't wear a crown, or act superior to anyone else. He doesn't even dress differently. But I guess being a ruler here could be different than on land, different from human governing systems. Okay, so maybe he's a king of sorts. But a Greek God? That's insane.

A loud ruckus erupts as spear-strapped Mer splash through the air barrier, two at a time, causing the film to wobble threateningly with vertical, sloshing waves. I bite my lip and pray the magical seam protecting against the seawater holds. I swear some Mer are intentionally belly-flopping across, as if dared. Even ten feet away, I'm getting soaked as if I'm standing poolside.

After they've all torn, splashed and leaped through like ten-year olds at a birthday party, I can breathe again. I walk up to watch the scene from the wavering window. It's like a dream. Actually, exactly like some dreams I've had. All the figures have shifted into Mer- dark tails glimmering and in the fading light from above, dangerous long spears in tow. They swim off like darting minnows, becoming enveloped by the darkening sea. Every distant Mer has tooth-pick-like spears attached their backs… I gaze out at Poi's exceptionally long midnight blue tail, his three-pronged tridents, and I have to ask.

Kiara is standing beside me, watching too.

My voice is strained, "Are those… tridents? That Poi is carrying?" And then I realize how strange the name "Poi" is. It's kind of similar to Poseidon. This is getting real weird.

She sideways glances at me and winks. "They are."

I knit my brow, watching the dots disappear into a murky haze. "Do they all use those?" I ask, but I know no one else was carrying them.

"Nope. Just Poi…" She purses her lips, but they sneak into a full smile.

"As in… like the mythical Greek God of the Sea? Poseidon?" My voice is weak. I can barely believe I've asked the question.

Her eyes brighten but she flips a hand nonchalantly. "Oh… the Greeks went overboard. They absolutely glorified the Guardians. Poi isn't God in a literal sense. The Abyss and the Great Ocean Spirit are closer to what you would call a God. Poi's just a Guardian. King Guardian of the Sea."

An odd tingling sensation pricks the base of my skull. Mermaids, sure, I guess. But anthropomorphic god-like Guardians? I feel faint. "So… why did the Greeks think he was a God?"

"Oh—they probably saw his abilities. You know, before he was more careful about staying hidden from humans. The Ancient Greeks were obsessed with beings like him."

Ancient Greeks were obsessed with beings like him? How old is this dude?

Kiara continues, fingering the spears hanging on the wall, "Several humans witnessed that he— ah, I should let him tell you…" She sighs, and we begin walking out of the armory, towards the dining hall.

She pauses, and I stay quiet, hoping she will continue. With a quiet thrill, I wonder if humans are allowed to know this stuff.

"And then… the Greek culture spread, and the myths have spread too." She glances at me as we approach the dining hall. "So yes, Poi is Poseidon, but not in the way you think."

My stomach is churning with nerves. "So… what makes him a… Guardian?"

She squints at me coyly. "I'm not sure how much I'm allowed to say…" and then glances at the buffet and groans. "Ugh. Good thing they're going on a hunt… I am not touching that barreleye. Yuck!"

The fish is on its side, nearly paper-thin and blackened with spices. Yet it's open mouth and crusty nose remind me of a mummified Egyptian. The large eyes must have been orb-like at one point, but they look deflated like raisins. I have to agree with her. That is repulsive. That doesn't qualify as food.

I wrinkle my nose and pull a face. "You couldn't dare me to eat that."

She laughs. "C'mon. Periwinkles are safe. Escargot! Chewy and good." We each pick up a clamshell of spiraled tiny snails, and another of shredded seaweed like pasta.

We head over to a table, and I'm beginning to feel at ease around her. She sits across from me. I pick up a snail, staring at the crusty inner slug with equal parts disgust and hunger, realizing I don't have the slightest idea how to eat it.

I just look up at her, and she laughs at my expression. "Here," she reaches to the center of the table where tiny toothpick-like, carved fish bones are arranged. She hands me one with an ornate and miniscule clamshell carved at the tip, and I wonder at the artistry in everything here. Time is spent on creating lasting, functional art. "You have to poke the side here," she demonstrates, "and pop it out." Then she pokes it with the bone like an hors d'oeuvres on a toothpick, and pops it in her mouth.

Hesitantly, I scrape the bone along the sides of the shell, but the snail doesn't "pop," instead, I'm just destroying it. My stomach grumbles testily. She just watches me. "You got it. Try skewering it now. Yep. Try yanking it out now."

It pops. She cheers. "There you go!"

I taste it, and it's buttery like lobster. But chewy. Definitely chewy.

After I struggle with a few more, I pick up the conversation again. "So, you said Poi is a King Guardian... does that mean he's sort of a King of the Mer?"

She sighs, clearly not eager for this line of conversation. "Yes... he is."

But I'm pretty good at getting answers. "So he's in charge of... this fortress... are there any other Merikoi Kings in the sea?"

She frowns, "No, it's not like human culture. We don't like war."

A bit affronted, I exclaim, "I don't like war! Lots of humans don't like war. The problem is the military-industrial complex makes a lot of money off wars. They get them started just to make money—"

Her eyes widen at my enthusiasm and holds out a hand to stop the flow of my impassioned speech, "Yes... but before that even, humans have always been at war with other humans. Across the ages. Mer are not like that. We don't fight with each other. We stay centered and peaceful."

I'm starting to get a little offended, but I realize it's not productive. I'm actually feeling a little combative, which annoyingly, proves her point. Humans do tend to fight with each other. So I decide to try to get more questions answered. "So… what sorts of things make him more than human?"

She spins her seaweed salad on a fork like pasta, bobbing her head as if weighing her thoughts. "Well… you know, some different types of magic… I really feel like it's not for me to say."

I can tell she's getting uncomfortable, but I can't help myself, I've just landed in this magical world, and I would like some answers please and thank you. "Are humans not supposed to know?"

"Something like that." She smiles.

Then, she gets a devilish gleam to her violet-flecked eyes, "Now, it's your turn to answer questions…"

A little flicker of fear twists inside me, as I wonder how personal this is going to get.

"What was your life like on land?" Her eyes are hungry with curiosity, "Did you have a car?"

I breathe out, smiling at her innocuous question. "Yep."

She swiftly extracts a snail and pops it into her mouth. "I love driving—I've only done it a few times though."

"Sounds dangerous."

She smiles sweetly, "I was a natural."

I wake, and wander outside. I stand before the wide orb of ocean meeting the cloudless sky. Bright light dances off the endless seas, and bounces back into the limitless blue. A sense of stretching happens in my soul. My heart expands to fill the open space.

This place of boundless wild beauty flaunts a certain freedom. I can feel my vivacious nature stirring from its slumber. This glimpse into who I am, contrasted to what I have been living, is stark. I never realized how much I had been giving up and over-accommodating before. It was an unconscious swap, a surrendering to everyone but myself, a slow and steady wearing at who I am and what I believe in. My chest clenches at just how far from myself I went, for the sake of feeling accepted and loved.

I decide I won't deny myself this feeling of freedom again. Just like the ocean refuses to quell its burgeoning waves, I won't trade my sense of truth and self for anyone again. The only type of love that is real and freeing is being loved for all of me. When I go back into love one day, that person will love me even more for my opinionated nature. I know what I think of the world. That's important. I won't be ashamed of having a brain.

A tawny seagull cuts through the empty air with paper airplane wings.

Biting my lip, I feel heavier again. It might be a long time before I am emotionally ready to be with someone. I just know that men subconsciously expect me to pander to them. I don't want to get sucked into that dynamic again. I don't want to lose myself in someone again. I clench my jaw, staring at too-bright light. I have to be ready to be alone for a long time. I stare out at the flat horizon, so far away. So separate.

It's okay. I've found my whole self. I will now coax it out of shelter. No more hibernation. The stirring deep in my soul seems to stretch out again. The briny wind catches in my lungs, and I can breathe again.

Staring out at the sea, I realize I could easily be home again with this view. It's the same tepid blue. It's a link to my truth. This whole time, all I really ever wanted to do was help the ocean, and sea creatures. Rather than laboring to uphold a fake identity for the sake of trying to be lovable, I'm just going to do what I want and love myself.

I stare down at the bright sea, knowing beneath holds a long-trailing fortress full of Mermaids named "Guardians of the Sea." They have the same goal as I do.

I feel incredulous. This magical world I have found myself in is exactly the reality I belong in. With the Mer, I'll find out how I can help protect the oceans. This is who I am and where my opinions have led me, and this what I want to do.

The day goes by quickly. Kiara and I return from another long tour of the fortress, so now I've learned just enough to get so sufficiently lost I would die trying to find my way back to the main halls. Depending on the height of the Ridge, there are give-or-take six stories of this fortress that run indefinitely North and South, and that would be enough for easy navigation if it were not for all the blocked passageways and specific stairwells you have to take to certain floors in order to have access to a hall that actually runs all the way North-South. Many of the Southern halls are blocked off, so Kiara spent hours showing me all the beautiful outlooks along the Northern Ridge. All the best vantage points from the wobbling windows were from communal lounges and private living quarters, I met many more Mer, and I hope I won't be expected to remember all their names later.

Finally, dusk arrives, and so do the hunters. Like warriors, high from battle, they stroll through the dining hall and towards the kitchen, carrying spears over their shoulders like skewers. Rows of gelatinous, dripping jellyfish trail their streamer-like tendrils lifelessly. I feel my nostrils flare and lip curl up in disgust, unable to hide my repulsion. Those aren't edible either. I hope that's not the only meal option…

Nonplussed by the chunks of slime slipping to the floor, Kiara and the few people who did not join the hunt cheer and hoot happily.

"To the hot springs!" Kiara announces happily.

I sit up stiffly, still aching from the miles of walking, extremely pleased with the mention of hot springs.

When we reach the grottos, there are many series of circular pools steaming enticingly. It reminds me of my first night, just two days ago, where I recovered from crossing half the Atlantic with Poi. But that was a private grotto hot spring. This is more of a social event. The torch lights are dancing off the water merrily, and most of the Mer are already here, lounging in the black waters and chatting in their lilting mysterious tongue.

Some Mer dip below the surface, and seconds later, appear in different pools, and I realize the springs must be connected. It's strange to think of Mer swimming beneath the rock floor, in secret cavernous spaces filled with warmth.

Nervously, I follow Kiara, Laude, and Poi to the pool Hades is already lounging in. The white swirls of steam curl around Hades' bulky dark shoulders. The others slip into the spring, and my toes gingerly kiss the surface. The black water nips heat around my ankles as I ease in slowly. The warmth encircles my torso and chest, lapping all the way up to my shoulders. The water caressing my skin makes me realize how much I've missed being touched. Sitting on an underwater ledge, my eyes find Poi. He's watching me closely. I'll admit it, he does look like a god in this light. The shadows play seductively around his carved chest and shoulders, his long neck and protruding adam's apple, his defined jawline, to the high planes of his cheek bones, and his symmetrical, rectangularly shaped face. His almond, dark amber eyes are glittering with reflecting light. His sculpted lips turn up in a tentative smile.

Adrenaline swirls against my insides. I really don't know how to be normal around someone this gorgeous, but I smile back awkwardly.

Kiara laughs and I realize people are talking around us. I listen in, grateful to not have to continue the unnerving staring contest.

"Levi nearly gutted Hades." Laude's wide red orb eyes are bulging with humor. Her tiny scissor smile makes me want to edge away, but I don't want to be rude, so I stay firmly seated.

Kiara shrieks with laughter again, shouting, "You idiot!" and splashing Hades, drenching his face.

He smirks, water dripping down his chest. "Levi was out of formation."

"Bullshit." Laude chides. "You weren't listening when we were talking tact. My bet is you were still doing the Yiadeiri." She smiles smugly, raising an eyebrow at him.

He twists his lips like he's trying to keep a smile in.

"Guilty..." Kiara taunts at him, and he cuts his eyes to her and winks.

"So..." Poi's voice is low as he stares across at me, "Do you have any questions? How was your tour of the Ridge?"

I bite my lip. His stare is going to be my undoing. "It was..." I fumble for the right words, needing to look away from him. My mind flashes to the stories of stacked caves and grottos, the gorgeous library and expansive lounges, and countless private suites we toured. The bare, beachy, rustic decorating style blew me away. All the repurposed relics of discarded human debris astounded me. The eye-popping collections of exquisite shells, stones and dried corals would be enough to make the curator of the Natural History Museum drool. I gaze up into Poi's dark amber eyes again, finding my voice. "It was eye-opening. You have such a beautiful way of life here."

His eyes warm and smiles, "Thank you," he rumbles. Despite his youth, his demeanor is that of someone far older. "Do you have any questions?" He repeats.

I purse my lips, and glance down at the flickering lamplight on the water. "Um, yes." I don't know how to say it without sounding outrageous... but somehow, I have to ask him outright, if he's a Greek God. I seriously hope Kiara wasn't messing with me. I glance at her, and realize she's staring at me quietly. They all are. I drag my eyes across Poi's sculpted chest again, and up to meet his gaze. "Are you Poseidon?"

His curved lips twitch into another smile. "Yes."

I feel my jaw drop, a little. "So... wait. What does that mean? Are you a— Greek Gods aren't real..." I trail off, not sure what to ask.

He smiles kindly. "I'm not a God, in the sense Humans detail in their myths, lore, or religions."

I squint my eyes at him, not sure what the name Poseidon would mean then, aside from just a name.

"I'm King Guardian of the Sea. I lead the Merikoi in protecting every living thing which inhabits the ocean."

I nod, but the label doesn't really help me out at all. "So... you're ... not a God. But... you're more than a Mer?"

"Right."

He doesn't explain much more, so I decide to go for a different angle: "So what about Greek Mythology then, what did they get right, and what did they get wrong?"

He squints up at the low, rough ceiling, thinking. His jaw lifted, I internally whimper at the exposure of his muscled neck, his Adam's apple pushing forward, and the smooth planes of his carved chest. "Well, I don't have the power to create earthquakes, and I have no infatuation with horses."

The other three laugh, but I don't get the joke. Apparently I know very little about actual Greek God mythology. Maybe the Ancient Greek version of Poseidon had an affinity with horses? Seems strange for the supposed God of the Sea.

"Despite the hopes of ancient humans, I've never had an interest in controlling the rainfall patterns over land." He continues, "I also didn't sire any monster children, and haven't been with countless lovers. So, I'm pretty boring." He shrugs his thick shoulders, and I have to disagree.

The word "ancient humans" echoes in my mind. He knew ancient humans? His visage is so... stunning... he just can't be thousands of years old. Maybe he doesn't age...?

"So you don't age then?" I ask him bluntly.

He inclines his head, "I do age, just... very slowly."

The concept is strange to me. I don't understand it, but I have so many more questions barreling through my mind, demanding answers. "So are all Greek Gods based in some truth?"

I realize Hades is giving me a "how stupid are you" look. And it clicks. Hades. God of the Underworld. I can't help expelling my shock: "The God of the Underworld is a Mermaid?!"

Laude and Kiara screech with laughter that ricochets around the echoey, already noise-filled grotto. Poi's laugh is guttural and makes something deep in my chest sing. His burgundy lips peel wide, his eyes dancing with humor as he watches at his brother's reaction.

Hades has a dangerous smile on his face, and is slowly shaking his head. "Trouble... you are in for some trouble. No one calls me a mermaid and gets away with it."

But Poi, Kiara, and Laude are crying with laughter, so it feels like an empty threat. I think of Dante's seven levels of hell- fires, and tortured souls. I think of a faceless, hooded grim reaper, and of a classic red-horned devil- with pretty Mermaid tails. I am trying so hard to bite back the erupting giggles.

His sage green eyes narrowed, Hades waits for me to compose myself. He drawls like he's explaining something to a very young child, "The main entrances to the Underworld are underwater, so Mer form is necessary. I am Immortal. You think the mortal forms I take define me?"

I shrink a little under his striking angelic stare, and realize I have technically affronted a god. I back down, "I don't know..."

"Mermaid!" Kiara erupts with giggles again.

Laude shoots her a "settle down" look, and Kiara bites her bottom lip, attempting to quell her laughter.

Hades sighs and rolls his eyes, slipping further into the water, sinking his chin to kiss the surface and narrowing his eyes at Kiara. Poi smirks at me, and it feels like there's some funny secret between us. It makes my heart get all jittery.

"To answer your question..." Poi speaks, and I don't know if it's the soft lighting, or if his gaze looks nearly suggestive, but his dark eyes could make me melt. "The Ancient Greeks were often far off the mark. Some of their so-called gods never existed, and everyone else was inaccurately portrayed. We could spend days talking about this."

And I want to spend days talking about it. As long as I get to be with him. Then I catch myself. This thought is very scary. I'm not ready for falling for someone again. I'm not ready to pander to another man- or worse, a freaking god. Not that he technically is- but he totally is. He lives forever and has magical powers. In my book, that equals a Greek God. Anyway, not that he'd be interested in a human. I look away from him, and try to collect myself. I cannot be crushing on a Greek God. That would be very stupid.

# CHAPTER 8

POI

The water slides off her skin as she gets out of the pool, her swim suit wraps around the body I knew as home, but I look away before she feels my gaze. The three women wrap themselves in silken cloaks, and Thalassa's wide gaze meets mine again before they leave the Grottos. I know her well, and in her lasting gazes, I read fear- as if she's anticipating me to hurt her. It makes me wonder what human men did to her. She thinks she's broken. I want to wrap my arms around her tiny frame and hug her. I want to kiss her like polishing a weathered stone until she shines bright again.

Every time she walks away, every time we part, I feel like I'm holding my breath. I want to follow her- to cocoon ourselves and only exist in the world between us. She's so close now, but I need to vigilantly keep a grip on myself. Any wrong move on my part, and I could ruin everything- her own chances of surviving past this one short human lifetime.

I could really use a human counsel for dating. I tried to talk to her, but out came my identity, and she appeared intimidated. There's just so much for her to adjust to. Time, it's just going to take more time than I want it to. I shouldn't even try to estimate how long.

"You're thinking hard." My brother drawls from beside me, and I realize he's been staring. "Trying to calculate how to flirt, rather than scare the shit out of Thalassa?"

I whip my head towards him. "Don't. Don't call her Thalassa. Sometimes I think you want to destroy everything."

He smiles at me flatly.

"Call her that again and I will banish you from the Ridge." I growl.

"Sure, sure." He rolls his eyes at me.

His competitive little crush on her never bothered me until now. If he could find some way to keep her in Hell, I'm sure he would. But I want to believe that deep down he cares about my happiness. It's only a little relieving to know that Hades is unlikely to tell Thalassa the truth simply because her knowledge that she was my soul mate and Queen, would hardly lend her towards choosing Hades instead. I'll just have to watch him closely. My heart tightens around the idea of him pursing her, but I can't excommunicate him for that. I have to believe she will choose me again.

I stare as the water stretches the torchlight, transfixed with a head full of new memories of Thalassa as Stella... as a human. More than just the fearful way she eyes me, she's less centered in general. The way she speaks, the way she holds herself around others- it's like she doesn't fully trust herself. It does makes sense- she doesn't know her full identity. This identity-searching, struggling version of her just makes me want to tell her the truth even more. But somehow, she has to fall in love with me first.

"Here's a tip—human women like when you grab their asses." Hades' hand clenches around the white steam.

Laughing, I swear "Fuck you," in Merglossa, and pull myself out of the pool. My brother is the last company that I need right now.

In an attempt to not smother her, for the first two days, I asked Laude and Kiara to show Stella around while I maintained my usual duties. But today, I'm going to spend with her. I can't convince myself out of it. Not alone, not the whole day, but I'll ease us into familiarity.

When green light begins to filter through the windows, I stop trying to sleep. I pull back the crimson sheets, and sit at the edge of the bed, rubbing the prickly stubble of my face. A knock resounds from my door.

"One minute… who is it?"

I hear Laude's gruff voice as I stretch towards the ceiling. Yawning, pull on a white T-shirt and jean shorts. I open the door to her stiff frame, face pinched with concern, and buggy scarlet eyes glancing behind me, as if she thought I might have caved and seduced Stella. I thought she knew me better than that. But if nothing else, Laude is thorough. She takes her post as my top strategy advisor a little too seriously.

I raise my eyebrows at her, "You're here early."

"We have to plan for today." She strides past me, and stands in the middle of the room, straight as a pole, and more alert than I have energy for.

"How long have you been awake for?" My voice is coarse.

"Guarantee I slept more than you. I knew you'd be awake."

"Hmm." I grunt at her, closing the door, and crossing to sit on my desk. I scoot the chair out with my foot for her to sit.

She perches on the edge, and shakes her head. "You're holding it together, and I don't want you to crack under the pressure."

My heart warms, and I can't help a small grin. She does know me well. "Thanks Laude. That's very kind of you."

She raises her platinum brows with an air of all-business. She's always been like a military general with the way she hides her soft heart.

"You've spent two whole days away from her, you're successfully stemming any suspicions insofar. I think you could afford to see her more today."

Immediately my jaw clenches. She has no right to tell me when I can and can't see Stella. Breathe. She's just trying to help. But a flicker of anger burns in my chest. I can't handle anyone trying to keep me from her now. I breathe until the anger is gone. This is what happens when I get attacked before I've even had time to shave. "I agree."

"You've got the Waste Counsel today—do you plan to keep that meeting?"

"Yes, of course. We can do both. I'm not going to spend all day with her. I don't want to frighten her."

She nods quickly.

"Will you and Kiara join me in showing her the gardens today?"

I'd like to go alone with Stella, but I believe it's too soon for that. Not with her fearful gazes.

I've never lounged so much in the dining hall, just waiting for her to walk in. My nerves are crackling fire. I can see that outside of my skin, the empty cavernous hall is peaceful. The cooks haven't arrived yet. I watch the familiar rays and schools of fish soaring above the broad skylight above. The world Stella knows is so shockingly different from the world we knew as one. How can she even relate to me and this strange world? What if she won't? What if she demands that I return her to the shore? My throat constricts. I don't have room for these fears. I have to keep believing. I have to believe that some part of her soul will recognize me, or at least be able to fall for me again.

My tumultuous reverie is disturbed as Mer wake, and it seems everyone wants a first-hand account of how this new human Thalassa is adjusting to the Ridge. I stem each query quickly, as she could walk in at any moment. After reminding many curious friends of this, Levi walks up. His curly sandy-blonde hair catches in his eyelashes, the bridge of his nose is slightly crooked, and his sapphire blue eyes are set slightly close together. His breakfast shell clangs on the table, and he sits. I have to talk to Levi. Not only is he a close friend, but also perilously curious. I need to squelch his dangerous inclination for knowledge. No one can be asking questions about Stella. I can't risk her overhearing a word of this.

"So she doesn't remember anything?" He asks, inhaling opalescent cooked jellyfish.

The words, put so precisely, are like a rushing rouge wave dragging me across a rocky sea floor. I breathe slowly.

He continues, "I mean, she looks exactly the same. She acts the same. She is the same. But she doesn't have her memory? How is that possible?"

"Levi, I know you have the urge to figure this out, but you need to keep it all inside."

His face crumples into a grumpy childlike grimace.

"There's nothing to be gained from you figuring out this puzzle. The Prophesy has laid it out for us clearly: She can't know of her identity, and I have to find a way to have her fall in love with me again. No one can speak of this. I can't risk her overhearing a word. So I ask that you become mute on the topic. Will you promise?"

His broad shoulders hunch over the last of his sautéed jellyfish. He sighs and looks up at me with itchy disappointment. "Fine. Sorry. I was just bored."

I keep my face even.

"So, how's it going with her, have you—"

Behind him, I see Stella's head of strawberry blonde messy hair as she walks into the dining hall. My eyes drink in her heart-shaped face, wide green eyes, full lips, and sprite-like form. My heart stutters. I have so missed her. She's wearing her old plum cloak, open to worn jean shorts and black tank- it's an appropriate hodgepodge between Mer and human realities. She searches the hall, and her weary gaze meets mine for a heartbeat. She smiles uncertainly.

I smile back, certainty written in every aorta of my heart.

Like a skittish ally cat, her eyes widen, and she turns her head and beelines towards the dining line. I can't help chuckling. This version of her is certainly amusing. Maybe she's as bad at this as I am. The thought is somehow comforting.

I glance back at Levi, who is smirking. "So it's going like that."

I grin back at him, rolling my eyes. "Like I said, it's not up for conversation."

"Human women are a difficult species. Trickier. They say they don't want something when they do, say they want what they don't—I still can't figure most of them out."

"But you try."

He winks at me wickedly, "If that's the story…"

I smile and shake my head at him. He's been single for decades now- not the sort to believe in soul mates, and instead prefers more carnal interactions with women. Mostly humans, actually.

"If you need advice… I'm here…" His eyes twinkle mischievously.

"Thanks…" I raise my eyebrows, knowing I won't be asking.

Clamshell of breakfast in her small hands, Stella keeps her eyes averted from me, and sits alone.

I debate for an instant. Either she wants the space, or she's uneasy around all the Mer. I stand and walk over towards her empty table. She sees me from a ways off, and gazes at me like I'm some sort of scary leopard seal. My heart aches for her faulty sense of weakness. Who is this meek girl? I know my Queen is in there somewhere.

Her blonde hair is a messy twist of a bun on her head, and in the bright morning light, it's clear how little sunlight she's had in this life. Her beautiful features are pale, there are purple shadows beneath her eyes. Her sweet face is full of concern, and I physically fight the impulse to round the table and embrace her, to pull the pain from her lips.

"Can I join you?" I ask with a smile.

She presses her lips together before answering, "Sure."

She stares at me, wide eyes catching between mine. I get lost in the textured, twisted green of her irises. There's less certainty there- I could almost map the ways that she's lost herself. My heart aches for her. She'll find herself again. I'll help her.

She loses her nerve and stares down again.

"How did you sleep?" I ask her gently.

She gazes up at me again, more guarded and less open than before. "Um, it's a really beautiful spot, but honestly I was a little cold."

I nod, mentally noting that I will have to bring blankets up later. "I'll address that."

"How did you sleep?" She asks, nerves brightening the tenor of her voice.

I grin. I'm the host, she doesn't need to ask that. But I reply, "Very well, thank you." Total lie. I was up all night thinking about her.

Our eyes catch again. It almost feels like our hearts could be beating in synch. She bites her lip and looks down again. She blushes as she stares down at her kelp toast, and takes a bite.

Yes… I believe I can read even this nervous version of her. She's attracted to me. My heart skips with gratitude. But that's just a step. Attraction and lust are not love. They're not the whole package. And I want her to come back. For her own sake. And yes, my own selfish reasons too. I do love her.

Chest lightened with hope, I remember to ask, "Kiara, Laude, and I would like to show you around the gardens this morning."

Her eyes brighten, as I knew they would. "Alright, that sounds cool."

I feel myself grinning, and she smiles back. My heart catches. It keeps hitting me that she's right here. After all this time.

Her eyes meet mine uncertainly, and she bites the edge of her lip. I inwardly groan. I'd like to do that. I've never had to hold back with her before.

"So, Mermaids and Greek Gods are real." Her face is matter-of-fact.

I laugh from deep down, something only she could pull out of me. "Merikoi," I glower teasingly.

Suddenly emboldened by curiosity, her voice is honey-like, like she's trying to tease a secret out of me. "How have you kept this hidden all this time?"

My heart stutters. She's leaning towards me, and her earnest expression is entrancing. The tension between us is rippling, and I am going to have to take this down a notch if I want to ensure that this human form of her doesn't just get caught up in lust. Humans have a reputation for being more focused on lust, than spiritual-emotional connections which are the basis of real love. I wonder if her human form will have a harder time falling in love- will she just skip straight to lust?

The coiling tension building below my core is reminding me I am not immune to lust either.

I lean back just a little, exhale slowly, and cool my tone. "We used to live along the coastal shelves— closer towards the shores of all the continents. But as modern human societies sprawled and covered nearly all the temperate seashores, our secrecy became endangered, and we displaced ourselves. Now many of us live within this Mid-Atlantic Ridge. This and underwater mountains around the world."

She blinks quickly, and straightens a bit in her seat, her head at the level of my shoulders, eyes glittering with curiosity. "But what about human technology? Surely a submarine has gone by and seen all your lights?" Her distanced tone seems to mirror mine. I curse myself, wondering if any form of distancing is actually a bad idea.

"Remember the entrance from the island?" I guide.

Her eyes flicker with recognition, "Some sort of cloaking or invisibility magic?"

"Indeed. All of our fortresses appear to be a natural formation of vegetation-encrusted rock. As long as we are within it, humans cannot see us or our fortresses."

"What about when you're not in a fortress?" Her interest has been displaced from me to the topic, and I don't know whether to be relieved or not. But I do admire her animation.

"Poi!" Kiara's voice rings out from directly behind me, and she sits down at my side. Laude's ghostly, limber form slips down beside Stella, and Hades lopes up and sits on Stella's other side. Too close for my comfort, but he doesn't look at me, so he doesn't catch my prolonged stare.

"Are you telling the human all of our secrets? Is that wise?" Kiara smiles at me widely, and I have to admire her playful role-playing here. She's probably right. I have to treat Stella like a normal human that can't know all our secrets.

I clear my throat and address Stella again. "Kiara's right… you're a human after all…" I smile at her, but she looks deflated. I can't seem to figure out how to talk to her and keep her safe at once.

Kiara, Laude and Hades overrun the conversation with Ridge gossip, and that is probably best, as I can't seem to trust myself with Stella. She gazes at me, and I realize I need to have a better approach to getting close to her.

Stella jumps through the cold water towards us. I chuckle at her ungraceful akimbo limbs, and admire her honey-colored hair billowing out like silky seaweed. Before, she would have tied or braided it to avoid knots. I approach her haphazard froggy swim as her eyes flick shyly to assess my shoulders, chest and stomach, and then fixate on my long tail. I tighten as my eyes graze along her familiar lines I know as home, the chest I've kissed, the tight muscles down her abdomen, the poetic sway of her hips, and the nook between her sprite-like legs. I grip her cool arms, covered in goosebumps, and pull her close. Her wild hair sprawls out around her beautiful face. Her eyes widen and pupils dilate as she stares up at me like I might eat her. I certainly want to devour her, but in a less literal sense.

Holding back the hurricane inside me, I place my lips against hers. I don't allow my body to touch hers. I separate her soft lips with mine, and blow air into her lungs until she is full. My heart yanks with joyous torture. I close her lush lips with mine, and I linger for just an instant, as only a shadow of the desire inside me slips out. I pull away, and her eyes are big, like she could feel what I wanted it to be.

I can't acknowledge it. I don't want to cave to that lust- it would be our ruin. I place my finger against her warm lips as a reminder not to speak. Mistake. Touching her lips just makes me want to kiss her again. She stares up back at me shock and disbelief. The air cycles in her lungs as her chest rises and falls. I pull away and since we're not going far, allow her to navigate towards the gardens on her own. I suddenly don't trust myself to touch her in a way that doesn't relay my desires.

Kiara leads the winding way through kelp as tall as trees, varieties of vegetation, and the hard white blooms of oysters barnacled to rock faces, colorful starfish clinging. Keeping my distance from Stella, I can't help but grin at her silly froggy strokes, and her enthusiastic mime-like communication over the passing schools of fish. But I don't trust myself to be close. It's like she can smell my desire for her, and it's too soon for that. I need to reel myself in before I can be near her again.

# CHAPTER 9

STELLA

It's my fourth night to sleep in the little cottage on the open dome of the sea. The windows rattle with the wind, and I tug them downwards, shutting them without much effect. June's cool night air seeps through the old glass panes. But a fire is lit in the stone fireplace, burning purple around the bone white driftwood logs expelling heat into the damp room. As if magically sensing my presence, the flames grow, and heat increases. I will not get over how cool that is.

Newly placed, a woven rug lays on the cold slate-like floor. The large oval rug nearly reaches the walls with hues of wildflowers melded with blues which mirror the moods of the sea. Bundles of thick wool and woven blankets are stacked neatly on the bed. I know he's only being a good host, but the fact that Poi remembered to bring blankets up, sort of melts my heart. I bite my lip, because somehow this makes me sad. I think I'm too eager to get the wrong idea with him. He couldn't want me. If he wanted me, he would have delivered the blankets in person- it would have been an excuse to be alone together, to talk. He's just being a good host. I grab the thickest woolen blanket, dark charcoal and scratchy, and wrap it around myself, immediately warmer.

I stare around at the old furniture in the room. It's definitely centuries-old, and carved from dark mahogany- domineering and intimidating to mirror Poi's beauty. Just thinking about him makes a heady adrenalized tonic brew in my core. Despite his good manners in the treatment of human guests, I am not getting sucked into a crush again. I'm not strong enough for the idea of love yet. And he is far out of my "league," as they say. I'm human, and I'm sure he only dates other gods- or "immortals," rather. Sighing, I realize I'm in for a riotous battle between my head and my heart, and either way doomed to lose.

A little desk sits pushed up against a darkened window, across from the fireplace. I pull out the Celtic-carved wooden chair, swiveling to face the fire, and leaning forward elbows on knees, watch the flames dance as they sizzle and crackle happily. Despite the growing warmth of the room and the comfort of the heavy blanket, the wind still rattles the windows dangerously, and whistles around the edges of the rock.

My mind flickers with unbidden images of Poi. The way his giving me oxygen felt more mind-blowingly passionate than any "kiss" I've ever experienced... and he barely touched me… Heat flares up deep within me, surprising me. I shove it aside, scolding myself and reminding myself why I want to stay- to help the oceans. And not to get wrapped up in dead-end, disempowering crushes. I need to set boundaries for my heart, and formalize the dynamic here- to tell him how I really do want to help protect the seas. This, at least, I feel more certain about than anything.

The dining hall is teeming with strange Mer, each of them not quite human. I can't see Poi anywhere, and rather than exposing myself for the lost human I am, I enter the kitchen line. I'm behind a woman with thick green dreadlocks braided high on her head, exposing fin-like ears. She's looping arms with a wiry guy with feathery blonde hair. I pick up a clamshell that's carved down to a convenient bowl shape. The wiry guy looks back. His irises are nearly a translucent white. His black pupils look freakishly tiny. Hot seafood chowder spills on my hand as I miss the target. He smiles politely and offers a cloth napkin. I thank him quietly, stunned by the opalescent, rainbow-quality to his eyes. I would say it's enticing, but it's more eerie than anything else. He smiles politely again, and the two of them file into the dining hall.

The masses of eccentric Mer intimidate me. They're all milling around the tables, not quite sitting down properly as they eat. It's hard to see past the crowded tables. There's maybe four hundred people in the cathedral-like hall. The echoing chatter and laughter is high pitch, musical, and distinctly alien.

I walk slowly past the first few tables, then see a familiar jolt of messy black hair. My stomach flips. My mind chides my knee-jerk reaction. I'm human, I better remember that.

He doesn't see me yet, he's sitting with a group, talking animatedly. I'm walking slowly towards him, unsure of myself in this foreign world. When his eyes catch mine, his gaze holds me still. My heart stutters and my brain turns off. Something about him just hooks the core of me and pulls. He excuses himself, stands up to his full height, and strolls over.

His dark hair skews thickly over his handsome face. His walk is both languid and certain. I am caught by the luminosity in his amber eyes as he draws closer.

My brain is blank. I bite my lip and remember what I had meant to say. Something about boundaries… remembering gods aren't into humans…

He stops an arm's length away, warmth lifting his features, "Sleep alright?"

The question makes me blush, because I dreamed of him. Instead I attempt to keep my train of thought, "You know, I've been thinking, and I really did mean what I said yesterday. There's nothing more important to me than saving the oceans. I want to be here, I want to do this, I want to help."

His mouth breaks into a smile and it feels like sunshine. "You're in the right place."

He guides me back to the table where Kiara, Laude and Hades are chatting. His voice measured and yet somehow musical, "To start, I was hoping you would be up for some lessons."

"Alright. With who?"

He smirks. "Me, of course."

My heart flutters. Damn. He's not making it easy to focus on my goal of no men.

"Don't you have better things to do? Aren't you a king, or ruler, or something around here?" I try to sound nonchalant. I'm pretty sure my voice sounds even.

He shrugs and looks around, "Nah... people know what needs to be done. I can spare some time for our newcomer." He smiles and I notice his teeth are perfect too. I scold myself- stop being superficial! Focus on goal! Ocean.

"So... what are you going to teach me?"

"Merikoi culture, human threats-" he ticks off his long fingers, "Which I don't have enough fingers for- and maybe I'll teach you a little Merglossa." I cock my head and he continues, "Merikoi language. How were you at languages in school?"

"Terrible. Don't get your hopes up." I say flatly.

He chortles and shakes his head. "We can try. It would be helpful. For example," he gestures up at the skylight above, "Glieasos."

"Glieasos." I parrot.

He smiles and gestures his hands open as if to say, 'see, not so hard.'

"Tviata." I hear Hades voice cut in as he slides onto the bench next to me. He points at Poi again, and repeats "Tviata."

"I don't trust you." I say plainly.

Poi laughs hard.

"You can say it- Tviata. It means 'ruler.'" Hades cajoles.

I narrow my eyes. "No it doesn't." C'mon, does Hades literally think I'm 5?

"Pshhh- you're no fun." He deflates.

I look at Poi. "What does it mean?"

He smiles amusedly at his brother. "Armpit."

"Easily confused with 'ruler.'" Hades shrugs and starts shoveling sushi into his mouth.

Poi teases, "Uh-huh, so that's why the Underworld is in such great shape these days…"

Hades squints and talks through two rolls of sushi, "Shut up."

Poi smiles happily.

Underworld. Hades. I'll assume if the Greek mythology of Poseidon is somewhat real, so is that of his mythological brother, Hades.

"So this is why I don't have Merglossa lessons with Hades."

Poi winks at me.

"She's clever for a human." Hades shovels in another two sushi.

I smile innocently at him. "And you're not so damnably evil for the supposed Ruler of the Underworld."

He whips his head towards me as Poi laughs from deep in his gut, head thrown back.

Hades eyes narrow, as his voice pitches up, "Who's calling me evil?"

"Um, how about half the world religions? Isn't the Underworld just another word for Hell? Isn't Hades just another word for… the devil?"

He twitches an eyebrow and pinches more sushi between his fingers, "See it the way you want to. The Underworld isn't all sunshine and happy dolphins, and neither am I."

Poi frowns and glances at his brother, "Hades drew the short stick when it came to ruling an Earthly domain… he was given a "fixer upper" as humans might call it, but there's nothing inherently evil about the Underworld, or him, most days."

Hades grins and leans in, "But it's more fun if we call it Hell, isn't it?"

"A little bit…" I whisper conspiratorially with a wrinkled nose. "But what's it really like down there?"

His sushi freezes halfway to his mouth. His upturned eyes squint at me. He speaks slowly, "I can show you sometime…"

"No." Poi interjects, voice overly harsh. His dark brows low, dark-lashed eyes flashing warning at Hades.

"But I'm curious—" I insist, turning back to Hades, "What happens when we die?"

Hades sighs and leans back, eyeing Poi uncomfortably, and gazing back at me with his stunning pale green eyes, "You won't end up there, love. It's only for factory rejects. You know— send it back!" Hades flicks his arm through the air as if wafting away a bad odor, and I'm horrified by his indifferent attitude towards his patrons.

I can't help laughing a little too. "You can't be serious…"

His voice is deep, "I completely am."

I cringe at the thought of souls so corrupt they're not worth saving, "That's so sad…"

He shrugs, "Not my fault."

"But can't you help them at all?"

He stares at me like I'm stupid, "Stella. We're talking about murders and rapists. You can't fix that level of psychotically wacked."

I heave a sigh, feeling like he's wrong, but not sure how to argue with the Ruler of the Underworld on how to do his job.

He leans back, upturned eyes bright with amusement above his pronounced cheekbones, voice off-hand, "Love, you are more than welcome to visit, and tell me all about how to do my job right…"

I am suddenly gripped by a want to do just that- I'm immensely curious…

Poi tenses beside me. "Hades, I would appreciate you retracting your offer…"

Hades meets his brother's gaze innocently. "It's her choice."

Poi is silent for a moment, then turns to me, composed. "Stella. Are you ready for your first lesson?" His velvet voice is inviting, his poetic features are warm, and the intensity in his amber eyes is totally distracting.

My heart skitters madly, "Absolutely," I squeak.

Poi's quiet as he leads me through the halls. He's about a head and a half taller than me and his legs carry him along efficiently, so I find myself taking wider, quicker steps. He opens a heavy oak door, exposing the library I saw during my tour. Book shelves are carved into the stone walls, leaden with leather volumes. A fireplace burns orange behind a few comfy-looking lime green metal-studded leather armchairs.

He turns to me, head lowered, his brow lowered slightly with concern, "Stella… I—I hope you don't take Hades up on his offer…"

I tilt my head with confusion, "Why? It's not like the Underworld is dangerous, is it?"

He blinks, and purses his lips before speaking, "Well, no… I'm just, concerned it may take away from your focus here, as Human Council to the Mer. The Underworld has a whole host of its own problems, I wouldn't want you to feel obligated to resolve them. You've already been so generous in offering your help here. I wouldn't want you to be stretched too thin…" His voice is solemn, but a part of me wonders if there's something more than curtesy and logic to his statement. I am sensing just hue of competitiveness with his brother. Strange that I would be in the middle of that. There are plenty of humans that would love to help—

My thoughts can't go any farther. Poi's looking down at me with his dark melt-me eyes. Here in this quiet space, with the torchlight flickering yellow, I really feel insanely tempted to lower my guy-ban.

Being with him makes me shaky, but I try to sound level, "I'll… keep that in mind." My eyes linger on his delicately sculpted lips, and I can't believe, even considering the oxygen-depraved circumstances, that I know how soft they are. With an effort, I force myself to stay focused on the fact that there will be a "lesson" coming up, and not what I want to be doing with him… which includes far less talking.

I look away to get my thoughts to move on. A beat passes. I'm wondering if there's a chance his thoughts are flickering to where mine went. I look at him curiously, and it seems like there is a wall down, and his eyes flicker to my lips. My blood pumps harder, like surging seas lifting with a high tide.

He clears his throat and looks towards the door, inching away from me. "So today, I was hoping to show you the Rescue Clinic."

"Oh, ah. Sounds great." I talk through a haze as my mind flickers back to reality. Of course this insanely sexy god-like being is not into me. I would be crazy to think that. Get with it brain!

He ushers me out of the heavy oaken door, and strides down the hallway quickly, as if eager to get out of the intimacy of that space, and I jog to catch up.

We arrive in front of a submerged room, and as I look closer, I see that it is the size of the dining hall, with hundreds of Mer hovering cloud-like in crowds.

Without warning, Poi splashes through the barrier, soaking me. Open mouthed, I look at him incredulously.

He raises a rebellious eyebrow at me, smirking, as he floats past me easily, already shifted. I can see him better in this light, his midnight blue tail bulges with strange muscles, the fin wide and curved elegantly, with beta fish tendrils. His tail alone, is easily ten feet long. I am no less fascinated by his shirtless torso, which is perfectly toned and causes an acute, resounding pang below my navel.

His long-fingered hand gestures, and my heart beat quickens as I realize what he's suggesting. I walk forwards and put my head, shoulders, and arms into the freezing water. Pushing off with legs, I attempt to propel myself gracefully into the water. Then, horrified, realize my feet are still on the ground. I'm stuck. Flailing, I try to swim with my arms towards Poi, with no luck. I then try kicking myself back into the room. Panicking, I look up, and see Poi convulsing with laughter. Furious, I give him my most reproachful glare.

He sobers up and leans down to grasp my arm, and pulls me across. Poi threads his hands into my hair, cocks his head to the side, presses his warm lips to mine, opening my mouth with his. The pang turns into a wrench, and I want him. I feel the heat of his body near mine. Warm, fresh, air gusts into my lungs. His lips are gentle. In a flash, his mouth is retreating from mine. I feel an intense tug to stay close to him as he pulls away. My heart beats frantically. What just happened? Why is my body doing this to me? I can't have a crush. Panicking against my reaction to him, I try to swim.

He's already floating towards the nearest group of Mer. A woman with braided white-blonde hair is grappling something in her arms. Her sunset orange tail is flicking steadily, and I can feel the water stirring like a gust of wind. I swim up, and see she's holding a giant sea turtle. Her boxy head is larger than a grapefruit, and mottled tangerine and white. Her eyes are shut, and her upturned snout shakes slowly side to side. She's about the size of a car tire, and her paddle-like flippers are swatting through the water like she's excited about something. Two other Merikoi swim before her- one wielding pliers.

I wonder what they could possibly be doing, when Poi gestures towards me, and murmurs something through the water. I swim closer, noticing the woman's pointed face is red with effort. An arm's distance away, I see the turtle's eyes are not closed, but squinting slowly, her mouth opening and closing. Poi taps his nose, and looks to the turtle. I see a small white circle encrusted within her nostril. I can't figure out what it could be, or why we're all gathered here to look at a turtle's nose.

A Merikoi woman with flowing dark hair and a grim expression, approaches with pliers. I wonder how they have tools down here, but then realize, with all the shipwrecks and trash humans leave, it's likely nothing unusual. And a third Mer- a man with a forest green tail and sapphire hair grasps the turtle by her squat little head. I clench my teeth as I watch the grim-faced Mer approach. The turtle obediently hangs her head, until the pliers make contact with the little white object. The Mer pulls with the pliers, and the turtle gasps her mouth open in pain, squinting her eyes. The Mer tugs, but makes no progress.

Tight-limbed, I watch for another ten minutes as they twist and pull at the object, until a little cloud of red seeps from her nose. Finally pulling it one inch out, blood flowing out more heavily, I see that the embedded object is a striped fast-food straw. I gape, wondering where the other ten inches of it are- in her brain? I notice the Mer have paused to glance at me, and shame floods over me. I've used straws. Who knows where they ended up.

They twist and pull the straw as the turtle flaps it's flippers quietly gasps with pain. Eventually, an entirely whole, twisted straw is extracted from the turtle's nostril. My eyes sting. The turtle ceases floundering. Her eyes close, and she goes limp with exhaustion. The sunset-tailed Mer swims the turtle towards the open sea entrance.

Poi glances at me over his shoulder, and turns, "Merikoi usually don't intervene with individual lives…" His voice seems so close under the water. "But this isn't balanced. We're just trying to mediate the impacts of human waste."

I look around, and see Mer wrestling down injured and fishing-line knotted sting rays, dolphins, some fish, and even a manatee. I spot another sea turtle and gape. With the head of a brontosaurus, black flippers like oars, and nearly the size of a car- she's like twelve of me. She's entangled in a mess of ropes, line, and buoys as if sporting a morbid Halloween costume.

As Poi begins to talk again, I watch two Merikoi methodically cutting through the thick layers of the fishing lines entrapping her. "We usually try to free the animals on the spot- but this is where we take the serious cases. We bring in a lot of turtles. They get caught in everything. Have terrible eyesight." He grimaces, "Had enough?"

I nod. I'm not feeling so great about being human right now. I think back about all the fairy tales I've been told in my life. Humans fighting off the evil magical creatures. Humans versus vampires, sirens, witches, werewolves, giants, ghouls, ghosts… the list is endless. The same story told in different ways. The fairy tale always seems to be that humans are always the well-intentioned, innocent beings just fighting to exist in a realm of evil monsters.

As I look around the space of tortured sea creatures, and the opposite seems to be true. Humans are careless, wasteful, and from my experience, intentionally ignorant. In this age, our biggest threats are the issues humans create. I can't help but think how the Merikoi must see us. They must hate us. Glancing over at Poi, I realize he would never date a human. We're the evil creature in their bedtime stories.

Although I promised myself I wouldn't get caught on another man, I can feel already that my heart hasn't listened. My heart can't be told what to feel. I have to feel it. And it feels leaden. Like a rusted anchor dropping into unknown leagues of watery darkness.

# CHAPTER 10

STELLA

Just as we're within reach of the wobbling, tenuous, magical wall, I hear an urgent voice cry "POI!" The sound is both an echo and an inch away.

Just ahead of me, he turns around, navy tail whipping through the water like a knife. I spin in the whirlpool of his movement.

"Yeah?" He calls forward, already swimming back into the cavernous space.

I marvel at his profile. Lean and muscular, his sinewy arms pull through the water, shoulders bulging. His tailfin flips up and down powerfully, the trailing gaudy fibers looking dark, gothic, and somehow lethal.

A bit late, I decide to follow the ruckus. Poi has already crossed about two hundred yards. The ocean is fairly clear here, but it's still not like looking through air. It's hazy like looking through columns of dust swirling in light. Poi's eyes are probably made to see through this, but with my human eyesight, all I can see are three blurry blobs at the cathedral-like entrance to the cave. I wouldn't have known it was Poi if I didn't see him swim off in that direction. I make my way over relatively slowly, arms burning, and lips pressed together to remember to not gasp for air.

I begin to see strange outlines. Three Mer, and something very large seems to block most of the entrance. I stop in shock, realizing it's alive. Fear trills through me as I approach the massive creature. Its warty, jutting jaw leans on the rocky bottom of the cave, the length of its long body extending out into open sea. A humpback whale. I see Poi gathered with the other Mer outside, and head that way. Swimming over the long, dark body feels like a dream. The whale's whole body is too big to take in at once, so I look part by part, savoring the amazing experience. I smile as I inspect the blow hole- just like a huge, upside-down nose, with deep nostrils attached to his back. Well, that's what it is. A nose. But it really looks like a human nose. My eyes drag along the back of the smooth beast, noting white scar marks against the black. And then I see. I see why he is here.

Just above the tailfin, his body is nearly severed in half. The pink, fleshy gash is not a clean cut, but mauled. Deeply feathered with ripped flesh. There is a surprisingly small amount of blood clouding around the wound. It looks hopeless. I can see from the Mer's sideways glances, they think so too.

"Stop! He needs to Shift!" Poi directs, but I don't see the whale moving. In fact, the whale looks eerily still.

"He'll need your help," calls a tanned blonde Merikoi guy with whale tattoos wrapping around the side of his ribcage and along his shoulders.

Poi glides over to the side of the whale's massive face, holding the head lovingly, staring into its black eye. He's speaking, but it sounds more like singing. His tone is low and deep, and carrying. Below his hands burns neon green light. The light creeps like a spider's webbing over the whale's entire mass, stretching until the whale seems to be glowing green. The light is growing stronger, Poi's hands guiding the energy, until it's so bright I can no longer see the whale.

Poi pulls back his hands, and the light fades into darkness. I blink out the bright haze burned into my eyes. A Merikoi man remains. Shock flutters through me, Merikoi can shift into animals... Immediately, I look for his tattoo. A humpback whale. It clicks. The tattoos indicate what they can shift into. My whole world flips, and I decide I need to stop thinking I have anything figured out. Hmm. I wonder why Poi has no tattoos…

I return my gaze to the injured Mer. He's very still. The gash is deep in his teal tail, where thighs would be. No blood is seeping out. The healers give him space.

Poi swims forward and grabs the man's pale hand.

The once-whale Mer flutters his eyes open, barely able to focus on Poi. Mer speech slips out of him like flickering candlelight.

Poi bows his head, responding throatily.

At that, the man lets his arm float to his side, and closes his eyes.

Poi recites something that sounds like a prayer, in lilting musical, deep tones. I long to know his words like a beautiful dream I wish were true.

Suddenly it seems like a moment so private, that I should not be witnessing it.

A white glow seems to hover brightly around the man, dim, and float out with the current into the abyss of sea.

My feet slap the dry rock with water, my footprints arched and inky black against the smoky gray. I shiver as I pull my emerald cloak over my wet bathing suit-like bra, and shorts. My hair drips loudly on the floor. Poi has walked over to the side of the room, where a shelf is carved out from the rock, and is taking notes in a large journal. I look around tentatively. The hall is empty, silent. The room has a low rough ceiling, and another day it might feel intimate, but at the moment, it feels cramped with my human guilt. His scribbling scratches stop. Poi looks around magisterially, his dark brow furrowed and serious.

"I have funeral arrangements to attend to." His professional manner is cold, and it bites me.

"What happened to him?" I inquire softly.

"Cruise ship." He clips.

A twenty-pound weight drops on my shoulders. Humans again. "Ah."

His tight eyes are already looking down the hall. It's clear he's not interested in talking. A small part of me wonders if this death just reminded him of how little he likes humans like me. Something inside of me is twisting and shriveling.

An awkward silence passes. Then a thought strikes me, "But how could that have happened?" I pause, not wanting to sound rude, "I mean, cruise ships don't drive that fast do they? Why didn't he notice it in time?"

He looks at me distantly, "He may have been logging—whales have incredible, prophetic dream states. We use that information." He stiffly brushes his sleeve. "Naido took a calculated risk."

"I'm… so sorry." And I really do feel like I'm at fault. Because who else will take the blame?

Holding his wet hair up with a hand, he sighs, "I've got to go tell Eldridge… so… I'll see you later."

I bite my lip and watch him walk off.

Uncertain about what to do with the rest of my day, I return to the sea cottage, climbing out of the dim cavern and into the misty gray light. The little rocky island seems to tower over the tepid sea. The ocean has pulled far back towards the horizon, leaving much of the earth barren and exposed. Seaweed is stranded in clumps, all the rock is dry, and the sea seems too far away to hear its whispers. It leaves me feeling lonely.

Having no idea what time it is, I drudge up the rock face towards the heavy wooden door, wrench it open, and don't bother to close it before climbing into the messy covers of the four-poster bed. I feel a deep sadness clinging to my heart like a cold, wet day. I'm not sure if it's for what humans are doing to turtles, whales, and sea life, and how I am inextricably connected to that crime… or… how much I want Poi, and how impossible that is.

I grit my teeth as I feel my heart has already surrendered itself to a man who could never want me. I twist the sheets with anger as tears brim. This second form of rejection is crushing. I think maybe if I curl up, I won't feel so alone. I bunch the blankets around me and wait, but the sadness does not ebb away. I feel a mournful emptiness echoing in the space above my pelvic bone. I realize the sadness is not something that can go away right now. Emptiness will be there when nothing else is.

## POI

My knock is heavy against the familiar oak door.

"Yes?" Eldridge's voice sings clearly from within.

I wipe the wetness from my eyes. I clear my throat with a swallow. My chest is leaden, but I have to be strong for her. "It's Poi—can I come in?"

The door swings open to the home I have countless times been a guest to. Their rooms smell like rose and dandelion. Mocking memories filter through the space like the yellow light glowing from the large living room window. At these netted Kombu swing seats, the couple served me herbal teas from land flowers as Naido relayed his prophesies and insights, and Eldridge wove gorgeous blankets for the Mer.

Eldridge sweeps the door open, and the large features of her small oval face tighten with concern. She sweeps a curl of her blonde hair behind her ear. Her slightly gawky frame is swallowed by a yolk-yellow silken robe, reminding me of an innocent child. Eldridge's wide brown eyes appraise me, fear knitting a deep line between her fine brows. "Poi, are you okay? What's happened? Why are you here?"

"I'm sorry—" My voice breaks, "Naido has passed."

Her features fall. She stares at me silently in a moment that stretches on. Lightning fast, her fist strikes my chest, "No!" Her voice is manic. She collapses to the ground, still not crying, barely hearing her own screams.

I don't reach out. I don't try to calm her down. I have seen enough death to know I can't stop the reaction felt by the living. Instead, grief surges in me as I watch Eldridge succumb to hiccupping, desperate tears as I cry my own silently. Naido was a very close friend. Seeing Eldridge in this sort of pain is torture. Yes, I've seen a lot of death, but Naido's death was exceptionally gruesome and sudden. Excepting human-caused deaths, our ends are usually calm and peaceful events. Death for the Mer is a highly spiritual experience- an event the participant readies for. An event loved ones have time to prepare for.

Eldridge stands again, arms shaking as she holds her elbows. Her pointing chin juts up at me as she stands to the height of my chest. The whites of her eyes are pink with veins. "What happened?"

The words cut through me as I speak them, "He was dream-state logging, and hit by a cruise ship." I feel responsible. Although as a Whale Shifter, his impulse and passion is to pull in prophesies, requiring the dangerous sleeping state of a Whale, we could have had Mer on guard for him. We should have had someone watching over him. Tightness wraps around my chest, guilt gripping me.

"I'm sorry—"

But she doesn't hear me.

She spins towards the empty room and screams a stumbling line of swears. Her knees bang the floor as she collapses again.

This time, I sit on the floor with her, and place a hand on the round of her bony spine as she rocks. She gulps air between her ranting cries. "Why did this happen? How could this happen? How could you let this happen? Why would he do this? How? How?"

Her back is hot with sweat as her body attempts to purge this pain.

I have been stupid. I had lost sight. Feeling Eldridge's pain under my palm, hearing her cries, I remember my true purpose here. Thalassa's return is more than simply helping her regain her memory- than regaining our love. Naido's prophesy tells us that somehow, Thalassa's return is about saving our entire community, and the oceans, from humanity's destructive force.

## STELLA

The light in the room is sideways and projecting yellow. I feel groggy, and without a sense of direction, I can't tell if it's just after sunrise or just before sunset. If I could just lay in bed, I would remember my dreams. I close my eyes shut again. My dreams feel so important. I think of Poi and feel grit in the arteries around my heart.

My dresser creaks as it shuts, and I jolt up. Laude is standing there, her bright scarlet eyes and pale skin nearly glow in the dim light. I still haven't gotten used to her inhuman appearance. She's holding up a black silken dress, with long, tapered sleeves. "We're headed down to Naido's Wake. Put this on. Starts shortly. We'll go down together." Laude is already wearing a black dress with gauzy, cobweb-like sleeves, and buttons secured neatly up her high collared neckline.

My limbs are heavy. With effort, I pull myself out of the cocooning sheets. My feet slap the cold stone floor. Rubbing my face, I walk towards her. She tosses the extra dress towards me, and doesn't ask me how I'm feeling. I'm grateful for it.

The silken dress is slippery and chilly between my fingers. I span it out to appraise it's flowing lines and scooping neck and back. Not as conservative as her dress. I begin pulling off my shorts and Laude turns as I change. The bony line of her spine is exposed, and the pink ruffles of ravaged whale flesh push to the forefront of my mind.

I assume she knew the severed Naido. Everyone seems to know each other here. "Were you and Naido close?"

Her angular shoulders lift and settle, "Not close. But he will be missed dearly."

I lower my head. "Who was he?"

"He was our best Oracle."

"Oracle? As in a fortune-teller?" I clarify.

"No, fortunes are for individuals. Our Oracles relay the interwoven Fate of the Mer and the Ocean."

I don't believe in Fate. I believe people have agency, and that life isn't a pre-set maze we blindly walk through. But I know there's no time to discuss this, so I just politely say "Hmm. Interesting," and finish buttoning up the side of the silky charcoal dress.

The waistline silk tucks perfectly against my skin, hugging my subtle curves. I'm struck by how perfectly all these clothes fit me. When did they measure me? In my sleep? Maybe Mer have a knack for sizing people up.

I toss my other clothes aside, and Laude turns to face me. "We need to head down now. The wake begins before sunset."

Involuntarily, I glance out the window, orienting myself westward, and noticing sunset will be in about an hour. I glance into the mirror in the ajar wardrobe door and I throw my hair into a quick messy bun. My disoriented, melancholy mood has not drained from my ivy eyes. I wish I were better at composing myself. I sigh. "Let's go."

Mournful, violin-like notes carry through the chilly waters. The water is darker, and it's hard to see all of them, but I know there are hundreds of Mer surrounding me. Their dark shadows blot out the light from the gray-green surface hundreds of yards above. The shadowy, foreboding forms of boat-sized whales encircle us.

Below, looms a deep cavity dropping deep towards the earth's core. Laude holds my hand, to keep me in place.

A deep, natural baritone moans slowly. A chill runs from the soles of my feet and up the back of my body. Several dips and calls shudder through my bones, my every organ, as I hear whale song all around me. It feels both like a higher reality and a dream. My heart seems to swell, and my eyes feel hot with tears.

The song ends, and I'm left in shock, wondering how a whale can speak to a deeper part of my soul than any human could.

Poi's voice cuts through the reverberating silence, but it's hard to hear what he says. I realize he must be speaking in Merglossa. It sounds so much more natural in the water than English. It makes him sound both ethereal and feral.

Laude's voice carries soft through the water, translating, "We were honored to have Naido among us. Not only was he a kind to all, and good partner to his other half, but our most gifted Oracle. He risked his life countless times while gathering truth and wisdom for us. We thank you, Naido."

Poi continues to speak, but Laude stops translating. Instead I hear his familiar velvet tones lilting and pronouncing in Mer. Floating in space, my mind tries to wrap around the sounds, but none of them are recognizable.

"Thank you, Great Ocean Spirit, we return your son." Laude continues translating as she gestures a pale arm forward. A shadowy body falls limply through the twilight murky water, like a leaf to the ground. The darkness slowly envelops him. "We return him to the Abyss, hoping his spirit will return again. Thank you, dear brother. Don't wait too long before rejoining us, we rely on your insights to survive. Rest well, learn much."

As the limp form is totally lost in the deep darkness below, it calls to something deep inside me. With a mixture of profound terror and philosophical curiosity, I picture Naido's limp body falling all the way down into the chasm, swallowed by endless black, and wonder how his spirit could ever return. Hot salty tears seep into the sea.

Laude stops translating as an eerie song breaks out amongst the Mer. She joins in their long, mournful notes, interspersed with high-pitched, keeling cries. Each sound feels closer here. As they continue, it wakes up my mind, clears a space in my heart, and I feel lighter.

The water begins to swirl around, pulling towards the surface. Like a column of fish, the Mer glide upwards, current rising from their tails. Laude releases me, and I drift in the shadowy mass of dark tails, trailing like gothic wedding dresses, joined with bodies clad in silk and shells. Their somber faces lift upwards, streamlined bodies flexing as they swim. Maybe it's just the dim twilight light, but I swear I've dreamt this before.

Like bubbles destined to burst at the surface, we stream upwards. Breaching past the line of ocean and air, my lungs expand with calm night air as it buffets my face, smelling of brine. I hear sighs and soft chattering all around me, still in the strange tongue of Merglossa.

Faint hues of drained yellow cling to the dark horizon. The sky drips sapphire blue, and a few stars hesitantly wink.

At dinner, everyone is still dressed in dark attire, and with the subdued manners and softer talk, it seems to be a continuation of the wake. Each table, long and pale, is dressed with black silken runners, and white shells contrasting like bones.

The room is painted with somber and pained expressions. It seems Naido's death was very unexpected. A stiff-moving woman is guided towards a table by two other Mer. Her brown eyes are wide- not quite fixating on anything. I realize she must be Naido's widow, Eldridge. Her gorgeous blonde hair curls haphazard and wild around her head, as if refusing to obediently accept her new reality.

"That's Eldridge." Kiara leans across the table in a low whisper. Her purple-flecked onyx eyes hold tangible empathy. She gazes back at the shocked woman, continuing, "Her and Naido- they were very in love. Have been together for two lifetimes. Sometimes that's all you get. But we're all hoping he returns."

My mind halts. "Um. Two lifetimes? What?"

"Reincarnation." Laude interjects.

They briefly catch each other's eye, and look back at me. Their mouths are solid lines, no twitch of a prank. Not that they would do that in this somber atmosphere.

I turn over the concept in my mind. "So... you all believe in that? You're... Buddhist... Mermaids?"

Laude husks a low chuckle.

Kiara wrinkles her nose, "No... I wouldn't call it that."

"It's not believing," Laude levels her blood-red gaze with mine. "We remember."

I look between them, flummoxed. "How?"

Laude shrugs, "Magic?"

Kiara rolls her eyes. "Our spirits have a memory. We go into the Abyss, which is like lucid dreaming, and after one to three years, we might return. After a few rounds, if we do enough good in the world, become a good enough soul, then we can pass on to the next, higher level of reality."

I squint at them. Have they been smoking Mermaid ganga? I lean back and fold my arms, "Okay, I'm actually really gullible, so please don't mess with me..."

"They're not." A deep male voice jolts me to my senses, and Hades slides into the bench beside me. He drawls, "My last life, I was just as much of a pain in the ass."

Kiara's face breaks into a devilish smile, "Don't lie to her! You were a sweetheart in your last life!"

His jaw tightens and he looks away. "I was an idiot."

She twists her lips with just a touch of a frown, "No..." she whispers.

I can see that some sort of secret is being acknowledged between the two of them, and I can't imagine the history that piles up between multiple lifetimes. But I can't focus on their private dilemmas. This reincarnation business has hooked me, and I want to know how I play into things. "What about humans?" I direct my question to Laude, "Do humans reincarnate?"

I'm already wondering who I could have been in a past life, what I could have accomplished, who I loved. Strange to think about having a whole different life, but still being me.

"Hopefully." Her voice has an edge of terseness.

I deflate a little, but intrigue continues to barrel through me. "What about your last life? Who were you? What did you do?" I fire.

"I was me. I did the same things." Her mouth is set, like she's done giving up Merikoi secrets to a curious human.

I fiddle with my fingers anxiously, fueled with an overwhelming hunger to for answers, but knowing this topic has finished. Hades and Kiara are whispering privately. I look around for Poi. He's milling around, consoling the bereft. His dark hair is unkempt, almost awkwardly, like he could do with someone dragging their hand through it and smoothing it out. I feel a painful tug in my chest, knowing I want to be that person. I pull my eyes away.

I jump as Hades slaps the table, "That's it. I'm not shifting anymore." He stage-whispers across at Laude and Kiara, "Why the fuck would anyone shift after today?"

Laude's thin eyebrows migrate to her hairline.

Kiara lets out a puff of air. "I really don't blame you. I mean, protecting other species is really impossible if we can't even protect ourselves…"

"You know that's practically heresy." Laude's voice is level, but I can see a fire in her eyes. I have no idea about what, but I keep my mouth shut, hoping to hear more secrets spilling out.

"For you, but I don't play by those rules." Hades taps the points of his fingers together, his angular face laser focused on Laude. "Do you even know how many close calls I've had?"

Laude grips the table, leaning towards him, poison in her quiet voice. "Yes, Naido risked his life to protect the ocean. That's the deal down here." Her words whip, "If you don't want to worry about anyone but yourself, give up your tail and go stay in hell."

Hades raises his hands and leans back, laughing humorlessly. "Calm down, Laude. I'm not causing a rebellion or anything."

Her snake eyes squint venomously. My stomach tightens. Poi's lucky he has her to protect their cause. She can be downright scary.

"We can't all be hammerheads. You have it easy." He folds his arms, leaning back. His light eyes dance, like he's enjoying this unusual chance to fire up Laude.

She laughs coldly. "We're nearly extinct. Every year, nearly two hundred million sharks are massacred by humans. For their fins. They suffocate to death and fall to waste. That's not having it easy." She scoffs.

"And what are you actually doing to help by becoming a shark? Aside from taking the death tally? Because I'm not into martyrdom."

"Eselk Veilisous." She hisses, and elegantly leaves the table.

Hades' eyes fire up, "Ooooh. Laude never swears…"

He glances over to Kiara, who's glaring his way with her color-sparked black gaze, and chides. "You fool."

For the first time, he looks chastened. "What? She gave me a hard time. She should be able to take it."

"That was a low blow. You know it."

He shrugs, and glances around the room, as if disappointed that his game has sizzled out.

I'm trying to string together the facts in my head… Naido had the whale tattoo, and could shift back and forth from being a whale to Mer. Laude has the hammerhead tattoo, and can shift back and forth from that animal. How many different animals can they turn into…and why? Laude was pretty adamant that the purpose of the Merikoi is to protect the oceans and all that live in them. And although it was a harsh point to be made, maybe Hades was right… they can't keep up with the destructive forces of humans…

"So… did this whole protection thing work better before… humans?"

Hades surveys me from the corner of his eye, "Astute."

"Merikoi are older than humans?" I pry.

He smirks. "Of course, humans evolved from the Merikoi who gave up on protecting the oceans."

The words hit me hard. We crawled out of the seas and created destruction on earth.

"Wait that's not fair," Kiara joins in, "Some committed Guardians followed the careless ones, and became Land Guardians under the watch of… your lost brother…" She whispers the last part so it is barely audible.

Hades gives her a hard look, as if she just said something out-of-bounds. My mind grips onto her words…A lost brother? Another God?

Hades' commentary yanks me back, "Guardianship did work before human technology developed in the last three hundred years. Really, the last hundred have been shit. Every year, they've got some new way to strip all the life from the ocean bottom or try out explosives, the list is exhaustive… So, no. It doesn't work now. Anyone who thinks we can still protect is deluding themselves."

Kiara bites her lip. "You didn't have to be such an ass to Laude. She's just trying to do what's right."

"We would do more good if we weren't lying to ourselves. Our powers of shifting are obsolete." His eyes squint at her with pale green fire, "She's wasting her time. She would do better to see reality as it is."

Hades has a point. I mean, I know I still know nothing about this world, but, there's no sense in holding on to old approaches that don't work. It's something I've tried to do in my life too- to see reality not as I want it to be, but as it is. Then work from there, with the facts. I wouldn't dare say that out loud though. Not after that row.

The rest of the night is pretty quiet. Laude doesn't return to our table the whole night (I really don't blame her), and Poi doesn't find the time to circle over towards us. I spend the evening sucking down raw oysters and munching on seaweed salad while watching flakes of lime bioluminescence float across the skylights high above like sands in a tide.

# CHAPTER 11

## STELLA

I wake to the chilly cottage room, hearing gentle breeze batter the sills. It's been three days since the wake, and I feel edgy, anticipating another day of revelations of my inherent human evilness. I don't know how to single-handedly face all this responsibility.

Staring out the old glass panes of the cottage window, I brush my fine hair out slowly, thinking. The ocean reflects the clouds back to the sky like Monet. I study the colors like it means something. As if somehow, if I could understand the translation, the murmurs between sky and water, I could figure out how I make sense here. The shadowy grays and opalescent silvers reveal nothing.

A knock resounds from the door. I can't help thinking Kiara or Laude wouldn't knock that loud. My heart starts battering. "Come in?"

The door swings open and Poi is standing in the frame, ducking his black shock of messy hair under the beam, slowly stepping into the room and making my heart race. His face is poetry.

"Sorry I haven't been making enough time for you," he murmurs.

My lips part in surprise. He's sorry? He hasn't been avoiding me? Or he's sorry for avoiding me?

"I know you may have been pretty shaken up after seeing Naido like that- I feel like I owe you an explanation." His eyes seem to narrow in on mine, and the room feels hushed, like even the wind is holding its breath.

My legs feel wobbly. I lean against the wardrobe, stabilizing myself. "It's okay, I know you were busy…" I trail off, still not really sure why I was the one he chose to help them in these dire straits. I'm hit hard with a reality check- despite my being in this with all my heart- I'm pretty near useless to their cause. It would only make sense that I would be very low on the list of priorities for him. But I don't say this, because I get the sense that he's so kind, he might pull a white lie to make me feel better.

"I've got a few meetings to attend, but… walk with me?" He raises a dark eyebrow.

I press my lips together as I think yes, anywhere. Instead I squeak, "Sure." I roll my eyes at myself. Please try to keep your cool.

In a surprisingly human gesture, he holds open the door for me. I walk past him into the bright white light of day. The waves of receding tide are half-heartedly toying with the silver speckled boulders. The expansive sea is still secretly whispering back to the sky in painted shapes and colors I can't translate.

We're silent as we wind down the tight, dark stairwell. When we reach the passageway, we fall into step, and he glances at me sideways in the flickering torchlight. "So, fill me in. What have you gathered about us?"

I bite my lip, immediately remembering Hade's painful logic- the idea that everything Poi is attempting is a lost cause. I try to focus more on the basics. "Well, a lot about how the Mer are guardians of the ocean, and you can shift into different animals- the ones on your tattoos…" I trail off as I realize I haven't seen him with any tattoos, and I wonder why… "Hey, take off your cloak." Oh shit. I stare ahead, blushing as I realize how that sounded. Even though I swear it was innocent, I just wanted to check him for tattoos…is all… but I realize my subconscious just won out on me that time. The battle continues.

When I look up at him, he's smirking crookedly, raising a bemused brow, and slowing down to face me, "Can I ask why?"

My eyes are wide, horrified with my lack of tact. "Um, I never saw your tattoos…so I don't know what you can shift into…"

His eyes flicker with something unreadable, and he shrugs off his cloak. "Alright. Inspect me."

My stomach reels with adrenaline.

His tanned torso is a topographical map of muscle. Feeling hot, I squint, like I'm not noticing his washboard abs, but rather looking for microscopic tattoos there. I don't dare glance up into his eyes, I inspect his broad shoulders, his muscled arms, and circle around to his back, which is also ripped, of course. Mer lifestyle could be seriously marketable in the human fitness world. Sighing at his perfect shoulders, I walk back around to face him. "Nope. No tattoos. You must be human."

He narrows his dark amber gaze, black lashes intertwining at the edges. "Not funny," he grumbles with a smirk.

I shrug, glancing down just one more time, "Well… you look human… no tattoos…"

He raises a quick eyebrow at me, "So, you're done?"

I nod, attempting to hide my regret, "Yes."

He swings his cape over his shoulders and fastens the buttons, satiny midnight blue swaying around him.

"So… what does it mean, you can't shift?"

He starts walking again, and I follow, "I can. I'm not limited to one species."

I stop as this hits me, and involuntarily grasp his thick arm. I quickly let go. "Wait. You can be… anything?"

His singular nod is so slow and discreet, it feels like he's telling me a secret.

"Wow…" my voice is hushed.

He begins walking again, and I follow.

"So, what's your favorite?"

He squints off into the darkened hall, "The seal I guess."

His answer makes me press my lips together. I don't need things in common with him, it will just make it harder. Why did he have to pick the seal? I casually pry, "Hmm, why? If you could be anything? They're so… common."

He shrugs again. "They're playful. Very intelligent. I get attached to them."

I can't help but smile, liking the modesty of his answer. He could have picked any fearsome creature in the sea. But despite being an immortal, he's not into inspiring fear, or being showy. He likes playfulness and connection. I like him for it more.

I think back to all the seals I've seen in the wild, the ones I swam with as I grew up, wistfully wondering if it was ever him. Suddenly an image pops into my head. A dark block of a seal head. Wait. A light goes on in my head. The seal I saw before I was captured. My gut tightens. I flicker my gaze towards him. No way.

I stop again, he slows and turns towards me, a few feet ahead, clearly eager to keep going.

"Were—was that you… the seal… before the massive wave when you took me?" My blood thunders through my ears.

His dark gaze is steady. Not denying it. As if willing me to understand… something. Body frozen, my heart starts thudding erratically.

His face opens, "I had to confirm- to know with my own eyes, it was you."

My mind is thrown by a centrifugal force. "Why does that matter? How would you know what I look like?"

Some foreign comprehension dawns in his eyes. His jaw flexes.

"I thought… this was random-" I gesture towards myself, "—right place, right time sort of a thing…"

"It is." He says curtly. "Convenience."

"Then why," I glare directly into his liquid amber eyes, my heart squeezing, "…did you have to know it was me? How would you even recognize me? I never met you before in my life!" I pause, flabbergasted, "Have I?"

He stares for a moment, stoic. "No."

My mind is whirring, my instinct piqued like heckles. I wait for more of an answer, but he doesn't give one. I square my body to his, putting my hands on my hips, "What exactly am I missing here?"

His mute gaze continues, and I realize how close I am to him. I can see his chest slowly rising and falling as he breathes, smelling distractingly sweet and musky.

When he speaks again, his voice is low, "There are some things I just can't reveal to you. You won't feel like I'm giving you enough information. I apologize."

He's so tight-lipped, there's no way I will get more than that out of him. But there is definitely something strange afoot. Maybe I can get information out of someone else…Kiara? Hades?

His jaw flexes, and his dark amber eyes flicker quickly between mine, reading me. "No one will be able to tell you."

What? How can he read me so well? I roll my eyes in exasperation. "And now you're a mind reader too?"

He starts walking yet again, and curtly responds, "Yes."

This is more than I can handle. Horrified, anger boils up in my chest. So he knows how much I think about him? All the stupid, useless, pathetic yearning? I spit fire, "Would you give me a WARNING? Geez! I mean, I think I deserve a little privacy…"

A hiccup of a laugh escapes from his smirk, then more laughter, and he's shaking. He's holding his stomach, bent over.

Incensed, I put my hands on my hips, raising my voice further, "Wow. Seriously? You've been reading my mind this whole time, and you think it's just funny?" My embarrassment is totally smothered by my rippling anger. I can't believe him. I thought he was a good guy. Conniving, more like.

Hands still on his knees, he looks up at me through his messed dark hair, eyes watery. "I'm not a mind-reading vampire," he wheezes through a smirk, standing up to his full height. "I think human novels about vampires have impaired your judgment."

The dust settles, and my glare is totally ruined by my stretching smile. I shake my head at him. "Not fair. If mermaids can be real... don't fault me for thinking mind reading is too. It probably is. You just don't have that skill."

He playfully places his hand on his heart like I've insulted him, "Now, don't make me get all insecure..."

I smirk and just shake my head at him. "You're a very good liar."

"I am related to Hades, after all." His eyes sparkle.

The words pop the bright bubble of this moment. I frown, annoyed. Hades is always getting pushed under the bus, and I think it's just because his ideas are different. I can relate to that, and I'm feeling myself get pretty defensive for him.

As if sensing my thoughts, Poi back-peddles. "Alright, alright. That's not fair. Since I'm the older brother, I'm the bad example." He drags his hand through his dark mess of hair again. "Speaking of being a bad example, I really am going to be late now... look, I was actually hoping you might want to come along?"

"Okay."

We're walking faster now, and I'm noticing as we take a turn from the familiar doorways, and downwards, deeper into the underground mountain. It's a bit freaky. The lanterns flicker on as we approach, flicker off as we pass, leaving us in a bubble of a light surrounded by shadow.

"The meeting is about human threats, so it's pertinent to you. I'll want to hear your opinion afterwards. We can meet in the gallery to discuss it." He's talking faster, and it's making me wonder if we're close to our destination. "I won't be able to explain much while we're in there- it's a pretty fast-paced gathering. Alright, we're here."

He swings open a thick cherry door, and the room has a huge orb window on the far wall, the walls covered with maps of the ocean and land. There are easily twenty people gathered in the center of the room. As we walk forwards, the crowd parts to face him. And I see the woman with lilac hair. What the FUCK.

It's like a hand with treacherous fingernails has impaled my stomach and is twisting. My mind rewinds to the time in the dusty attic, where she stared at me, and started whispering to her partner, with the wide, wild eyes. He's standing beside her now, staring at me with the same discomforting electric green eyes.

So… this kidnapping was far more planned that Poi wants to admit. Clearly they were scouts. For some reason, they picked me. And I need to find out that reason. Because I don't think it was purely out of the idea that I would be the most helpful to their cause. Sure I was at an environmental action meeting, but I mean, they didn't even talk to me. They just saw me.

"Stella—" Poi glances back with an arm outstretched, and realizes I'm about ten paces behind him. He follows my gaze, as he seems to clock my thoughts. Damn, he's good at that for not being a mind-reader.

The room seems to stiffen as he exchanges a glance with the fake human couple. Maybe he really is hiding something. Everyone has stopped their conversations, and is watching us.

Poi sighs and faces me, beckoning me forward, "Stella… this is Leyra and Marc."

My eyes are burning his with questions. But his jaw is high, and his expression is stony and regal. Surrounded by this serious group, it doesn't seem the time to ask more questions. But they will definitely be asked.

Poi's tone is tight, "Leyra and Marc are some of our land scouts."

I look to them. Swanky lilac eyes is smiling encouragingly, exposing her set of sharp teeth, which totally ruins her intent. I realize Marc's right eye can't quite focus on me.

"Hi," I say awkwardly, because 'nice to meet you' doesn't fit the situation.

They reach out their hands and shake with mine in a human way. I look closer, and with a small stab of jealousy, see that Leyra's vivid irises are natural. She's wearing a black leather t-shirt, and jeans. Marc is wearing cargo pants and a tie-dye shirt. Human clothes. I look around and realize everyone is wearing human clothes. It's strange, in this underwater room.

"Shall we begin?" Poi is already walking towards the gaudy chair before the window, facing the crowd. Everyone else takes a seat in the old carved chairs creating a circle around the room. Suddenly it feels like musical chairs, the music has paused, and I have no idea where to sit. Inevitably, I'm standing in the middle as everyone else has found their seat.

I bite my lip and look towards Poi. He gestures to the seat beside him, which is also old and gaudy, the pair to his. I hesitantly walk over towards it quickly, feeling all the strange colored eyes on me. The two seats tower over the others. It feels too powerful and dominant for a human observer. But I don't see another seat.

Not wanting to stall things, I gingerly sit. I avoid putting my arms out on the deeply carved armrests, and fold my hands in my lap.

"Carter," Poi's deep voice drawls, "Give us the skinny on DC."

My eyes bulge. I guess I shouldn't have expected any less.

At the far end of the room, a man with thinning gray hair and a fitted charcoal suit looks out of place as he sums up highlights of American ocean and environmental policy of the last month. "...congress is lifting protections in the Atlantic for the sake of expanding oil mining." His face is grim. "Goes into effect as of January." His face is apologetic, "Poseidon, you know how little sway I have against the oil lobby."

Hearing his whole name out loud makes me feel squirmish.

Poi holds out a long-fingered hand, as if to physically stop the man's apologies. "It's undemocratic. I understand. Thank you for your report." His smile is more of a grimace, and his gaze flicks to the other side of the room, a seat very near me, filled with a woman in her fifties, with short blonde hair, and bright blue eyes. "Dianna, could you catch us up?"

She straightens, folding her hands in her lap, addressing him, "The US Military is currently proceeding with the same projects- experimenting with missiles in the

Gulf of Mexico, invisible destroyers are on track between DC and the North pole- and as climate change continues, there may be a tussle with Russia. The US Military's sonic weapons experiments continue, as you know—" Her bright eyes flicker to mine for an instant, "along the New England coast- just past the Georges Bank. They are experimenting with a new technology, so tests are heavily scheduled for October. Every Tuesday through Thursday, all day, it is unsafe to be in the region."

I can't take this all in, somehow, this woman has access to top secret military information, and is frequently passing it all along to the King Guardian of the Sea, Poi. I want to laugh. Well, at least this starts to level the playing field a little.

The strange conference continues, and I discover Poi has stashed Merikoi consultants all across the globe- informing him of military statuses, politics, environmental policies, and even top-secret military technology that's not even fully developed. I have to say I'm impressed. He's covered all his bases. I'm looking at him with a new perspective and yet another layer of appreciation. Maybe he'll figure this out after all.

His face is impassive as he takes on the news of the world above. News he has no power over, and yet threatens his entire kingdom.

The meeting ends with a narrow-faced Japanese man, wearing a simple black suit, speaking with flawless English. "The Japanese government maintains its position on Taiji's dolphin and whale massacre. They believe that dolphins and whales are a threat to global fisheries, and see them as competition for scarce resources. Not to mention, OceanZoo and countless aquariums from around the globe are paying hundreds of thousands per animal. If we could stop the financial incentive of the round-up, the murders would be harder for government officials to defend. I look towards your wildlife activist contacts. They must petition world governments to outlaw the imprisonment of cetaceans." His eyes are fiery, his nostrils flaring as he gazes at Poi.

"You're quite right, Yimoto. We understand that Cetaceans have a knowledge that expands past our own, and should be treated as equals in human policy. However, we know money rules the law on land. That's hard to change. In the meantime, your reports are priceless, Yimoto. Thank you."

I knew about the murders of dolphins in Japan… but down here, surrounded by this panel of serious Merikoi, it all feels more real.

"Yes, but who is addressing the issue of Cetacean policy?" Yimoto's voice is cutting.

A black woman in a bright purple suit holds up a thin hand to Poi, who nods at her, and she addresses Yimoto. "I am, Yimoto. But until humans are open to understanding they're not the brainiest beings on earth- which will never happen- they will think they have a right to capture and exhibit everything on earth- for their five year-olds to harass." I notice she has a streak of gray in her tight bun. I notice a fin tattoo on her neck, escaping her polished suit. "I am working with the top cetacean neurologists in the globe, and lobbying the the US government, as well as having meetings globally, with any government official who will meet with me. Problem is, cetacean suffering isn't a priority for any government."

Yimoto's eyes flick back to Poi, "This doesn't sound like a solution."

Poi is unmoved, his voice easy. "It sounds like you might have a better idea, Yimoto. Please, share."

Yimoto narrows his eyes at Poi. "I guess, use more human methods. It's their system. Enlist more human protesters. Grassroots. Make more movements."

Poi raises his eyebrows appreciatively, leaning back in his chair, "That's… a great idea. Let's do it. Yimoto, Natasha, Tyrone, Liana, Reuder- this is a priority between now and our next meeting. Reach out to your environmental contacts. Create a connected strategy of grassroots protests at aquariums. Make sure there is social media coverage. Are we missing anything, Yimoto?"

Yimoto's expression is softened, "We need a campaign name to pass along."

"Smarter Than You- Cetacean Rights." The slender woman in the pink suit smiles widely.

Poi smirks, "I think this is something you can figure out later on a conference call. But, it's a good point. Organized effort, do it the human way." He breathes in, "Okay, thanks everyone. I think that wraps things up. Any last comments?"

A man speaks with an Indian accent, "A lot of us are pressed by land schedules, are we still having our meeting on ocean acidification metrics and species population tallies before we head back to shore?"

"Absolutely. Tomorrow same time. Can everyone make that time?"

People look around stiffly, as if they are looking to others for answers.

"Do we need to make it sooner? Tonight, after dusk?"

There is a murmur of consent.

"Great. See you in a few hours then."

Like a jury being adjourned, they gather their belongings, and chatting, file out into the hall.

Poi keeps his eyes on them as he speaks to me, voice low, "They spend barely any time in the ocean. It's like they're just itching to get back to their human lives. If they're not careful, they'll forget they have tails."

I'm surprised to hear him lower his guard. I'm not really sure how to respond. "They wouldn't want to be human though, would they?"

It's just us in the room, and he shifts to face me, lounging in the towering grand chair. "I think they forget the magic, the thrill, and the call of the ocean. But they're very loyal."

A thought hits me, "Have you ever spent time on land? There are thrills there too."

"Sure, I have. It's not bad. But it will never compare to the freedom of shifting." He pauses, regarding me seriously, "When it comes to land, I try not to risk it. Merikoi that die on land reincarnate as humans." His eyes seem like they contain leagues and leagues of emotion. It draws me in like gravity. His liquid amber eyes drop from mine, his long lashes fluttering down. His lips press together, like his thoughts are pressing at every recess of his body, trying to come out. He seems to be at war with himself.

"What are you thinking right now?" I ask gently.

His eyes meet mine again, and his eyebrows peak at the center, like he's sad for some reason. His voice is a rough whisper, "I really can't tell you."

My heart tugs towards him, I don't know what it is that's haunting him, but it makes me want to give him a hug. I want to fix it for him. I try to lighten the mood, "Well then, it's a good thing I'm not a mind-reading vampire."

He throws his head back and laughs. It makes me smile.

He smirks at me and flips up his wrist, his large hand open. "Shall we?"

I stare at his hand, heart thudding quickly.

I slowly float my hand towards his, glancing up at him to see if I've read his signs wrong.

Leaving his hand open, he flicks his fingers, like he's waiting for my hand. Time slows to a waltz.

Carefully, my hand touches his warm palm. My heart melts. Heat erupts in my center like crackling fire. He folds his long fingers around mine. I am gripped by an overwhelming sense of rightness.

I stare up at him in astonishment.

His expression is serious. His enigmatic dark eyes hold mine. Time is stuck somewhere in space like a fly in honey. I'm afraid to breathe- it could shatter this moment. My throat is tight.

He stands, pulls me up beside him, and fluidly drops his hand from mine. "Have you eaten?"

I can't manage words, I just shake my head. The memory of his hand still wraps around mine. The door to the hallway is ajar, and he holds it open for me. In a state of confused shock, I feel like I've entered a fairy tale all over again.

# CHAPTER 12

STELLA

We walk, and my heart is pumping up visions of romance and love to overwhelm my mind and blur my vision. I struggle to maintain a hold on my logical brain and fight hard to suppress the whimsy. The hand-holding was simply helping me up, and the door-opening gesture was politeness.

His chuckle surprises me. "You're quiet."

I rack my brains for anything to say but what's on my mind. It would be unwise to let my brain turn his millisecond of chivalry into romantic interest. So, I force my mind back to the meeting, and with a jolt of adrenaline, remember the woman with purple hair. "Um, well I meant to ask you…" I turn to him, and we are pausing again in the dimly lit hall, dark rock carved around us.

He tilts his head forward just slightly, gently raising his brow with curiosity. "Yes?"

I notice how close we are, how alone we are, and it's really hard to breathe. I rally my thoughts back. "You said this was happenstance." I point to myself. "But that woman with the purple hair—"

"Leyra." His face is already squinting, as if he has detected a bad smell.

"Yes, Leyra. I saw her and her partner at an environmental action meeting in Maine, before you brought me here." I stare at him. I know I don't have to ask the question. He knows exactly what I'm asking.

He closes his eyes and breathes deep. I love the chance to stare at his beautiful face. When he opens his eyes again, he speaks carefully. "There was… a process of picking you."

I scrunch my brow in bafflement. "And that was…"

He glances away, shaking his head, looking agitated. "Look, I really can't explain it. Yes, they saw you, and they told me where you were and I planned to take you. That's what you can know."

The idea of being wanted by him on any level releases a brutal fiery adrenaline in my veins. I steady my voice, "Look, I want to help you. I want to fix what humans are doing to the ocean. I want to be here. But—" I narrow my eyes up into his dark angelic face, and step closer, making my heart race.

Unmoving, he regards me from his full height, expression closed.

I whisper threateningly, "I'll get answers about why I'm here. And you might not like who I get them from. But I have a feeling he'll tell me."

His eyes flicker at me, anger flashing. "You wouldn't."

I raise my eyebrows, shrugging as I back away. "I have a right to know."

Breathing heavily, his dark eyes rake over me in disbelief.

Fed up, I turn and start to walk away.

His long legs catch up quickly, and he spins to stand in front of me. Looking frazzled, he draws a hand through his disheveled hair, and looks at me pleadingly. "Please, just listen."

"I have been…" I concede, "But there's no information. That's why I'll go to the one person with reason to explain." Hades, despite a little playful misdirecting, seems to want to let me in on the secrets here more than anyone else.

I start to walk past him.

Sighing, Poi rolls his eyes, and closes the distance between us, gently grasping the backs of my arms and pulling himself up to me. He's so close I can feel his warmth radiating. I'm at the height of his chest, and look up to his painfully gorgeous face. My heart riots.

His dark amber eyes flicker between mine, his face pained. "I would tell you," he whispers roughly, "But Stella, I'm afraid I don't make all the rules around here. God, I wish I could tell you." His fingers flex gently around my arms, and his eyes flick to my lips again. "Would it be enough to say Fate has its rules?" His dark eyes are pleading like a seal pup. "Stella, will you please stop asking?"

I hesitate, not really sure about his belief of "Fate."

He clearly reads my face, and his becomes stern. "It's dangerous for anyone to tell you." He growls.

He's very sexy when he gets all bothered. But I don't believe in "Fate." However, I don't think he would take that very well. So I just blink.

He releases me and sighs dramatically. "I really don't know what to do with you when you get like this. You get stuck on an idea, and I just can't get you to leave it alone…" He runs a hand through his hair again. "I know you'll just keep going till you get an answer, and then fuck it all up."

My eyebrows sky-rocket. "Excuse me?" I laugh open-mouthed. Maybe he's a touch insane. He doesn't know me. My voice comes out haughty, "How do you suppose to know me that well? Takes a lot of nerve to tell me I'm going to 'Fuck it all up,' when you barely know me at all!!"

His open mouth becomes a closed line. He looks like a misbehaving child caught in the act. He stills and bites his lip. Then he starts to chuckle to himself (insane theory is winning out), and glances up at me with a surrendered smile, "I apologize. You're quite right. I must be mixing you up with someone else."

I survey him suspiciously.

He just looks at me and shakes his head. "C'mon. I can't stay at the dining hall, but I'll walk you."

I stay rooted to the spot, glaring at him, torn. Every bone, sinew, and synapse in my adrenalized body is firing to follow him anywhere. But my mind is stuck on needing to know why I was picked to be here. I will not be satiated until I know the answer. And I'm a little peeved that somehow, he hit the nail on the head. He kind of knows me exactly. And it's really weird.

He starts to shuffle backwards down the hall, "You going to make me walk all alone down these dark passageways?" His voice is nearly seductive, and I'm wondering if he's aware of that.

He does somehow know me. Being all playful and cute like that is the only thing that would work to make my feet walk forward impulsively. Like now. Grr. How does he know me so well?? Maybe he is just really, really good with people skills. He, technically, is a King. He would have to master people skills. I catch up to his backward gait, and reach up to push his shoulder playfully. "Don't be a baby."

He caves in to my touch, and pulls my arm, bringing me close. Breath catches in my throat. His gaze flickers to my lips again. He leans down slowly, and moves towards my ear, whispering into my hair, "Give it up."

His breath sends a chill down my neck. "You don't play fair!" I glower.

He's chuckling.

I back away gently, spin around him, and sprint on the balls of my feet. After a considerable lead, I shout down the hallway, "Hades will tell me!!"

"Oh fuck!" I hear him running up to try to catch me, I manage to reach the dining hall doorway.

I see Hades is in the dining hall line, chatting with the cook. He senses my stare, looks back, and I see an incredulous expression cross his face as a force thumps me out of the doorframe and against the outside wall.

Poi's body is pressed against mine, our chests heaving. His warmth and heady smell makes me dizzy high with lust. He inches back, hands gently gripping my shoulders. His eyes are wide with alarm. His deep voice is threaded with threat,

"You don't want to know the answers to your questions." He looks at me like I'm a hyperactive house cat he doesn't know how to tame.

I flicker with anger, because I deserve to know why I'm here, and I'm sure I'd like to know the answer. That's up to me. I'm not going to give up. Maybe he picked the wrong human. I glare up at his caramel-flecked eyes glowing through the shadowy light, and will myself to focus not on his magnetic proximity, but my own agency here.

"Wow... am I interrupting something?" Hades' voice drawls from beside us.

"Yes. Go away." Poi growls at the same time as I speak: "Hades, what am I doing here?"

I manage a glance at Hades, and he looks thoroughly entertained.

"Don't." Poi cuts at him, but continues to stare me down. Something infinitesimal in his expression has shifted, hardened, and his eyes aren't glowing anymore.

"Hades, I know you want to tell me. What's going on?"

Poi glowers down at me, hissing "Stubborn."

"I would love to," Hades leans up against the wall, creating the effect of an intimate threesome. "But unfortunately," he speaks melodramatically, as if this is all just some stage play, "I already promised my ol' bro that I wouldn't speak a word."

I look at him, open jawed. "But... but why now are you being good?" I stutter at his unpalatable joker smile.

"Because love, it's for your own good. Didn't Poi tell you? Poi, are you being a bad host?"

Poi's warm touch is lighter, as if his mind was put to ease, but at Hades' term of endearment his hands had flexed ever so slightly. He shifts his gaze to Hades, who's only inches from my head. Poi's voice is still tight. "Thanks."

"Uh-huh." Hades stares between us, smiling with intrigue, waiting for the next move.

Poi grits his teeth, "Could you give us some space?"

Hades purses his lips and shrugs away, calling "Boring…" as he slips back into the hall.

Poi's warm hands slip off my shoulders and graze my arms as he pulls back and crosses his arms, still just inches from me. All the tiny hairs on my skin are standing up as if a static current has passed between us. It's not just attraction… it's a strange feeling I can't place…

His serious molten stare connects to me like a physical thread. His voice is low, dangerous, "Anything you want—it's yours. But do not try to figure this out. It's the one thing I cannot give you."

Curiosity flares up in me like fireworks. Why does this matter so much? I have to ask. I find myself whispering too. "What makes you think Fate is real?"

His barely-withheld tortured look resurfaces. I wonder what he's battling. He just stares at me a moment before responding. "Experience."

That's hard to argue him on.

"Convinced?" he says doubtfully.

I smile uncomfortably. "Not really…"

He somehow smirks without humor. He tilts his head towards mine, and he steps just half a step closer, so we're nearly touching again. "I know you're not easily convinced. I certainly won't convince you here—like this." A sheepish expression flickers across his face, but it disappears into seriousness again, "But I need you to promise me. I need you to promise you won't go looking for answers on this." He pauses, his body heat emanating and engulfing me, his voice softening. "If for nothing else, please do it for me."

I feel hot. Heartbeats pulse my whole body. "This is unfair," I whisper.

His brow knits in confusion, "How?" he whispers.

I bite my lip, not wanting to tell him the effect he has on me. I'm not really sure if he's doing any of this intentionally, or if it's just his nature. With his body so close, I really don't want to think about the "Fate" thing, or why I'm here, anymore. I just want to collapse the inches between us.

He locks eyes with me, seeming to sense my weakness. "Promise." He whispers.

His face is too angelic, eyes too deep, and I find myself murmuring, "Okay."

He closes his eyes, and hangs his head over me a moment as he breathes. When he opens his eyes again, they are filled with relief. "Thank you. I know you're usually good on your word."

I don't know if this is a guilt-trip, or if somehow... he thinks he knows me better than he should. Again. I am good on my word. Mystified, I feel a strange sensation stir in me.

His face clears slightly, "I'll find you before the next counsel gathering."

Without touching me again, he turns and leaves.

I feel like my insides were just melted. I lean my head back against the cold rock and breathe slowly, trying to recover my senses.

The question builds up in me like a balloon expanding in my chest. I feel like I have to ask about it. Why am I involved in this? How am I involved?

I am the type of person that needs answers. And this is exactly what I was talking about when I promised myself not to pander to men's needs. Geez—I haven't even properly kissed the guy, and I'm promising away things I have a right to. I mean, he technically kidnapped me. He's very lucky I that am beyond joyous to be in this fairytale world.

This is one promise I can break. It didn't even make sense that I promised to it. I was coerced. His proximity, penetrating gaze, and model aesthetic makes the agreement void.

My brain comes to a halt with one idea. Leyra and Marc. They helped to capture me, so they must know something. I glance around the bustling dining room, hopeful that I might see her lilac locks.

Scanning, I quickly see that there is no purple hair. I squint my eyes, trying to think of where she might be. As I remember her sharp teeth, the idea of cornering her alone is a tad alarming.

Spotting Yimoto, I decide he may know where she is. When he notices me approaching, he stiffens, and lowers his fork.

"Stella, nice to see you." He nods politely, but his face is guarded, suspicious.

"Hi Yimoto." I feel awkward, suddenly. I realize I'm approaching one of Poi's senior advisors, and probably some prominent figure in Japan. How do I even start?

"Um, I think it's great how you corralled the panel into committing to a grassroots effort to stop the Taiji murders."

His eyes narrow, as if trying to puzzle out my strange human motives. He just nods once.

I suspect he knows I didn't come to just chat, and I feel he's silently willing me to get to the point. I twist my fingers before saying, "Ah, do you know where Leyra and Marc might be?" My voice chirps up at the end betraying my nerves.

He purses his lips, like he wants to know what I'm up to. I seriously hope he doesn't ask, or out of loyalty to Poi, try to stop me. I rock back on my heels.

"I suspect they are enjoying their brief vacation from duty. Maybe they are swimming along the mountainside, maybe they are visiting their tribes in private quarters. I do not know."

I appreciate that he's being so honest with me. But I feel a little deflated. There's no way I can find them in the ocean, or would even consider knocking on tons of stranger's rooms. Dead end for now. "Well, thank you, Yimoto."

He smiles stiffly, and as I edge slightly away from his table, he puts his head down and resolutely focuses on his salad.

I find myself pacing around the hall, wandering as my mind does. Light is streaming through the four stories of open air, and it seems brighter, less green. The hall is half full with about two hundred people. The long tables are lined up end-to-end in rows. Who else would know about why a human is here... who else...

I know that Laude must know something, but there's no way she wouldn't know of Poi's wishes, much less betray them.

The rest of Poi's advisors must be somewhat of experts at Merikoi-Human relations… but I can't embarrass him by going around and asking them all about it. Unless I did so discreetly… which I totally could…

Now I'm sizing up the room differently, looking for any Merikoi that dress like humans… anyone who had just been in the council meeting…

Dianne stands out like a firework with her pink power suit and stout frame. I think of all her restricted-access military knowledge and cringe. Too intimidating. Several others are in a group, chatting, mostly likely about the meeting. No. I want to find someone alone. Not to corner them, per say, but to not have too many people knowing what I'm asking about…

I recognize a balding blonde guy sitting on his own. Bingo. I don't really look his way as I approach, wanting to appear incredibly casual and not on a mission to get Mer to divulge their secrets to a human. He doesn't seem to see me until I'm sliding into the bench across from him. He flinches like a cinder has landed on his button-up shirt.

"I'm Stella. You were at the council meeting, weren't you?"

He's looking at me like I just said I'm an alien. It's strange, it's almost like the council members like humans less than the ones that never see them. I guess I don't blame them.

"I was," He finally says with a German accent. "I'm Reuder."

"So how did you think it went?" I have to start somewhere.

He looks at me uncomfortably, like he's not sure if he wants to play along with a human. "Generally, good." He pauses. "They always focus a little too much on American politics if you ask me."

"Happens on land too." I smile, happy to start edging the conversation towards humans.

"Yes, American politics is like loud-mouthed Americans." He chortles. I notice he still has seaweed stuck between his teeth. A bit affronted by his digs on Americans, I decide not to tell him.

I smile uncomfortably, "Right…" I have to think of how to get to the topic of humans…

"But you are from America, am I right?" He seems to be highly entertained by this fact, his light brown eyes dancing merrily.

"Yes, I am. I'm from—"

"How do you like it?" He huffs over my words, I realize his breath smells a bit stale. Like he has smuggled some alcohol down here or something. Maybe this is why he's sitting alone. He's being an anti-social drunk. Well, too late to avoid him. And… perfect person to spill the beans about Merikoi-Human secrets…

I answer, "I like it. Freedom of speech, women are generally respected, the wilderness is pristine… lots of pros."

He scratches his nose, seemingly disappointed with my answer. "But the people. How do you like the people? I find them to be loud, uneducated, and obnoxious, hey?"

I quell my annoyance at this stereotype, and redirect. Time to take charge. "Do you see a lot of Americans down here?"

His face falls just a tad. "By here, you mean the Ridge, not Germany, eh?"

"Yeah…" I try to appear vague, disinterested, merely conversational.

He pulls a small vial out of his ragged gray suit, swigs it, replaces it, and scrutinizes me. "Nope."

"How about…any… other humans?" I throw caution to the wind.

He continues to fork his skeletal fish into his mouth, bones and all. Eventually he pauses to say, "You're the first, the only, that I know of."

My jaw drops. "Why…" I pause, trying to keep my cool and not cause him alarm, "…do you think that is?"

He squares me with a look. "You're helping him, aren't you? Human perspective. Hard times."

This answer disappoints me. It's so logical. So reasonable. This answer holds nothing of what Poi is hiding. And Poi is definitely hiding something from me. Otherwise, why would he practically tackle me? That was completely out of his otherwise composed character.

"Do you think he's going to be bringing more humans down here? More Americans?" I add just for luster.

He raises an eyebrow at me lazily. "I really don't think so. One is enough."

I furrow my brow. This is totally confusing. "Why would he have picked me then? I'm not some government advisor, or anything."

He pauses and just looks at me for one long moment. A musty whisky cloud reaches my nose. He speaks gruffly, "I think that's a question for him. Don't you think?"

I want to roll my eyes with frustration. Like Poi will tell me!! I grit my teeth, realizing I'm getting nowhere with this. "A human girl from a boring office job gets pulled under the waves to help mermai- the Merikoi." I quickly amend, watching him bristle. "What's your theory?"

His nostrils flare as he heaves out a heavy sigh, and reaches for the flask in his jacket. "We don't have any other office workers down here. It's a hot commodity." He can't say it with a straight face. He was already chortling at his own joke before he finished the sentence.

I drop my head into my hands, dragging my fingers through my hair miserably. "I guess I'll never figure it out. I just don't get why it's some big secret."

I look up at him through my fingers, and I'm not sure if I'm imagining it, but it's like I almost see pity on his face.

"I'm not regretting being here." I amend, "I love it. It's amazing here- and everyone cares about saving the Ocean. I'm not complaining." I straighten it out. I don't want to start spreading the wrong impression, and get sent back. No way. I wouldn't want that. I don't know that I could go back now, not after knowing all this magic exists. And that Poi exists. No, I want to be right here in the middle of it all.

"Then stop worrying so much. Enjoy the moment, you lucky human." He takes another long swig of his flask. Hiding my exasperation, I thank him and swiftly retreat to an empty table.

I stake out the dining hall nearly half the day, hoping to see Leyra or Marc. I don't luck out. Reuder's words don't really settle in. I am so overwhelmingly curious about being their human experiment, I can think of nothing else. Eventually, the hall starts to fill with eclectic Merikoi, and the human-like Mer start to filter out. I follow them back to the meeting room, shuffling like a pouting child.

Poi is already sitting at his (it can't be called a chair), throne, with a small folding desk before him. His posture is so calm and relaxed you'd think he doesn't have a care in the world. He's nonchalantly gesturing a ballpoint pen towards a Merikoi woman, not a council member, and I realize that normal, ocean-dwelling Merikoi are filtering in to this meeting as well. I avoid the chair beside him, feeling it incredibly inappropriate to sit at the head of the circle again and quietly pick a less ornately carved chair closest to the door.

Mer continue to shuffle into the room and stand behind the occupied chairs, as the meeting has already appeared to have started.

"Fifty-seven thousand." Says a woman with pale blonde hair and large black eyes.

Poi records the number in his ledger. His eyes flick to me, and he squints for a moment, as if trying to tell if I've been up to anything. I feel hot under his gaze, but he seems satisfied with my general frustrated air, because he returns to the ledger.

The pointing and numbers continue. As people settle in, a grim silence falls, cut only by numbers.

"Eighty million." Says a man with brilliant silver eyes, and dark black hair.

The woman beside me has a husky voice which captures the room, "Three hundred and fifty. Seventy breeding females, and no calves again this year."

The room stills. Time seems to slow and warp with heaviness. Poi's brow furrows as he loudly draws the pen across the page.

The counts continue quickly around the room, and I ask the woman beside me what her numbers meant.

Her toffee eyes tighten as they focus on mine. "That's the remaining number of Right Whales in the entire ocean. Three hundred and fifty." My eyes graze down to her arms, covered with ink etchings of whales. She continues, "Humans have projected the Right Whale to go extinct within twenty years, but it may be sooner."

Stiffening, she refocuses her gaze at Poi recording tallies, and once again, I feel another stab of guilt for being human. The guilt is starting to feel like mercury I can't hold in my hands, or in my body.

A man grimly speaks, "Eight ."

My eyes bulge and I see an inked porpoise species trailing up his arm and towards his heart. Each low number feels like a dart holding me to a wall.

I look around the room, wondering how long the Mer have been around for, wondering how much their culture has changed since the Ancient Greeks named Poi a god.

Finally, seemingly two hours later, the tallies finish. Everyone in the room seems to be holding their breath, and gazing at Poi. He sighs, closes the front cover of the massive leather-bound volume, and looks around the room. "You all know, we are in a bind." He touches his fingertips together, as if thinking the best way to phrase things. "Humans… are causing a mass extinction on land, and in the oceans, as you can see by the dwindling species numbers. With humans overfishing, fishing with dangerous technology, polluting, destroying habitats, creating a painful cacophony of noise through oil exploration and drilling, causing ocean warming and increased acidity… the list goes on… everyone is struggling." He says it all with calm composure, as if regaling the weather. "We all know this. We know that when a species dies out, the Mer tribe associated with that species dies too."

No one moves. No one seems to breathe.

He pauses, placing his long fingers over his mouth for a moment before continuing, "I would ask, that we all do our best to remain calm. All we can do is work in the present moment to support the species and try to keep them alive."

The air is so thick with questions I can almost pluck them out and answer my own.

"This is…" His deep voice is somehow calming, "…happening quickly. More quickly than we had predicted. However." Subtly, he lifts his chin, and I admire his ability to stay so grounded in a time so stricken with panic. "We are making progress with humans on land. As they remain unaware of our whereabouts and existence, we sway their ocean policies and regulations. It is working. We are not at a point where anyone should feel emboldened towards extreme action. I am grateful that we are all united in our approach, and anyone with new ideas should collaborate with the Human-Relations Counsel."

Assessing the crowd, he seems to remember one last thing to say, "We must endeavor to keep in mind that humans are not intentionally destroying the world. It is important to not hate them for their ignorance. They have forgotten their way as Guardians, and it is no longer taught or a part of their culture. The only way is to slowly teach them to protect the Earth they depend on for their own survival. Hating them will never help us. Teaching them will help the world."

Suddenly, everyone is bowing their head as if in agreement. Despite his words, anger batters in my chest like a blind rabid bat. The oceans are literally apocalyptic, and human cultures aren't even acting to try to stop it. Why are the Mer being so nice about it?

Poi's sentiment is beautiful, but insane. Taking population tallies and subtly affecting policy isn't enough. Biting my lip with pity, I realize that none of their plans will work. The only thing that can fix this mess is human technology. They did this- they need to undo this.

These tragedy-imposed, peaceful people are struggling to survive, just like every other species in the ocean. As human, and guilty by association, I feel more responsibility to help. I set my jaw, realizing that I am willing to risk anything, even possibly my life, to reverse this mounting, human-created apocalypse.

# CHAPTER 13

STELLA

Despite the mild summer air, the sky appears cold. The bumpy patchwork quilt of frozen ice hangs way up in the air and wraps around infinity, sun stained with defiant magenta. The heaving waves echo back a dance of liquid gold, rose, cabernet, and aquamarine. Beneath the glittering surface, lurks black.

The rocks are cold below me, and the wind is wicked this evening. But I'm grateful to be out here by myself, to get some space to process, before the council members meet at the bar tonight. Before I see Poi, at the bar tonight. There's so much pandemonium battering around in me, it's like there are three baboons trying to inhabit my one petite body.

Being here is amazing- but human guilt gnaws at my appendages, and an unattainable god haunts my heart.

I'm a bit hesitant to even let myself entertain Poi as a real possibility... I pretzeled myself so far last time... I still can't believe my blind willingness spraying weed-killer on what makes me colorful, just for the sake of being tame enough to be loved.

Now, I'm less afraid of my own opinions. Fully acknowledging my mind, I've realized so much more of myself. I've embraced what I suppressed, and I love my wildflower fields. I'm opening to my defining factors. It's okay for me to feel such deep grievance for being human, it's okay for me to be opinionated about it. It's okay for me to care so much. It hurts more to say it doesn't matter.

Being alone feels precious. It's a space where no one's judging my mind, where no one's telling me what thoughts to have. Why the hell would I want to pretzel myself again?

And yet, a compulsive part of me tracks Poi. I always seem to be aware of where he is, or wondering. Not in a needy sense, so much as a sort of awe. I've never felt this for someone before. Just knowing he exists makes me feel better about the world. Okay, I do want him. So maybe a little needy... but not in the delusional sense that he might be interested in me. And not for a need that his love could define me as someone worth loving. My fascination for him is not an egotistical, self-flattering, or conquesting sense. It's more pure than that. I'm enthralled with him- his unrelenting and steadfast passionate approach to saving what he loves despite the odds. His relaxed and grounded nature- as if despite the melee, the world is a place one can be calm in. His thoughtful and observant demeanor- how he seems to always have so much more in his mind that what he says aloud. And his clear appreciation for others. Despite being a ruler of sorts, people are just at ease around him, because he's not judging them, he seems to accept them, faults and all. And that's worth gravitating to. It's like his immense age has taught him what really matters. And I admire him for it.

The light has faded around me, but far off and above the horizon, molten crimson burns on the edge of the sea. These bold lights we are graced with twice a day don't come often, but do, occasionally and reliably, reach earth. A little crack in my reality of what love could be, shines through the ruby red. Maybe one day, I'll be in a relationship where both parties are whole, and just coexist in easy appreciation together. That would be nice. But I don't feel whole enough for that yet- I feel like a kid, wearing an oversized jacket I have to grow into.

The dimly lit long room immediately reminds me of a bar- real and human-owned, but more naturalistically designed, and less sticky beer floors. Dozens of lit candles have been placed along rock outcroppings which has been left rough, which actually looks rugged and hip. To the left, a bar runs along the length of the room. Mellow music carries from the back, where I assume there is a band. The land-dwelling and ocean-dwelling Mer are mingling in groups, chatting and tipping up conch shells as they drink. Despite their fancy attire, I grin as I notice no one is wearing shoes, and realize they never do shoes down here. My kind of people.

Laude approaches, looking amazing. She's wearing a swanky, deep neck, shimmering navy-blue gown, with gold strings of pearls across her flat chest like a flapper. The outline of a hammerhead shark delicately repeats and winds itself up and around her right bicep and towards her back. Her short, platinum blonde hair is styled wildly around her head. She smiles with her set of sharp little teeth, "Kiara and I were just talking about you, come sit with us."

She guides me past the tattooed and exotic Mer- some wearing revealing evening gowns, some dresses so skimpy they could nearly be bathing suits. Gorgeous shells are embedded in their braided hair, hanging from necklaces, and sewn to dresses. Some of them seem to be wearing glitter across their cheekbones and eyelids. Many of the men are wearing no shirts at all- only loose silken shorts or trousers, also adorned with shells and shark teeth.

I'm wearing a silky Mer number I found in the cottage wardrobe- it fits me really well… it's low cut, skimpy, and a burnished shade of lilac that contrasts with my eyes. Gazing around at the festooned Mer, I kind of wish I had been bolder with my shell accessorizing.

Kiara and Poi sit at a beat-up round wooden table that looks like it was once an industrial spool. It's small, and in the middle of the loud crowd. Poi's leaning over the table, staggeringly handsome, his bulky shoulders stretching his white shirt. His cropped wavy dark hair is messy. His dark eyes look me up and down so quickly I almost don't notice. It's a jolt to my stomach. I bite my lip, wanting him.

"Don't look so shocked," His amber eyes glint, "We know how to have fun too." Don't read into it. Don't. Take it for face value. I smile demurely, "It really does seem like a normal bar."

Kiara laughs, and I notice her. She's wearing a pale pink silken top that compliments her warm mocha skin. Her turtle tattoos climb elegantly up her arm, and disappear behind her exposed shoulder. Her tone is pointedly saucy, "It is a normal bar- to us…"

Laude's unnerving red eyes are gleaming with amusement.

I fidget, "Right." I don't try saving face. How am I supposed to make any sense when so much adrenaline is kicking around in my stomach?

But I notice his eyes are still on me. As Kiara and Laude talk, and the crowd mills around us, I feel a magnetic pull between us. His face is almost sexier in the shadows.

"Don't you agree?" Laude's voice is asking, and she leans in and catches Poi's eye, who drags his gaze from mine.

"I heard nothing- what were you saying?" His voice is gravelly.

Does he feel a magnetic force between us too? Fiery adrenaline twists below my navel.

"—pain in the ass." I hear her say, "The damned Octopi tribe has been sneaking around. I caught Levi in the far north passages- it's totally abandoned! What the hell do you think he's up to down there?"

"Ah- he gets bored." Poi waves a hand. "Levi's excessively intelligent-he's too cooped up here. I think the Octopi must miss living at the coral reefs more than anyone." For an instant, his eyes are far-off. "So, I've asked him to brainstorm potential human visibility threats. That'll be why he's searching down the abandoned ridge."

Placated, she huffs, "Fine."

He grins at her affectionately, "Maybe you need a few extra projects."

She shrugs, "Bring it."

"You going to drink something?" Kiara asks me, gesturing towards a conch resting sideways on its spiny spindles.

I peer between the blushing pink and bone white, and see a mysterious red substance.

"It's wine. From Italy." She smiles at me, and I lift it up in two palms, perplexed.

"We do a discreet business with one specific vineyard." Poi explains. "He doesn't exactly know we're Mer... but I think there may be local legends there."

"But how can you...afford it?" I ask.

Laude barks a laugh. Kiara is literally screeching with laughter. It's nearly drowned out by the steel drum and cacophony around us.

Poi's expression contorts, failing to hold back a bemused grin. He shakes his head condescendingly, "Oh...little human... so much to teach you... do we have the time?" He looks to Laude.

"Oh... she's a quick learner, she'll pick it up." She winks a red orb at me.

He shrugs, playing along. "If you say so..."

Kiara rolls her eyes, and leans forward conspiratorially, "Do you know... just how many ship wrecks litter the oceans? We're not just talking treasure here. Scrap metal, antiques, you name it. People will pay big money for shipwrecked wooden beams..."

Poi grins at me casually, "We take their trash and sell it back to them."

"Cheers to that." Laude lifts her shell and we chink. Poi's eyes are still on me, staring into mine.

I feel a breath-taking urge to close the distance between us.

Instead I take a sip. I navigate the liquid down the narrow stem of the conch. Earthy and smooth, it's very good wine. It's comforting to have something that grew from a tree, from the earth.

A pale arm reaches over Poi and rests on the table, a woman with full lips and braided ginger hair leans over and starts talking to him, "Speaking of our haul, did I tell you that Juniper discovered a shipwreck off the coast of Oman? Recent, and massive. Must be the doing of Somalian pirates. They must have bit off more than they could chew."

"Really? What type of ship?" He's already climbing out of his seat and following her. I presume "Juniper" must be around somewhere. I am hit with an unwelcome frisson of jealousy, watching him recede into the crowd of glamorous Mer.

Kiara lands me with a mischievous stare and alarming smile. "Now. Just us girls. Let's hear the dirt."

Laude laughs, "Now, don't harass her."

Kiara raises her eyebrows innocently, "Asking personal questions is polite in human culture."

It's my turn to laugh, but I turn it into a cough as she just looks confused.

She's already asked me tons of questions about human life in general, but from her expression, I worry she may be emboldened by her wine, and ready to start asking the harder questions. I just hope she doesn't ask about guys. I would never want to admit I like Poi. How embarrassing for both of us.

"Did you have kids?" She whispers.

I laugh, not having expected that question, "Nope."

She pauses for just an instant, "So how do you feel about Poi?"

I freeze.

"Kiara!" Laude slaps her arm reproachfully. "Don't be pushy."

Kiara raises her eyebrows at me, eyes glinting. "I think he's into you…"

My heart starts thudding and I hope she's right but I worry that her saying this will just feed into my hopes more than reality.

Kiara starts again while Laude rolls her eyes and sighs exasperatedly. "So… have you noticed how he–"

She's cut off by Hades. "Ladies!" He practically shouts. He slips into Poi's place. He's holding two drinks and one is clearly his back-up. "Did you see Operram by the door? He's got a *wild* jellyfish sting. Was in with the healer for a whole hour. Now, what are we talking about?"

His presence is demanding.

Laude blinks a few times, "Treasure- you know, they found another sunken ship- probably the Somalians. Arabian Sea."

He takes in our expressions, "Bullshit. You were talking about guys."

"Pshh how did you *know*?!" Kiara cries.

"I am very good at bullshit myself. So, bullshit knows bullshit." He beams, clearly very pleased with himself.

He gives me a sultry stare, "So who are we talking about?"

I raise an eyebrow, "We're not. Topic exhausted itself."

He shakes his head at me with a devilish smile, "Pretty little thing like you? I highly doubt it."

I raise my eyebrows and look to Laude, hoping for help.

"Hades—" she begins matronly.

"So, did you have a little human boyfriend? What was he like…?" He rests his head on his hands and stares expectantly.

I huff. I really don't want to do this. "Human, okay?"

Kiara laughs, "Go girl. Don't take his shit."

I decide to turn the tables. "So, who are you guys dating?"

They all straighten up in their seats, moving back infinitesimally. Well that changed the mood. Aha. I should have tried this before!

"Hades, you first." I demand.

"Well that's not fair," he pouts, "I didn't get to hear any of the dirt, and now I am fed to the sharks?"

"Hades loves his single life. Can't settle down." Kiara volunteers.

"Won't." He flashes a grin that could be on the cover of any dental flyer.

Under cover of the loud bar, Laude bends to my ear, and murmurs in hushed tones, "His Queen, the famed Persephone, left him centuries ago. It crushed him. He's still in denial about the whole thing."

I'm sure Hades can't hear Laude's comment, but his pale eyes dart between us with suspicion. I get the feeling he is very protective of this knowledge, despite it being common lore. He stole a woman from the Earth, she ate a single pomegranate seed in the underworld, and was therefore trapped there with him for three seasons of every year. I wonder intensely which parts of this fable are true. Mostly, I wonder if she was there voluntarily. Did she ever actually love him? He looks between us uncertainly again, and sloshes back a significant amount of his drink.

Laude continues to the group, "I have a partner who is often on land. She's embedded into the US military, and is a reliable source of crucial information." She sighs, "But, I don't see her enough."

"She said she's going to take a break soon." Kiara interjects.

Laude rolls her eyes, "She's been saying that for years…" She sighs, "But, I get to see her at least four months of the year- she's worked in a ton of vacation time. And honestly, we'd probably drive each other crazy if we saw each other all the time."

"You would." Hades nods emphatically. "Petrika drives me nuts all the time. I don't know how you stand her."

Laude grins her sharp teeth viciously. "I'll be sure to tell her. She'll make more time for you her next visit."

Kiara smacks his bare arm. "Trouble-maker, behave."

"And you, my sweet. Too good for everyone, aren't you?" He grins down at her with a flirty smile.

She smirks but her eyes wander across the room, and I follow them. A tall, slightly lanky, blonde guy reaches over the bar and helps himself to a drink. One of his long arms is wrapped in elegant tentacle tracings, which lead up his arm and snake under his loose silken vest. Glancing back at Kiara, I watch her sticky gaze return to Laude who is now talking to Hades.

Apparently at least one guy meets her standards.

Speaking of that. I realize that this is my chance to get information about Poi... If he's dating anyone. There's no real subtle way to do it... but does it matter? Do I want to be discreet? Absolutely. The last thing I want is for someone to hint to him that I may like him. I might have misread the chemistry I felt. My stubborn hope blinds me. If he were into me, he'd have returned to the table by now. Maybe I will ask just Laude, later.

I decide asking about dating in general is easier. Simple curiosity. Any human would ask. "Do Mer mate for life?"

"Not this one." Hades boasts.

Laude ignores him. "Some do. I suppose it's kind of like humans. You wait to find the right match."

"In the meantime..." Hades stares unabashedly at my tight dress before looking at my face, "We experiment."

Right...I narrow my eyes. Wishing Poi was still sitting there instead of him.

"Some a bit too much..." Laude glances over towards a couple along the wall.

Kiara watches with a slight frown, "Good for them."

I turn to look around the dim bar, and notice quite a lot of couples are very affectionate. A man bites the ear of another. The red-bearded healer from the clinic is leaning over to massage the slender black woman from the council meeting. She's now wearing a pale pink dress instead of a suit. He's whispering something into the back of her head, making her eyebrows raise. The couple against the wall is outrageous. And then my eyes bulge as I realize I recognize them from earlier this morning. The woman with mossy green hair is now wearing a skimpy red satiny excuse for a dress, and is pinning the milky-eyed man against the wall with her leg suggestively up resting on the rock like she's about to climb the wall. He leans his white-blonde head down to her, wrapping his tattooed arms against her back as they suck face. I'm astonished at the flagrant PDA.

"Doesn't everyone... have private rooms?" I ask.

"Sure, but I think they like showing off." Hades is squinting, as if inspecting their form.

"They're just in the moment." Kiara states. Then her eyes glide back over to the sandy-haired guy, who is wrapping an arm lazily around the pretty red head who had extracted Poi from us in the first place.

I'm relieved to see Poi isn't with her still, and try to suppress my disappointment in his not returning. I wonder again if he's seeing anyone. The thought makes me want to bolt.

I realize it must have gotten pretty late into the night. The Mer party harder than I can, and with Poi not anywhere in sight, I'm so ready to give up here.

As if reading my mind, Laude announces, "I'm turning in."

I sit up quickly, realizing this is my chance to ask about Poi. "Me too." I allow a yawn.

As we leave, I keep imagining that Poi might see us go, grab my arm, and say- "You're leaving?" with a puppy-dog stare, and say, "Why don't you stay…" and we would end the night making out Mer style. But that doesn't happen. I even look around through the throngs, and don't see him.

The din of the bar echoes into the hall.

I don't know where Laude lives, so I get right to it: "Laude, can I ask a question, and you not tell anyone I've asked it?"

She pauses and turns to me, assessing. "Sure."

I hold my breath, thinking this might be a better time to ask about why I was the only human on earth plucked off of land to be living amongst mermaids. But there is one question that is elbowing out all the rest. "Is Poi dating anyone?"

Her smile is easy, "I don't believe he is."

My lungs feel lighter. "Good. I mean, I was just curious." I fidget awkwardly, and she waits. "Did he… has he… dated a lot of women?" I am not sure what to think about his… he's so insanely gorgeous, but, on the other hand, he's so reserved…

"No... he doesn't date. He's very focused on the job, you know. Pretty busy." It's a fairly generous amount of information coming from Laude.

But I'm not done. "Has he... ever dated anyone? I mean, he must've."

She hesitates. "Only one."

The words hit me like a stone. She must have been pretty important. I wonder if anyone will ever compare- if he will ever get over her. If I could ever compare. "What happened? Where is she now?"

Laude looks down the hall for a moment, distracted or uncomfortable. After thinking she may not answer, she speaks. "She died."

"Oh." I'm not sure how to respond. "I'm... sorry. Was it long ago?"

"Long enough." Laude leans her head, and we begin to walk again. I'm sensing she doesn't want to say any more.

I think about Poi's past love life. No ...I obsess about his love life as I walk the rest of the way up to my room. Only one. Damn, she must have been special. And the way Laude talks about it... it was like he actually hasn't gotten over her. I'm fretting over a woman who's no longer around. Mind, I demand, he's single. Focus on that.

But I can't help but wish I had left the conversation drop after finding out he's single.

# CHAPTER 14

POI

My eyes skim across text without reading the words. I shut the book with a snap. My nerves are crackling like the fireplace. I've barely let myself be alone with her, I've eased us into this, and now is the time where, I hope, we start all over again. It's so hard to pretend I haven't known her for a sizable fraction of eternity. I can't reveal anything, and I have to keep fighting the impulse to drop my guard.

Tall bookcases loom above me and box me into the end of a library aisle. None of the bindings on the shelves can capture my attention. The room is still, holding its breath. I've just worn the aisle down with pacing, but apparently it wasn't enough. My foot won't stop tapping.

The brass nob rattles as she twists from the other side, opening with a dramatic creak. Through the gaps in the bookshelves, I see her walk into the room. My heart beat jars my chest. Her high cheekbones and small, upturned nose are rosy with sunburn. Her delicate brows are knitted with nervousness as she bites her lip and looks around. She's wearing just a loose t-shirt and shorts, hair tied back in a messy pony tail. I'm still getting used to her human look- it's so different from the silken garments and intricate braids of her past life. She gazes around the room, and lingers at the peridot fireplace. Not seeing me, she heads to the stone alcove embedded with carved bookshelves. For an instant, I debate playing a trick on her. That would go over well in her past life, but this version of her is so skittish already, I don't dare.

She comes back to the middle of the room, wide emerald eyes darting over the pages of a small leather volume in her hands. She stops, reading a passage, and continues to walk, until she leans and sits on a desk. A desk between two plump leather chairs. Now that's more her style.

"What are you reading?" I've walked up pretty close without her noticing- the closest I'll go to playing a trick on this version of her.

"Jesus!" Flinching, she flails off the desk to stand on one leg before rebalancing. Her eyebrows raise at the edges in confusion, "You were here the whole time?"

I can't help chuckling a little. "I was."

"Where? Back in the shelves?"

I nod, biting back a wide grin. I miss how we used to be- playful. We were gods, but we were children.

Scrunching her forehead, she raises her eyebrows further, assessing me with a hint of who she used to be. "I'll never play hide and seek against you."

I grin. "I'd rather be on the same team."

Her eyes bulge and she blushes. Oops. I can't help just falling back into what we had before. Boundaries. "What are you reading?"

She picks up the book from the floor, and I can't help but admire her nimble fluidity. She brushes a flyaway hair behind her ear, exposing her heart-shaped face, and angles the book cover to me as she hands it over. "The New World- it was written in 1578!"

I take the volume from her, and my hand brushes her chilly fingers. Electricity bolts up to my heart.

Her eyes widen, but she looks back at the book with a determined expression. "The Portuguese settlers listed the Merikoi as one of the coastal Maine Native American tribes. Did the Merikoi really live in Maine?"

"We lived along many of America's coastal shelves. But I loved living in the area which became the Maine coast, we did a lot of trading and socializing with the Penobscots and Passamaquodys."

She gasps and gazes up at me with her wide eyes, "You lived in Maine? When?"

"Oh, about three hundred and fifty years ago."

"Holy shit!!" She stumbles back, leaning against the desk for support, full lips parted in surprise. "You're crazy old!!"

I can't help smirking at her theatrical manner. "You know I'm immortal…"

"Yeah, but, you look- maybe twenty-eight…" She squints her eyes and eases off the desk again, walking closer. My heartbeat hitches as she raises onto her tiptoes before me, gazing up at my hairline. "Do you have any gray hairs?"

My lips pull wide, "No."

She cocks her head, stunned, which is very adorable. I withhold every impulse to close the space between us. "How does it work?"

She stays near, inspecting me with heart-breaking curiosity, and my chest clenches with the need to pull her closer. I keep my tone even, "Mer age differently than humans. They reincarnate a few times, and pass on. I am immortal in that I reincarnate eternally. I always come back the same, with a continuous memory." I stare into the eyes of my long-lost queen, who is completely shocked by the concept, and a heavy sadness descends through my ribcage. At any point, she could die a human, and never return. I wish I could change everything for her. I wish I could give her back her life.

"But what about when you're a kid? Who rules then?" She's eases back infinitesimally, solidly resting on her heels again.

"All the Mer are Guardians. They know what to do. We take care of each other."

She squints, nods slowly, then disarms me with a penetrating look. "So how old are you, really?"

It's a good thing she asked a question I can answer. I could have spilled anything. "Eight-hundred and ninety-six rotations of the earth around the sun."

Her jaw drops and her nose crinkles on one side, eyes squinting oddly with what is most likely horror, or repulsion. I inwardly flinch. I didn't predict my age to be problem for us, but it might be. She shifts her weight forward, as if to get a better look at me. Her voice is a whisper, "How is that possible? Reincarnation- sure, but how can you age so differently…?"

I shrug, feeling a frisson of age-shame for the first time in my existence. "Heartbeats. Our hearts beat slowly. We're designed for the pressure of the ocean- even in this air-tight room."

She squints at me, as if trying to calculate heart beats and ocean pressure. Wildly, blood surging with trepidation, I take a half-step forward, and reach down to grasp her chilly hand. Her whole hand fits into the concave of my palm. Gently, I draw her fingers up towards my pulse, and she steps closer, expression terrified, which is never a good sign. Maybe I'm just an old god to her. But I swear she's flushing.

Reminding myself to breathe normally, I pull her cool fingertips up to my neck, against my jugular vein. I don't think she's breathing. I've missed her being so close that it makes me reckless. I want to tell her everything. I want to kiss her awake. But my actions could be the death of her. I wrap up my emotions in silence. I keep her fingers against the stubble below my jaw, and look down, waiting for her to feel a pulse.

"Don't feel it, do you?" My voice comes out a rough whisper.

She shakes her head, staring at my neck with concentration. Maybe this was a terrible idea. But I keep holding her light fingers to my neck. "My heart hasn't beat yet." My voice is low.

Despite the racing feeling of adrenaline burning through me, the seconds drag on as my blood makes its slow circuit. She's biting her lip now, and I stare off into the room, not wanting to make her nervous. Finally, I feel the slow thud of my blood beneath her cool fingertips.

Flickering her eyes up to mine, she whispers, "There it is."

I hold her with my gaze, saying all the things I can't speak. Her ivy eyes hook into my soul and pull. I forgot what it was like to be this close to her. The magnetism nearly knocks me off my feet, amplifying between us, and it's all I can do to just stay still.

Her light brows furrow together, and she blinks a few times, looking down. "So…you're older than Shakespeare. That's hard to wrap my mind around."

I chuckle, and recklessly reach for her chin with my fingertips. She's very still, and she looks more fearful than eager. It's going to take time to earn her trust. Painful want grips me like a fist as I linger slowly on her skin, tracing across to her jawline, tucking my fingertips under the silken flesh of her exposed neck. Her breathing hitches, and her skin flushes hot again. Maybe I'm not so repulsive after all. A corner of my lips twitches up. Catching her vein, my eyes widen at her jittery pulse, "Way too fast. Are you okay?"

She blushes, looking away, "Yeah, I'm fine."

I drop my arm slowly, shaken by the visceral reminder of her ticking clock. Her human life is running past faster than I know how to track. My heart twists painfully. Her heart is beating too fast… "Okay, hmm. I don't know, is that normal for a human?"

She's burning crimson now, looking all around the room but at me. "Um, I think so…" she squeaks uncertainly.

I narrow my eyes, not buying her answer. She's nervous, and it's eating up her lifeline. Worse, it's caused by her proximity to me. "Maybe our lesson will slow your heart rate back down," my tone comes out gruff. I pull out a chair for her and gesture for her to sit, noticing her shallow breathing, which isn't healthy either. I need to stop measuring her mortality. I can't control it, and I'm driving myself crazy with this worrying.

I force air deep into my lungs. I round the table and sit across from her. My whole body is rigid. Without any disasters, she has a couple of decades if she doesn't fall for me. I gaze into her deep emerald eyes, knowing I would give up my own rationed heartbeats just for hers to one day restart again.

## STELLA

The walk down to the library this time isn't any easier. Fiery, electric adrenaline oozes out of every cell of my body. My energy seems to ricochet off the rough rock walls and potentiate into an unbearable cocktail of wobbly legs and shallow breathing. I seriously hope he doesn't try to take my pulse again. But another part of me super wants that. Just to be close to him. I notice my mind has to take considerably more effort to lasso in all my female instincts. Calm down! My brain screams at my body. But I know it's not just wanting him in a carnal way. It's my heart. Something about him has lodged deeply into the beating part of my soul from very early on. Maybe it would be easier if it was only hormones. Suddenly, the impossibility of my crush is a heavy fog crowding in on me.

Human pulses freak him out. Another reason he would never go for a human like me. Not only am I evil by association, but I could only ever live for a small fraction of his lifetime. He's a classy, commitment, sort of a guy. He's only been serious with one woman. She probably lived for a very long time, just like him. He wouldn't want to date someone who's only a minute of his eternity. The sudden heaviness of my heart is tonifying. I slow down, I breathe. I remember what I'm doing here. I'm just here to help save the oceans.

When I push open the door, he's already in that same seat at the table. He smiles up at me, like he's been wanting to see me all day, and my weary heart can't help but skip hopefully. My mind reminds me that he likely has this manner and effect with everyone.

I try so hard to dampen my physical reactions as I sit across from him. I'm clenching my stomach and reminding myself to breathe at once. I look around the room to distract myself. The space is still, quiet. The sweet smells of cherry wood, musky leather and old books fill the air. Bookcases carved into black rock line the room, while tall cherry wooden bookcases create a handful of aisles packed with books. Torchlights burn against the walls, and there are no windows revealing our location beneath the sea. It almost feels like I have stumbled into some privately-owned human library on land.

He narrows his dark honey eyes at me, "You alright?"

Cursing my transparency, I try to breathe normally, and say brightly "Yep." I don't know if he's just better at reading me, or simply pays closer attention than most people. Either way, it's unnerving. And my nerves are already doing their best to stay in-line.

He raises a dark eyebrow at me, his lips strained into a firm but crooked smile. "You're not getting away with it. I know you're unnerved about something. Speak up."

My lips part in surprise as I stare back at him. My mind viciously quips; Um sure... it's just unrequited love for a hot, incomparably admirable, immortal that would never date a perishable, evil human.

His dark gaze is penetrating, and makes me feel too still.

"It's nothing..." I manage to breathe out.

He nods once, as if he's done what a proper host would do- ask if I was okay. And now that I've refused his query, he has permission to move on to more important topics. He is polite above all else. "So." His dark eyes flash playfully, "How much stock do you put into conspiracy theories?" His question catches me off-guard. He intertwines his long fingers before him, waiting.

I smirk. "Very little... why?"

He shrugs, "I'm looking for leads. I don't have enough people with access to highly restricted military info. I've heard great things about the videos humans watch on the internet- a lot of those military conspiracies turn out having some thread of truth to them. How much time have you spent on the YouTube?"

I grin widely at his funny way of speaking, and actually impressive knowledge of human culture. I try to answer honestly. "Probably the normal amount for anyone working a desk job. Which is a lot. I have to admit I have spent a few lunch hours engrossed in conspiracy theory videos…"

He smiles broadly, "Perfect. So what have you…I won't say learned…but…" he squints over my shoulder while he grasps at the right word, "…what's the hearsay? Could you list anything to do with military technology?"

A thought dawns on me, and I cock my head at him and gaze with horror. "You're not planning to start a war or anything? You won't win."

He rolls his eyes impatiently. "Of course not… that would be… extincticidal, to coin a new term. I just need to know if we need to adjust our security in any way."

"Alright. I guess you didn't live this long by being incautious." I take the paper in hand and begin to write a list.

I feel him watching me write, but honestly, I like it. I'm useless at his project though. Feeling silly, I title the page, "Possible Technology." I write the first thing that comes to me, even though it doesn't really fit the category, "Remote Viewing,"

He immediately asks, "What's that?"

"It's a military term for being psychic—for being able to see what's hidden and locate important threats." I watch his expression turn sober.

"Well, we aren't a threat," He sighs, "but it was certainly an advantage when modern humans didn't believe they had any spiritual or psychic ability…Damn. There's not much hiding from that."

He leans back in his chair and runs a hand through his hair with a sigh. "They're really not giving us much breathing room here."

Suddenly he looks worn and vulnerable. It makes me want to give him a hug. But I hold my arms down on the table. My voice is soft, "Have you ever thought about…I dunno… negotiating your existence with humans?"

A blip of shock crosses his face, then he squints at me with what I swear is suspicion. Maybe regret for letting a human in on Mer secrets- and seriously hoping I don't blab. Another beat passes, and his expression shifts to: "don't be silly." His voice is as near condescending as I've ever heard from him, "You know that wouldn't work. Humans fight for peace. We don't have a military. The only thing we know how to fight is our food. We're better off with staying hidden as long as possible." He stares off into the dusty shadowy spaces in the library. "At some point, we may not be able to stay hidden. I do not want to think about that day. But increasingly, it seems like that time is edging closer and closer. I absolutely dread that moment. It would mean total annihilation."

I have nothing comforting to say. Nothing useful. Humans are at risk of destroying each other each day, and another species? Well, we're destroying more than we can count at record speed. Scientists are talking about a sixth mass extinction in progress. I don't think these sentiments would be useful right now. Instead, despite a hummingbird of a heart, I just reach my hand across the table, and gently place it on his. "I'm very sorry."

He looks at my hand on his, and closes his eyes. I can't imagine the pressure he is under- nothing like that of the ocean- no being is built to sustain this amount of pressure.

As my hand lays still and cool over his warm hand, I'm shocked at my calm, but my heart is heavy for him. I wish there was some way I could lighten his burden. I want to flip his hand over, and gently massage his palm with my thumbs. But I know the instinct is too intimate, so I stay still. He keeps his eyes closed, and I want to wave a magic wand and make all this trouble turn into dust.

When he opens his eyes again, he keeps his hand in mine. His expression is more open than I've seen. The shadows seem darker around his eyes, his black brows pull in with concern, the elegant planes of his face are etched with emotions I can't read. I realize that this abundance of feeling must be the reason he often comes across as so reserved- he just hides it all. His voice is rough, "Thanks."

I hold his dark gaze, trying to understand all his emotions that are pouring forth. "Sure… Anytime." I amend. I really do wish he could always be this open around me.

He looks around at the flickering torchlights, without windows it's hard to judge the time that has passed. "We should head to the dining hall."

I look around, resistant, "Right."

I start to pull my hand back from his, but he catches my wrist with a quick movement. He lowers his mouth to my palm and softly presses his warm lips against me. His dark gaze is bare, intimate, and suggestive.

My breath catches. Is he into me? My neurons are exploding as my heart riots.

And just as suddenly, he gets up, and promptly seems to forget the moment. He barely seems to look at me as we head out into the hall.

My mind is reeling. Maybe I was wrong? Maybe a little human does have a chance at a fling with a god? But my heart can't quite keep the beat, because it still knows I wouldn't be a serious encounter for him. I want to think less of him, for wanting an impermanent fling, but I can't. I want him. With every spinning atom in my body.

# CHAPTER 15

STELLA

It's no surprise that my dreams were filled with Poi, but last night my subconscious was a considerably more hopeful narrator. I hear the waves spraying up on the rock. The sunlight is so bright I see it before I open my eyelids. Deep in my chest, a hopeful fire is burning.

I swing out of bed like a lithe ten-year old, excited to go to school to see a crush. Opening the wardrobe doors, I catch a glimpse of myself in the age-spotted glass mirror. My messy hair is streaked and stained light blonde from the sun, my evergreen eyes are somehow catching more light, and even my skin seems to be glowing. More tiny freckles splay across the bridge of my nose, a signature of summer. I look happy.

I pull out a silken emerald cloak to throw around my t-shirt and shorts. The fabric slips around me like water. I sigh, checking out my Mer look in the mirror, and deciding to fishtail braid my hair around the side and add a few shell pendants for fun. Strangely, I finally know what feels like me, and it's this. This world.

I look at my right palm again. I have thought of Poi's kiss so many times that I have utterly sucked it dry. Staring at the tell-tale wrinkled lines of supposed fate, and blood swimming in veins below, I wonder what overcame him when he kissed me there. I wonder if the scorching look in his eyes was lust, or if I am misreading some sort of typical Mer gesture of gratitude for emotional support. I sigh, starting to doubt myself a little.

As I walk down the gray light passageways towards the dining hall, passing the waterlogged rooms shedding muted light, feet padding on cold stone, any confidence I had in the sunlight seems to slip into the murky shadows. The scrawl crawling and cut into stone looks increasingly foreign, the more I stare, the less it looks mandarin, and the more it looks alien. Despite my lust and obsession with this world, I just don't understand, or fit in. I'm slowing my walk as I near the gold-gilt doorframe, reaching up to my hair, considering removing a few shells when Kiara appears.

"Perfect. I was just about to come find you." Her words gush out as she slips her warm arm around my elbow and guides me through the dining hall which smells like fresh cooked lobster. Despite her strong hold and attempts to pull me directly through the hall without food, like a misbehaved dog on a leash, I determinedly drag her through the breakfast line. Sensing we won't have time to sit, I just grab two pieces of green toast and look longingly at the thick claws of steamed lobsters.

Kiara catches my gaze, tugging at my arm gently. "Poi is about to leave- it's his turn to do rescue, and he wanted you to join."

A jolt hits my stomach, and I stare at her, "He didn't tell me I was supposed to meet him this early! Are we going to miss him?" Nerves crawl like caterpillars in my intestines.

She shrugs her cloaked shoulders, "Not sure."

We're already walking through the tables towards the other end of the hall, zig-zagging between the crowds of strange exotic Mer. I'm shamelessly cramming as much seaweed toast into my gullet as possible, not sure what I'll need to prepare myself for.

When all the toast is gone, and the roof of my mouth is scratched from eating it too quickly, my nerves take over again. Led by Kiara's quick step, I'm not sure which is more overwhelming; learning about more human destruction, going out in the open ocean, or that Poi wants me to join. I keep getting stuck on the last one. But my mind starts to get a grip again. Of course he wants me to, it's sort of my job here.

We approach the front hall- a domineering wobbling wall of air spanning two stories in a cathedral-like arch. The wide-open ocean is full of green light, and yet everything is hazy and endless. Kiara impatiently huffs, and taps her fingers together.

"Ah, they're already out there… damn." She peers through the wall of air, and waves her free arm in a half jumping jack at the small figures that are too far to see us, and not even looking in this direction.

My heart starts to dip, realizing I lost my chance at another day with Poi. But I know I'll have more lessons with him, I won't let myself be disappointed. And there's really no point in hoping anyway, is there? The ghost of his kiss returns in my palm.

"You're coming with?" I hear his gentle voice from behind me. A shiver spirals up my spine. I turn and his dark hair is dry, messy and sticking up in places. His warm eyes smile down at me. He waited.

My heart tugs at him like it always does. I really don't understand how he already has such a hold deep in my heart. "Sure. But I hope I don't hold you back too much…"

He shrugs with an amused smirk. "You will be slow. But your education is important."

He starts stripping off his cloak and for a moment I just stare at his beautiful tanned shoulders before I realize my terrible manners and look away, and do the same. I strip down to my Mer silky undergarments. Still unsure of what their Mer customs are with nudity, I take my time attempting to fold the emerald cloak- which is a good way to pass the dragging seconds because the slippery thing doesn't want to be folded into any recognizable shape. Finally I hear him splash into the ocean.

He's warped behind the wall that rolls threateningly between ocean and air, as if gravity caught a case of vertigo. I take a deep breath and leap in with abandon- the cold water hits me like a brick wall, but I sink through. The salt water burns my eyes as I keep them open wide.

With his brows raised, chest shaking, Poi's laughing at my entry. My heart flutters at him, then starts to race as I realize what's next. Air. From his lips.

He comes close, and looks down for a moment, a flicker of hurt runs across his face. He raises his fingertips, and I feel them gently trace my lips. A green glow fills the space between us, and I feel the ease of breath again. I feel warmth spreading in my veins, his magic protecting my skin and body from the frigid cold pressure of the ocean.

As he pulls away without putting his mouth to mine, my heart starts to sputter with maddening confusion and hurt. I'm sure it shows, but he's averting his eyes. Maybe he doesn't want to give me the wrong impression. Suddenly the hazy green sea gives the unnerving feeling of floating in space. I feel exposed and human. I also feel like crying. How dare I let myself believe. My eyes burn again.

Then he grabs my waist and pulls me into the empty ocean. As his pace increases, it's really hard to keep my torso up against the drag, and he slips his hands up beneath my armpits. Totally unromantic. But it's easier to hold my head up. He swims above me, torso just inches from my bare skin, as water pulls fast around us. We suddenly jolt as if in turbulence, and the water isn't pushing against me from the front, it's carrying us forward so fast I can't guess at the pace. There are about five more Mer around us coasting in the current, their strong tails flipping and torsos undulating like Olympic swimmers doing a marathon. I'm watching the fire-red tail of a woman with curling blonde hair pulling loose in the currents. My inner five-year old is jumping up and down screaming "real mermaid!!" I am totally awed at the long tendrils of her beta fish tail speeding in the current. Sensing my gaze, she glances across at me, and I am met with Eldridge's sandy brown eyes. I stare ahead quickly, feeling rude. But I'm struck. Just days ago she was barely able to walk with grief. I guess this is better than sitting at home surrounded by objects that only remind you of the one you lost. But I'm sure it's not easy for her to be here.

I look around at the crowd more closely, and realize Laude is far ahead of us, her blonde bob only a prick of reflecting light. I also recognize the green braids of Juniper, and the sandy-blonde octopus tribe guy- Kiara's crush. His thick arms are tight by his sides as he propels himself forward. His tail is so dark green it's nearly black. When he gazes back at me, I realize how incredibly aware they all are. Suddenly feeling even more rude for staring, I quietly look out at the open ocean for a long time.

I can't get over how empty it is. The ocean floor raises into view- we're flying above mountains and deserts. The watery sun follows us as we pass acres and acres. My heart is aching with the beauty, and it's refreshing that it's not for Poi. A school of swordfish comes up on us like a herd of buffalo, I jerk in surprise, just barely remembering not to gasp in salt water. Their stabbing Pinocchio noses thread between us with terrifying speed.

We slow, and the water pressure increases at our backs. I sigh internally, extremely aware of the new aches in my neck from the strength it takes to look up. We coast in the current, until Poi pulls us against and through the wall. Suddenly, the water is eerily still, sluggish.

A darker haze filters the light before us. As we proceed, I see shadow specters hanging in the open-mouthed green murk. We ascend, and small particles float around us like dust motes. In front of us, a bright green plastic lighter slowly drops. A red and white straw floats aimlessly. Fragments of clear plastic haunt the still water like ghosts. Darkness shrouds the waters in a false cloud, as a small continent of human waste spans the surface for farther than I can see.

I learned about this- the plastic breaks into small pieces that leech toxic chemicals. I start to worry about Poi's gills. He pulls me far into the mess, and the lifeless particles swirl around us. It's sickening. I don't want this trash to touch me. I don't want to be around all this plastic melting in the sun and leeching out toxins. But the Mer swim bravely forth. To quell my anxiety, I focus on the superficial breaths cycling through my compressed lungs.

His grip tightens on me, and then I hear a single, nasal moan through the water. Poi accelerates. At the surface above, juxtaposed between the floating waste and sky, flicks the unmistakable, finger-like tail fin of a harbor seal.

Poi releases me, and his long-fingered hand is already stroking the silver speckled side of the seal. It's nasal cry tears at my heart. It half-heartedly thrashes, as if somehow restricted. We crest the trash, and break the surface with plastic clinging around like an overfilled bathtub of toys. The seal's cries become more desperate- it's moan raspy like a neglected child. A mess of clear nylon fishing line has wedged itself into the seal's red flesh, creating a deep ugly wound. The clear nylon is knotted into a heavy mess of thick green fishing net- a snowballing of more debris- and it's a wonder that she hasn't drowned yet. Her black eyes are glazed with pain and thick with goo.

Poi winces and gently coos to her as he reaches into her inches-deep collar wound with a pair of scissors. She yells gutturally, twisting and flailing her tail, but not trying to get free. I hear the snip of the filament, but it does not come free. He places the scissors between his teeth and squints at the wound as he eases his fingers deep into the gash. The seal screams again, but her exhaustion keeps her from thrashing. Such empathetic pain is written across Poi's face that I'm suddenly struck with unbidden, overwhelming love for him. It nearly swells out of my chest and there's no controlling it. I am both horrified and mollified, because my subconscious has won out, and is screaming at me that I already knew I loved him. My heart strikes a fast tempo and my head swims with the full recognition of what had been growing, secretly, in my soul.

I force myself to watch his fingers as they extract the blood encrusted wire, gently peeling it from around her neck. His hand disappears as he places the scissors back in his pouch. He sighs, "She'll be okay."

He murmurs in Mer to her. With incredible tenderness, he places his hand above her gashes. She whimpers softly. Whispering, his hands emit a neon green light, absorbing into the three-inch deep wound around her neck. Like lightning, it grounds to the glossy flesh and snaps in a way that sounds painful. With astonishment, I watch as the wound becomes gauzy and stringy as flesh attaches to itself, healing before my eyes. I blink up at him in shock, almost more surprised at this magic than the existence of the Mer. After several minutes, the wound is merely a pale pink scar dividing her beautiful silver coat.

He's still watching her, and pats her back gently, his voice soft. "Go on."

She looks at him, and barks weakly. She doesn't go.

"Maybe she's tired, maybe she can't swim away." I suggest. Feeling my own aching neck from just the swim over.

His glance holds intensity, "You're probably right. Alright, let's rest with her. Then we can help her home."

We don't talk. I take in the scene. It doesn't look like the ocean anymore. It's a gray sludge of melting toxins. There is a tire near my elbow, a broken plastic fork in front of me, floating colorful caps, a laundry detergent container, a sun-bleached razor, a doll without arms, and countless plastic bottles. My head spins as I recognize all this stuff as the innocuous convenience of my human life. I thought I was all aware and cared, but I've used all this stuff, and some of it could easily be mine… my throat tightens. Looking around the expanse of endless human convenience, floating in its own disturbing immortality, the guilt is nauseating.

My eyes catch on Poi. His dark gaze is unreadable. This is his world that I've helped to destroy. My heart twists, and I feel like sinking. Of course he doesn't want to kiss me. But, regretfully, this won't make the love go out of my heart.

His form is strong and muscular as he silently treads the water, holding the seal with one forearm. His dark eyes are serious as he stares back at me, quiet and unnervingly still. His drenched, tousled hair is littered with a confetti of plastic and styrofoam. The warped bottles, a white coffee-lid, and nameless deformities of plastic crap nudge at his perfect rippling torso. He does look like a Greek God. Surrounded by a wasteland of trash.

A hurricane of emotion swells in me, threatening to rip the marrow from my bones and reroute the rivers of my blood. And despite all my energetic fury, I have no idea what to do.

The ocean is gray, blending to a gray sky without a horizon to separate worlds. I sit alone on the cold rocks looking out, gathering two layers of cloaks around me, which barely hold out the chill of the salty wind. I'm haunted by what I saw. I just needed to get away from it, to get the space to think.

And I knew I loved him, on some level, but recognizing it so fully, so quickly, is really scary. It makes me feel entirely powerless. Maybe part of me thought that if I could just push it away, the hurt of knowing he'd never want me back would never crawl in. I sigh. But now that I have, accepted it, I love him… It's all the more reason to help him. And I will find a way to help him.

I look out at the gently rolling expanse, deceiving in its perfect platinum reflection of the sky. I could be back in Maine, seeing the same view. I have seen the ocean from so many vantage points, and yet it hides so much. The edges of the world, where the ocean breathes against the earth, impresses us with the flash of sunsets, reflections of sky, and play of colors dancing before our eyes.

But it's only a light show. It's only a fraction of the truth. The light show is not the ocean. The ocean is battered, starving, and poisoned. It puts on a pretty smile, but it's struggling to breathe. And it's nothing to do with natural patterns. It's humans.

My lungs are leaden. My chest is stiff, ribcage constricting. It all seems so impossible from here. I see why Poi wouldn't want to tell humans about the existence of the Mer. Humans don't have a good track record- the only impacts they have on the ocean and all their creatures are negative. I could see that from Poi's perspective, there's no reason to think that humans would want to clean up the oceans. They, we, operate by toxic convenience, not earth-saving stewardship.

At the same time, there's no way human patterns will stop until we suffocate ourselves with all assortments of trash, and starve on delusions. Unless, we recognize, and decide to live in harmony with nature's limits and patterns.

I squeeze my fingers nervously, staring at the haze of gray where the horizon should be. Would humans stop trashing the oceans if they knew about the existence of Merikoi? Would they really change their behavior if they knew they were suffocating all the life out of seventy percent of the earth? Humans are wading thigh-deep in trash on earth too. Despite attempts to hide and contain, humans refuse to face their societal habit of plastic defecation. I think back to the environmentally friendly fractions of society, and their weak voice compared to the sheer force of the masses in their compulsive compliance to materialism, consumerism, and convenience. With the memory of today vivid in my mind's eye, I know that if we let industry continue to steer our will, we will suffocate in our own crap.

How will we change our ways in time?

I watch the white cut-out of a gull, like a marionette in flight. But beneath her white feathers, her muscles fire quickly, pushing her forward. She directs her energy, she chooses her path.

This reality doesn't feel fated. This feels like a crazed dystopia crash landing. Somehow, despite its disastrous state, this world doesn't feel any less magical than the first day I was here. In fact, the worlds have simply merged. The human world and Mer world are the same. And it's all magical. And I do believe if humans could see this magic, know they were part of it all… felt the connection in their hearts… then maybe they would appreciate this world enough to be responsible for it. To care that their own actions always harm or help the Earth.

That's what it comes down to- can humans take responsibility for themselves? And someone needs to ask the question. And that requires the Merikoi revealing themselves.

I let out a gust of air. The Merikoi need to act fast. Poi needs to reveal the Merikoi ASAP. And somehow, I have to convince him of that.

# CHAPTER 16

STELLA

My intestines are cringing. Technically, I'm about to advise Poseidon on how to do his job... I remind myself I am down here as his human... counsel. It's my place to give him advice on humans.

Poi is doing all he can to hide the existence of Merikoi, and I'm simply going to ask him to reconsider. For the sake of both Mer and Humans. He himself admitted that this hiding game can only go on for so long.

Speaking of hiding, I can't see him. I am supposed to meet him here for another "lesson," but either I'm late, or he's already in the waterlogged room. The wall of air is easy to see through, and the room before me is a cavernous extension of the mountainside- with colorful vegetation embedded in uneven terrain. Fish flick quickly into the hall, travel in broad winding circles, and leave in dynamic formations. Several Mer are perched along rocks in the room; an idyllic scene that could be out of a children's movie. Eyes closed and very still, their gills flutter along their ribs with each slow breath. The long tendrils of their fins sway gently in the current with the corals. I wonder if this is how Merikoi sleep.

"Cultivation." He says, causing me to jump in surprise, splashing my hand through the icy barrier, and pulling a spill of chilly water over myself. He chuckles. "Sorry to surprise you."

All the plastic bits are out of his hair, and he looks right again. More than right, downright godly. But that's not for me to judge. I'm human. I'm the enemy. There's no space for my oozing heartbeats. Anyone would fall for him. It doesn't give them a right to him. My love is meaningless. I harden my heart, but my stomach twists again with the thought of giving him counsel. I remind myself again that's why I'm in this fortress in the first place.

"They're cultivating." He clarifies, gesturing with a tanned arm towards the sleeping Mer. I look at a woman with jet black hair and mahogany skin, just as a school of fish circle her like a flock of birds. She doesn't seem to notice. She stays perfectly still. They spiral away, pursuing the corals with their tiny gummy mouths.

"Is that Mer for sleeping?"

"Humans call it meditation."

My eyes widen as I realize all the seemingly sleeping Mer are perfectly alert. I think of our last trip out in the sea, their eerie sense of my gaze, and wonder if they know they're being watched now. I wonder… "Why do you do it?"

"Our abilities to direct energy and Shift reflect our commitment to Cultivation."

He says it evenly, like it's a very straight-forward concept, but my mind is bending around the concept, struggling to consume it. He's saying…meditation is how the Merikoi has the ability to Shift into any creature, and use magic? My thoughts leap to his extra abilities. "So… since you can Shift into any creature, and have lots of abilities, so you must be doing this all the time."

He shrugs modestly. "I have a daily practice."

"So, are you all like monks?" I think again of my conversation with Laude about reincarnation. She scoffed at the comparison to human spirituality. "Why does it work? Why weren't the monks turning into fish?"

He smirks. "Monks have accomplished plenty that you would consider magic." He gazes out at the sitting Mer. "We cultivate spirit, which is fourth-dimensional and belongs to the Abyss. It is this Spirit that is our core existence. This is what many humans seem to have forgotten. We, all beings on earth, belong to more than this three-dimensional world. Honoring this inner connection allows our spirit to choose its three-dimensional, physical, form. The spirit has the power to change the three-dimensional reality, through the mind."

A flame burns hot deep in my chest. Goosebumps ghost cold up my spine. I don't fully understand the concept, but something about it... feels right. "So, if I meditated- or Cultivated- I would be able to change form?"

His mouth pulls to one side, "It would take a human a very long time to reach this level of energetic awareness. It helps that we live for centuries, and remember our past lives."

I purse my lips, feeling a bit like a kid that was just told they couldn't join a cool, exclusive club. I touch my fingers against the cold, jelly-like wall of water, watching it ripple, and wondering how so much magic can be around me, and yet so inaccessible.

He touches my shoulder, sending serious voltage into my skin. "I didn't mean to insult you." He says gently. "It's just, you're not Mer, so I didn't want to get your hopes up." He removes his hand from my shoulder, and velvety static snaps across my skin.

I sigh. More than just the magic is inaccessible. I decide I may as well speak my mind. "Hey Poi—"

He gazes down at me with dark amber eyes framed with black lashes. "Yes?"

"I know we're here for a lesson—but I actually have something to mention..."

"Sure, you don't have to ask..." He turns to me with muscular arms crossed, brow smooth. His gaze is expectant.

My gut slithers uneasily. He's so damn intimidating. I know he doesn't mean to be, but still. He is. I start, "Well, you brought me here, a human," I realize I'm nervously miming the words to him, and smirking at myself, drop my arms and breathe. "You brought me here to help the Mer the best I could, to give you my opinion from the view of an average human, right?" I can't say things straight when I get nervous. I know it sounds like I'm beating around the bush, but I hope he's following.

"Sure…"

"Well, as a human, as… your Human Counsel," I quip, "I would advise…"

He's staring at me with those dark kaleidoscope eyes with such intensity that it's very hard to remember my thoughts. I look away from him a little, and start again. He might not want to hear this, but he needs to hear it. I clear my throat. "Humans need to take responsibility for their catastrophic dissonance with nature…" I glance up at him, quickly gauging from his subtle nod that he is listening. Suddenly throwing caution to the wind, I decide to just be myself. Opinionated. Fuck it.

I level my gaze with his, feeling fire in my chest. His expression shifts infinitesimally towards hesitant. I continue, my pitch strained and high, "Humans know they're killing the earth, and most of them don't care. The mess will keep piling up. The overfishing will continue until there are no more fish, and nothing more to eat but sand. At this rate, they're not going to change. Certainly not in time for the Mer to keep living." Let him hate me for saying it, let him hate me for being human, but his is what he needs to hear. "Unless you shake them out of it. Your best chance is to stop hiding, shock them with the reality of how magical this world still is, how they are a part of it all, and inspire them to be responsible for their own behaviors." The more I talk, the more his expression flickers like candlelight- from open-mouthed shock, to rapid-blinking disbelief, to a mortified glare. Unstymied, I continue, "I know you hate it, but the longer you wait, your chances of survival shrink. Everyone's chances shrink. You have to reveal the existence of the Merikoi in order to save yourselves, and everyone. Humans need this too."

His silent glower is withering. I don't remember him being quite this tall, or this big. I have never seen him look downright dangerous, until now.

I cross my arms. "You wanted my opinion." This is who I am. If he can't take it, I shouldn't have a crush on him anyway.

He's shaking his head with an expression of disbelief. "I don't mean offense, but I really don't think you understand enough on this matter to advise me to that degree."

"The matter of humans? I think I do." I put my hands on my hips, matching his dangerous glower with my own.

His eyebrows lift. "Fine, you know about humans." His voice is tight. "But you know very little of living here. The risks of exposure are so great I won't even consider it."

"The risks of secrecy are worse." I can't believe he's so blind with fear.

He laughs once, humorlessly. "You know nothing of it! If humans knew of our existence, they'd eviscerate us! They would pull us out of the sea, decimate the Ridge, keep us in experimental labs like every other breathing thing on this e—"

"I know plenty—" I cut in, "Humans won't change their behaviors unless someone shows them their own ugly truth. You can do that by revealing the Merikoi and how you're being crowded out by their waste, and it's only a matter of time until they get suffocated too. If you could just inspire them with your guardianship, with your magic—"

I take a breath to continue, but he is bursting to interrupt me. "We will never reveal our magic to Humans." He's barely containing his volume. I've pissed him off. Crossed a line. But that's okay. Maybe I need to shake him up first. Before he changes things in a real way.

"You revealed it to me…" I look at him questioningly.

"That's different…" He grumbles testily.

"Why?" I cut quickly.

"You're—different…" His tone is moody, and he doesn't finish.

I'm quiet. I'm waiting for another hint at why I was picked to be here.

His eyes flicker with something I can't place before he looks away with a violent expulsion of air.

"How?" I press.

He shakes his head. "That's aside from the point. It's obscene to suggest revealing our magic to humans—"

All the pressures I've seen him under suddenly are bursting to get out of me, and I just can't let him stay blind with fear. Because conveniently, his fear of humans is holding at bay another fear which is far more daunting. "It's insane to let humans continue to tear up, trash, poison, and suck the life out of the oceans. If you don't Reveal, the Mer will die at the hand of humans. The impact is too much to contain, you can't handle it anymore—"

He stumbles back with one foot, like forcibly hit.

My heart pulls, as if physically attached to him. Gritting my teeth for the kill, I continue, "There is a breaking point, and you're past it. This isn't a waiting game. You need to ask them to step up and take responsibility. They're the only ones that can fix this."

All the sinews in his body stiffen. He doesn't speak another word to me. And it looks like he never will again. Expression hard, he turns around, and swiftly walks down the roughly carved passage, leaving me in a state of shaky-legged, popcorn heartbeat, shock.

My breathing eventually slows and I can move again. The flames in torchlights around me burn simply, upwards, and predictable in a way I wish I could harness. I try breathing more, and I realize the hallways are still filled with the glorious scent of steamed lobster.

This normal, appeasable, craving soothes me, and I realize I can walk again. Loosening my rigor mortis joints, I find my way towards the gold-gilt doorframe of the dining hall, dim with the dying light of pre-dusk.

Without really letting any thoughts in, I go through the dining line, and pick up a piping hot two-pound lobster. I splay it on a large carved clamshell plate, squeezing its claw and delighting to find that it is soft-shell, the tastiest type. Lobsters just make me feel like home. A little guiltily, I realize I have barely thought about home at all.

Assessing the milling dinner crowds but not really wanting to have a conversation, I work my way over to the corner of the room, where an empty table leans up against the tortoise-shell adorned wall. Home feels like here, already. Despite it being so foreign, something deep inside me tells me I belong here. If Poi will let me stay…

I allow my brain to thaw, and process our argument. Well, that's certainly not how I pictured it going. I definitely got the point across, but I didn't predict how insulting I would be... I'm a little embarrassed I couldn't frame my thoughts with better words. But it really doesn't matter if he's mad at me. He doesn't have to like me. I just hope I can convince him before he kicks me out or something.

I crack open the largest, bumpy red claw. Peeling back the soft shell, extracting the meat, I pop it into my mouth. It's sweet and tender and the texture is like al dente pasta. At least one thing is right in the world.

My mouth is happy as I stare off at dust motes catching in the gray light filtering through the skylight above. I can't help but notice how full space is, after spending so much time swimming through water. I continue the lobster revere, ignoring everything else.

Sadly, lobster doesn't last forever. And as I sit, digesting, my heart feels restless, as if I have done something admonishable. But I refuse to apologize. I was right. He's just letting fear keep him distracted from a greater fear. I won't let him blindly pick destruction. I'm going to formulate a plan for Poi. He might be resistant, but I have to try.

Hades slips into the pale driftwood bench across from me. His smooth dark skin contrasts against the table like stars and night. His lips part into a crooked smile, and his eyes twinkle. "You're plotting."

I knit my brow in shock. How am I so transparent here? Are Mer just better at reading expressions? Or more forthcoming about what they notice, and I've always been this expressive, and just never knew? Either way, I am profoundly perplexed. "How could you tell?"

He shrugs, pulls back the tail of his lobster until its back snaps, swiftly shoves his finger down the tail, and the fleshy white meat slips out. He takes a bite as if it's just chicken, and stares at me.

I look expectantly at his striking seafoam eyes. He nonchalantly waves a lobstery hand in my direction, talking while chewing the last of the lobster tail, "You were really spaced out, and that's always a dangerous thing."

I squint at him with confusion. "Wait, me in particular, or spacing out in general?"

"No." He snaps off a many jointed front claw, snapping off the smaller bits and eating the white flesh before reaching the three-inch pincer. He pops white meat into his mouth. "It's dangerous when you space out."

I laugh bemusedly, "How would you know?"

He raises an eyebrow, and slows as he devours the tender pink claw meat. "Observation."

I nod. "Creepy. Do that less."

He smirks. And it is compelling. He angles his chin towards me, voice low, "So what's that mind working on. Let me in on a secret."

I twist my mouth, thinking. The dozens of hall tables are nearly empty, but it's not like I'm trying to keep quiet about my ideas. I clear my throat, "Well, I was just trying to convince Poi, to reveal the existence of the Mer to humans—"

Loud barks of his laughter interrupt me. They rocket around the room like missiles, and the handful of people who remain glance over curiously. Smack! His palm hits the table, and I jolt. His laugh is caught in his throat and his eyes are watering. His laugh has turned so silent as he convulses that I'm worried he might actually be choking.

"Are you going to make it?"

He breathes in with some effort, and weakly squeaks, "Unbelievable…"

"Okay, I know it sounds like an insane idea, but actually, humans are the only ones that can actually fix this. Poi is doing great things- saving sea creatures and all, but really you guys aren't in a position to keep up with the torrent of human impact…"

His smile is incredulous, eyes wickedly bright, "And you told him this?"

"Yes…" I'm suddenly wondering what Hades knows that I don't.

His smile widens. "I wish I could have seen that. What did he say?"

I think back, "Well… he didn't say much. It was more he was so insulted he walked off…"

Hades claps his long-fingered hands together childishly. "Perfect!!"

I narrow my eyes. "Not perfect. I'm trying to convince him here. Any tips?"

He looks off past my shoulder for a moment. "I'd guess start by realizing he won't budge."

I sigh exasperatedly, "But he has to. He has to change his mind! The longer he waits, the more mess builds up, and the harder it will be to fix anything. Mer can't fix this. Humans have the technology and ability to make this mess, and they're the only ones with the ability to fix it."

He shrugs his broad shoulders, grins wide, and his pale eyes twinkle, "You can certainly try."

"I am going to convince him. He'll have to give up at some point." I cross my arms over the smooth bone-dry table.

Hades' smile just looks more and more insane.

"I'm going to make a plan, something to suggest to Poi." I look at his slightly deranged and gleeful expression, and throwing caution to the wind, decide to let him in. "Want to help me?"

"Absolutely." His expression disturbingly fanatic.

I try to twist my expression into a smile. Maybe he's not in it for the right reasons, but any help is good help, right?

# CHAPTER 17

STELLA

I've decided I need a more concrete plan before I approach Poi again. Less insulting and more helpful. He's already freaked, so I simply have to coax him towards reason. Hades knows him well, and knows this world, so he'll be helpful even if he doesn't believe it will work. I'm meeting Hades in a room I've never been in or even seen before. He said I'll know it by piles and piles of stored furniture from shipwrecks.

The end of the hallway is swallowed in darkness, and it's unnerving to walk towards. Wet damp clings to me as I walk, and my feet slip uncertainly across the wet rock. The hall is lined with doors of unique motifs: woven rope art hangs around oaken doors- as if wind chimes and spider webs had a shell-art child, others are decorated with eclectic found art made from human litter, but surrounding most doors are patterns carved into the rock with varying degrees of skill.

Knowing that behind most of these closed doors are private living spaces, it feels a bit like walking down an insanely long hotel hallway- if hotels were freezing cold, the walls slick with slowly dripping sea water, and were sparsely lit with magically flickering mounted torches that light as you approach and dim as you pass. Actually, it feels nothing like a hotel.

I'm on the sixth floor, South Side, and I have to go until I get to the end of the hallway, with a closed door, that won't be locked, and continue through. The iron-framed oak door grates with a loud whine as I slowly push it out. A forceful draft of icy, damp air whisks around my robes and goosebumps threaten to pop out of my skin. The long hallway is filled with darkness. I stiffen. I hold the door open from the lit hallway, hesitantly staring out at the dripping stalactites which threateningly bite towards their matching stalagmites in an unnerving sneer. It feels like an alien wilderness. Pressing my lips together, I allow the hallway door to close behind me. The only source of light crawls across my feet from the cracked door to my right.

I hear Hades' voice yell, "C'mon in!"

The room is less damp, but remains freezing cold. It's expansive, maybe as large as the dining hall. Nearly the entire space is shoved tight with old furniture. Some of the pieces are visibly damaged, but possibly repairable. There are off-kilter and broken chandeliers, hangings and flags which dangle from the ceiling, including a few authentic-looking, tattered pirate flags.

A thick woven blanket comes flying at my face. I catch it just before it smacks me. "Ah- thanks!" The air is a white cloud with my breath.

Hades is already sitting on an old leather armchair. "Welcome to the warehouse." His long arms fling out dramatically, matching his flourishing tone.

I raise an eyebrow. "That doesn't sound very Mer."

He shrugs, "That's what you call it right? It's a storing spot? This is where we keep all the shipwrecked furniture that no one's using. Pretty great secret meeting place, right?"

I inwardly cringe at the word secret. I'm not trying to keep anything secret from Poi. I'm just trying to come up with a more concrete plan he can get on board with. However, it seems like Hades is relishing in the idea of hiding something from Poi. I wonder how much Hades actually cares about asking human societies to take responsibility for their mess.

I fall into the cushy leather chair across from his. The dormant chill of the leather seeps through my silken robes and dress. I pull the thick blanket around my back, and curl it forward and around my sides to keep out the cold. I feel his gaze on me, and I look up at him. The God of the Underworld has his feet propped up on an old treasure chest between us, and is tightly cocooned in a knit blanket with a bemused expression on his face. I suppress a smirk.

He jerks his jaw at me, "What's funny?"

I shrug, "Nothing…"

He narrows his eyes.

I quickly focus on the matter at hand, "So… do you really care about asking humans to be accountable for their mess?"

He sighs dramatically, "Not particularly…"

I cock my head, "Then why are you helping me?"

He gazes at me for a moment before answering, "You're good company."

I look down and knit my brow. I don't want to give him the wrong idea here. This is purely about planning a Reveal. I swipe away his lingering words with my own, "Thanks. So why don't you think humans will care?"

He's silent a beat. "They don't seem to mind swimming in their own filth on land, so why would they care about the sea?"

I bite my lip, it's a good point. But I'm not ready to give in to apathetic logic. The situation is far too dire for that. I appraise him with a raised eyebrow, wondering if I can convince him to wholeheartedly help me with this, or if his help will be like squeezing lemon juice from a beetroot. He's currently nestling the blanket around his neck with his chin.

Inwardly steeling myself, I get to it. "Product-pushing, industry-run human governments aren't going to suddenly pick perspective in exchange for cash. And certainly not in time for the Mer, or any life in the sea, to survive. So really, the Mer speaking up about this catastrophe is our last chance to wake up the human masses so they hold their governments accountable before their- our-" I amend guiltily, "-habits wipe out life on earth."

He smiles languidly at me, big arms crossed beneath his blanket and wiggling deeper into the chair. "Well you have given this some thought. I'm impressed… but it won't work. With humans, it's always a losing battle."

Beetroot. I sigh out a ghostly fog. "But you'll still help me?"

His lips twist to one side, eyebrows peaking with a trace of theatrical pity. "As long as you know you'll fail. Sure. I don't want all your hopes and dreams to get crushed."

I shake my head, agitation like rug-burn heating my skin. "I don't need you to believe. I just need you to answer some questions."

"I can do that…" His voice is low and suggestive in a way that really confounds me.

"To be clear- I'm not doing this to piss off Poi. I want to help him." I curl my cold bare feet under the blanket, shivering.

He shrugs, deep voice gruff, "Either way, it'll be entertaining. I'm all in."

I roll my eyes. "I don't know if you're going to be helpful at all with that attitude."

"Me either." His smile is mischievous.

I sigh. My white breath swims out in front of me. Of course I would pick to ally with the wild card…

I straighten, "Alright. So, the purpose of this meeting, is to determine the most beneficial way to Reveal the existence of Mer to Humans."

He fixes me with amused eyes. They're a unique hue of mint green. I brush off his entrancing stare and focus on the real matter at hand, continuing: "The purpose of the Reveal is to get humans to take responsibility for the mess they create. So, what's the best angle for that?"

He raises his eyebrows. "You think that makes a difference?"

I already feel like throwing things at him. "Of course it does!"

The rest of the conversation, Hades is similarly unhelpful, but I feel like I've learned enough about the Mer to make it worth the battle.

We've met in the warehouse twice now, and I find myself walking more quickly to get there this third time. It's refreshing to be around someone who's not spooked by my mind. Although he's less interested in the actual point of our meetings, and more interested in just talking about random stuff, he has still helped me get closer to a plan, and I'm hoping to solidify it today.

I open the door, already talking. "Okay, so, I've thought about it, and I think we should Reveal first to environmental action groups. I'm thinking a short documentary. The top groups I have in mind are Sea Shepard, Oceana, Parley, Ric O'…" my voice trails off uncertainly.

Hades isn't in the room. Confounded, I look around at the dusty hall filled with forgotten furniture. "Hades?" His name is swallowed by the dark shadows between the lifeless inanimate objects. "Hades?" I try louder.

No response.

The door creaks open again, and talking as I look around, I say "Hey Ha—" A stone drops into my stomach.

Poi is filling the doorframe, the picture of fury. I kind of feel like I'm suddenly in a horror flick. The doorframe is a victim to his gripping fist, and his dark eyes are on fire. His tenor is scalding, "What the hell are you doing here with Hades?"

I bite my lip, and suddenly wish I could slip into one of the thousands of hiding spots around me.

He waits. His broad shoulders rise and fall with each breath, as if he just ran here.

I twist the blanket around my fingertips. I remember this was never supposed to be a secret. Although it suddenly really feels like it was, in this unsuccessful hiding spot.

I find my voice, and feign the calm I don't feel. "I was just coming up with a plan for the Reveal… to tell you about- ahh… to suggest." I amend quickly, my heart a deaf bat fluttering around my ribcage.

His dark eyes flash, and he removes his hand from the doorway, and pulls it through his messed black hair as he walks forward. He appraises me, the ceiling, me again. "Stella- I appreciate that you're trying to help. But please stop." His eyes are surprisingly soft.

It makes me feel like a flame in breeze, or maybe melting candle wax. I grit my teeth, and cross my arms. This isn't about if he likes me, it's not about pissing him off or not, it's about helping to save him and literally everything else. "You haven't even heard my plan."

He breathes in slowly, staring down at me. His poetic features are unnecessarily dramatized in the near darkness. His carved lips mold into a hard, curved line. He speaks quietly, stiffly. "Okay. What is it."

Heart batting violently, I breathe. This is more important than me and my confused senses. "Your best bet is to start by Revealing to environmental groups who can produce a documentary, then release it in potentially supportive countries, all at once, so the truth can't be suppressed. Then you'll have a global platform to speak to humans, and you can challenge them to clean up their act."

His dark pupils constrict in horror. He looks like I just told him an unstoppable plague is obliterating lives on its way to us.

But facing his fear is unavoidable. In fact, entirely necessary. I impulsively rest a hand on his arm, which sizzles with static. I pull back, zapped. "And, if you Reveal, then you won't be taken off-guard by human discovery, and you'd be more in-control."

Turning away, he seems to swear in Merglossa. "I can't believe this." He begins to pace, and looks off into the sea of dusty artifacts. "And Hades was helping you with this?"

"I feel like you're not hearing me…" My chest is tight with frustration. It feels insanely important that he hear me. I don't understand why he can't seem to hear logic.

He glances at me, and laughs incredulously. "Oh, I am. It's just unbelievable."

He doesn't seem to like my opinions, much less an opinionated me. I want to squish the burning feelings I have for him. But I can't. He's walking closer, and my pulse becomes increasingly frantic.

"Did Hades… convince you of any of this?" His brows are raised, hopeful.

I'm insulted. "Of course not." I cross my arms, chuckling darkly. "You think he cares?"

He glares through black lashes. "Hmm."

I realize this is the haphazard Reveal presentation, right now. I redirect the conversation. "So… you'll consider it?"

His eyes widen as he shakes his head. "No… No. I definitely won't."

It seems cruel to ask him what his brilliant plan is. He's operating out of fear. And I really don't want to make him feel worse. He's acting like he has everything figured out, but clearly… it's not a real long-term plan. He's just surviving in the short-term.

He narrows his eyes at mine, searching. He's so close I could reach out and touch the dark stubble along his jaw, or his white t-shirt. I can practically taste his pheromones. It makes me feel woozy. His voice is low, "You're judging me. But you don't know."

I feel wide-eyed and transparent beneath his stare, but I still know I'm right.

"I have lived along-side humans for millennia. I know how they operate-ownership and war. If we Reveal, they won't even hear our message. They will only see that human-like creatures are living in their oceans. Greed will fuel all their actions."

A sensation of a blunt knife stabs just below my sternum. Some sort of sticky sadness bleeds into my stomach. In this moment, I fully realize he would never be interested in a greedy human. I am evil by association. I don't think I operate out of greed, but maybe compared to a Mer, I do… the thought is chilling. My heart beats drag their feet.

He brazenly continues, arms crossed before him, and it looks completely imperative to him that I understand, "If they believe the ocean is a livable space by any means, they will want it for their own. They would want to own us and our secrets. It would mean the end of the Mer. We have to influence without identity."

Chest heavy, I look up into his heart-breakingly handsome face, and my heart limps. His dark amber eyes are accentuated by his onyx-black lashes, off-kilter shock of hair, and the unshaved stubble accentuating his jaw. Does he talk this close to everyone? It's very distracting. Something about his argument isn't right, and I can't figure it out just now. Wanting to clear my head, I back up just a half-step.

He glances down at my body as I do, noticing my bid for space.

A part of me wishes I hadn't created distance at all. But I'm an evil human, what does he care? And, he clearly hates my ideas, so in the crazy world that my being human doesn't matter to him, he still wouldn't be down for my mind... And I'm not looking for a love where I can't be all of myself.

I force my mind to stay on-topic, "What if you don't have the time to wait and see? Have you heard global warming projections?"

He sighs, and backs up as well. He rests a palm against the dusty desk behind him. "Of course."

"Well, maybe you need more drastic action than human grassroots movements." It's a not-so subtle jab, and I'm starting to wish I had more time to rehearse this.

He squeezes the desk and his knuckles protrude against his skin. "Stella, I'm doing what I can. If you have any suggestions that don't include a Reveal, I'm open."

I purse my lips and shake my head silently. "Maybe we're not all quite as evil as you think." My eyes warm with salty tears.

His face fills with concern, his voice gentler, "I didn't mean you."

I shrug, wiping the wetness away quickly. "It's okay." He stares as I take a breath and compose myself, "You're right. Lots of humans are greedy and materialistic. They end up trashing the earth in their twisted, transactional search to get connected with it…" I trail off, not sure if I'm making sense anymore. "Ultimately, we all operate out of a want for that sense of connection, just like you. We aren't that different." Suddenly can't bear to look at him any longer. I stare at the oriental carpet beneath my feet. My heart is twisting and thumping like an overloaded washing machine.

I hear him push off the desk, and walk towards me, close again. My heart pulls into my throat without my permission. I was not supposed to let myself get upset over this inevitable wall between us- my being human. He won't see past it. I thought I had braced myself for this. But as usual, my mind underestimates my heart.

His cool fingertips tug loosely at mine, and shock spiders up my arms. Like an injured bird, my heart flutters frantically, surprised at his proximity. I look up. His waiting eyes hold mine seriously. I wish he wouldn't talk so close. I want him so bad that it literally hurts.

His lips gently frame the words, "You are so far from evil, Stella." He pauses, and so does my heart. "I'm generalizing, and that's not fair."

I look at the worn carpet again, feeling like I am too close to the sun, and I am burning. Not in a sexy way, but in third-degree way. His fingers are still somehow intertwined in mine, as if he has forgotten them. But I can't hope. "Far from evil" is eons from what I want to hear...

His voice is a whisper, "You are..."

He trails off for so long that it's like my nerves are stretching on a medieval torture rack. I keep filling in the blank: materialistic, human, opinionated, strong-willed, stubborn, dangerous. That's the one. I'm dangerous. I'm dangerous to the status-quo here.

I can't stand the dragging silence anymore. I look up as I say the word. "Dangerous."

His brow knits, "That's not... what I was going to say..."

"But it's true."

He bites his lip, staring back at me, his rutilated eyes brewing mysteriously. "Yes... it is true... your opinions are dangerous..." He glances to the side for a moment. "I would ask that you don't spread them around."

I press my lips together in frustration. His fingers are locked with mine. Why is he still so close to me? My mind flicks to the idea that maybe he's trying to contain me on some level. I won't have it. I decide to bring us back to the point.

I look back into his deep eyes and try not to stagger off the edge. I know he's the God of the Sea, Poseidon incarnate, but he needs to hear me. I don't want him dying, the whole ocean falling apart, because he was too paralyzed to make the right decision. The Reveal has to happen. It comes out as a breathy whisper, "Danger is inescapable now."

I slip my hands from his, which tugs at me like a sweater unravelling. Holding my breath, I walk out. In the hallway, the icy chill tackles me. It worms its way down my trachea and into my chest. I can't help but wonder at what he was going to say.

# CHAPTER 18

STELLA

I haven't given up on planning the Reveal. I've doubled down. Focusing on this allows my mind to not circuitously obsess over what Poi's real fill-in-the-blank answer would have been. It allows me to not think about how much I want him. It allows me not to think about how Poi is yet another guy who would label me as "too opinionated." And especially, I am not thinking about how yet another man I have fallen for doesn't appreciate my mind. And I seriously want someone who doesn't feel like they have to "put up" with me. I want someone who wants all of me. And that isn't Poi.

I've found a black ball-point pen, and I am trying not to dig it too deeply into the blank, yellowed pages of the leather journal I found in the cottage. Sliced eel left untouched on the plate before me, I scratch the ink into potential Reveal statements:

"We reveal our existence out of pure necessity. We prefer to live in secrecy, but our hand has been forced. We can no longer stand by and watch our food supplies diminish with improper fishery management. Human waste infiltrates every iota of ocean space, catches in our gills and poisons our food. We ask you to no longer consider yourself as separate from this earth, but rather entities within an inescapable web of existence, influencing all life."

I place the pen between my lips, thinking. It's a little too finger-pointy. Even though it's exactly their fault… people are touchy. They won't want to be told that so directly. They need something… more empowering, more positive… I try again.

"We were once the same race. We live in guardianship of the sea, you were once the guardians of the land…

Brainstorming, my eyes travel out to the space before me- filled with yellow morning light, making the expansive hall feel even larger. It makes me feel lighter, like things could be easier today.

I imagine the Reveal as a video that becomes viral… footage of the plastic gyres, of sea creatures mutilated by mindless plastic waste. With a tweak of my innards, I imagine Poi, in his midnight blue robes, speaking out from a screen, and inspiring people to care again… If anyone could make the quarrelsome nations of the world hush their childish prattle and just listen to the dire state of our existence, it would be Poi.

I watch the Mer crowd around a table three away from my own, arms outstretched as they compare scars and gashes. The Mer can be violent, too, I note. But, these are marks of hunting for survival, or protecting the world, rather than trying to conquer it. They each have elegant black tattoos, signifying the Dolphin tribe. Despite their variety of skin tones, they all have electric cyan eyes and platinum hair tied high in dreaded braids.

Dressed in black robes, Poi stalks past me at a distance like some lithe mountain lion, keeping an eye on a rabbit. In a useless Pavlovian response, my heart beats. Drawing no nearer, he glances at my journal and pen, and raises an eyebrow. He lowers himself onto a bench between an olive-toned woman with hooded eyes, and a caramel-toned guy with an upturned chin, both with the signifying piercing pale blue eyes of the Dolphin tribe. They immediately start speaking in quick Merglossa, gesticulating with their hands as if planning a sports play.

The hide journal pulls from under my hands, and is in Hades' bony fingers.

"We Reveal our previously secret-" He intones in a tremulous, melodramatic voice, which resounds through the entire hall, causing Poi to glance over and narrow his eyes at us.

"Shhh!" I shove Hades in the rib.

He slaps down the journal with his palm and clears his throat. "Oh right, wouldn't want Poi to overhear your secret plans for the Reveal…" He sits across from me.

Poi is watching us closely, frame stiff. He's not engaging in the animate conversation around him. Although it is his kingdom after all, it still feels like he's being overly controlling. A prickle of rebellion stirs restlessly inside me.

Looking away from him, I lock my gaze on Hades. "Oh, he's heard them."

Hades' eyebrows raise to his tiny dreadlocks which hang over his forehead, adorned with a few cowry shells. His face really is something to behold. Certainly a Greek God in his own right. His pale eyes gleam, "When?"

"When you ditched out on me yesterday." I say flatly, not sure if it would be worse if Poi were to walk in on us both plotting.

His eyes are fixed on mine. "I was late- I just thought you didn't show."

"Nope. Poi found me and I had to explain the Reveal plan. Somehow, he knew you and I had been meeting there. I guess someone must have seen."

His lips spread into a devilish grin. He lowers his voice, eyes shining mischievously, "He must have been apoplectic."

I sigh, wishing I could do more than just stir up brotherly games. "I certainly didn't convince him to Reveal."

He purses his lips with impatience, "Well, we knew you wouldn't. If you want to Reveal, you'll have to do it on your own."

I drop my jaw in shock, glaring at him. "No way! I couldn't do that for all of you! It's up to you! I would never do that to Poi."

Hades shrugs, twirling his kelp pasta and pink shrimp with an antique silver fork. "Do you want to Reveal? That's probably the only way."

"I just, I couldn't do that to him…" But the idea is tempting. Maybe I just need to prove to Poi, on a small scale, that it could work.

Hades inches his finger onto the page, and wiggles the journal under my gaze.

I roll my eyes and look up at his. "Poi would never forgive me."

His eyes lock with mine. "Why does that matter?"

Something about his look makes my stomach flip. My face feels hot, and I'm acutely aware of how Hades is just inches away from me.

Suddenly I hear footsteps behind me, and the hide journal is snatched out from my fingers again.

I'm starting to recognize Poi's Merglossa curses.

I turn, and watch his eyes tearing across the page, rereading lines in disbelief. He slowly hands it back to me, and my lips part with shock. I really expected him to tear it up. Poi's amber eyes flick between Hades and I, expression unreadable.

Keeping his distance, he lifts his jaw and addresses me with a formal tone. "Stella…" His voice is strained, as if his normal casual manner is difficult to maintain. "I'm going on a trip tomorrow. Would you like to join?"

Immediately I panic. Sure, a "trip." More like he's going to drop me off at shore and be done with me and my dangerous ideas. My heart ricochets against my ribs. I'm not ready to leave. I love it here.

My voice is faint, "Not… really?"

Infinitesimally, Poi's eyes narrow as his dark brow knits.

Hades laughs gaily, and stretches a long arm over the table to pat my shoulder rather roughly. "Ohh… turned down by the human. Ouch."

Poi's lips harden. He really looks like Poseidon, standing there, his poetic features all grave and serious. Like he's sick of looking after a dangerous, independent-minded human. If he's planning to get rid of me, maybe I can pull off a small-scale Reveal before he extracts me from the magic.

Despite it being exceedingly clear that he could never want me, my heart tugs madly at my insides, making a bid to get to him. I can't follow it. Probably wouldn't even have the time.

I smile uncertainly, which probably looks more like a grimace. "Thanks though."

"Hmm…" He looks down at us again, his own expression crossing over towards something severe and dangerous. It makes me feel twitchy. It makes me feel like I have very little time here. Poi's alarming gaze studies me for so long I think he might consider just grabbing me now and forcing me back to dry land. Eventually, he blinks, as if breaking a spell. He starts to back away slowly, "I'll see you later." And it sounds like a threat.

He turns, black cloak billowing, and I breathe.

The electricity seems to drain out of my veins. I hold myself up my elbows, and run a hand through my loose blonde hair, sighing. I really, really don't want to be forced into leaving here. The Ridge is the only place in the whole world that strangely feels like home. I can't go.

"That was interesting." Hades voice rumbles.

I groan. "Do you think he's going to kick me out of here?"

His deep laugh fills the hall, and it relaxes me. "Probably not." He accentuates all the consonants, and it sounds definitive, but it doesn't make me forget Poi's threatening tone.

I drag my hand through my hair again, nervous. "Well, I'm pretty convinced that he is."

He assesses me through his piercing pale eyes. "Aha."

My mind is spinning scenarios, wildly imagining scenes where I convince Poi to let me stay despite my "dangerous" opinions… but even my mind can't bend reality that far. All the scenarios end with me on land, severed from the Mer, knowing about so much magic in the world and being even further removed from it. The idea of knowing Poi is in the world, and entirely inaccessible, with leagues and leagues of ocean between us, is enough to make me crack. Having a breakdown seems inevitable. Head hanging and hair surrounding my face, I feel my eyes starting to well up.

"So… what are we doing tomorrow?" Hades voice languidly cuts through my nightmare reverie.

I pull back my hair, startled. I quickly brush away the wetness around my eyes. "What?"

"What are we doing, tomorrow?" His tone is drawn out, slow, like a gameshow host.

I let out a puff of air, confused. Tomorrow? Will I even be here tomorrow? And then I realize how strange his question is. "Since when do we hang out?"

He shrugs his broad shoulders. "Last few days, I guess?"

I sigh shakily, feeling like a vulnerable seven-year old. I think I'll need to ask him for help. I just don't know what else to do. I'm afraid to pull myself together and ask later, because there might not be a later… "Do you think…" My voice pitches up, and cracks, "if Poi wanted to kick me out… you could somehow… I don't know… help me stay?"

Hades' face reflects my pain. It makes a part of me soften. As if instinctively, he walks around and sits beside me. He pulls a warm arm around my back, swiftly presses his lips into my hair, and I didn't realize how close I was to totally falling apart. His voice is gravelly, "Absolutely."

# CHAPTER 19

STELLA

Avoiding the dining hall and any chance of seeing Poi, I brought seaweed toast to the little rocky island. The heavy wool bedspread from the cottage is spun around me like a cocoon. The chilly air rushes in and fills my lungs. The sun is high above, and the day is brisk and clear. It feels like a cold early summer day on Spear Island, and the thought is not comforting. I don't know what I'll do with myself if I have to go back.

Hades would help me stay, somehow. Although I don't like to think about the logistical arrangement, which might include some seriously creepy neighbors. It's not the same as the ridge. It's not the Mer. It's not... Poi. Thinking of him is like taking off a blindfold and seeing sunlight so bright it hurts my corneas. He's just too much to think about.

"Stella." His voice makes my back stiffen. I hadn't heard Poi approach.

I turn and look towards him, squinting in the bright sun. His face is unreadable, and crushingly gorgeous. "Yes?" I say uncertainly, my gut clenching.

"I'd like you to accompany me on a trip today." His words crash around me like high tide. This is it. He's kicking me out.

"You're… sure?" I can barely breathe the words. I was holding out some wild hope that he might let me stay.

"Yes." He squints and looks me over quickly, "I'd like to leave… soon, so, could you be ready to go… now?"

I glance down at the seaweed toast, suddenly not hungry at all, stomach clenching in heavy fear. "Okay."

He nods once, and I follow him out of the bright sunlight, leaving the blanket exposed to the elements. It's not like I will need it again.

"We'll be going with a troupe— the Dolphins." His tone is very business-like, all hints of possible friendliness, or once-imagined intimacy, gone. Cutting the ties. Ready to cast me and my dangerous ideas away.

Scrambling for a grip against his quick pace, I say, "Can I quickly say a goodbye to Hades first?"

He glances down at me with hostility, "We're in a hurry."

Damn. Not good. I step quickly, trying to keep up with his long strides. I realize, if Poseidon wants me gone, there's really very little I can do. Maybe from land I can figure out some Reveal. It will be hard, not being here, but I'm not going to let distance stop me from helping.

We reach the Dolphin crowd at the front hall. They're not in hunting gear, only loose cloaks, waiting to shift. At least it will be cool to swim with dolphins. A proper send-off.

Silver bodies surround us in the crystal waters. They slip against each other, weaving invisible patterns into the sea. Their clicks and calls resound around us. Secure for now, Poi grasps around my underarms, his fingertips crossing my chest. Despite his end goal, my heart squeezes desperately at his touch. Placidly, he swims us forward.

I haven't been told where we're headed, but I'm assuming back to Spear Island. It doesn't take away from the magic of now. In fact, maybe I had gotten used to this absurdly beautiful world to some degree, because right now, everything is hyper-real.

The sea is a crystalline topaz glowing with threads of dancing light. Cold water rushes past my face, pulls along my body, and slips through my toes. Recycled air gently expands my lungs. Real dolphins join the shifted Mer, and our troupe has expanded to more than thirty. We dive into the current which glides us forward with impossible speed. We dip and curve with the force of a roller coaster. I hold my arms crossed and tight against my chest. The dolphins joyfully thread around us as if in a constant sports play.

After a few dizzying hours, we spin out of the current, and are met with fields that appear to be rusted iron ore in the pattern of upended tree roots. The water is nearly as warm as my body temperature. Immediately perplexed, I realize we're nowhere near my anticipated return spot in Maine. For miles and miles we pass the strange, interwoven brown briars. Some of it is swaying with wooly threads- molding.

The air blazes blue above the break between sea and sky. A school of iridescent fish the size of my pinkie swim at us, around us, and away. I see color in the far distance. It blooms into a forest of large plate-like growths, of bouquets of alien dandelions, blue lace, and the jelly-like fingers of tangerine anemone hiding little nemo clownfish. Fish are swarming the tiny city, and the strangest whispered cacophony of purrs, grunts and groans meets my ears. A lightning-bolt painted fish as thin as a playing card turns its beaked head our way, clicking in warning.

Just as suddenly as the world came into view, we pass, and the flowers turn to stone, the fish disappear, the fleshy white brain-like corals rot into spider webs, and the squishy anemones harden to bone. The dead expanse continues as if in a dark fairy tale with an evil queen whose spell has caused all the land to wither and die. For many more miles, the twisted corroded skeletons lead us toward the shore.

We break the surface, and the air is thick with heat. The coastline is a cluster of towering hotels. Honking cars, city white noise, and barreling groans of speeding eighteen wheelers accost my ears. Gray and white buildings crowd the coastline, interspersed with palms making their bid for wilderness among the black tar parking lots.

Poi swims along-side me, taking in the view. The dolphins blow out air around us, and pop their heads out, assessing the urban coastline.

Totally thrown, I ask, "Um, where the hell are we?"

"Miami."

Salt water splashes into my mouth. "What!!" I look around in horror. Considering his knowledge of the human world, this drop off is a little shocking. I doubt he has a plane ticket for me. I place a hand on his slippery shoulder. "Wait. I thought you were making me go back home. This is a bit too far for me to get back okay…"

Drenched, he looks back at me in alarm. Gathering wave sets heave us upwards as we tread. His voice is rough, "No, I'm not bringing you back— unless you want to go…" He's suddenly right in front of me. The crystalline water laps around his muscled chest and broad shoulders. In the magnified sunshine, his dark amber gaze burns gold. He's looking at me with a fervent searching expression, and I can't get used to being around him.

"I don't." I say quickly, stunned and not quite being able to process relief.

He squints against the sunshine. "Why would you think that?"

Dolphins swarm around us like a pack of excited dogs, trying to get us to move along. One slips against my arm, spurting air and salty sea.

"Because I keep talking about revealing your existence to humans. And you think it's dangerous."

He grimaces. A wave lifts us three feet higher, and drops us again. "I don't want you to leave." His voice is even, serious, but there's something beyond the words that pulls at my heart.

My throat constricts as a wave gently casts us skywards.

He holds my gaze silently, then says, "I just wanted to show you something… on land."

I find my voice, "Thanks for not… asking me to leave."

His penetrating gaze melts me. "I'll never ask for that."

It's strange walking along a sandy beach with Poi, surrounded by seven dolphin-tatted Mer. They all stroll with preternatural muscular swagger. They're eyes are so electric blue it's noticeably unhuman. They're all hovering around Poi's height of just over six feet, including the women. Their ethereal beauty really, really doesn't fit in here. The beach is ridden with tanned bikini clad plastic bodies on colorful towels and plastic recliners.

The sand clings like stubborn glitter to our salty bodies. Having thrown our t-shirts and jean shorts on in the surf, our clothes are as wet as the ocean. The cling of the damp clothes compresses with the sensation of sticky heat in a nearly intolerable fashion. The sun is blindingly strong, and my eyes are wishing for the muted light of the Mer world.

We stop before the black asphalt, and Poi hands me a pair of flip-flops. It's even more strange, sitting in a cab with him. The cab feels small, with his long legs cramped behind the passenger seat, and his head bent downwards to the window. He looks out, watching the neon signs pass. I try not to notice how his wet t-shirt molds to his muscular torso.

The streets cut a grid into the coastline. Cement towers blockade the road, allowing only glimpses of the sea which shines a jewel-like turquoise green. The cab enters the highway, and Poi continues his silent stare out the window. It makes sense. He isn't often on land, so when he is, it must be exceedingly strange to look around at human civilization.

"Every time I visit," his voice is low, as if he doesn't want the driver to hear it above the sounds of the engine, "…it seems like human population has boomed again."

"It doesn't stop, I guess…" I say quietly, remembering all the sacrifices the Mer have made to stay alive within the limits of dwindling food sources. Again, I feel hit with the guilt of being human, and add yet another reason he wouldn't want to be with me to my mental list. I stare at him staring out the window. His cut jaw leaning out, tousled hair still damp and resting on his ears. He looks so innocent for being the one trying to take on all the problems of the world.

"They do have a lot of momentum…" He muses quietly.

"Back there- those brownish brambles- were they all dead corals?"

He glances at me from the corner of his eye, "Yes."

He resumes his stare at the arching concrete twist of highways, sighing. "Stella, as you pointed out to me recently, the ocean is warming. In an attempt to cool the atmosphere, the ocean absorbs most of the heat, and that current is dragged around the sea causing coral reefs to bleach, rot, and die. This is only a small fraction of what has happened in the last thirty years."

He's silent then, and I am bursting to fire at him: "All the more reason to Reveal…"

But I don't. Because silent waves of relief are still rolling over me. I'll be able to return to the Ridge, his home. I don't have to say goodbye to him. He said he'd never ask me to leave. My heart hitches with a crazy hope.

We stop on a road lined with bushels of green palms. An old, Easter blue and pink building boasts in large cartoony lettering: "Aquarium of Miami," accompanied by a fat dolphin.

I cringe. Okay, he's trying to make a point here. Humans force other creatures to be their captives, and if they knew of the Mer, they could do this to them as well… I don't understand why this needs to be demonstrated.

Poi pays the driver, and we stand below the tubby dolphin sign. Despite the humidity, my hair is no longer soaking wet, and our clothes are merely damp. Waiting for the other Mer to get out of their taxis and join us, with just the two of us standing below the aquarium sign, it almost feels like we're about to go on a date. The thought sends manic butterflies ricocheting around my stomach.

The many-toned, tall blonde Mer lope towards us. In this setting, their dolphin tattoos stand out so clearly, they seem to be in a cult devoted to the cetacean. Hopefully the aquarium workers will not think they're some sort of PETA action group, and refuse our admission.

"This is where they filmed Dolphin Days!" A matronly woman with a festive visor exclaims to her teenagers.

"What's Dolphin Days?" A freckly preteen boy asks lazily with his eyes glued to his phone screen.

Loud peppy music blares through the speakers while we wait in the hallway to enter the show. I notice a tall pale Mer beside me unsheathe a knife and surreptitiously slip it along the wall, cutting a handful of black wires. Just as stealthily, she slips the knife back in the inseam of her loose torn up jean shorts. My hands sweat with fear. The Mer are up to something, and I really don't want to get arrested… I glance at Poi, but he seems not to have noticed. I remember my spark plug experiment, and fully realize I never would have had the guts to actually go through with it.

The ticket attendant opens the door, and the crowd filters into a glass-domed building. There is a teasing view of the turquoise sea. Below the amphitheater seating, is a concrete pool lined with tall plexiglass barriers. Within it, floats a black and white orca; massive and beautiful. Noticing the tall, striking Mer, the orca immediately swims towards the crowd, placing her head up against the glass, calling like a transistor radio. She barely has room to move, much less do tricks in a few moments. Four dolphins pop their heads out of the water, and immediately seem to stand on the water, backing up and showing off.

"Oh!" A tiny blonde trainer squeals enthusiastically into a megaphone from a small platform in the whale tub. "They're very social today! Excited to see the kids!"

The trainers start rhythmically clapping with such pep and enthusiasm it must be insulting to the cramped and constricted cetaceans. I shuffle down the aisle to sit between Poi and a tea-skinned lithe Mer, a few rows from the pool. Already disturbed by the arena, a damp cold sags between my ribs.

The team of four trainers start handing out fish to the dolphins that flip or spin for them. A tiny blonde ponytailed trainer is staring at the orca, dangling a large fish and clapping violently against her leg. Ignoring her, the orca is staring up at the Mer surrounding me, her mouth open wide and calling in a mournsome high pitch squeak which abruptly shifts to a buzzy nasal intonation. Her riveted focus makes me think she's is communicating something vital. And then I realize the Mer might actually understand her.

Poi's muted voice reaches my ears despite the blaring music and clapping. "Lolita, they call her, was taken from her wild pod as a child."

Calls between a cat screeching and a door opening peel past her pink tongue, lined by her perfect set of rounded yellow teeth.

Poi continues, "Her mother is now 85, and the rest of their pod is in the Pacific, protected by an environmental law. She, however, doesn't count."

Manically smiling, the trainer is increasingly aggressive with her calls to Lolita, but the orca continues her buzzing calls towards us, pacing back and forth. I feel the tension of the Mer around me thick like a thunderstorm. None of the Mer are moving, much less breathing.

A ballistic whistle ricochets around the glass room, and the Orca immediately spins to face the ponytailed trainer, swimming over in an impulsive Pavlovian response. Anger boils in my chest as I think how that swift reaction must have been broken into her. The trainer holds Lolita's big head between her hands, as if mutely reprimanding her, before relinquishing a fish.

"Years ago, there was another Orca in this show, but he repeatedly bashed his head against the wall. He died of an aneurism," Poi's voice is suspiciously level.

I feel smaller in my seat, reading between the lines of his words. Humans don't care. Human amusement is a higher priority than the wellbeing of other sentient beings. Maybe Mer would never be stuck in a glitzy show like this, but he's showing me that humans will always put their interests first, at the expense of all other life.

The show begins, but every time Lolita gets near us, she slows and calls. The tiny blonde trainer has the whale swim on her side, fin in the air, and stands firmly on her silky skin. A plastic ecstatic smile smeared to her face, the trainer waves like a queen at the cheering children and clapping parents. When Lolita reaches us, she rolls. There is an expression of muted horror which interrupts the camera-ready smile before the trainer is dunked into the pool. She doesn't scream, but quickly front crawls to the platform. The Orca swims around behind her, and the massive form of the whale slides onto the platform, as if doing a trick. Her black and white beak sends the peppy trainer into an ungraceful jumping jack and into the slopping water again.

The glistening, truck-sized orca balances her weight like a seal, fins splay out, as she assesses the crowd of screaming parents, laughing children, and quiet Mer. Her dorsal fin sways to the side, as if deflated. The trainers back away from her fearfully: two are isolated on the edge of the platform, looking towards the water as if considering an escape. It's clear that Lolita just performed a show faux pas, and the peppy drones seem to be recognizing their misguided attempts to rein in a top predator.

Poi's soft voice carries to my ears again. "The emotional brain of an Orca is far more advanced than any human brain. They have complex neuron structures that humans haven't even developed." His eyes are steely, and suddenly, I notice maybe a hint of determination.

A spittle of water lands on my arms. Watching the chittering dolphins and magisterial whale, I see the dysfunctional show isn't the source. Suddenly, it's raining inside. Alarms blare mechanically, lights flash on timers. Children are wailing as their parents hurriedly grab the stuffed whales, strollers, and children's hands and file them out of the madness. In the water, the orca joins the chorus of chaos with helium squeals against the glass barricade between us.

The blonde trainer is on her feet, a frazzled look on her orange face as she stares around at the sprinklers shaking and buckling as they spray impossible amounts of water around the room. She screeches into the megaphone, "Show is cancelled! Please exit… call for refunds!"

She paces quickly to join the masses scurrying to the exits as if they've never been caught in the rain.

Edging at the end of my seat, ready to stand, I glance over at Poi, who hasn't stood. His eyes are glancing up at the sprinklers, focused. His fingers look stiff, as if pulling at some invisible force. And then I get it. Buckets of water are pouring from the ceiling, and he's pulling it out.

"You…" I say under my breath, while water drenches me, and the alarm lights flash, and bells continue to blare.

He does a little grin, still staring at the tarnished pipes above. All the trainers have rushed out the exits, not seeming to be bothered that a couple of soaked hipsters remain. The dolphins, however, sensing something strange, are lined up towards the nearest edge of the pool, staring at us.

"Now, Poi, they're gone." A Mer with ebony skin calls from the aisle.

He nods once, subtly. "Video is down? Doors locked?"

She nods quickly, her platinum dreads jangling around her face.

Then he sits back and looks out at the turquoise seas, and I follow his gaze. The horizon looks taller. I let out a tiny scream as I realize a tsunami-like wall of water is headed our way. I hear it crashing through the glass on all sides as Poi grabs my head and presses his lips against mine. Out of passion or fear, I grab him back. My heart throbs painfully as I grasp his shoulder and around his tight torso. My stomach swoops as his lips part and he sends air into my lungs, his body blocking mine from the initial force of the wave as a thousand tons press us into the back of my seat. It's crazy, but I revel in the closeness. Just as quickly, Poi's hand pulls me through the wave.

I open my eyes, praying we avoid the shards of glass as we swim in the massive swell. A cacophony of ecstatic dolphin cries fill my ears. The other Mer have shifted to dolphins, leading out the others towards the sea. The orca swims directly towards us, rather than towards freedom. Poi swims us forward quickly. Turning, she trails us past the broken barrier and over the outside encampments which abut the sea.

Circling us, her sleek predator's body passes like a dark cloud, and I stop breathing. The black painted over her eye makes her look ready for battle. She passes so close I could nearly kiss her. Pausing, she gazes at us with one mahogany iris which coveys more sadness than I could ever hold. And I know, there is no way to undo the decades of torture and isolation she's already been through. My heart drops as she swims over Aquarium of Miami's walls and into wild sea.

# CHAPTER 20

STELLA

I don't even care if Poi likes my opinions now. No, I do. But that was incredible. My ridiculous crush has grown to an impossible weight. I need to cool it. I'm just totally high off that prison break. I need to remember I'm human, he's not interested, and if I don't want to be totally crushed, I need to stop....

The dining hall is dark at this late hour, lit with only a few torches. It's only our group, crowded around two pushed-together tables, shoveling down the day's leftovers. Despite the exhaustion in my saggy bones, I am so relieved to be back here.

Green seaweed toast in hand, I watch the gesticulating Dolphin clan recount the event: the mortified expressions on the trainer's faces when things went off-plan, and stories from the show dolphins. Poi can't stop grinning- his whole face is lit up.

Hades, Kiara and Laude are beside me, eagerly listening, and popping escargot into their mouths like popcorn.

"I wish I could have been there…" Laude growls, scarlet eyes roving jealously over the excited platinum blonde Mer.

Kiara bulges her eyes at Laude with incredulity, her voice squeezing with emphasis, "As a hammerhead, you would have scared the oxygen out of those circus dolphins."

Laude sighs, grabbing more escargot shells from the large clamshell at the middle of the table.

"So, did Poi prove his point to you?" Hades asks me in a low voice from my side.

I look into his curious face, and squint. "Maybe."

His smile falters, he sighs and looks away.

I stare at the crowd with their post-battle glow, and that was pretty incredible, but I have no idea how many hundreds more aquariums just like that exist. But I do know that it would be fairly suspect if worldwide, all aquariums had creatures escape due to unpredictable, entirely focused, tsunamis. How could something like that work for all of them? Will small scale guerrilla tactics actually work in every case? It seems like a whole mountain range of work.

The thing that still gets me, is that he's making this decision for everyone. What about the other Mer? They will all certainly live to see some drastic changes for the worse, and who knows if they will survive it. Don't they have any say in their destiny?

My mind clicks. A vote. We need to have a vote. Poi may never agree to this, so I will have to arrange it…

"Hey Hades…" I look up at him, and suddenly feel his burning thigh against mine. Reflexively, I pull my leg away.

"Yeah—" he says distractedly, still apparently listening to a story from the breakout.

I keep my voice low, worried Poi might overhear. "Could you… distract Poi, you know, keep him busy, from breakfast through lunch tomorrow?"

His eyes snap to mine and a sly smile returns to his face. He whispers, "You're up to something."

I raise an eyebrow, but feel a guardedness in my heart. His willingness to just be against his brother for the sake of it is starting to send off a red flag. "Can you?"

His smile is wide. "Definitely."

He hangs an arm around my shoulders, overwarm. I want to cringe out of it, but I leave it there, determined not to throw off the plan by insulting my main ally.

Poi's eyes halt on the two of us. My heart pauses. His brow furrows slightly. I stare back at him, remembering how the last time his lips were on mine- it felt like a kiss. He drags his eyes away as the retold circus tales continue.

## POI

Sleep doesn't come. Light from the nearly full moon cascades through the moving waters, and through the wide skylight above my bed. It reminds me of a night with Thalassa. We had gone to shore together, for two months, our longest time on land. The industrial revolution was in full swing, and human pollution was just beginning to exponentially increase. Europe was filled with smoke and sludge, with poor people fighting to make a living but sleeping in bunkhouses. Europeans were stealing Africans from their homes and forcing them into slavery, and committing a massive genocide of the Indigenous peoples in the Americas. Everywhere we turned, those in power were blindly pushing for an idea of progress in exchange for any standard of morals.

Home felt too close to all the pain. Thalassa and I vowed to each other- to never rule the seas with such greed. We moved all our colonies to the Ridge, and underwater mountain ranges around the world. Our first night here looked like this- magnified silver light quivering in waves across the satin bed and black slate floors. Different from the bright corals we knew and loved, we held each other close that night, unsure of what the world would bring.

My chest is a cavern that aches. I just want to hold her here with me. It's been a while, and I need her so much closer. I don't know how to do this. My attempts have been disastrous… she thought I was going to excommunicate her… torment wraps around me.

I look up at the slippery moon, a pale ball stretching in the waters- what can I do? My chest constricts, and slow tears leak from the corners of my eyes.

My thoughts begin to repeat, and I realize I cannot think clearly about this. I need advice. Levi. I groan. I don't want to talk about my love life. But I also don't want to obsess. I need some perspective. A second opinion could be useful.

His room is a mile North, two stories down, and the walk through the empty halls calms my mind. I nearly convince myself I don't need to talk. But I do.

I knock, and lean my palm against the door frame. I wait, and knock again. He grumbles a garbled question at the door, and I announce myself. Several moments later, Levi pulls open the door, wearing a sage cloak and squinting at me with puffy mid-sleep eyes.

"Where's the fire?" He croaks with a voice out of tune.

I suppress a grin and shake my head. "I apologize for the hour… I was hoping you could give me some advice."

He rolls his eyes and steps back, sweeping me into the room, "Finally!"

I grin. Maybe he's right— maybe I've waited too long.

The door shuts, and we walk towards his lounge which faces the dark sea gleaming with the occasional bioluminescent fish. The lounge seats are tightly woven seaweed, filled with sea sponges, and mold wonderfully as I sit to face the panoramic view.

"Gin?" He shakes a crystal decanter with a raised brow.

I hesitate. He pours two. He sits on the next seat, facing the sea, and passes me the drink. I twirl it, sigh, and throw it back. We sit quietly for a moment.

"What do you want to know?" His voice is scratchy sandpaper.

I sigh with more force than I realized I needed to release. "I don't know... I just ... I don't know."

I can hear invisible currents flowing past the window.

"She likes you." He states quietly.

"Does she? It's hard to tell." I grimace. It's hard to read this human version of her. I think she sees me as weak for not wanting to Reveal.

"Yes... but you haven't exactly laid out your cards." He pauses for a moment, "You better be careful... I think Hades is competing with you."

I raise an eyebrow and look at him. His side-glance sapphire eye holds warning. His voice is gruff, "You can't tell me you haven't seen it— he's liked her since Persephone left him. But now that she doesn't remember... the future is far more open to influence."

My heavy sigh lifts my shoulders as I look out into the blackness again. I have seen it. He put an arm around her today, and the image keeps flashing into my mind. But I can't tell him not to- he knows it's wrong. And I want to win her over. I should be able to. I cringe, uneasy with the idea of having to compete for Stella's love. It was always just there between us- something we always worked on, but would never go away. I have to believe that deep down, that same love is still between us.

"So what do I do?" My voice sounds more desperate than I want it to.

"Woo her, Poseidon." He turns in his seat to face me. "You want her? You have to show her. You're the God of the Sea, and she thinks she's just an insignificant human. She's not going to make a move. You have to be the one."

I furrow my brow. I didn't see it like that. She's so beautiful- even though she doesn't know our world, I just assumed she would be confident. She doesn't think she's enough? That's so far from the woman I knew her to be. My heart sinks lower.

"You need to act. You need big gestures, you need physical contact."

I pull a hand through my hair. "Physical contact I do not need—the Prophesy...?"

"Ah. It says you can't have sex until love—it doesn't say you can't kiss the woman. How is she going to know you have feelings for her? I think you forget how she sees you. You're definitely more handsome than any human, or Mer, she's ever seen. You've gotta know that, man. She's intimidated as fuck."

I raise my eyebrows and shake my head. I don't evaluate myself by those standards. I never needed to- Thalassa and I were paired for eternity. But I can see what he means, objectively. Maybe she is intimidated.

I take a breath. "Okay. It's been so long since our first life in the world of gods, when I first courted her. Of course, I was always wooing her in every life, forever, but I can't just jump back into that… now that she's a human…I don't know how to not scare her away with it… she's a human who doesn't remember me…"

He looks at me, expression disbelieving. "You're not going to scare her away. She wants you."

I nod once, heart hurting, unsure. Pain like nausea swells up from my gut through my throat, threatening to pour out. I bite the inside of my cheek, trying to hold it in. I will not cry here. But I cannot speak.

He won't look at me, as if he knows of the secret storm in me. Eventually, he asks, "So what's your new plan, Poi?"

I'm silent, I can't speak yet.

"You always did so much for her as our Queen… just pretend she's the same, because deep down, she is."

I nod, thinking of her favorite gestures. She loved surprise Balls. She loved dancing. I wonder if she still does. One way to find out. My heart lightens. I reach out and grip Levi's hairy forearm, and squeeze it affectionately, "Thank you Levi. I think I know what to do now."

His smile stretches easy and wide, his eyebrows are high, and his expression is relieved. "No problem, Poi. I'm rooting for you."

"YES!!!" Kiara squeals as she slaps my chest. Her smile is contagious. "Of course I will. And the band preparations will be no big deal. We've been practicing— we need a Ball!! It's been too long. Poi! This is perfect! This is how you're going to get her back! She's always loved the surprise Balls you threw for her. Oh my god, YES!!!" She fist pumps the air.

I'm shocked she has this much energy at four am. I can't help laughing.

"Oh, Poi. This is perfect. Finally. I'm glad you're doing this. And the KING TIDE BALL!! Those were always the best!!"

My heart hurts a little at the words. I stopped all the Balls when Thalassa died. The idea of a big party without her hurt too much. But now I realize… I was being selfish… everyone else's lives went on. They probably would have appreciated a Ball now and then…

I gaze seriously at her effusive expression, "You're sure you have time… to make it?"

She claps her hands together, "If I start right now, I should have time for it all!"

My brows peak, feeling guilty. "You are the best. Have I mentioned that?"

"Yeahyeahyeah. I just want to have a big party!! And see you and Stella get together!! About time!" She shoves me towards her doorframe, ushering me out. "Now getout! I have to get started!" Her glowing smile makes my guilt recede. It's nice to know so many people are behind us, wanting for this to work.

STELLA

My hands are shaking as I push out the papers across the table. I have folded a paper up to say: "Voting Station." Several Mer are eyeing it cautiously. I might be pushing my luck here. I'm heavily relying on Poi's promise to not kick me out. I feel a little guilty for doing this, but the Reveal is a matter of survival.

I have spread out several sheets with the same statements. A summary of arguments for and against the Reveal. There are tiny squares of paper I have ripped, ready for votes to be written and cast into the large tortoise shell I found.

After a few moments of nervously looking around and bouncing my heels under the table, a woman walks over. She has skin as pale as a moon, hair as blue as the sky, sharp fins lining her fish-tattooed forearms, and a guarded expression. She looks at me uncertainly, picks up a pen, guards her vote with her other hand, scribbles something on the sheet, folds it, and tosses it into the tortoise shell. First vote. My heart thuds nervously.

Seconds later, a group of Mer with octopus tattoos crowd the table, speaking quickly in inscrutable Merglossa, exchanging pens and hiding scribbles, and tossing them into the shell.

As more and more Mer visit the table, I get jittery like I've had a few expresso shots. I sincerely hope this works. I hope they now can choose to Reveal themselves, and work towards a better future with humans. I've empowered them. I smile to myself.

Kiara's eyes are massive as they catch on the sign. She practically runs over. "What are you doing?" She grips the table in her hands, purple-flecked eyes roving over the summaries. "Oh my god," her voice is faint. "You can't do this... Poi will be so mad!!"

My throat is dry, but I shrug. "He said he's not going to kick me out."

She laughs frantically. "No, no, seriously!! You can't do this!! It's up to him to decide! We can't- we don't *vote*." She says the word like it's a sin.

"Sure you can. Here." I proffer a pen and a ripped piece of paper.

She looks at it open-mouthed, horrified. "No..."

"Don't write your name on it if you're worried, but you deserve to have some say in your own fate. The Humans are creating an apocalyptic end to this earth, and taking down the Mer with them. Poi is refusing to see that hiding is not the answer. Vote."

Staring at the paper and pen, she slowly takes them, and leans over the table to read the summary of arguments. Then, hesitantly, she votes.

I feel like skipping. The plan is working. I sit for hours, from early breakfast to late lunch. The pile of votes is overflowing the turtle shell. Someone came up to me and gave me a large seaweed weaved bag to put most of the votes in. Total success. Poi is nowhere to be seen, Hades is totally helping the cause.

Smiling happily, I begin to pack up, stuffing the final votes in the bag, and straightening up the papers to leave. Looking around the hall in total shock, feeling like a burglar with a penchant for good deeds, I haul out the bag of Reveal votes.

Spread out on the woven rug of the tiny cottage, I pull the first vote out of the bag. It's illegible.

The curling vertical lines scrawl Mer. I set my jaw. Damn.

Pulling out more notes, I see nearly all half of them are written in Merglossa. Sighing, I scoop them back into the rubbery knitted bag.

I could ask Laude to count up the votes, or Kiara. But I have the feeling... that they would not want to be involved in something against Poi's will. I could have Hades read them... but Poi will have to find out eventually... My head starts to pound. I can't imagine Poi would destroy the results without reading them first. At the least, he must be curious. As I'm already out the door, lugging the votes back, I decide we can discover the result together. I have a feeling he won't be too happy. But a majority vote might be enough to open his mind. Wild pride surges in me.

After asking around a little, I discover Poi and Hades are in the counsel room. I have no idea how Hades has kept him there for so long, but I'm extremely grateful for it. I push open the heavy door, and hear Hades' voice saying, "It's the virus, you can't see that? Just look closer..." A small pink octopus is suspended between Hades' dark hands like taffy with a killer grasp. Poi is bent over, holding a magnifying glass to her slippery limbs, inspecting. As the door clicks shut, Poi glances up and does a double take. Hades has the most mischievous flicker in his eyes.

The bag feels incredibly heavy over my shoulder. I heave it to the ground. Hades smiles wickedly, and Poi paces over slowly.

Before Hades can out me, I speak. "Poi. I know you don't want to Reveal your existence to the Humans." His expression is wary. I continue rather quickly, "But considering the dire straits you're in, I figured it's not only up to you. You are deciding for everyone, and I thought there should be a vote. So here are the votes."

He stops in his tracks, glaring at the bag as if it holds a wild boar. Or maybe a human. "You did this?" He whispers up at me, shocked. Then he turns to Hades, dangling his magnifying glass between his fingers, "A distraction?"

Hades is beaming madly.

Poi swears in Merglossa and runs a hand through his dark hair. He looks back towards me, arms folding. His voice flat, "What was the result?"

I squirm. "Actually... I still don't know. Half the votes were written in Merglossa... so... I was hoping you could help me count them up?"

His dark eyes bore into mine.

"Aren't you curious?" I say lightly.

He looks down at the bag, unceremoniously opens the drawstring, and pulls out a scrap of folded paper. He furrows his brow.

"What's it say?" I whisper.

He just looks up at me through his dark lashes with a stubborn look. "Let's count."

Gleeful, I sit across from him on the carpet as he goes through the tiny notes, one by one. His broad shoulders are hunched over the bag as he sits cross-legged, expression muted as his long fingers quickly sort. The pile on his left is considerably larger.

"Which one is that pile?" I point at the larger pile, curious.

He looks up at me mutely, clearly not surrendering to the entire process. I bet it's the Reveal pile. My heartbeats quicken as I try to peer at the scrawled notes, but he pulls them closer to his legs, not even looking up.

He reaches around in the bag, grabs nothing, then holds it by the end as the final note falls out. It lands on the floor, open. "Reveal."

He picks it up, glances at me, and gently places it atop the smaller pile. His eyebrow raises with an apologetic expression carved into his godly features.

"No!" I look through the pile, and see all the tiny scrawl, several in English reading "Reveal." "How could this happen?" I look up at Poi. He's saying sorry with every handsome feature. So annoying. How could this plan not have worked? "Did you cheat? Hades- check the bigger pile for Reveal votes."

Hades gets up from the couch with a dramatic groan, and squats next to the larger pile on Poi's left. He picks up a few notes, nodding, and placing them in a third pile. He sifts through all of them, relocating none in the "Reveal" pile. As the last one drops, Hades looks up at me. "Sorry babe. Looks like no luck."

I groan madly, looking up towards the hanging chandeliers, glowing contently with bright butterscotch light. How did this happen? Are all the Mer just as afraid as Poi? That must be it. They're all too scared to make the big moves they need to. Damn, I just gave Poi's argument more weight.

I look back at Poi, who's still on the carpet across from me, his dark hair a mess. He's silently surveying me with his disarmingly warm amber eyes. It gives me a vertigo heartbeat, and I'm glad I'm already sitting. My mind slows to a stop. I grapple to regain my thoughts, and appreciate that he's at least not rubbing in the vote. Yet. The votes really do all the work for him. Gawd, am I mad at myself.

I sigh, "Fine. They might agree with you, but it doesn't mean you're right."

He breaks eye contact, and gathers up the notes into the bag.

"Allow me," Hades voice drones from the couch. Poi drops them out of the bag, midair, and suddenly they all burst into dazzling violet flames, ashes falling like gentle snow to the carpet.

I purse my lips, and sigh in frustrated defeat.

# CHAPTER 21

STELLA

Without another word, and not wanting to acknowledge any sense of surrender, I walk back towards the cottage on the sea. The sun leaks tangerine into the skies, clouds alight neon coral. Glittering gold-tipped rose waves push calmly against the gray rock, hushing and popping musically. Looking out at the pristine view, I realize the Mer aren't so different from humans. They just want to enjoy the sunsets. They just want to live their lives. They don't want to take big risks when they can survive for the moment and pretend things will pan out fine.

I'm not satisfied with sitting and waiting to see, but now that the vote is out, and I have to respect the wishes of the Mer. It's not my secret to tell. Damn, I should have seen how I was setting myself up for failure.

"Stella!" I nearly jump out of my bones when Kiara's voice cuts through the sound of gentle surf. Looking around, I see her decked out in a gorgeous silk dress. Muted salmon in color, it wraps flatteringly around her generous curves, festooned with hundreds of tiny shells. She glows in the tangerine light. "Poi told me to come get you. Did anyone mention to you the King Tide Ball tonight?"

I stiffen. Now her dress makes sense. But I was not warned of a ball of any sort.

With judgmental eyes, she assesses the cloak I've been wearing for the last three days over jeans and a white t-shirt. "I'll take that as a no..." She starts towards the cottage, calling over her shoulder. "Alright, get your bum up here. I have a feeling we'll find something striking enough for a King Tide Ball."

I scramble up from the rocks, taking a last look at the burning edge of the red sun slipping into the sea. I hate giving up ground, but my hopes of a Reveal will have to be put to bed for a while. Until I can think of a better approach. I've been so goal-oriented, maybe taking my mind off the Reveal for a little while will be healthy. I can come back to it with a fresh mind later. Awkwardly, I decide to just let myself enjoy the magic of this world without worrying about its impermanence.

Skipping quickly over the uneven rocks, I enter the old stone cottage to find the wardrobe's contents all over my unmade bed. My eyes catch on an intricate blushing plum dress. I haven't seen it before, and I've looked carefully through the entire wardrobe. It's ornately sewn out of watery silk which racily cuts up between the thighs in a fin type shape, mirrored by the low V-neck with spaghetti straps. Fabric gathers at the waistline, secured by three tiny gold buttons which line each side of the bodice. It's accented on the sides with dark gossamer trails.

"What do you think?" Kiara stands next to me, buzzy with energy. "It's an edgy new Mer style."

I nervously pick up a gauzy train. "It's beautiful... but isn't it a little... overkill? I mean, I'm not Mer..."

"Who cares? You can't overdo it with a King Tide Ball." She shimmies a little, and the pointed spiral shells on the neck line and hem of her dress tinkle.

I laugh at her vogue-like expression, but I know exactly who cares that I'm not Mer. I brush it away from my mind, and focus on the gorgeous dress before me. "Alright, but who made me this dress? I'm sure I haven't seen it in the wardrobe before..."

She hums thoughtfully, "Well... actually, I made it, and snuck it into your wardrobe." Her glee is bubbly. "At Poi's request."

I gasp as adrenaline runs a lap in my veins. Why would he do that? It feels like a romantic gesture, but is he just being a good host?

I grab Kiara's hand. "This is incredible!! You could be a fashion designer for humans!"

She glares teasingly, "I prefer to design for Mer."

Suddenly, I wonder if everyone here is a little prejudiced against humans. I can't really blame them. "Well you're incredible. This meticulous craftsmanship is stunning."

She smiles proudly, "Thanks."

I bite my lip, trying to keep my voice even. "And Poi… asked for this to be made? Is that… normal?"

She raises a thin eyebrow at me. "If you're asking if he's having dresses made for every female at the Ridge, the answer is no."

Hot adrenaline claws at my guts. I push it aside. Hard. It's not real. He won't date a human. This dress is simply a symbolic gesture of peace between Mer and Human cultures, as I represent his Human Counsel.

I swallow, taking in the gorgeous dress and wishing that maybe I could pass as a Mer for tonight.

The dining tables are gone, the hall is lit entirely with aqua-teal flames in the iron torches, creating a dusky romantic ambiance. Long strands of glittering pearls hang across the empty four stories like streamers. A massive edifice of the full moon precariously looms from the fourth-floor balcony, spinning as if not fully tied down.

Steel drums plunk, ping, and patter with tropical rhythms that make standing still impossible. The dancing throng reminds me of clubbing in Boston. All the Mer I've ever seen and more are crammed into the spacious hall. They're reaching their arms up and dancing ferociously like smartphone videos don't exist. And they don't here. They're screeching and laughing as they dance in an utterly flabbergastingly uninhibited display of glee.

Walking around the elevated Mer, their giddiness is contagious. With shells wound into my high braids, and the pretty plum dress tight at my sides, I secretly feel like a Mer.

I scan for Poi, biting my lip, and despite myself, hoping I'll fool him for a moment too. Kiara and I weave our way towards the drinks.

The table is crowded with tons of Mer I've never seen before. Their tight vests and skimpy dresses expose their intricate tattoos, strange Mer features, ripped muscles. Laude beelines towards us, a tiny Thai woman on her arm. She smiles broadly, exposing her set of sharp teeth, "This is Petrika! Petrika, Stella."

Aha. This is the much spoken-of partner of Laude, and harasser of Hades. She's not how I pictured her- as a terse, fair-haired Russian woman. Instead, she smiles benevolently, her dark silky hair is loose around her shoulders, a horseshoe crab tattoo repeating itself around her arm towards her simple gray dress. "Nice to meet you," her accent is distinctly American.

I smile back, relieved she doesn't extend a hand in formalities.

Kiara grabs my shoulder. "I have to head over—" she gestures towards the densest part of the throngs. "I'm on the xylophone tonight." She smiles, and with a glamorous twist, grooves towards the set.

Petrika and Laude are chattering in Merglossa. I take the chance to look around the room for Poi again, and see him kneeling on the balcony above a colossal constructed moon, ropes in hand, and tying the celestial symbol into static submission. Yanking at the ropes to finish the knot, he leans around the banister to check his work. He glances up through the dark skylight where the real full moon looms above the surf, adding a white glow to the torch-lit hall. He strolls along the balcony, past the groups of unfamiliar Mer, and disappears again.

A complex rhythm drops in with the steel drums. The masses keel and shout. The full-bodied tones play expertly across octaves, totally irresistible. I smile, Kiara is good. I can't help twitching my hips to the beat. I consider heading to the dance floor and skipping the drink line entirely.

But the line is thinning. Turtle shells the size of car tires are filled with mysterious red and green liquids. From partying at college, I learned to avoid this gamble, and go for something more predictable. Unfortunately, I don't see a cooler of beer, or a box of wine, and I'm not surprised. A conch shell holding glowing green liquid floats near my face. Instinctively, I edge away from it.

"Here, don't wait in line." I glance over to see Hades, holding a brilliant pink conch near my shoulder. He's wearing a pale green vest which accentuates his unusual eyes. His exposed dark skin is insanely muscled, just as I suspected.

I notice he's looking at me too. I resist the impulse to fidget with the skimpy skin-tight dress, silk rising further up between my legs, dropping lower on my chest, than I would have chosen. I cross my arms to create a barrier. His eyes finally meet mine. "You look sexy in that."

I feel myself blush, and shift nervously, surprised at his bluntness.

He shifts closer, and I wish he wouldn't. "Ah relax, I tell everyone that. Poi threw a little hissy fit when I told him he looked sexy in his trousers."

I chuckle a little, "You did not."

He looks a bit guilty, and I contemplate just how good their genes are. If it works that way with gods. "Well, maybe not." He holds the extra drink between us again, grinning, "Here's to you not getting kicked out."

I breathe out with relief, grasping the spindly shell and shaking my head, "I don't know how…"

His eyebrows scrunch up his forehead, "And you pulled off the vote too… Really pushing your luck little lady."

He winks as his conch shell clinks mine, and a twinge of guilt works over me. I don't feel like celebrating anything- I've upset Poi, and there's no way to Reveal.

I survey the mysterious green liquid held in the pink lips of the conch. The shell spindles fit between my fingers as I whirl the viscus drink around, hesitant to sip, "So," I say tentatively, making conversation, as I know no one else around, "Do you have a guess as to what they put in this?"

He peers into his own conch shell, "Oh I'm sure they ferment snails guts or something."

I automatically stick out my tongue and he laughs.

Despite myself, I sniff the concoction, which smells somehow fruity. I take a small sip, and squint. "Definitely salty. Could be snail guts."

He throws his head back as he laughs, then looks at me bluntly, "Drink up."

Petrika's wide black gaze finds Hades, and she steps between us, short yet demanding. "Laude tells me you couldn't wait to see me."

I bite back a laugh at Hades' exasperated expression. He looks at me as if trapped, and I drift further away, glancing around for Poi again. Poi is leaning over the edge of the highest balcony, watching the crowd below. His muscles flex with the weight of his shoulders, and even from here, I start to feel all melty inside. As if sensing my stare, his gaze flicks to mine. He stares down at me for a disarmingly long beat.

I freeze as my heart swoops into my gut. I bite my lip. I feel exposed in this teeny dress. With a dangerous jolt of adrenaline, I wonder if part of him wanted to see me in this.

His lips part into a smile, and he leans back and starts sauntering towards the stairwell. I forget how to breathe properly. I have to look away, I can't just stare at him as he finds his way over.

"—well that's not the point, Hades." Petrika glances up at Laude with a snarky eye roll.

Laude gives her a "settle down now" stern look.

Petrika can't help herself, addressing Hades again, "The studies show... that if more young women are educated about family planning, human populations will naturally decrease. There's no need for governments to regulate the number of children..."

Hades stares down at the petite woman like he would rather pull out his short dreads than listen to another word. I snigger at his expression. His eyes flick to mine.

"Stella! Why don't you, talk to…" He attempts to spin Petrika around at me, but she smacks his hands and remains planted.

"If you could just grasp, that women need to be empowered in every situation, including not being physically shuffled around by men, your perspective would be much improved."

He bulges his eyes in frustration, and it's hilarious. Laude can't help smirking. I love Petrika.

I cast around looking for Poi, and see him walking over now. Hit with a wave of nervous nausea, I turn away, distracting myself with watching Petrika talk at Hades without really seeing her.

Body, stop. Stop reacting. I force myself to breathe normally. Remember, technically, I'm still mad at Poi. He has the fate of his people in his hands, and is being a wimp about it. It doesn't matter if he sees the votes as encouragement that he's doing the right thing. The Mer are just as freaked out as he is. Blind leading the blind, I would say. But to be honest, I'm still a little embarrassed about that vote. I mean, I really thought the Mer would know better.

His fingertips brush my arm, and I involuntarily shiver. I turn, and barely breathing, look him over. His dark visage is stunning. More of his tan, carved muscles are exposed than I'm used to, and it's painful how much I want him. He's wearing a loose black vest and silken pants adorned with black pearls. His wavy black hair has been tousled in a way that looks nearly intentional. His dark amber eyes are warmly smiling down at me.

His voice is velvet, "You look like a Mer…"

My heart frantically beats against its cage. If only. "Thanks," I squeak, feeling my whole body blush. "Um, it's really nice of you… it's a really beautiful dress, thank you."

He smirks at my stuttery awkwardness, "You don't wear dresses often, do you?"

I bite my lip. "No."

His sculpted lips turn to a dangerous smile as he raises a dark brow, his gaze flicks over me again. "We will have to change that."

I blink. I'm not really sure where he's going with this. Is he… interested or polite? When he's right in front of me like this, it's really impossible to think straight.

He turns and gestures towards the moon façade. "So, what do you think? Is it crooked?"

I glance over at the bright white moon fastened above the teeming hordes of dancers. "Um, it's a circle. It can't be crooked."

With only a twitch of a smirk, he gazes down at me with burnt gold eyes. Mind forgotten, my everything else is aching for him.

He purrs, "Shall we have a vote on it?"

My mind flickers on. I glare up at him, but can't help a teasing tone, "Nooo. You'd rig it."

He chuckles. "I am known to do so."

I bite my lip, staring into his darkly angelic face, my heart and mind warring violently.

His deep eyes stare back. He proffers his hand regally, "Do you want to dance?"

I feel my eyes bulge, and I'm not sure I'm hearing him correctly. But his serious lips turn into a grin as he waits. My kneecaps decide to stop being bone. I slip my hand into his and a pulse like a memory jolts through me. He gently guides me forward with his hand on my exposed lower back, sending tingles up my spine. My heart is in my throat, and my brain is gone. I'm not sure I could talk if I had to.

We wind around the Mer whose quick footwork and flailing arms navigate downbeats and distinctive rhythms with precision. I can't help but be impressed with the dancing. Poi turns to face me, bending over and grooving as he drags me into the center of the insanity. My body is addicted to the beats. He pulls me closer, swaying to the beat and looking down at me, smiling in a way that melts me. Gawd, he's handsome. And damn good at dancing. Grinning, he puts my hands on his broad shoulders and wraps an arm around my back as we groove to the beat. I can't help smiling back at his expression. It's just so easy, being with him.

I feel my heart relaxing, tentatively thinking maybe this could be real. He spins me unexpectedly, my wild laughter is eaten by the cacophony, and he pulls me in closer. My hands land against his hot torso, his arms wrap around me, and we've paused. His dark gaze is almost grave. My heart is thudding harder than the steel drums. His expression deepens as his eyes catch between mine fervently, as if looking for some answer in me. His fingers tighten around my back. My stomach swoops.

The beat drops, and like someone clicked "resume" on a video, the moment is gone. He tilts his head back and grooves to the beats, and his hands grip my buttoned waist. I feel his fingertips against my bare back as we find the rhythm again.

Eventually, he bends over and whispers in my ear, "Would you like a drink?" His breath on my neck makes me shiver. I'm still holding his torso close.

I don't want a drink. I want to stay here. This close to him, in a dream. But I realize that his question is probably a polite way of him saying he needs a drink, or a break, so I nod.

He gently grasps the back of my neck that's wet with sweat, but it just makes a cold chill roll down my spine. He leans in and grazes my ear, his breath is warm on my neck, "Thanks for the dance."

My heart is just under my skin. I'm a little scared of turning to face him, his lips are so close in proximity to mine. I don't move. I speak a little shakily, "You're a fun dancer."

He pulls back and just smiles at me gently, not taking the compliment, but not refusing it either. He wraps an arm around my waist and navigates us through the crowd which has somehow intensified in their dancing fervor. He pulls me towards a table with a barrel of freshwater and shells. He casually signals for me to wait with a finger, and I do. He pours water into two conch shells, and gestures towards an alcove with a private table.

I slip into the bench, wondering how we will hear each other over the wild beats and gaily screeching Mer. But then he slides into the bench next to me, and I'm certain I am visibly shaking. His body is slick with dancing, his black hair is entirely tousled, and tonight his eyes are like fireflies.

He puts his hand gently over mine, and it's just not real. It can't be.

"Stella. I have to make an announcement tonight… and you're probably not going to like it."

My eyebrows twitch together.

"The vote confused a few people. And now rumors are going around. With all these visiting Mer… I need to make an announcement before the rumors can be spread all around the seas. I can't risk a rebellion. We need to stay united." His dark amber gaze fixes on me, as if willing me to understand the importance of this. "I have to ask you to not keep this up. Please just trust that the Mer can handle themselves, and we really don't need to add to the chaos by starting any sort of rebellion. So if the thought has crossed your mind, drop it."

His sudden harshness is shattering the night. "I never even though of a rebellion. But thanks for the idea," I half-heartedly joke. Suddenly, my chest is overwhelmed with a different feeling entirely, heavy disappointment. Totally overstimulated, I realize I want to cry. For just a moment, I totally forgot how much he hates my ideas, and my vision for Mer and human survival.

He slowly shakes his head. "Seriously, don't. Please, I'm asking you to stop."

I take my other hand from my lap and rest it over my lips. I don't know what to do here. I have wanted him badly for so long, and didn't think it was possible. Now that he might want me, it comes with a weighty clause which says I can't express what my heart knows is right. Determined not to cry, I meet his gaze. "I promise to not start a rebellion." I can agree to that. That's fair. But I'm not surrendering the Reveal.

He seems to read between the lines, and purses his slightly pouty bottom lip. "Fine." He pats my hand. "Okay, I need to go make the announcement."

He glances at me again before he walks through the throngs again. A hot tear slides down my cheek, but I quickly wipe it away. A moment later, the music stops. The dancers slow like wilting flowers, and look towards the band. An eerie silence crosses the room.

"Welcome back to the Ridge. I'm glad you were all able to make it for the King Tide Ball." Poi's voice is clear across the motionless hall. I wonder if he's speaking in English for my benefit.

I get up, walking my way towards his voice.

"As you may have heard, there was a vote held to determine if we should Reveal our existence to Humans as a means to ask them to take responsibility for their negative impacts."

I edge around the room, until he comes into view. His arms are motionless by his sides, his chest slightly raised.

His voice projects clearly. "Your votes came back with a strong majority against a Reveal."

I feel incredibly small.

"Remaining hidden, and influencing without an identity, is, and continues to be, our safest, most effective, option." He scans around the room magisterially, as if hoping to instill this truth. "A Reveal is not an option for us. I ask that we all stay united in this. If anyone questions the validity of this approach, I ask that they come directly to me. We cannot afford a divided community. We cannot afford to be caught off-guard by a faction of individuals with rebellious views."

I cross my arms. He's totally downplaying the enormity of the human threats they face. Their plan sucks. I understand that he's doing what he thinks is best. But clearly he can't really open up to anyone else's ideas, otherwise he'd see his fear for what it is. I can't listen to any more of his political jargon. He'll never appreciate me for my mind. Heart dragging with defeat, and mind brutally screaming "I told you so," I walk back towards the drink table. I haphazardly attempt to fill my empty conch shell with mysterious red ooze. It splashes on my hand, and I don't care.

"Nice dancing." Hades whispers under his breath, side-eyeing me and refilling his drink with far more finesse than I had.

I stare at him flatly, not in the mood for compliments or small talk.

He turns to lean against the table, facing me, and whispering, "Good speech, huh?"

I narrow my eyes at him, still silent as Poi's voice carries across the miraculously mute hall. "Human governments would see our existence through a frame of greed and ownership. Humans would want to own us, own the Ridge..."

Rolling my eyes, brimming with frustration, and aching with disappointment, I turn and walk towards the exit.

Sipping my drink as I walk down the dark corridors, Hades hand touches my arm, and I spill again.

I spin at him, hissing, "What."

His ebony shoulders roll back as he lifts his non-drink hand in surrender. Frozen, he looks like a surprised cat.

I turn and walk away again, Poi's words echoing in my head, causing a disjointed clatter like mixed radio signals as I also remember his fingers around my waist as he drew me close. Pull me in, then lecture me, then publicly embarrass me? Not cool, Poi. This is bullshit.

I was so drawn to him being all attractive, and a god that saved baby seals, that I was blind. He's just like any other guy. They want women for how they look, how they're cute, how they fit in a convenient little box. But they don't respect them for their opinions, they don't want them for their minds either. I fiercely growl into the empty hallways, "I'm done with men!"

After proclaiming this statement, expecting to feel relieved, anger recedes to emptiness. I feel totally alone as I wind up the staircase towards the rocky outcropping on the sea.

I sit in front of the green flames, wishing for warmth and feeling hollow. Maybe everything I thought was going on with Poi was just contingent on me not having opinions. And I'm back just where I started. Stupid me. The flames crackle and dance, and I wish for that kind of freedom.

# CHAPTER 22

STELLA

Surrendering, I curl before the emerald flames of the cottage fireplace. Buried very deep inside of me, an ignored girl just wants love. I've let her come to the surface. Her wants are daunting. Is it even possible to be appreciated and loved for my mind too? I want a love where I can remain whole, but it just doesn't seem to be working. Because all I am is alone. A bubble of pain warps up through my lungs and tears up through my throat. My stomach twists painfully.

I can't bear it if Poi doesn't want me for all of me. He pushes my ideas away so hard that it hurts. He can't push away part of me without pushing away all of me.

I convulse with tears, trying to purge how much I really want him. I have to be free of him. It just hurts too much to not be loved fully.

The night drags on, and eventually I just gaze into the green flames, blankly transfixed.

The cottage door creaks open, but I have no energy for adrenaline. My heart twists with a sick hope for Poi. I pull up on my forearm, and see Hades standing in the doorframe.

"Hey." I whisper flatly, and look back at the fire. He must register my mood, because without a word, he joins me, cross-legged, before the peridot flames.

"Can I…?" He gestures to pull me into his lap.

I narrow my eyes at him suspiciously. I shake my head. Suddenly I don't want to be touched.

He shrugs his broad shoulders and gazes into the fireplace lit with his magical flames. The strands of light pop and fizz. He side-eyes me. "Do you want to talk about it?"

I shake my head stiffly. "Not really." I whisper. It's still too painful.

The fire crackles expectantly. The words grate out of me in a ragged whisper, "I just don't think Poi and I… will ever see eye-to-eye."

I glance over at him, and his eyes are tightened ever-so-slightly. He's silent for a moment. His voice is low, "I think you could, but he won't change his mind on the Reveal."

I roll my eyes. Poi made it very clear tonight. He won't consider my ideas, perspective, or respect my opinions. He doesn't even trust me. There's no way he would like all of me. I drop my head into my knees with an exasperated moan.

"You look like someone beat you up. Are you sure you don't want that hug?" His voice is teasing, and I look up beneath my messy hair. His broad torso is concave with his shoulders rolled forward, and I suddenly crave a hug.

Hesitation catches in me like sticky spider webs.

"Who are you trying to impress, tough girl?" He looks at me like I'm being ridiculous by not taking a hug in this state.

"Fine." I huff deflatedly.

His warm arms scoop under my legs and around my waist, and pull me onto his crossed legs. I keep my eyes down. I can't look at him. I'm embarrassed by my completely distraught state. But it's comforting to feel his heat around me, his bonfire smell. His arms wrap around mine, pulling me against his fiery chest. Pain swells in me again as I can't help wishing this night had gone drastically differently.

Torturing myself, I impulsively wish that it was Poi wrapping me close to him. Tears start streaming again, but I hope Hades doesn't notice.

His lips nestle into my braids, and his large hand rubs my back slowly. I feel like a small child in his arms, and it is totally comforting. "Thanks Hades," I mumble against his t-shirt, now wet with my tears.

"You got it."

Deep inside me, a dangerous rip tide pulls me towards Poi, threatening to drown me. My mysterious need for him is all-consuming, tearing me up from the inside-out. I forget my surroundings, awash with worn-out hopeful moments of Poi mixed with soul-tearing disappointment that we could never be what I want us to be. Equals.

An immeasurable amount of time later, I resurface. Realizing how disgusting I am, I mumble, "Sorry I'm getting you all wet."

Hades laughs, his voice deep, "Yes, I hate water."

I force a chuckle. It was funny. Maybe I just need a distraction. Maybe my brain has simply gotten water-logged, causing an unhealthy and unrealistic obsession over Poi. "Tell me a story." I ask Hades, feeling even more like a child, and reveling in it. He is a TON older than me, after all.

He grunts bemusedly, and squints at the fire. "Once upon a time there was a beautiful little human girl who got swept up by a big wave and brought to the Merikoi Fortress. She fell in love with the power-hungry King, and didn't notice his devilishly handsome yet modest brother who had a wicked crush on her—"

I stiffen and edge away from him, glaring, but his arms are still tight around me. Did he really just say that? Right now? Bad timing. To say the least. And no luck, 'cause my heart is already tied to a mooring for a ship that probably doesn't even exist. I evade his implications, voice tight, "That's not the sort of story I meant. I wanted a distraction, not something that made things weird."

"Stella..." His voice is chastising, then gentle. "Be real. We're good together." He rubs my back again in a way that had been comforting, but now just makes it spasm. "I'm not asking you to change a part of yourself. You don't have to be going through all of this for him. Look at you—you're tortured!!" His voice is gruff and strained at once. His brow knits together in concern, eyes searching my face as if investigating a crime scene. He raises his large palm from my back, gently tracing away half-dried tears with the backs of his long fingers. His deep voice is silky, "I would be good for you."

My heart thumps painfully, disagreeing like a juror's mallet. Hades' eyes are so forcefully fixated on me I push myself to consider his words. Logically, I see he would be good for me. Hades is supportive, sweet, funny, intelligent, and insanely sexy, but hearts don't do math.

My eyes widen in surprise as his fingertips trace to my chin and tip my face upwards to his. "Just let me try to persuade you." His upturned teal eyes are deep with a vulnerability that catches me off-guard. The beauty and symmetry in his immortal face would make a model cry. In my blip of shock at being desired by a god, he drops his head to mine. His plush lips push against mine, and my heart twists in confusion. Could this be right? Am I just being stupid about wanting Poi? Poi seems to want to do surgery on my personality- wants me without my opinions, and that's not a pattern I'm keen to repeat. Maybe I somehow look for terrible relationships. Maybe I should consider Hades. He's definitely a good kisser.

His tongue rolls persistently against mine, and I feel mechanical, wishing this could make my crazy, painful obsession go away. Wishing I could pick the logical choice for myself. It would be easier, I concede.

"This is too much—" My heart is scratching wildly to get out of his grasp. It feels so wrong- like the world has spun off its axis, and I'm nearly nauseas with strangled grief. It turns out adding more emotions in when I'm already worn-out is a recipe gone very wrong.

A flicker of pain in his expression is replaced quickly by playfulness. "That wasn't a very long trial period."

I roll my eyes, leaning back from him and standing up out of his hold. His hands grip around my legs, holding my waist to his face as he stares up at me. "You haven't even given me a chance to take your mind off him."

My heart jerks with it's insane truth, "I don't want my mind to be taken off him."

He raises an eyebrow and rolls his eyes at once. "I don't believe that after that kiss."

Looking down, locked in his stupidly handsome gaze, I sigh with frustration. "Hades, this has been really sweet of you, to come here and comfort me." I lift my hands and cradle his smooth angel's face. "You're perfect, and if I was logical, I'd pick you. But I can't. I'm sorry, I think I need to be alone right now." It's only a hint at my suddenly overwhelming need for him to get gone.

He shakes his head once, sighing with frustration, breaking our gaze to stand. He cups the backs of my arms and draws me to him close. My heart wobbles for his sincerity. He gazes down at me fiercely, "You're so stubborn. This would be easy. You don't see how much happier you would be with me. Have I ever made you cry?"

"No, but that's be—"

"Have I ever asked you to change your mind?"

"Yes."

"When?" Confusion tightens his intent gaze.

"Right now." I raise an eyebrow. I'm totally sick of this convincing.

He purses his lips and rolls his eyes. "This doesn't count."

I raise my brows impossibly high, "It totally does."

His eyes burn into mine, "I'll convince you."

I think of Poi, and healthy or not, how entirely stuck on him I am. I feel ill with it, like it's an irreversible curse. "You won't," I say miserably.

"Stella—" his voice is ragged with frustration. He draws me in nearer, radiating heat. "Give me time," his voice is pleading, leaving a trace of ill-disguised desperation which confuses me.

My eyebrows knit with sadness, I've been totally blindsided here. I'm getting a sense of the depth of Hades' inexplicable and confounding crush, and it scares me a little. How could I have never seen this before? All those times he comforted me, and I just thought he was being a friend.

It's too much. Too much after tonight's disappointment, too much after all the emotional turmoil. Exhaustion drops on me like a heavy blanket, refusing to let me calculate any more. My mind finally fixates on something instead of Poi. "Look, I need to sleep…"

He sighs quickly, "I didn't mean to lay all this out tonight—it was bad timing." I nod.

He studies my face before quickly pressing his warm lips to my forehead, and releasing me. Finally. I didn't want to be rude, but I was about to be.

His voice is gruff, "I'll see you later."

The words feel laced with too many implications, but I'm too tired to argue. "Okay, goodnight."

After the door closes, I feel frozen with shock for a long moment. When it recedes, I can finally breathe again. Hades likes me? That's the last thing I needed to add to the mix. It's not a convenient distraction, it's pressure I don't want and can't handle right now.

I have the strange sensation of my head being pulled apart like wool as I stumble towards my bed. Thank some sort of deity who's not hitting on me, sleep takes me quickly.

Sleep's strong undertow keeps me from waking. Poi and I are together, being together. My heart is in exactly the right spot as I gaze up at his warm amber eyes. He smiles at me like I mean the world to him. I'm at ease.

"Do you want to tell them, or should I?" He nods towards the videographer hiding behind his black camera apparatus, and a woman standing before him with a boxy microphone that says Channel 3 NEWS.

Confusion is a thorn which nettles me back to reality. Before I even open my eyes, disappointment swarms around me like bees. It's really inconvenient how hopefully imaginative I can be.

The gray afternoon light compliments my sudden heavy mood. Pelleting rain droplets blur the windows. The waves are crashing violently around the rocks, and I'm impressed with myself for sleeping through it.

I groan as I attempt to sit up as if I've been in a physical fight. Trying to wake myself up, I blink groggily around the room, and remember that's what Hades had said- that it looked like someone had beat me up. Nope, just me, torturing myself.

I pull my knees into my chest, and fall sideways back on the bed. I just want to go back to sleep world, where Poi loves me, where we do the Reveal, where Hades isn't making things weird. Poi loving me had felt so real. I close my eyes, desperately willing myself to return to him. But I can't get there.

Pain ratchets around my chest, and I'm not sure which will be worse- seeing him again- the real version who doesn't accept all of me, or wallowing over the loving dream version of him here. Both options suck. There has to be another option.

I push myself up and stare out the window again. Light wind rattles the glass as rain thrums against it. The ocean is a churning mob of waves which call to me. Mesmerized, I slip out of bed, change, and wrap myself in a silken cloak.

Pushing open the heavy oak door, briny ocean air sweeps into my lungs. I breathe out heavily, and suck in the clean air. Walking out along the slippery dark rocks, cold rain patters against me, waking me up and washing me clean. The wind whips gently around my neck, my bare legs and arms, as if brushing off all the sadness, all the things lost that I never really had.

Rain spits down endlessly. White haze diminishes every horizon. The ocean roils with exposed power, surging and throwing itself against immobile rocks. For all the emotion in the world, I can't change reality. Poi's not going to change, no matter how much I want him to want all of me.

The ache in me is demanding like the waves, and reality feels harsh and cold like the jagged rock beneath my bare feet. I sit. Warmth spills down my cheeks, mixing with the rain. The ocean is my companion, and I root for her as I stare out through the spittle of half-hearted precipitation. I keep wishing she could wash this little island away. But maybe she doesn't want to. Maybe the rock should be allowed to exist too. Maybe I'm just wanting Poi to change too much for me, and my heart just needs to realize we're not good for each other.

Emptiness echoes through me in a frighteningly expansive way. The panoramic eternity of wide, expansive sea seems to leer at me. What am I supposed to do with this much nothing?

## POI

The current pushes at my right and pulls around my torso like a slow breeze. My gills are tight at my ribcage, tense as they drag in fresh saltwater. I sit atop the empty mountaintop of the Ridge, gazing out at the turquoise sea. I know well that meditation is the only cure for this lovesick obsessing. I wait for my mind to go blank- to only feel the immediate present…

But why did she leave last night? Was she really so angry with my public address and denouncement of the vote, that she couldn't bear to see me afterwards? It must be, because before that, it seemed like we were finally connecting… holding her close, I could almost forget that she has forgotten.

Thanks to Levi's advice, I was letting down my guard about the physical connection… realizing that some contact might be a way to start all intimacy. And it was working- Stella was relaxing around me. Until I had to make the announcement.

I don't know how to do this. I knew it would be hard... but I never expected her to pick up our arguments right where we left off. I thought falling in love was supposed to be fun... not torture...

A burnt orange dot catches my eye at the foot of the mountain, and I track it. Ascending, a brain-like sack of a head is followed, flanked and propelled by many-twisting legs. The tentacles collapse and squeeze through the ocean- opening and fisting like a many-fingered hand. Undulating and elegant, the Shifted form of my brother reaches me. He circles around my body several times, his many-suctioned tendrils furling and unfurling, twirling the sea, turning a deep amethyst with excitement.

It lightens my heart. Hades has been in pain since Persephone left him four hundred years ago. For centuries, he has denied his grief- transmuting it into unhealthy habits and projecting it into dead-end relationships.

He floats up to my tail, and lazily hangs before me like a giant spider. The fleshy sack of his brain, and one-third of his neurons, sags behind his pale green eyes. His fleshy purple brows are lifted, as if finding something humorous.

I chuckle, and speaking in Merglossa, exclaim, "Out with it, Brother! What has returned your spirits to you?"

His twisting form abstracts into an amethyst cloud- floating outwards. His haze radiates to the edges of his Mer form. For an instant, Hades is a ghost filling in with flesh. He's not smiling as I expected, but his teal eyes are glowing to match the sea around him. For some reason, he's suppressing it, but haven't seen him this happy for half a millennium.

His torso stays level with mine as his opalescent green tail circles in the open water, gleaming in the bright morning sea.

I smile broadly at him, happy for whatever caused this shift, curiosity wearing away at my patience. "What has happened?"

I'm guessing it's a woman, because that's generally what raises his spirits. He doesn't know how to be alone with himself. He doesn't enjoy his own company, or pour himself into projects, but rather is dangerously dependent on the female species to improve his mood. An issue from which I have spent centuries attempting to divert him.

But there couldn't have been the time for someone new. We knew everyone at the ball last night… I guess I could have missed a latecomer.

The gills knitted into his ribcage flutter as he exhales deeply, squinting at me and flexing his jaw. "There's something I have to tell you."

I tilt my head, frowning slightly. Something in his tone sounds off.

"I have to admit I've had feelings for Thalassa for a long time—since before Persephone left me…"

My gut drops as my chest constricts, my words are an ambush, "Why are you telling me this?"

He looks away, and back to me again, pale eyes squinting as if he could shield himself from seeing me. "I think she might pick me, Poi."

I lean back from him in horror, rage tearing a gaping hole in my chest. "How could you even say that? You know she's been my soul mate for eternity—you know if she picks you she'll never return to her whole self—and somehow the whole ocean's fate depends on her! Why the hell would you say that?"

His brow knits, eyes sad, "She's changed, Poi. I don't think she's going to change back. I can love her as she is now—but if she never changes back, she will never be enough for you."

Rage rears in me as the truth grips me hard, "She will always be enough for me."

"But what if she doesn't pick you, Poi? What if she picks me?"

"She won't."

He's silent for a minute, then softly speaks, "She has. She doesn't fully know it yet, but she has."

I don't know whether to throttle him or laugh. "There's no way, Hades. I'm sorry… you need to move on. We have to talk about this… it's high time you move past what Persephone did to you…"

"No. Poi. I'm serious. We were together..."

The words hang for a moment, before my heart gets slowly impaled by a twisted spear tip. My heart beat stutters, I clear my throat, "No... you couldn't..."

"We did. Last night. I thought you should know."

My gills are frozen. I can't breathe.

"Poi, she's not coming back. I'm good for this version of her."

"YOU AREN'T." I shudder, "HOW COULD YOU DO THIS TO US?"

"I love her too, Poi. You know that."

I sink into black seas impervious to daylight, barely breathing. Thoughts tear through my mind like hooks destroying flesh. My gut is hard rocks tumbling painfully against organs- nauseous with pain.

Darkness reflects darkness. Compression is the only comfort. I could lose myself here. Black eternity swallows the present whole. Time is gone. Everything is gone. Heavy ache pulls me deeper. Gravity is the only thing that makes any sense now.

I thought she loved me, my heart whispers circuitously.

Darkness is quiet. I remember she is not the same now. She doesn't remember our eternity together, what we had, what we might lose—

My heart beats once, echoing slow in blackness.

Maybe she never knew I loved her.

Maybe she will never know.

The infinity of darkness swallows me, again and again, compressing me harder like the never-ending belly of a colossal beast.

Is she coming back?

Pressure crowds in thickly, threatening to suffocate me.

My heart blips an S.O.S.- she has to.

Thoughts flood into my mind again. Why did I let my fears keep me from getting close to her...? Before... How could I have let this happen... Why did I never kiss her?

My blood circuits once with every question, as if looking for an answer, and finding nothing worthy. My heart aches with the compounding pressure, blackness pressing like walls against my every fiber.

The image of her floats to my mind, serene as she stands before me- her wide emerald eyes clear, the sweetness in her face etched into my heart, into every sinew of my soul. I could never let her go- never. Jolting madly, my heart wakes me up like hot water cracking ice. My quickening my pulse reverberates against the constricting seas.

I won't give up on her.

# CHAPTER 23

STELLA

Shivering with cold that has seeped dangerously deep into my bones, I have the urge to slip down to hot springs. I've never gone by myself. Barely remembering the circuitous route, and shuddering with cold and relief, I finally take in the private grotto. The rough, dark walls of the circular room dome to low ceilings dripping with condensation. The flickering torchlights reflect off the mysteriously deep black pool, and catch in the white steam as it pulls off the water. Poi brought me here my first night, he carried me against his chest. I wonder if I ever had a hope of not falling in love with him. Heaviness crushes me from the inside out, imploding any sense of sanity I had found by the sea.

I pull off my soaking cloak, and peel off my wet shorts and shirt, getting a strong sense of de'ja'vu. When I first came here, I thought it was all a dream, it was too perfect- a mouthwateringly handsome guy, mermaids, ocean conservation. I had no idea these circumstances could be the perfect ingredients for torture. I was so freaking naïve.

My big toe smarts as I dip it into the searing heat. I definitely stayed out in the rain for way too long. I sit on the edge, awkwardly hovering my feet above the water. Whenever my skin touches the surface, I have to bite my lip with the pain. Eventually, the steam warms me enough to slip my feet in. My mind has a numb quality to it, as if it's completely overwhelmed by the ache in my chest.

Staring past my knees into inky water, I swirl my feet in figure eights. Can I stand to be here with him if he doesn't want all of me? The idea of losing him completely is not an option. How did I get this bad? I'm flummoxing myself with this level of needing him. This invisible pull for him is like getting sucked out to sea- hopelessly and against my will.

I bury my head in my hands, wondering where I went wrong, wondering at the point where I could have kept my sanity. I'm so far from it I can't even pin-point a time. So will I give myself up for him? If he asks, will I give up my opinions, and everything I care about, everything I am, again? I'm horrified by the voice inside me that says "yes" with no hesitation. I can't do that. I can't allow myself to get lost in a man. I can't repeat that pattern of self-destruction. Gawd, is Poi a formidable foe. I grit my teeth and stare at the waters again. The steam pulls away so easily, as if separation of elements is a natural thing. I can't believe I'm letting myself go again- how can I let him be more important than my identity? My heart doesn't answer in logic. It just aches.

Maybe it's like a cold that will pass- or a fever that has to break, and recede. Maybe I'll get better. But I know I've never felt this way about anyone before, and I probably never could again. Now my mind is ganging up on me too. How the hell did he become the most important thing in my life? How did he so easily displace my love of the sea, my desperation to save humanity and now the Mer? When it comes down to it, I'm selfish. I want him.

But what then- if I am so ridiculously lucky as to jump from a night of hot dancing, to him actually wanting me… (of which the chances are ludicrously slim- why am I even worried? That would never happen…). But for the sake of hypotheticals and humoring my obsession- in a crazy world of him actually wanting me, what happens after? Would I miss the old parts of myself, or would I be like a brainwashed bimbo, forgetting everything that I am? Would he really want me to be incomplete? The thought of it makes me angry at him, even though I know this is all imagined. I start pulling my feet in figure eights again, trying to distract or comfort myself. It doesn't work.

"Stella." His voice is rough behind me. My back straightens with shock as a blush blooms across my body. My heart thuds hard. I'm suddenly super aware of how naked I am. And how messy my hair is.

Red-faced, keeping my chest facing the wall, I angle my head around, chin kissing my shoulder. "Hi." I say nervously, high-pitched tone betraying my cool. "What's up?"

Even from this strange angle, his beauty is devastating. His dark hair is soaking wet, twisted around his square face, masculine features, and strong jaw. Still standing in the entrance, practically filling it, there's an odd expression on his face- like he's uncomfortable too. He's not quite looking at me.

"I didn't expect to see you here…" His voice is tight with something I can't place.

I suddenly wonder if this grotto is off-limits to the public- his private pool or something. Oops. My heart thuds impossibly harder. I worry my eyebrows and bite my lip, "Um, sorry, should I leave?"

He's looking at me now. A shiver erupts along my spine. "No." He says tightly. He looks over my head again as he speaks, "I meant to find you after I—" His gaze falters down at me again, and he looks away. "I need to ask you something. Could you get dressed and meet me in the hall? You can return after."

"Sure." I can't believe how much my voice quakes in that one syllable. A tremor that has nothing to do with near-hypothermia runs through me. I feel hot and cold at once. What could he possibly need to ask me?

He retreats to the shadows of the hallway, allowing me privacy. My mind immediately goes to a dark place- maybe I accidentally did start rebellion with the vote, and he's really going to kick me out this time. But then why would I be able to return to the pool? Maybe he's being nice about kicking me out, because he did swear he'd never ask me to.

Through all my panicked thoughts, I don't even notice the process of pulling on all my damp clothing. As I turn out of the steamy grotto and into the damp hall, his eyes sear into mine with emotions I cannot place, but fury is definitely a strong contender. Shit. Some sort of rebellion, for sure. He's really going to ask me to leave this time.

Ache compounds with rattling heartbeats and I wonder if I can have a heart attack at twenty-six. It definitely feels like it.

The poorly lit hall flickers with a single torchlight twenty feet from us. Poi is more than a little intimidating in the gray shadows. His arms are crossed, stance at shoulder-width- a wall of tall black cloak stretches across his muscular frame. His olive skin is slick with saltwater as it drips off his nose and from his inky tendrils of messy hair. He must have just left the sea. His thickly-lashed, dark amber eyes bore into mine with such an intensity that I couldn't move if I wanted to. We're silent for a long moment, and I don't dare start the conversation.

His eyes rake over me quickly, eyebrows pulling together. "You look cold."

I shiver involuntarily, as if remembering. "I'm okay."

He strides closer. Only inches of space separate us, and my heart jerks violently, like it's trying to get to him. He grasps my hands in his broad palms, his eyes widening, "You're an ice cube… What happened?"

His large hands are warm around mine. If he's really going to kick me out, he's making this so much harder than it has to be. Maybe he won't. He did promise. My heart is ricocheting painfully around my chest, and my lips part in confusion as I stare up at him. Why is he so close again? Isn't he mad at me? Staring up at his transfixing beauty, I speak plainly, not capable of any advanced brain function. My voice is hushed, "I sat out in the rain."

His eyes flare with frustration, before his thick banded arms fold around me and bring me tightly against his core. The feeling of him so close is intoxicating. My heart flops around hopelessly, and my fluttering stomach is totally deluded. I can't help nestling my head against his chest, and resting my palms against his hard torso. Even though he was just in the sea, he's warm. His indefinable, delectable manly musk filters through his salty garments, and trying to be conspicuous, I breathe in deeply. It feels so right here, everything else so easily drops away. It's scary.

"You're soaking wet." I state helpfully.

"Yes, but I'm warmer than you." His voice rumbles through his chest into mine, and a fiery thrill fractures out to my every appendage like lightning. What am I going to do with myself? Terror ebbs at me, tearing me in two directions.

"Stella, I have to ask you a question…" His voice is rough, and his heart pounds hard just once.

Extracting myself just a little, I gaze up into his shadowy face. The edges of his almond-shaped eyes are tight, his dark brows are peaked, and sadness is etched into his face. It pulls at my heart. "What's wrong?"

He blinks a few times, expanding his chest with a tight breath as he lifts his chin and looks around at the room. His breath doesn't seem to leave him. He looks back down at me, still looking like he's going through some sort of physical pain. "Do you have feelings for Hades?"

My lips part in surprise. My heart flutters in a panic. Does he know Hades kissed me?

Poi's face flinches with pain. I realize I've been silent too long. He leans back as his arms slide from my back and to my arms, edging me away from him. Panic sweeps in like the cold air. I fumble to find my voice, "No, I don't."

His brows twitch together, his amber eyes pained, voice tight, "I don't believe that."

My eyes go wide, "What? Why not?"

"You slept with him." His words crash in on me like a tsunami. His large hands fall from my arms and he backs up a step, as if removing himself from the path of the storm.

Tears prick my eyes, and my heart whips around like a caged bird. My voice is chopped up by my tightening throat, "What? I didn't. Why would you think that?"

His expression hardens further. He exhales as he stares over my shoulder, refusing to look at me, arms crossed. "He told me."

It's like I've been trapped in an arena with a bull which I am now expected to battle, but I have no red flag, and no skills to speak of. My heart aches madly. How could Hades do this to me? I say the only thing I know for sure, "He lied."

Poi's dangerous gaze flicks to mine, locking me in. He really does look like the dark, foreboding God of the Sea. "Did he?"

My heart won't stop kicking violently in my chest. "Yes." My voice trembles. "He doesn't lie to me."

"I'm not lying." I feel like something in me is breaking.

Poi's expression is hard, as if there is some raging fury threatening to crack through his composed façade. "Then what happened."

I swallow, "Hades came to my room last night, and he kissed me. That's all."

Poi's face contorts with pain. Swearing, his long cloak swings around him as he spins to face the empty dark hallway. He swears in more Merglossa and it echoes faintly.

I ache, not knowing how to fix it, but just plea, "I don't want to be with him."

He shakes his head, turning around as he pulls his long fingers through his disheveled inky hair, "Then what do you want, Stella?"

My heart stutters. "You…"

He blinks, and looks around a lot, and I notice his eyes have become watery. He clears his throat. "Then why did you leave last night?"

I sigh, thinking of his embarrassing public renouncement of my Reveal vote. I look at him in exasperation, but when I see the water in his eyes, I can't help whispering, "You really don't know?"

He sighs expulsively, "Of course not."

"You… you really hurt my feelings," I feel silly saying it, but it's true.

His eyes bulge wide and he steps back a foot as his head juts forward, his voice is incredulous, "How?!?"

I hate that I have to spell it out for him. I hate that he doesn't know. It makes me feel ridiculous for how I feel. "Because…" I sigh, "I was publicly embarrassed by your speech. Not to mention, you told me not to speak my opinions, and you actually thought I would be so rude as to start an uprising… I mean, you don't even trust me!"

He opens his mouth, then closes it firmly. His eyes narrow in on mine again, his dark brows are set in a permanent furrow. "I didn't mean for you to take it that way…"

I lift my shoulders, suddenly a bit angry. "Well I did."

He sighs again, dragging his hand through his damp hair. "Your vote could have destabilized our entire community, and could have put us all at risk of a Reveal. I had to make the announcement. I had to ask you to not take it further. For all our safety."

I nod, tightness gripping my chest, and look away. The tension rises up through my throat, and squeezes tears out of my eyes. Aha. And this is why we can't be together. We will never see eye-to-eye. He can't respect my opinions and my mind. He'd only ever want a piece of me. He'll never want all of me. I feel like I'm getting wrung tighter and tighter, and it's hard to breathe, and the world is so blurry that nothing makes sense.

He steps forward and wraps his arms around me, holding me in close. His musky pheromones taunt me, and the feeling of him against me again is torturously heavenly. "Hey," his voice is low, "I'm sorry. I didn't mean for you to take it so personally…"

I yank back, pushing him away from me, and glaring at his surprised expression. "But it is personal. You can't stand me! You can't stand my ideas and my perspective—we could never get along. So I don't even know why you hold me so close." My voice cracks miserably.

"And that's why you kissed Hades." He states it blankly. "He convinced you that he, in contrast, does like your ideas."

I look away. "I tried to make myself like him instead. But I can't."

Poi's quiet a moment. When I gaze back at him, his eyes are so serious that my knees are weak. His low voice is soft, "Stella. Just because I don't take your advice doesn't mean I don't respect your opinions. Yes, they are the opposite from mine, yes, it's been challenging..." He grins with a raised eyebrow, then sighs, "But in truth, I love that you have made the effort to get thoroughly informed, that you make up your own mind about the world, and that you care enough to have the strong will to act."

I squint at him. Well that's hard to believe. "You haven't been acting like you love it... you've been acting like I'm a pain in your ass..."

He grins widely, shaking his head, and looking off and looking back to me. "It would be easier if you were on my side..."

I raise my eyebrows, putting my hands on my hips, "Come over to my side then."

He smirks again, eyes twinkling. "This is what I'm talking about. You never lose your fire, you care so much about the world, always. You hold to your vision... even when you think it's at the expense of us."

His words usher a hush into the darkened, damp hallway. Possibility hovers like ice particles.

"Isn't it?" I whisper.

"No." His voice is resolute.

"But I don't want to change my opinions to appease you."

"I'm not asking you to."

"Aren't you?"

He sighs, "No. I'm asking you not to start a rebellion and overthrow my rule. I respect your autonomy, I know you have a brilliant mind, Stella. Just because I'm not choosing to rule by your opinion doesn't mean I don't respect it."

It clicks. I have been pushing so hard for the Reveal, that I couldn't see the truth in our dynamic. In all my self-empowerment zeal, I really missed out on seeing the obvious... He respects me. He's right- just because he doesn't make my opinions his own, doesn't mean he doesn't appreciate them. Hmm. I guess that's what you'd call a sore spot, or a blind spot. Definitely a smudge, of some sort.

Well, this changes things.

I look at him uncertainly, and he's squinting at me, as if assessing. "So... you're saying... you like me for... my mind...?"

He grins, nodding and sighing, "Yes."

"Oh."

I'm not sure what to do with this version of reality.

His voice is serious, "Can you, as well, respect my mind despite the fact that my opinions are different from yours?" He just stands just an arm's length away, as if he is also paralyzed by the enormity of the moment.

I consider this. I guess this was the big problem all along. It was my judgements blocking us, not his. Reality has contorted. Can I respect him for his mind? His resistance to the Reveal is hard pill to swallow. How can I respect him for being fearful of humans? Maybe his experience has trained him to be so... oh this is hard... I guess it's a question of: can I respect his mind, while also asking him to see a new angle? Maybe. Damn, is that all I can really give him? A maybe? Don't I want him?

I glance towards him again, nervous that my offer won't be enough, "I will try... But I'm still going to try to convince you like crazy."

He grins wide, "I wouldn't expect anything less."

Ache throbs uncertainly in my chest. "You won't be disappointed."

His megawatt smile blossoms in my chest and warms me from the inside out. I find myself smiling too.

He collapses the space between us, stopping just before me with an expression that melts me. He gently presses his hand against the small of my back, pulling me nearer. The beating in my chest heats the rest of my shaking body. His broad frame encircles mine. My heart jerks madly. His fingertips gently trace up my jaw until his warm hands cradle my head below his. His thumbs hook beneath my jaw, and angle my face up towards him. His voice is rough, "I want all of you, Stella. Even that rebellious heart."

My heart beats once, registering his words, and soars free. Maybe it was my heart all along, that wanted good for the world. Maybe he knows me better than I thought.

His amber eyes flick between mine with a burning intensity. His black-lashed gaze drops to my parted lips. My heart swoops like a plane in turbulence. He's going to kiss me.

I forget to breathe. He lowers his mouth to mine, gazing at me until our lips touch. Heat explodes in my chest, a fluttering release. His soft lips knead gently against mine, and it's so sweet it hurts. It just causes me to ache with needing him more. His arm bands around me, pulling me close against his muscled chest. His lips open mine, and I yield to his slow, tangling tongue. The pit of my stomach becomes molten lava. His mouth works prose across mine, pulling at my heart like a marionette. The moment stretches on sweetly, until my heart breaks, because how could I have been trying to hold this off?

# CHAPTER 24

POI

Storm brewing in my veins, thunder clapping with every heartbeat, I wait. Doors creak behind me as Mer leave their living quarters for dinner. I stare at the oaken door at the threshold of the wild Ridge, and Hades' path to his living quarters. It's all very clear now. All the extra time he spent here, socializing, when he very well knows he has his own responsibilities to attend to Beneath. Time contorts as I ruminate on his betrayal.

More than anything, it's unfair to her. He's putting his own selfish wants before restoring her memory and self. That alone should be enough to show him he doesn't love her. But he won't hear it.

The metal ironwork of the latch lifts from the outside, and the door swings open, ushering in a gush of icy cold, and Hades, stumbling with shock when he sees me. The door slams shut.

"Oh shit." It looks like he's smelled sour milk. Then he lifts his chin back and sighs, "You asked her, didn't you."

"I did." I remain still, the only way to keep fiery anger from overtaking me.

He shrugs, "Fine, I lied. But we did make-out."

I flinch at the image. Kissing sounds more benign. It's all awful. I grit my teeth. "I know."

"I just thought you should know I have a real chance with her."

"It's not a competition, Hades. It's her life."

He squints pale snake eyes, "You're all high and mighty because you're on the right side of the fence. What would you do if the situation was reversed? If you loved her, but she was meant to fall in love with me?" His eyebrow raised, arms crossed, he's stepped forward so I can see the tightness in his supposedly cool manner.

"I want her to remember herself, I want her to regain her immortal life, more than I want her for myself. Her life comes first." The words barrel out of me, scratching the soft flesh of my trachea. It's the truth, but the idea of us not being together is unbearable too.

Hades rolls his eyes and brushes past me. "Sure, you say that. Mr. High and Mighty, but you're not living it."

Fear bores into my chest. Would I be so weak if Thalassa and I weren't fated (with a plethora of fine print), to return to each other? Heat sears into me, and now I'm less sure. But I think of her, everything that she is, everything she's lost, everything she has to gain, and I want her to be whole again.

I wish Hades could know such a love. He's never really told us an unembellished, frank story of what happened with Persephone, but I know she wasn't worthy of him. Hades has already walked ten leisurely paces down the hall of brightly painted and shell-adorned doors affronting living quarters. "Hades."

He stops before a robin's egg blue door, and rounds slowly, "What…" his tone is exasperated.

"Why have you not tried to find your own Queen?"

He shakes his head. "Seriously? This again?"

I catch up to him, desperately needing to distract him from Stella, and honestly wishing he could find someone for himself. Right now, objectively, it's so clear to see that Stella and him wouldn't be good together. He just humors her- he doesn't engage her. She and I have a chemistry that can't be altered by lifetimes or memories, something in our spirits was in love before we even knew it. And after kissing her today, I'm on such a high I can't be down for long. Finally. I'm already feeling more level, picking up my usual, older-brother tone, "Hades, you haven't honestly tried to find an eternal match in a century. Have you given up?"

His eyes flame, "No."

"Stella is not an option. Spend your energy on someone that could work for you."

Baring his teeth, he talks through a clenched jaw, "She could work for me. Can't you see that?" He stabs a burning finger against my chest, "You made her cry. We kissed because I was comforting her. Maybe you should reconsider who is best for her here."

I am alarmed by how tightly he's gripping onto her. It's like coming up on a shark in murky waters when I'd thought it was a bait fish. I hold the line. "I am best for her, because I put her first. Twisted fates aside, that's the bare truth, and I'd do it no matter what. You need to find someone you'd give up everything for- including them."

Shoving his lips together in a pale line, his eyes glare with the words he doesn't have. Raw frustration and desperation play across his face. "I can't take this anymore, Poi, you don't even know what it's like. Some of us aren't fated for anyone."

The words hit me like a wave and crack my heart. My brother thinks he's not meant to be loved. That's hard to fix. My lips part, but it's my turn for no words.

"There's no space for us, but we just fall in love anyway, and cause disaster."

"That's not true…" I stumble, heart aching for him, recklessly wanting to pull a blowfish into a hug, "You're fated to be loved too."

"Oh really? Show me the Prophesy." He snaps, glowering.

"Just because it hasn't happened doesn't mean it won't." I mean it, but my heart is heavy, it's been a long time.

"It's been eons- it's not going to happen." He sighs expulsively, "I'm done with getting lectured."

He strides down the hall again, more quickly, trying to shake me off. "I just care for you, Hades. I want to see you find someone."

He pauses suddenly, I keep walking, and turn towards him. His expression is knowing, "Yeah, because you want to throw me off from chasing Stella."

Something clicks in my chest. I'm not all good. I clench my jaw. "Both."

He sighs and shakes his head, walking past me. I join, but he stares straight ahead as we walk towards the dining hall. Stella will be there. We need to wrap this conversation up. And I have to get to my final point. I put a hand on his burning shoulder, and he stops, but looks like he might punch me.

"What?" He swings his arms out wide, throwing off my hand, "Would you leave me alone?!"

"You need to apologize to Stella."

His gaze thrusts upwards violently, then smacks down on me like a festering beached whale, "You didn't have to tell her."

Fury boils in me like lava, volatile and unyielding. Shaking, I stymie all my reactions. I breathe stiffly. I choose less words, because more would risk an explosion, and I don't want to play his game. "You will apologize to her."

His lips curl at me with pure hatred, "Fine." He turns and strides quickly down the hall, burning off his own anger.

I walk slowly, trying to expand my constricted lungs and regain my balance.

She's standing outside the dining hall entrance in a decorated alcove with Hades. Her mouth is ajar, messy blonde hair askew, with an expression of abject terror as Hades stands before her. My heart clenches and I pick up my step. He's standing too close to her, and she's leaning against the rough stone wall, as if she's backed up too many times already.

"In the Underworld, you wouldn't age- you'd stay twenty-six forever. But if you stay here, Poi will stay young, and you- you'll get old and wrinkled—"

Oh my god. I pick up my pace. This is literally the worst thing he could be saying…

Stella's wide emerald eyes are swimming with tears. Her old expression of fear is back, as if she's absorbed every word.

I grab Hades' at the nape of his cloak and fling him to the ground. "Enough." I snarl. "Your impulsive behavior is putting others at risk, brother."

Laughing with an acerbic edge, Hades just lifts himself up to his elbows. He lounges as if he chose to be splayed prostrate on the cold, damp stone floor. "If you think my prerogative is endangering anyone, your perspective is laughably skewed. Isn't it clear? Your Queen is never coming back. So don't get your hopes—"

Terror and fury ratchet around my chest, dissolve my sight, and destroy my resolve. I direct water to materialize around Hades' head from the spirit dimension. Warping his features, Hades' head is stuck in a whirlpool of spinning ice water, contained to the size of a small fish tank. Hades spins onto his stomach, pulling up to all fours, spluttering contained bubbles, coughing bound water, and wheezing for air. He claws at it with fire in his palms, which only heats it towards a boil, and he quickly stops.

Stella inhales dramatically. "Poi! What the hell are you doing? Hades—oh my god don't kill him!!!"

Hades could last another minute without suffering, but I dissolve the water back into the spirit dimension. With no orb barricade, Hades' wheezes and coughs crisply echo off the walls. He shudders a ragged breath in, glancing up at Stella with watery eyes, "Some things are dangerous for you to know, love… but I won't hide things from you…"

My heart catches in my throat. "Thin ice." I grind out, ready to censure with water at an instant's notice.

"Relax…" Hades rolls his eyes, and coughs some more. He spins on to his back, pulling himself up to his elbows again, as if he still prefers the slick cold floor to standing. He's so stubborn. "Before you so rudely interrupted, I was just telling Stella…" Hades his tone is bland, bored. "If she's lucky, she'll get all pruned, aged, and gray. You'll have her for—" he glances up at Stella, scrunching up his face and coldly estimating as if she's an undesirable slab of meat, "Maybe fifty years?" He glances my way, shrugging, "If she doesn't get stung or drown before then. Then, she's gone forever— such a quick little jaunt through a perilous human life."

She bites her lip and appears to shrink as tears brim over and spill across her cheeks. She's so fragile and innocent in this state, so incredibly vulnerable, that my heart breaks for her. I wish that I could help her be strong. My whole body has seized up against Hades' words.

I round on him, "Apologize to her. That was cruel."

He won't look at me, he's just staring at Stella, who looks cornered. "You have options, Stella. Your time with Poi would be very brief, just the blink of an eye. But you could have immortal life with me."

The bastard. I withhold from kicking him while he's down. "She would be undead and trapped. That's not immortal life."

"It's close." He stares up at her, unblinking.

My chest clenches, because I'm really not sure what she's thinking. She can't be considering his offer, can she?

Leaning against the wall, glaring at him through her running tears, her voice whips, "I don't want forever with you. After your lie, I can't even look at you." Without even glancing my way, she pushes off from the wall with arms wrapped around herself and head down, speed-walking away with my heart.

## STELLA

I don't make it back to the cottage. In the stairwell just below the island, Poi's hands grab my waist and turn me towards him.

Frantically, I try to wipe away the wetness around my eyes with the back of my hands. I'm still shuddering with the sadness of not being enough for him, of losing him before I really ever had him. Gasping for air and embarrassed for being so upset I can't speak right, I flutter a hand at him, "Go'way."

His face is full of concern, "No."

I take a shaky breath, heart surging with new laments as I remember he's looked twenty-eight for about eight-hundred years. My life is just a heartbeat compared with his.

He tucks my hair behind my ears, and cups my face in his warm hand. His low growl is protective, "Hades shouldn't have said all that."

I shrug weakly, "He was right though, wasn't he?"

His dark amber eyes are unfathomably sad. "He may have been."

"I will only live for a second, compared to your eternity." The truth grates deep into my soul, like sand in my lungs, and I can't help the tears that stream down my face.

He leans down, and presses his lips against my forehead, whispering, "It will be the most beautiful, most memorable second of that eternity."

For some reason, this just makes me cry harder. I feel like I'm missing out on so much, even though I had no right to it in the first place.

He wraps me into his arms, and in the darkness, smothered by his warmth and sweet musk, I calm. Compared to my human life, this is more than I could have ever bargained for. I force myself to be grateful for what I have right now. Miraculously, I have him.

Then a scary thought hits me. "What about... the Queen? Hades mentioned you still think she will come back?"

He is silent for a long time, just holding me, and I start to think he might not answer. His voice is slow, careful, "The Queen has been gone, for a very long time."

Somehow, this doesn't settle my fears. In this jarring moment, I realize I have been stupid again. She's his true soul mate- a part of him is still holding out for, and I could never replace her. This is definitely worse than my being impermanent.

The light pitter-patter of rain is a metronome to my thoughts. They ping between Hades' cruel reminders of my life expectancy, and Poi's lost Queen.

I look up at the cottage ceiling, seeing nothing but darkness. It's no different than closing my eyes, but I can't sleep. Poi told me that he would kiss me goodnight after his late meetings, but Hades words are like a cruel spell, turning my anticipation into dread. The pat of rain is drumming a song of "im.not.enough, im.not.enough, im.not.enough."

When the door moans open, amplifying the rhythms of a light rain, my heart thuds deep and hard in my chest. I listen as Poi quietly shuts it, removes his wet cloak with a swish and a rustle, and hangs it by the door, before soundlessly padding over.

"You're not sleeping…" He gruffly accuses. His amber eyes reflect in the night like a cat's. Only there is no light they are reflecting, and I wonder again at his genetic makeup.

"You can see in the dark." I find it harder to take a breath. I sit up.

He chuckles, and I feel the covers sliding back as the bed pitches with his weight. My heartbeat radiates to every inch of me, mind in a state of frozen disbelief at what may be transpiring.

In the black grip of night, his irresistible musk floats to me. His eyes glow burnt copper like thin crescent moons. His hand tucks a lock of my hair behind my ear. Without stumbling, his warm thumb slowly traces my cheekbone, my jaw, the line of my neck, and rests on my trembling shoulder.

His smooth voice is low, "I was planning on just giving you a goodnight kiss."

His other hand touches my bare knee, causing electricity to jitter up my leg… My insides constrict. My heart thuds violently.

"But now I see that you aren't sleeping, if it's okay with you, I could stay the night."

Adrenaline swirls in my stomach. I fight to find my voice, "Ah, yes. That's fine."

His other hand intertwines through the hair at the back of my head, and his warm lips find mine. They knead and burn with intensity, opening my mouth to his, his tongue searching mine with delicate precision which melts me.

He pulls back, speaking raggedly, "But don't get any ideas. I plan on sleeping." I smirk in the darkness, unconvinced.

His mouth persuasively melds to mine, he leans into me suggestively, and he spins me down, into the pillows. Darkness around, his glowing ember eyes penetrate mine from just inches above. Parts of him are clearly warring. His voice is rough, "I need to wait."

"Okay," I whisper, confused. "Can you explain why?"

"Darling, I want to…" He leans down and his soft lips graze mine, pushing insistently, biting my lip. My arms tighten around his broad shoulders.

I whisper against his lips, "What's stopping you?"

I feel him lift off of me, and lay on his back with a huff. His voice is thick with frustration, "I am not going to explain it to you. Suffice it to say, I'll make sure we get fully acquainted in good time."

My stomach jolts at his words. He wants me, and it's going to be so good. But also, he is absolutely maddening. In good time? That would be now. I am barely holding myself together with all the desire roiling through me. But gently, respectfully, I lie my head against his bare chest, and sidling up to him, weave my arm around his warm, sculpted torso. He wraps his arm down my back, and holds my shoulder with his other. His heart thuds only occasionally, but when it does, it shakes his whole body. My chest purrs happily.

Despite my accusation, he falls asleep very quickly, most likely out of pure exhaustion. I feel a little guilty for trying to keep him awake, knowing full well all the things he is trying to accomplish in the day. As his breathing slides deep and calm through his lungs, and his heartbeats soften, my heart tugs for him painfully, despite his being right here, in my arms.

His radiating heat and sweet musky pheromones sing to me. I consider why he wants to wait.

The world expands, and everything else crowds in. A torrential rain pounds on the roof, a strumming of patterns too complex to ever repeat. But then it repeats. It is as relentless as the questions in my mind.

Does Poi want wait to make sure his Queen doesn't return, before fully moving on? Who was this woman Poi loved, this Queen? Of course, I picture that she was perfect, something I could never compare to. Why does Poi think she will come back? And what would happen to me, if she does? I hate to think it.

The rain continues to be an insane metronome to my thoughts. He said he would keep me company because I couldn't sleep, but this has been the perfect concoction for an all-nighter. You'd think my adrenaline would be tired of doing laps up and down my spine, but it has kept it up for hours. My wired mind is roaming across the dangerous frontier of jealousy, and if I'm going to appreciate my time with Poi, I don't want to feel constantly on-guard. I have to know why he thinks she could come back, and when. I need to know my timeline, and be ready for when I have to let him go. My heart squelches painfully.

As slowly as possible, I peel myself away without waking him. I unwind the sheets from my restless legs, and creep off the mattress. My feet touch the icy floor silently. I don't bother with the creaky wardrobe doors. Silently tip-toeing across the woven rug, I grab yesterday's plum-colored cloak from the wooden desk, and pull it on over my sleep shorts and shirt.

At the door, I turn the brass knob very slowly, and miraculously, the thunderous rain drowns the moan of hinges. I am soaked the moment I stand beneath the sky. The icy shower pounds my skull and shoulders, drenching every inch of me. There is no light. The rain cascades down on the sea like hail singing against endless pavement. The sound is more infinite than I can comprehend. Nor do I want to stand here and get more waterlogged. My body remembers the way, and with arms outstretched, I manage not to fall across slippery rocks before finding the damp stairwell.

I shake like a wet dog, but the water clings anyways. I don't have their canine form down. Shivering and mumbling complaints, I skitter down the passageways as the lone torches alight, and dim, as I pass. The quiet is serene and uncanny.

I push open the iron-framed oak library door, it creaks as it opens wide, and there is darkness for only an instant. Torchlights flame to life, the fireplace crackles with a burst of white hot fire which simmers down to a tepid orange. Pulling off the drenched cloak, I lay it across a chair to dry near the fireplace. I stand fingers out, watching the flames, until my bones feel dry again.

Roasting, I turn my backside to the fire, and look at the shadow-drenched bookcases looming in the flickering light. Dozens of shelves are carved high into the rock, and standing wooden shelves between those, all stuffed with dusty volumes that could contain the poisonous knowledge that I seek.

Finding out more about the Queen is like tracking down someone else's lost dog that also just so happens to have rabies. My stomach is a mess of maggots that thought they might one day be butterflies. When my bum begins to sear with the heat of the fireplace, I give up my nervous hesitation, and wander the shelves…

There must be records upon records of her. The question is if they will be in English, or Merglossa… I tap my fingers impatiently on the back of a lime leather chair, scanning the bindings on the wall. They're all nonsense letters and symbols. I stand and walk through the small passageways lined with books, and am shocked with a small selection of books with bindings I can actually read. Bending down, a maroon leather book with gold-gilt lettering catches my eye: "The Selkie Queen."

I wonder if this is her. Stomach roiling, I open it quickly, not really wanting to see. The print date is 1701 in Dublin, Ireland. Carefully moving tissue paper aside, black ink sketches illustrate Sulkies as seals which can turn human and back.

A personal account is recorded. When faced with famine, the people of a small coastal town in Ireland called upon the Selkies to save them:

*One day, when I returned to the rocky shores, a beautiful woman in a silken cloak stood before baskets and baskets of fish. Her hair was flaxen gold, her eyes greener than emeralds. She spoke with a strange foreign accent, but told me that the people would not starve. Every week of fall and winter, there were baskets of fish and seaweed along the rocks. The people of our region survived until the next harvest.*

*I asked how I could repay her, and she requested that the people always remember to respect the sea. I asked her if she be a Selkie or a God. She replied neither. But I will always believe she was the Queen of the Selkies, and the Goddess of the Sea, sent to help human kind.*

I shut the book, disgusted. Great, she was a fucking saint. I shove the book back onto the shelf angrily.

I'd rather not read through how magical and perfect she was. What I really want to know is… is she coming back? How did she die? Why hasn't she come back yet? I need to learn more about just the end of her life. That's all I need to know.

An idea clicks. If the Mer keep a ledger for species population records, it's likely they also keep a record for the lives of individual mer. It can't be that far of a stretch. Remembering the ledgers had been stacked on the shelf near the fireplace, I wind through the chairs and tables with eyes locked on the fat black bindings. Reaching them, I pray for English.

I breathe in anticipation as I see Merikoi scrawl paired with English. Scanning the stacks, my heart starts to skip in my chest as I read "Birth and Death," on one heavy binding, and haul the heavy volume off the shelf. It requires two hands. I sneeze as I drop it onto the cherry wood desk. I open it randomly, skimming over the words. My fingers trace along the mandarin-like calligraphy of Merglossa, and the disjointed English print below.

There is a mind-bendingly long stretch of years in between births and deaths. My mind warps as I see, beside each name, in tight font, several lifetimes are listed.

I stare into space with complete confusion. I wonder if I will reincarnate, or ever have before. Then I remember Hades' taunting voice; "Then she's gone forever, such a quick little jaunt through perilous life." What a cruel thing to say. I decide I need to give him more credit for being the God of the Underworld and Keeper of Hell. He knew exactly what to say to create a wedge between Poi and me.

I flip to the front of the book, looking for some sort of directory, but there is none. It seems birthdays are written in as soon as someone was born. Assuming, as the Queen is also a God of sorts, and she was likely born first, I scan the first records page with my finger.

I read her name: "Goddess and Queen Guardian of the Sea, Thalassa." A sensation like sand through an hourglass runs up my spine. I look around the room, feeling I've been here before, and had this exact same thought, looking at this exact same book. I shake it off and focus. Her birth dates start in Merglossa, and pair with English around 1100AD. From the sheer quantity of markings, her lives seem to span more time than western society claims humans have existed. Despite myself, I am filled with an awe for this woman, realizing she must have been very wise, for having seen so much. With an involuntary shudder, I wonder how it's possible to kill a god. I look at her last written date, a death. 1992. Two years before my birth. It's been over a quarter century since she was alive. I scan between all the other deaths and births, noting there is a gap of one to three years. The place behind my sternum loosens. Maybe she won't return…

The heavy oaken door groans open. Gripping the door, drenched, Poi pauses in the threshold looking like a model out of a Gucci ad. My heart batters wildly.

"It's so early. Why'd you leave?" His voice is gravelly.

Looking at him, I wonder that too. Then I realize he may not be too happy to see me thumbing through his Queen's previous life records. Regretfully, this book is far too large to casually swipe under my arm and pretend it's not there. I try to act casual. "I um, couldn't sleep…"

His eyebrows knit with empathy as he strolls across the room towards me, and for the millionth time, I appreciate how sexy he is when drenched. His voice is brooding, "I guess I wasn't any help…"

My stomach claws with feral adrenaline. My heart is in my throat. I wonder how I have any left of either. "No, I liked it… I was just—"

He's not even within arm's reach when he glances across at my reading materials, freezes in his tracks, and lands me with an expression of flummoxed horror. "You've got to be kidding me." His voice is deadpan.

I glance at the monster volume, and back at him. He looks like someone who just watched their car get hit and run. I fumble with my voice, "Ah, nope."

He quickly closes the distance between us, and rapidly shuts the volume's cover as I pull my fingers off the pages. He heaves the ledger off the desk, onto another nearby desk- away from me. He balances on his long fingers over the desk, leaning down with mutinous eyes. But if he's trying to impose any fear with that glare, it's really not working on me- I just want to jump his bones.

"What do you know," he demands.

I try to stay cool. "I was just looking at the Queen's birth and death days."

He blinks hurriedly. Eyes flashing, he looks around the room and stands up. He walks back a few steps. He drags his long fingers through his mess of black hair. He takes a breath. Clearly I've upset him. Guilt nestles into my chest.

He squints at me through his dark lashes. "And how are you feeling?"

It seems like an odd question, considering the conversation, but I answer. "Fine… a little jittery still…"

He rubs his dark stubble with his palm as he nods, apparently contemplating. "That's good."

I'm not sure I want to be polite and ask how he's feeling too. It's very clear he's upset.

He strolls back to the desk, places his palms on the desk, his strong arms constricting as he leans towards me again. His voice strained, "Look, you have stumbled upon... yet another path that is off-limits... I have to ask that you don't mettle in the Queen's past."

The mixture of exhaustion, concern, and torture in his expression is disarming. Maybe I've gone too far with my jealousy. Maybe this really is hurting him. Maybe this is one question, that I can leave hanging. She *has* been gone for more than a quarter century.

And whole-heartedly feeling it, I look into his pained dark gaze, and reply, "Alright, I'll let her go. I'm sorry I hurt you by bringing it up again. I was just, a little jealous. I was worried she might come back, and was trying to prepare, to know, how much time I might have with you..." My voice is soft at the end as my heart twists like a knife.

"Oh." He says it with genuine surprise. His guard down, he is by my side in a moment, sitting on the desk, cupping my chin in his large warm palm.

I realize a warm tear has leaked out of my right eye.

"You have nothing to worry about," he speaks roughly, his molten gaze is so filled with conviction that it melts my worry. I'll let her go.

But another worry pops up. "What about my being human? Hades was right. You barely age, and my life will be like- blip! Done. It will be hard for both of us."

Pain flicks across his face. He readjusts on the desk, one knee on either side of my chair, he grasps both my shoulders in his large palms, and inclines his head. His low, gravelly voice is somewhere between dangerous and seductive, "My interest in you is not conditional."

Caught off-guard, my lips part in surprise. This is not something you hear every day. It sounds... serious. His intense stare is threatening to burn me down. I meet his honesty with my own, voice soft, "I'll stay as long as you'll have me."

His sunrise smile returns, amber eyes blazing: "Then prepare to die here," he teases.

"That shouldn't be too long..." I sigh in faint disbelief of joking about my own death.

He glares at me through dark lashes, his face angelic beneath his messed wet locks, "We'll make it worth your while."

His tantalizing stare makes me stop breathing.

He traces my jaw with his thumb, voice gentle, "But for now, shall we try to catch some sleep before tomorrow starts?"

I nod, feeling guilty for keeping him up.

He leans in and presses his soft lips against my forehead, whispering, "You're brave."

Reaching up to my shoulder, I hold his hand beneath mine, and I just feel so exhausted and so far from brave. I close my eyes, whispering, "You're sweet."

"Come here," He stands, pulling me beneath his damp cloak, and holding me tight against his radiating heat. His hand grips under my hair, holding me against his slow heartbeat. I wind my arms around him, nestling in and feeling warm and whole and right.

Walking wrapped side-by-side, head leaning against his chest, we navigate through the empty corridors, the winding stone staircase, and back to the dusky gray light of the craggy island. The rain has ceased. The wind is sleeping with the night.

Through the dreamlike darkness, we shuffle into the cottage, peeling off layers. I slip into the bed with heavy bones. He stands beside the bed, pulling my covers up and hovering over me. "You won't sleep with me here, so I'll see you when you wake up."

"No..." I moan groggily. "I'm definitely going to sleep." I pat the bed behind me, nearly slurring my words, "Stay."

He hesitates, and then silently walks around the bed: it creaks as he climbs in. He reaches an arm around my waist as his body molds against mine. I am finally out of adrenaline. I lean against his warm chest, and let myself drift.

# CHAPTER 25

STELLA

I have a spoonful of squishy conch chowder, somehow almost buttery, and extremely salty. The Mer like their salt. It's almost as if they are so used to salt from swimming in it nearly all day, they need to shock their system with extreme amounts to actually taste it. Before I can actually continue to consume it, I add in water from my drinking shell.

Noon's bright sunlight streams down from the skylight dome above. The sea is a teal green, tiger-striped with focused rays of light. The light roams across the hall, reflecting and shimmying. I am in a strange state of grog mixed with bliss mixed with shock. My tired mind and ragged heart can barely believe that Poi has spent so much time with me in the past forty-eight hours.

Turtle-tattooed arms wrap around me, bear-hugging me, as someone's high pitch squeal resounds in my ear.

"Stelllahhh" Kiara sings as she rocks me side to side.

I can't help smiling. She knows.

She releases me and sits on the bench beside me, straddling it. Her fine eyebrow is raised higher than I have ever witnessed. "You, and Poi, are together…" She says it almost reverently, and I appreciate that tone, I feel like it is more than appropriate for the situation.

I nod happily, "I think so."

Her dark eyes are bright- the purple flecks nearly lilac. "He told me this morning. He's happier than I've seen in a really long time."

A warm bubble swells in my chest, and I sincerely hope her words are true.

"He told me to tell you that he'll be back late tonight. He's meeting with the Caribbean Mer. They're coral farmers trying to replant the reef species in cooler parts of the ocean before they all bleach and die with this year's record-hot, scorching El Niño."

The knowledge hits me like cold water. Once again, he's scrambling around doing his best to fix problems humans have caused.

"They're making good progress," She reads my expression, her tone hopeful. "About ninety percent of coral reefs in the Caribbean have died, but they've been able to replant about ten percent of that in cooler areas. I really think it's taking hold."

That is sad if she thinks that's encouraging. I palm my forehead. I stare into her pretty face pleadingly, "How can I convince him to Reveal?"

She looks down. "Stella, I really can't help you with that."

"Don't you see how important it is though? All around the world, coral reefs are dying en-masse. I know you know that's beyond the beginning of the end. The corals are the root of all the life in the oceans, and on earth, they're where life started!"

Her gaze is pained, her lips are twisted downward. "Stella, it's all the more reason to fear humans. I don't blame him. I'm scared of them too. What's happening now- it's disastrous, but at least it's somewhat predictable. What would they do to us, if they knew…"

It's my turn to look down. I feel really awful, because I know she's right. There's no guarantee all the world's nations would be kind to the Mer. It would only take one cruel nation to end them. What I'm asking, could potentially wipe out the Mer forever. But I have to believe that enough of the world would care. Forgetting nations, but the random people, from environmentalists to human rights people, the people that act not because they're getting paid, but because they care. Those are the people that make change.

She's gazing at me sadly, as if nothing we could ever do or say would make the smallest difference in the world. And I just cannot accept that. "Kiara," my voice sounds stronger, like a different version of me, "What's scarier—facing the fact that it's humans causing this mess, or the fact that the world might end if humans don't fix it?"

She looks away, uncomfortable.

I wait for her answer. It feels incredibly important to me that she sees this.

When she speaks again, her voice is soft. "For me, it's a question of: do we die later, due to humans, or do we die now, due to humans? The dying part, for me, that's certain."

Her words hit me like a hammer. I can't bear the idea of her death, or the extinction of the Mer and all the ocean life, due to humans. I breathe in slowly. "Can't you see, there is a sliver of a chance of survival, with the Reveal? Why wouldn't you pick that sliver of a chance?"

She gets agitated, rising from her seat, and glaring at me. "Because I want to live these next twenty years, before the whole ocean bottoms out, and dies. So please don't fuck that up for me."

I say nothing. She stalks off.

One thing I know: I'm not giving up on the Reveal.

I'm not really expecting to, but I don't see Poi all day. I ruminate in the sun, wondering how I can get the word out to some environmental groups about a documentary, without totally pissing off Poi. I play out different approaches, but everything ends in him being furious. My heart twists, but I'm less afraid of his fury than I am of the ocean's impending collapse. Does an action count as treacherous if you have that person's best intentions in mind?

I keep hearing: "Yes."

Darkness falls substantially, and I cave into the idea of not seeing Poi tonight. When I get back to the cottage studio, I notice all the mess I didn't see last night. There's a surprising amount of sand and built-up salt on the floor, and a few of my clothes are strewn around. Bending, I pick up my shorts and shirts, and place them in my washing pile.

Behind the wardrobe, is a broom I've never used. I pull it out, its tiny driftwood twigs spring in all directions. I succumb to brushing out all the sand and salt from the floor, and it doesn't take as long as I thought it might. I'm angling the broom to sweep under the bed, when my eye catches on the smallest corner of paper peeking out between the mattress and box spring.

I place the broom down slowly, as if approaching a stray cat. My fingers pinch the tiny corner, and pull. It becomes an unmarked envelope.

I open it. Inside is a printed letter, yellowed with age:

Dear Thalassa,

Threshold Independent Filmmaking is looking forward to our meeting on September 13th, 1992. As you know, our focus is the Ocean Wasteland documentary.

We appreciate your extremely novel idea to include folkloric images associated with ocean, harkening to a glorified and fairytale-like image society holds of the ocean. This could be a great visual contrast to the wasteland it's becoming.

We make no promises to use the reel; we'll have to see how authentic the film comes out, but we appreciate your unique efforts to add to the project.

In Solidarity,

Adrian Stone

Threshold Independent Filmmaking

My mouth gapes open as I re-read the lines. I hold the paper like it might spontaneously combust. My ears ring loudly, and I can't believe what I'm seeing. From the sounds of it, the Queen was planning a Reveal. To documentary film makers. Pretty much exactly the way I am planning it. The strange coincidence of it is overwhelming.

Suddenly, I decide I like Poi's Queen. She sounds very clever. As long as she doesn't come back.

The date on the letter surprises me too. I remember her death being in 1992, the same year as their supposed meeting. And because the world of humans know nothing about the Merikoi, I am going to guess she died before she could make it happen.

I feel like I just unwittingly stepped into a mire of quicksand. I wonder if her death was murder- because someone didn't want her to complete the Reveal. Who would stop a Queen? A King? It couldn't be… it couldn't be Poi… he loved her… The room is spinning. I can't quite breathe. I pull myself together. He loved her, he wouldn't kill her. Something must have happened.

But there is no doubt in my mind, that this death of a Goddess, was not unintentional.

Unsure of what to do with the note, and knowing Poi could walk in at any moment, I hastily stuff it back where it was.

Then a thought occurs to me, and I squeeze my arm between the thick layers of bed. I catch on two more pieces of paper. I pull them out gently, jittery with curiosity.

My Queen,

I have met with the Prime Minister of Canada, as you asked. I apologize for my late response, I had to meet with his advisors multiple times, as he was hesitant to meet with our company on such mysterious terms. After considerable coaxing, he has agreed to meet with you at Luis Lounge in Quebec City at 3pm, October 28th 1992.

With Respect,

Laude

I freeze, rereading her name. I can't believe that Laude would willingly go against her King's wishes… she's so incredibly loyal. But I guess she was loyal to the Queen as well. My mind is grappling to pull the pieces together. The plan clicks into place- the Queen had been setting up to meet with world leaders as the film was being made, setting the stage for worldwide discussions on the state of the oceans. I have to give her some credit, I didn't even think of that step.

I read the next letter.

> My Queen,
>
> You're insane for thinking your plans will work. But I admire your independence. I applaud it.
>
> You'll be happy to know the Prime Ministers of Australia, New Zealand, and Papua New Guinea have agreed to meet with you this Winter.
>
> Yours,
> Hades

I laugh in disbelief. Wow… she really was setting the stage… I am impressed, and emboldened. If only she had completed the Reveal twenty-eight years ago-maybe most of the world's coral reefs would still be alive. A buzzy, wild high fills my every fiber. I am going to complete her dying wish.

I wake to violet early morning light. The clouds out the window are bruised with grape and plum. I stretch awake, roll over, and realize I'm alone. Poi never came back.

Concern hitches in me. I tell myself that he's a god, and he'll be okay, as I throw on a shirt and shorts, braiding my hair back quick and messy as I walk outside. I barely take in the beautiful sunrise blooming across the day as I scamper across chilly jagged rocks.

I run down the tiny stairwell, and my momentum nearly throws me into Poi. I stop awkwardly, looking evenly at him as he walks up.

"Whoah," he smiles, "Where are you going in such a hurry?"

His voice is smooth, but exhaustion is worn across his face.

I regain my balance with my fingertips on his broad shoulders, "Looking for you, mister."

He steps to the stoop below me, winds his arms around my waist and squeezes me as he pulls me upwards, "Well, I'm right here." He heaves me over his shoulder, hooks one arm around my bent knees, and begins walking up the stairwell as blood gushes to my head and I laugh at the ridiculousness of his gesture.

His voice is gruff, "And we, are going back to bed."

I smirk, but I really don't think it means what I want it to mean. I bet after two nights of not really sleeping, he's a mess.

He manages to keep me over his shoulder across the brief trek to the cottage, and I see rose singeing the upside-down grape clouds.

"So did you sleep in the Caribbean?" I call up at him.

He laughs, and there is just a hint of hysteria in it.

He drops me onto the bed, and falls on after me. He promptly pretends to snore on my stomach. With his full dead-weight, I find it's very hard to breathe. Before he actually does fall asleep on me, I try sidling out from under him by pushing against his shoulders. After considerable heaving and huffing to the sound of his chuckling, I fail.

He looks up at me with puppy eyes, "Are you saying I need to lose weight?"

I laugh weakly, trying to get breath, and glare, "Only if you plan to sleep on me with all of it."

He groans and moves aside, releasing me, grumbling, "I'll consider it."

On his side, he props himself up with his elbow, and it looks like it's taking all his effort.

I want to know what happened in the Caribbean, but he looks way too exhausted to tell me the story. I just reach my hand up against his black-stubble jaw, and tell him, "You don't have to stay up and talk to me. You can just sleep."

His sleepy smile is so wide you'd think it was for the nicest person in the world. Which I am. I'm letting a sex god just sleep in my bed- not many people would allow that.

He falls back on the bed, and I jump off. I pull back the covers and he rolls around into them, murmuring thanks. I pull the covers up onto him, and his thickly-lashed chestnut eyes channel his last ounce of awareness as they penetrate mine. "You're gold. Pure gold."

I smirk. "Well thank you." I swallow all the cheesy jokes I could respond with.

I stroke his dark hair back as he closes his eyes, smiling through his serene features. I imitate his sexy intonation, "You won't sleep with me here, so I'll see you when you wake up."

He chuckles without opening his eyes, and nods. His voice is velvet through his sculpted burgundy lips, "That's true."

"Damn." I whisper, realizing all the letters are between the box-spring and mattress that Poi is currently, and indefinitely, passed out on. I sigh, and continue walking down the decorated corridor towards the dining hall. To be honest, right now, I'm a little bit glad to have an excuse not to immediately chase after the Reveal. After seeing Poi totally slammed with exhaustion and the literal weight of the world, I don't want to add to that.

My mind perks up: Don't go soft on him! You're trying to HELP.

I have to agree with myself.

Sighing, I wander to the dining hall, feeling utterly useless as a human. If I was at least a Mer, I'd be able to swim around without a babysitter, and maybe replant some corals or something. As it is, I am pretty much just on standby. It's maddening. There is so much to do, and I want to do it, but I have no clear route.

Frustrated with the monotony, I stand through the dining line, pick the green toast with some thinly sliced mystery sushi, and nearly resign myself to a seat amongst the driftwood tables, but I stop. The healing clinic. I can go and watch that at least.

By the time I remember where to find it amongst all the floors of winding halls, my breakfast is finished. I stand before the glassy wobbling door, and peer into the crystal-clear teal waters. I wonder at being able to see so clearly today.

Masses of still and disoriented creatures flood the wide hall. Five bespeckled, grumpy-faced, unicorn-tusked Narwhals lay listlessly near the entrance. Their twisting singular horns are nearly as long as their bodies, and their very tiny fins make them look like beefy body builders- a far more intimidating image than I previously associated with Narwhals. Mer swim between them methodically, pressing fingers beneath the fins for a few minutes, as if taking a pulse. I'm very quiet, standing close to the door, and I swear I hear the occasional thud-thud of their big whale hearts.

For hours, I watch the Octopus Mer unwind, unknot, and detangle fishing line, fishing nets, and plastic debris, from more sea turtles, dolphins, manta rays, sting rays, and fish than I can count. I marvel at their dexterity, and feel a small sense of release every time a turtle is ushered out into the open sea. But then more bundles of sea creatures torn by commercial fishing gear and trash are carried in. An angular-faced shark lies still, stomach sliced open, as a Mer calmly pulls out a license plate, a tire, a few cell phones, some pill bottles, and a dead squirrel. The Mer sews him up, and performs several more surgeries on docile shark patients.

"Poi is looking for you," Laude calls as she strolls towards me, her pixie blonde hair flat and scarlet eyes calm.

I think of her letter to the Queen, supporting the Reveal. I think of her as I know her, always on some errand for Poi. The two versions of her don't add up. I want to ask her about the letter, but I don't want to scare her away. I'm torn.

She glances at the Narwhals a moment, then back down at me. "He'll be in the counsel room for the next few hours, he said you can just walk in whenever."

"Thanks, Laude." Should I bring up the note? My gut is telling me she will tattle.

"Well, I'm headed for a swim, then helping to harvest some Kelp." She's already walking off past me, nodding her goodbye.

And I'm alone in front of the clinic again. Faced with the woes that are beyond typical life and death struggles- these beings are not equipped, evolved, or adapted for human-imposed obstacles. It makes me wonder what sort of life will be left, if humans continue to live carelessly. Probably enchanting rats, majestic seagulls, and magnificent mosquitoes.

# CHAPTER 26

STELLA

It's not the human-mingling Mer that join Poi in the counsel room, but an assortment of beshelled and bedecked Mer. A large table stands in the center of the room, and over a dozen of his Mer counsel are peeking at something on the table. He's standing amidst them, his messed, dark hair sticking at odd angles as he points to an expansive map. His voice is clear, as if he's had a full night's sleep and a week's vacation: "These regions here…"

The heads lean in, taking turns looking through the crowd. "…are projected to have cooler currents in the next few years. The West Pacific Mer were indicating that this region here… has been ideal for replanting corals. It may take several years for a reef to take hold— and your guess is as good as mine as to whether it will actually work— but we need numbers. So Yiere, and Juniper, I'm going to ask that you halt your shipwreck retrieval operations, and orchestrate sending people out for this coral replanting. Can you do that?"

A woman with frizzy, burnt-orange hair and moon-white skin nods professionally, addressing Poi from across the table with a voice I recognize from the night at the bar, "Sure can. We'll send people out in a matter of days. How long do you think this replanting will take?"

Poi's lips pull down to the side, exposing some of his white teeth, "Ah. I really don't know. We've never done a project on this scale before. But people can take breaks. They don't have to stay on-site indefinitely…" He pauses, and stares off into space, as if planning on the spot, "It needs to be livable. Let's schedule shifts, and we can adjust things as we go. Just keep communicating with me, let me know what you need."

This is hot. He is so on his game, so focused and driven that it really makes me wonder how I got so damn lucky to be with a guy this top-notch.

As if reading my mind, his gaze flicks up to me. He's leaning over his maps, arms flexing beneath his humble white t-shirt, surrounded by bedazzled Mer, and smiles. It's a private, sweet smile, that no one seems to notice, but it melts me.

When they break, his eyes hold mine as he strolls over to me, kick-starting my heart. His smile is easy and wide across his model-worthy face, "Thanks for letting me sleep this morning…"

He winds an arm around my back, pulling me into him and leaning down to my ear, breathing, "Promise I'll make it up to you."

My adrenaline spikes.

He bites my ear. In the middle of his milling council members.

It still makes me quiver. I put a hand against his chest, "Behave."

He groans and steps back just a tad, fixing me with his kaleidoscope dark eyes, "How are you? What did you get up to this morning?"

I want to be honest, but I'm still obsessing about the letters, wondering who I can collaborate with. Laude and Hades are pinging through my mind. I opt for his second question, "I went to the healing clinic. Do you know why the Narwhals are there?"

He squints his eyes a moment with a quick low hum. "I would guess something to do with melting glacial caps. But I don't know the specifics. I could find out for you. Rose—" He calls out, glancing to his left.

A Mer version of heavy-set, honey-skinned man with light pink hair stands beside him, voice deep, "What's up."

Poi turns to him casually, "Do you know why there are Narwhals in the healing clinic?"

A light flickers in Rose's magenta gaze, "Yeah. Humans have expanded their hunting into seas once covered with glacial ice." His voice is gruff and his stare intense, as if trying to beam all the information from his brain to mine with just his eyes. "When Narwhals get stuck in nets, they don't have a typical fight-or-flight response. When they get trapped, their hearts shut down and freeze, but their bodies panic and try to swim." His expression is solemn, "It's a real clusterfuck." He accentuates the cuss with a head nod.

"Oh." I say unhelpfully. "Sorry, about the… humans…"

He laughs from his gut, nearly crying, then sighs, and fixes me with his unnerving magenta stare again. "Funniest thing I heard all day. Good seeing ya, T—"

Poi shoves him away, hard, stopping him mid-sentence, then catches him. "Oops, sorry. Good seeing ya, Rose, it's been a while, hasn't it? Let's talk later."

I watch Poi guide the confused man, talking over him, and passing him towards Yiere. Poi mumbles something, she nods, and I am fully flummoxed at his act of random aggression. He clearly stopped Rose from whatever he was going to say, but it just sounded like he was saying; "Good seeing ya," and then about to say; "Talk to you later."

Sometimes, I cannot figure out Poi and his weirdo mysteriousness. When he walks over to me, I am staring at him as if he's a twenty-one-year old who's trying to go trick-or-treating. My arms involuntarily fold. "What was that about? Why did you cut him off?"

He shrugs, looking at the members around the room as he talks, "I owed him a good shove. It's just a game we play. Kind of like tag." When he's done talking, he looks at me, and it gives me the sense that he doesn't believe a word he is saying. And it's the strangest thing.

I state the obvious: "You are lying through your teeth."

He smirks and raises an eyebrow. "Maybe I am." His eyes flash, "I don't like lying to you, but it's a secret I can't let you in on."

I glance over at Rose, in deep conversation with Yiere. "Something he was going to say?" My eyes skip to him, considering just going over and asking him to repeat himself.

Poi's steps into my line of sight with his muscular frame, smiling dangerously, growling "Don't you dare."

I squint up at him. "Why is it a secret? What's at stake?"

His eyes flick between mine quickly. His voice becomes hushed, "Fate has deemed certain knowledge to be off-limits to humans like... you."

I nod slowly, not liking his answer. It seems to draw a line between us again. Him as the God of the Sea, me as a meek little human. Nope. Don't like that answer at all. I cluck my tongue with disapproval, turn, and leave him to his counsel.

There was a line before- between him being a slightly judgement-flawed god, and my being a devious human, but that shifted, morphed, and I thought gave way when I accepted his statement that he likes me for all of me. Despite the obvious, I was hoping for an equal partnership. It hurts to think we would act any different.

After renewed efforts in brainstorming the Reveal, it took barely a millisecond to determine that Laude would make a far better partner than Hades. Hades is my last resort. We have successfully avoided each other for several days now, and I would like that to continue.

Before showing Laude the note, I have decided to casually ask her thoughts on the Reveal. Maybe she's partial. Maybe I won't need to mention the letters at all. She's sitting across from me, it's just us, and it's perfect timing.

"Laude. Do you think it's worth risking the Reveal, if there's a chance of saving everything?"

Her fingers full of shelled, glistening escargot stop halfway to her mouth. She stares back at me, unblinking. "Why would you ask me that?"

I shrug. "I'm asking everyone."

She resumes the escargot trip to her mouth, "Are you trying to build up some sort of rebellion?"

I flinch at the words. "No, definitely not. In fact, I promised I wouldn't. I just… am asking a few people, I guess." You, and Hades, to be specific.

The escargot squelch into her many-fanged mouth as she speaks, "Logistically, I think a Reveal would be practical. But Poi wants a united front, so we've got to stick to that." Her eyes flick up to mine, surveying.

I ask, "Do you think there might be some way to… convince him?"

She pulls a face, "Highly unlikely."

"Why," I prod, desperate for more information.

"He's considered all the angles. Indirectly, he's been working with humans for… longer than your human brain can wrap itself around. He knows them well."

Poi sits down at the table, and I feel his stare.

She continues, "He's making an educated decision to handle it himself." Her words are sort of harsh, but her tone is completely wan of any judgement or worry as she continues to annihilate snail guts.

"It's possible that he's got it wrong though." I continue to ignore his burning stare from beside Laude.

"Poi gets most things wrong," Hades voice resonates beside me, and I stiffen, as he slips into the bench. He's close, but he doesn't touch me.

"Hades," Kiara cries as she sits down on Poi's other side, "You just like to play devil's advocate."

"Well, I do have that reputation for a reason." His voice is thick with pride.

Laude calls to Kiara flatly, "Why do you set him up like that?"

"Well, he was being an instigator." She shrugs.

Laude sighs, shaking her head.

The dinner continues with their bantering accounts of the day, and Hades doesn't so much as directly address me before he leaves. I breathe easy. Kiara and Laude fall into conversation.

Suddenly, I can sense Poi behind me. He leans over, and his voice croons in my ear, "You're not still mad at me, are you?"

Traitorous shivers spider up my spine. "Yes, I am."

He bites my ear again, "Come up to bed."

My breathing hitches, my I try to keep my voice level, "Hmm, that doesn't sound like an apology."

He kisses my neck, but Laude and Kiara don't seem to notice. His lips make me feel mercurial and wired at once. His voice is low, his breath is warm on my neck, "I'm not going to apologize for Fate's secrets. Can I apologize for anything else?"

I turn and look up at him, and he stays close. I whisper, "I know I'm just a human, and you're technically a god of sorts, but you just made it painfully obvious. It felt like you were rubbing it in."

He sits beside me. "How."

"The way you talked about yourself— as if you were blessed by fate, and I was some unfortunate human meant to be kept in the dark. It was very condescending."

His eyebrows raise minutely, "Aha. Well let's be clear. I am anything but blessed by Fate. Fate has totally banged me around for the last thirty years. And I think of my Guardianship as a duty- as my job. I am sorry I came off as condescending. I don't think I'm any better than you, or anyone else."

His brow is knit in earnest, as if he's confused as to how anyone could actually have the mindset of a pompous asshole. I am struck again by his complete modesty. It's so admirable and hot. I stiff-arm my curiosity at the many mysteries that are "out of bounds" for me here. I drop the accusations and nod, "Okay, thanks for clearing that up."

His gold-flecked gaze scorches me as he gently lifts my hand from my knee, flips it, and presses his lips softly into my palm. His tongue flicks across my lifeline. I take a sharp breath. His voice is tantalizing, "You, are very welcome."

His hand in mine, I sincerely hope my palms don't start sweating with my rapid heartbeat. I am jumping to conclusions as we casually stroll towards the cottage. What does the right moment mean to him? Once again, I wonder why he thinks he has to wait, and it clicks. Fate is his authority. Maybe he's worried that if we have sex, it makes the Queen's absence somehow permanent. Maybe he's still waiting for her. The thought makes me feel out of my league.

"You're quiet." He muses as we start climbing the damp stairwell.

Briny air swirls down and rustles my light hair. I try to let go of all the maybes, and just be in this lucky-as-fuck moment with him. "Just thinking…"

"About?" He prompts, turning.

I shrug, not wanting to keep ruminating, "Obstacles."

His cool palms press against my hipbones as he pushes me against the damp wall. His eyes are burning lanterns reflecting the scant torchlight. "It is high time that I convince you to forget those."

A burst of electricity traces my insides. I reach up to his gorgeous face, cupping his cut jaw, and drawing him down to me, whispering a challenge, "You can try…"

His palms grip my waist as he lifts me to his height, and pins me against the wall. I wrap my arms around his neck, smelling his intangibly sweet musk. His lips softly trace mine. He leans into me and bites my lip. I wrap my legs around his waist, feeling his warmth.

He tenderly kisses my cheek, then pulls me away from the wall. Still holding me around his waist, his rutilated amber eyes are thoughtful as he walks us up the stairwell, and into the sky.

Feathered wings of pulled-apart clouds span across the dome of the atmosphere, catching the bright white light radiating from the west. He pauses, appreciating the sky as well. His olive skin glows in the magnified light. His amber eyes catch and refract more light than the lowering sun. His poetic features are sculpted with something beyond the standards of symmetry and earthly beauty.

High waves roll in quick sets, threatening to overwhelm the tiny island, roughly smacking the rocks and spraying us with their wild dance. Poi doesn't seem to notice. Holding me to his stomach, my arms and legs still wrapped around him, he walks back up to the perilously situated cottage with an expression that tells me he's anything but tired.

He passes the threshold. His expression burns through me, and I am very aware of my legs wrapped around him. My heart rate skitters frantically. He slowly lowers me to the bed, as he places his forearms beside my head, and gazes down at me. Every fiber of me is shivering with a mutinous need for him.

His voice is so ordinary, you wouldn't think my legs were still wrapped around him as we lay in my bed: "How do you feel about me, Stella?"

I freeze. I'm bursting with- I love you. I've loved you for a while now. My second thought is: what is the right thing to say here? What does he want me to say? And the third thought is: I'm not going to guess what he wants to hear, and say that. But, I don't want to scare him away, either. He may still be just passing time, and waiting for his Queen to return. My lungs shrink with the thought.

"Stella?"

My voice is faint, because I want to say the truth, but I water it down. "I've liked you very much, for a while now."

He smirks. "Like, like you like lobster and sunsets? Is that what humans tell each other? What does "like" mean?"

Suddenly, I feel like I'm under an interrogation light, and I don't have my story straight. I try for watered-down honesty again, my words scurrying out fast from between my lips, "It means I like you so much I don't want to scare you away with which words I pick…"

His lips twitch like he's trying to hide a smile, and then he comes in close, his face just inches from mine, he breathes, "You are not going to scare me away."

My heart hurts a little, like it's afraid to get any bigger, or it might pop.

His eyes flick to my lips, and my breathing becomes shallow as he leans in. His lips softly trace mine before a need overcomes him and my lips yield to his rugged desperation. They move against me with a rhythm that radiates to our bodies, as we struggle to get closer- to encompass one another.

"Stella…" He growls, and I, very hesitantly, look up at him. His carved lips are pressed into a line, but he breathes heavily, broad shoulders raising and falling. His eyes are apologetic, and his voice is faint, "Please help me with this, we have to wait."

I breathe, "Why."

He closes his eyes for a moment, forcing slow breaths. He clearly wants to, and I just don't know why he would wait. Except for the Queen. My heart tumbles heavily, and the words slip out, "Are you waiting for your Queen?"

He shakes his head slowly, sighs heavily, "I'll convince you in time, that I'm just waiting for the right moment, for us."

Rolling my eyes, I fix him with my stare, "You. Are maddening. Do you have any idea how much I want this to be the right moment?"

He bites his lip darkly. Then, he smirks, "An inkling…"

I growl and throw a pillow at him, which he catches, and throws to the floor.

"Nice try," he grins, "On all accounts."

Cautiously, as if I might bite, he eases down onto the bed beside me. He slips under the covers, turns me away, and pulls me into him tightly.

I whimper, "You've got to be kidding me."

He leans down to whisper in my ear, "Don't turn around this time." His arms tighten, and he kisses my exposed neck. We lie there as electricity fizzes between us.

# CHAPTER 27

POI

I'm frozen. Her flushed body is in my arms, pressed against me, wanting me. I can feel that she's not really breathing. I bite my lip, inwardly groaning. My mind is full of different ways I could make love to her. If I get up to leave, I might change my mind and kiss her again, and that could turn into lovemaking. Easily…

I have clearly lost my mind. I can't trust myself right now. I force myself to think about the Prophesy. If we have sex before I know that she loves me… she's gone forever. I don't know if she loves me yet. I can't take any chances. I have to be really clear on this. She might think she likes me like she likes lobster, but that's not enough. This version of her has barely had time to get to know me. This is going to take time.

My grip on her loosens. The burning heat of my need begins to relent. I breathe deeply. Her hair smells so sweet… exactly as always. My heart melts. I kiss the top of her head.

"Hey Poi?" Her voice is innocent.

"Yes?"

"Did you ever date anyone after the Queen died?"

"No."

"Oh." Her voice is quiet.

The silence stretches on, and I hope she realizes the significance of us being together. From her human perspective, maybe that will give her confidence. I decide to speak, my heart aches with my whispered words, "I'm serious about you Stella."

She turns around in my arms, and I shift back, so there is space between my chest and hers. This is just too risky. I can't do this again.

Her wide green eyes and heart-shaped face glow with refracted moonlight, "Really?"

I stroke her hair back with my fingers until my hand rests behind her delicate ear. "I don't want to scare you away."

"You won't." Her voice is hushed.

I smile weakly, worried that I might. What I'm asking for is a lot for a human to hear. She barely knows me.

She closes the distance between us, her warm chest pressing against mine. Her fingers lace into my hair and she brings my head towards her. Her pillowy lips push against mine. I shiver with fierce need. I let her push me back, lying on me as she dips her tongue into my mouth.

Fighting my every screaming instinct, I roll her off me. "I have to go—" I breathe.

"Why—" her flushed lips hang open with the question.

She's gorgeous- my gaze runs down her elegant neck, her silk bandeau, to her tight waist, the tiny shorts stretching across her hips. Her light hair is an adorable mess around her head. Her black pupils are dilated, wanting me. I'm sick with need.

I back off the bed, feet hitting the floor.

I can't look at her with this want gripping me. I look around for my cloak and pull it on as I speak, "If I stay, I'll make love to you. And I can't do that."

I fasten the brass buttons on the cloak, and she watches me silently.

I frown, swiftly walk over, hold the back of her head and kiss her on the forehead. "I'll see you in the morning."

"Okay." She whispers.

When my lungs fill with night air, it's not cold enough. And I know one thing: I cannot go into a bedroom with her again- until I'm certain she loves me.

As I quickly pace back to my chambers, the truth slowly dawns on me. I was so close to ruining everything. Ruining her memory forever. And in some mysterious way, ruining the ocean's one true chance of survival.

How can I claim to love her, and yet almost destroy her?

Furious at myself, I break into a run. Each footstep echoes off the stone passageways. Torches flare alive as I approach, and die like candles blown out as I pass. I sprint past my chambers, and I keep running until I reach the deserted front hall. I strip, and leap through into the freezing sea.

The relentless, obsessive need in me is quenched by the sea's frigid embrace. I shift, dragging ice through my gills until my blood cools. I pull my hand through my hair. I swim aimlessly through the dark night. Thick water slips across my skin, reminding me of feeling her, and I wonder how I will stay away. Fate wasn't kidding- this is a real challenge. I'm really going to have to earn her back in Fate's eyes as well.

The night creatures have lifted from the depths, and the sea is full of jellyfish flashing neon green and electric blue. In a bedroom, it's difficult to remember that our decisions impact even these lives. As King Guardian I nearly failed them tonight.

My heart drags. I swim hard to release the guilt of what I nearly committed tonight. Dissatisfied, I shift into a manta ray. This form always calms me. My visual field expands. My fins span to a sheet twenty feet wide, and I glide through the night like a bat. It's a relief to not be in a human or Mer form. I flutter like a leaf as I catch a current, and let the invisible seas take me.

The low-lighting of the spacious lounge, the long window billowing with the movements of the dark sea, and the hanging hammock chairs, are a refreshing contrast to the overcrowded meeting room Stella and I attended all day. She glowed when, as a team, we discussed the coral replanting strategies. I think she's been wanting to help, and with this, finally she has a way. Maybe it will even distract her from her ardent Reveal plotting. But I highly doubt it.

She doesn't have the memory of compiled lifetimes, but I still value her perspective. Her human perspective is surprisingly useful. But I also have an ulterior motive. We were together, but not alone. I've decided she and I need to connect on an intellectual level, rather than physical. With all the distractions of the day, I'm not sure she's surmised my new boundaries yet. I haven't told her I'm not going near her bedroom again. I just hope she doesn't misunderstand.

Now we sit at the high-top round table, reconstructed out of an old mill spool, surrounded by Laude, Kiara, and Hades. Stella grins widely as she gathers clinking coins across the rough table and piles them in two tall rows before her. When we began the game, she marveled at the gold, silver and bronze coins- all shipwrecked hundreds of years ago. Human treasures don't hold much value with us, but they're fun to play poker with.

Hades grumbles as he shuffles the cards. "Verrry lucky. You can't rely on that. I'm coming for those." He eyes the two layers of coins stacked before Stella, who grins proudly.

He's already nearly out of coins- just three more silver coins, and a single gold. Kiara and Laude have just a few more than him. I have about two-thirds of what she has. The game will be down to the two of us. I have to say, I'm impressed that she knows how to play so well. I did not expect that out of the human version of her. I don't know what I'll do with my ego if she beats me.

"Oh, you're screwed," Stella relays to Hades as she beams at her cards, with a terrible (or impressive?) poker face.

I squint at her, trying to discern if she's bluffing. She looks up at me, her bright-ivy eyes twinkling, eyebrows raising with expectation. It's no good. I can't read this version of her.

My cards are rotten- the Queen of Spades and a Three of Hearts. The cards laid down are the Four of Diamonds and the Ace of Hearts. Stella's eyes keep darting to the Ace. I fold.

True to Texas Hold 'Em style, three more cards are dropped in the middle. Everyone shows, and Stella had pocket Aces. No one could beat Trip Aces. She draws in the remains of Hades, Laude and Kiara's coins.

She grins at Hades, and tempts fate by saying, "I guess I can rely on the luck." He chuckles once, and shakes his head, "Guess so."

Her gaze lands on mine, completely taken-over by her competitive nature, and ready for the next kill.

I can't help grinning at her as I shuffle the deck. "You want to share your secret with me?"

She raises an eyebrow as I hand her the cards, and quips, "Only if you share all of yours…"

I smirk, shaking my head, as I read my cards. Ace of Hearts and Two of Clubs. Too late, I realize her comment distracted me, and I totally missed my chance to read her reaction to her own cards.

The Jack and Queen of Hearts are the flop. She purses her lips and bets conservatively, clinking down the high blind of five gold coins.

Ace in hand, and thinking of a royal flush, but hoping to scare her into folding, I bet boldly. I push all my coins forward an inch. "All in."

She raises an eyebrow, and cannot suppress a smirk. Shit. I know that face. She has something good. "Okay, I'll go all in too," she pipes with slathered-on confidence.

Damnit. "Show?" I ask.

She shakes her head, grinning mischievously.

Beside the Jack and Queen of Hearts, I lay down the Jack of Spades, Ten of Hearts, and Three of Clubs. Shit. I have literally nothing. I was distracted. I don't normally play so impulsively.

I show first, and she grimaces unapologetically, eyes twinkling.

"Okay, show already." I growl playfully at her.

She lays down the Jack of Diamonds and the Queen of Spades- she has a Full House. Her gorgeous face is lit up with the joy of conquer.

"Ohhh!!" The others yell.

"Poi was beaten by a human!!" Hades taunts me. I glare at him apathetically.

Stella raises an eyebrow at me, "Bound to happen."

I scoff, voice low, "You know, I actually have a reputation around here… so… that statement is unfounded."

She shrugs, "I have a reputation too. Just not here—until now." Her smile is wide and provocative.

"Aow! Go girl!" Kiara calls.

I mock glare at Stella, who just grins. Playful and eyes alight, her magnetism is amplified with the glory of victory.

Laude starts stacking the coins into their box, silently calling order to the cajoling.

My grin falters, as I realize in a few moments I'll have to draw boundaries with Stella. My heart thuds once, uneasily. I don't know how to do this.

She gazes inquisitively at me, but says nothing. I consider asking to play another round, but I know it would only be more stalling. This has to happen.

We walk through the corridors, her small hand in mine, talking about replanting corals, and poker strategy. Before I'm ready, and with absolutely no time to think, we're on the island, with the warm wind whipping steadily East to West. My legs walk automatically beside hers to the cabin, but when we reach it, I stop.

Momentum causes her arm to tauten against mine, and she spins around with a confused expression.

"I can't go any further." I gaze into her emerald eyes, pleading silently for her to understand, for her not to be hurt by this, and for the boundaries I lay not to drive a wedge between us.

Her eyebrows knit, and her forehead creases. "Why? Because of—"

I nod, willing her to understand. Not wanting to delineate boundaries any more than absolutely necessary.

"Oh." She looks down. Her voice is a whisper, "I'm sorry if… I made you uncomfortable last night… please stay… I won't… do anything." She looks back up at me, looking a bit horrified with herself.

I hold her face towards mine, bringing her dangerously close. "I trust you. It's myself, I don't trust."

She bites her lip. Beneath the wind, her voice is barely audible, "I scared you away—you said I wouldn't do that."

"Oh—" I pull her into a tight hug, kissing the top of her head. My heart plummets. I haven't done this right. "You haven't scared me away. I'm right here." I squeeze her close.

She whispers into my chest, "But you won't come in, will you?"

"No."

She leans back to look up at me. "So I scared you away. I'm sorry. I won't—try to convince you to do anything—I'm sorry." Her voice cracks.

Her pleading makes my heart break. I wish I didn't have to do this. What I want to do, is to make love to her slowly, until all her doubts burn up between us. But I can't do that.

"Stella, I wanted you to do everything you did last night. I wanted more. That's the problem. Please understand. You're just too tempting for me to be in a bedroom with. I need to take it slow."

She whispers up at me, voice almost stolen by the wind, "Okay, so, I didn't freak you out?" A tiny crease is forming between her elegant brows and above her worried eyes.

I gently tuck her wild blonde hair behind her ears. "The opposite. Stella, I wanted to be with you so badly that I nearly caved." My instincts are cajoling me to drop my plan, pick her up, just walk through the doors, and make love to her like we used to. But I continue, "Dating is for me is more than what happens in the bedroom. Let's just take our time."

She raises her eyebrows, eyes widening, "Dating?"

I smirk, "That's what humans call it, isn't it?"

A shocked grin spans across her face, and my chest lightens. Finally, I said something right.

"Uh-huh." She says, still grinning.

I lean down and softly press my lips to her forehead, whispering, "Goodnight, cuddlefish."

Her eyes gaze into mine, "'Night."

I feel her watching me as I climb across the rocks, and force myself to keep walking away from her, and down the stairwell. When I get into the slick, damp corridors, I breathe out. I made it. I'm doing the right thing. My heart feels sore and stretched thin- like I left one end in her room, and I want to rubber-band back to her, but I walk on.

# CHAPTER 28

STELLA

At my bedroom threshold, Poi grasps my shoulders and slowly leans in to kiss my forehead, his voice muted, "Good night, cuddlefish."

The inches between us are chilly, and I gaze up at him through what feels like miles of molecules.

He tucks a stray hair behind my ear, smiling at me gently with tender eyes, "I'll come get you in the morning. We'll go out."

He turns, his black cape billowing in the whipping wind, and disappears across the jagged rocks.

This is how it has been since that night he spent in my bedroom. That was a week ago. His kisses are gentle and distant, his touches are sincere yet brief, and he hasn't crossed the threshold of the cottage since.

I'm not sure why the right moment is so important, but I'm trying to be respectful and go along with it. I sigh deeply, and the gritty brine in the wind circulates my lungs abrasively. I have to refocus.

I pull the yellowed notes out from between the mattress and box-spring, find Laude's note, and replace the other two, hoping I never have to use the one marked with Hades' name. My eyes linger on Laude's simple, scratchy handwriting. I imagine completing the Reveal exactly as the Queen had planned. Guilt seeps into my mind.

For the first time, I let myself fully recognize, that completing the Queen's dying wish, would be going behind Poi's back. It's more than dishonest, it's betrayal. When we first started being together, he said he wanted my "rebellious heart," but I highly doubt that meant: "be backstabbing." I stash the letter away. It can wait.

Long shafts of light pull through the surface, radiating as if through clouds in some heavenly scene. Either it is a very clear day, and blue skies above, or my eyes have begun to adjust to seeing underwater.

Far out, sting rays swim like gulls- their bodies gliding and fluttering in flight as if winged. Laude leads ten Mer towards a current that's warping the crystal waters. As Poi and I near, I hold my breath. It's like a tornado sucking us in. Once we're in, everything blasts by in a blur, but Poi is still pumping his tail.

We arrive on a gritty beach, sand whipping wildly against our skin and eyes as everyone throws on their hooded drenched cloaks. The sun is too bright. Heat undulates and warps the air before us, threatening to char broil us. The sand sears my soles, and I cry out and return to the shallow water as I pull from my pack the flip-flops Poi gave me.

Covered with a wet white cloak which clings to his broad shoulders, Poi winks at me before striding up the beach. Everyone seems to be scampering off with a job to do. I take in the surroundings. A burnt-orange arch reaches out of the endless dunes, and into the sea. I see no humans, no sign of civilization, not even a road sign, and wonder what we're doing in this desolate place.

Above the debris of the high tide mark, waves of heat shroud the gathered Mer. Shovels have seemingly materialized into their hands. Poi, sandy-haired Levi, and a handful of other Mer, dig into the earth quickly, heaps of sand building beside them. My mind swims in the heat and the confusion, and I wish I had asked for a bit more explanation about today's trip.

I near the group as Laude assembles a military-style, desert sand disguise screen. Kiara kneels beside the sand pit as Levi hands her a wad of blankets. Pulling them apart, she reveals a state-of-the-art camera with the longest lens I have ever seen.

I give her an inquisitive look, but she ignores me, screwing it into the tripod behind the screen.

Squinting against the glare, and sweating under her mauve hood, Laude points out towards the horizon. A gray, oxidizing barge lurks about a half mile out from the shore. Her voice is gritty and wheezy with the dry heat, "Someone's been illegally dumping radioactive waste into the ocean. We're going to find out exactly who they are, and make sure they get held accountable."

My eyes bulge. At the Ridge, it's easy to forget how the Mer are so tapped into the human world. I guess they need to be, as humans keep imposing toxic waste on every being in existence. Again, I am hit with a frustrated wave of guilt for being human. I grit my teeth and watch the Mer's scrappy attempts at holding the line.

Kiara is adjusting the lens, tweaking her hands minutely, if she's done this a thousand times. Maybe she has, but it's strange to see her so well-versed with human technology. With an eye attached to the camera, she explains with a slack jaw, "We're anonymously sending this video to the UN. We have to move fast, obviously."

I swallow without saliva, my voice scratches, "The UN? Where are we?" I glance around, wondering if maybe it's Africa, with all the dunes.

"Western Sahara." Poi says distractedly, while squatting over something that looks like a radio transmitter, and tinkering. "I wouldn't take you to Somalia, where the toxic dumping is really outrageous. Despite the considerable impact of this waste, the actual dumping is fairly small-scale. We should be able to take care of it. Okay we have signal." He stands and glances at Kiara.

"Great, hang on a sec…damn. The sand is killing me here." She covers the camera with her cape, and her voice comes out from under it in a hush, "There we go… okay, I see two of the guys… gotcha." Her camera shutters like a sprinkler on a hot day. "Okay, shhh, I'm taking video now…"

Kiara is glued to the long lens, Poi is staring like an overbearing parent at the blinking red dot on the transmitter, and through the blind holes, I watch the steely gray ship. The heat is melting me, but I'm not sweating. I wonder how quickly someone can die from dehydration out here. Best guess is three hours. I'm already looking at the water with desperation, and wondering how the Mer are surviving this dry heat.

The camera clicks, and Kiara shifts, her voice raspy, "Poi, did that go out?"

He's is already packing up the transmitter. "Yeah."

Beneath her cloak, Kiara struggles with the case, and emerges with the camera already protected against the whipping sands.

Levi grabs the camera and transmitter, storing them back in the sands. Laude deftly compacts the screen. Within a matter of seconds, all the supplies are beneath seamless sands. I walk between Poi and Laude as they stride down the scorching beach. "What's going to happen to the cameras?" I ask.

"Another pick-up, later." Laude expounds quickly, her voice cracking.

The heat is so thick that there's barely any air. The sands merge with sea, and with huge relief, I plunge into the shallow, dissatisfying, lukewarm water. Resurfacing quickly, I watch the Mer pulling off cloaks and gear and storing them in packs. Pulling off my flip-flops and storing them in my pack, I watch the offending barge with concern, realizing something disturbing. I place a hand on Poi's thick shoulder, nodding at the ship "Aren't you worried they might see us? Don't they have guns?"

He laces his long fingers in mine, and gently pulls me into the deeper waters, his voice calm, "Yes, they have guns. But they have no reason to suspect us of anything. And they aren't expecting to see anyone on this deserted beach with no roads, and no boats pulled up to the shore. Their eyes are on the water."

This settles my fears only a little, as the water is where we're headed. I hope he meant their eyes are on the horizon. I glance at the hulking ship one more time, and we submerge.

The waters chill quickly as Poi dives us deep, following the group led by Laude. They flit ahead like colorful minnows. They drop below us, and we hover above a second desert, with dunes raising up like hills, patterned in diamonds by the currents.

The barge grinds a metallic groan, clicks keening high notes, and chugs as if struggling to stay afloat. It hovers fifty feet above us. Laude and the ten other Mer emerge below us, tails flicking madly against the weight of a school-bus sized bundle of net. A cloud of silt-like sand sifts from the net as the Mer lift it upwards. Poi squeezes me gently around the waist, pecks my ear, and joins them. Muscles straining and midnight tail kicking vigorously, he hoists up a sagging end of the ropes. They charge upwards, to the rectangle shadow above. I watch through the clear waters, swimming upwards, frog-like. They reach the massive hull, which is like a dense storm cloud. They rig the ropes up to the boat, with massive magnets until the netting hangs like a hammock.

Warped voices shout above, and the twisted blue sky swirls like gasoline in the bright sun. A red barrel crashes through empty sky, falling slowly into the sea, liquids in tendrils pull upward as noxious waste seeps out. Fear jolts me like lightning. I hold my arms out impulsively, and before I really fully realize what I'm doing, my fingers are forming a triangle. Perplexed, I stare at my hands, wondering why I would have done that. Each of the Mer are doing the same- only they have light glowing out from their palms, stretching out and surrounding their bodies in orbs of protective green. Another two barrels fall. Heart thudding, I drop my hands as I stare at the brown sludge waste pooling out into the pristine teal sea. Poi's hands direct bright orbs of light like lightning bolts to each of the twenty barrels as they fall, attaching to the holes, plugging them, and keeping the rest of the sludge from leaking into the sea.

Green light twinkles around me like a web, then fills the spaces and surrounds me like a bubble. Immediately I look to my hands, but only light pink skin flexes before me. I don't know what I was thinking. I realize Poi must be behind me again, spreading his shield towards me.

I turn, and it is his shield. He's holding his hands up the same way I had. His dark eyes wide, delicate nostrils flaring, his brow deeply furrowed- his expression is urgently fearful. Electricity spiking my blood, I spin again, on guard. I expect to see a barrel emptying into space, but the Mer are already transferring each barrel into the gargantuan hammock. I turn back to him. His expression is still horrified. He's appraising me like I've suddenly grown a second head.

I shrug my shoulders and give him a "what" look.

He shakes his head slowly, blinks, and reaches a hand out to my jaw, and gently pulls me closer to him through the waters, his stomach undulating slowly with the muscles in his tail. His dark hair floats lazily around his worried face as his eyes meet mine like he's looking for something. I squint at him, unsure of his mood. I appreciate his romantic nature, but I'm thinking now is not the time. He draws away with a suspicious expression.

I jerk my thumb towards the boat, and he nods solemnly.

We burst back into air, splashing water all over the slippery black rock of the entrance hall. Mer are all around, chattering loudly and recounting the endeavor as they shake off water and slip on cloaks.

Poi messes my wet hair, "So that was strange- why'd you do that?" He sounds casual, but there's an undercurrent like he's interrogating me.

"You mean- this?" I hold out my hands like I had before- fingers forming a triangle.

His head tilts back, surveying me over his high cheekbones as his eyes tighten, "Yes."

"I don't know…" I confess, "I was scared of the nuclear waste, and then I was just doing it. It was really strange!" I think back to the moment. For an instant, it was like I thought I could do magic.

He presses his long fingers against his burgundy lips, and crosses his other arm against his chest. Towering over me, his dark-lashed eyes squint, assessing my sanity. "How are you feeling?"

Furrowing my brow, I take a minute. "Normal, I think. I hope I'm not going crazy from being underwater for so long."

He subtly shakes his head, and steps closer, "You're not going crazy." He looks down at me with a serious gaze. His cool fingertips trace up my jawline and rest behind my ears. I shiver. He looks at me a long time, and then quietly says, "Come on, let's head to the springs."

White steam rises up from the black waters, like swirling ghosts against the black grotto walls.

Toes first, I slip into the enveloping warmth. I sit on the ledge beside Laude. The water nearly kisses my chin. Poi's hairy legs pierce the water as he sits beside me. The water agitates violently, and I suspect that below the midnight water, he's shifted. My impulse is to reach out and touch his thigh, or tail, but I don't. It's strange that I've touched practically all of him, but never his tail. Suddenly, I realize I really want to.

He winds an arm over my shoulders, pulling me against him with more intimacy than I have felt in a week. It surprises me, but then I realize we're sitting in the pool with Laude, and now Kiara and Levi too, so he feels safe. Boldly, I stretch a hand through the waters towards where his thigh would be, and tentatively rest my palm on his tail. It's like touching a fish: silken yet rough, with tight muscles beneath. His gaze jerks to mine. His dark amber eyes are alarmed.

"Sorry," I whisper, removing my hand, "I was curious…"

He raises an eyebrow, humorously. He rumbles, "It's fine." His left hand finds mine beneath the water, and he places my palm back on his scaled thigh again.

"Does it feel different?" I whisper, intensely curious.

His sculpted lips twist into a discreet smile as he inclines his head towards me, "It's like having calloused hands."

I nod, feeling the strange silken leather of his tail under my palm.

"I'm surprised the magnets held all that weight." Laude is saying to Levi.

"Well, they didn't." Levi is smirking mischievously. His sandy blonde hair is tousled, nearly reaching his deep sapphire eyes. Inky tentacles wrap around his forearms, biceps and muscled chest. He's sitting beside Kiara, who's biting her lip and looking uncharacteristically nervous. I remember her eyes darting to him the night we spent in the bar, and I'm rooting for her.

Levi continues on, "A few anchoring hooks may have been set into holes previously drilled into the barge…"

Laude is affronted, "That's not safe. The whole thing could have sunken, and the waste would have been everywhere."

His fingers emerge from the pool as he gestures for her to relax. He speaks as if he's bored, "I made sure it was above their water mark, the ship made it back didn't it? And I'm sure it will be possessed by the Italian government, considering the mobsters were arrested."

Laude's tiny pale lips twist in disapproval.

I think about the twenty barrels of waste returned to the mobsters, and wonder what would have happened if they leeched into the ocean instead.

Poi's tanned hand hovers above the water, and swirls the surface up without touching it. The water raises like a small silken fountain, defying gravity. My lips part in shock. Sometimes I forget who he is, how he is actually the God of the Sea.

His dark hair is twisting and becoming wavy with the steam, he's so delicious to look at that it's entirely distracting. With his one arm around me, and his silken skin and tight muscles against me, I sincerely wish it was just us in the pools. But considering it isn't, I ask a question. "Hey, so, I know nuclear waste is bad, but what would have happened if you didn't stop that dumping?"

He sighs slowly, dropping his palm through the surface and shattering his miniature fountain. He watches the lamplight reflections stretching across the black water. He looks down at me, only inches away, as I am nestled against his shoulder. His smile is grim, "I almost don't want to tell you. I know it will only reignite your Reveal efforts…"

I patiently wait, cradled against him and looking up into his insanely gorgeous face. I don't mind waiting like this.

His lips twitch into a crooked smile, "Fine." Tucked beneath his arm, his fingers drum my ribcage, "You can't look at me like that. It's not playing fair."

I keep looking, "Like what?"

He smirks, and looks back at the water. Then he sighs, and his voice rumbles, "Effects of nuclear waste in the ocean are inescapable due to Fukushima, which dwarfs your Chernobyl. So that trip, although important to the immediate environment, was on scale, very insignificant."

"So what are the effects?" I prod.

Chin lifted, throat exposed, his Adam's apple bulges at his black stubble. The planes of his sculpted shoulders and chest are slick with steam and sweat. He stares at the ceiling as if he's being cornered into speaking, and isn't wanting to, but he does: "After Fukushima, fifty thousand Mer died due to radiation exposure." He looks at me seriously, "Much of the vegetation died, along with all breathing creatures. Outside of the highest radiation dead-zone, we saw sea life with some very strange birth defects. Creatures with smaller brains, shrunken to skeletal size, with deformed air sacks and appendages. The fine pattern of genetic creation was scrambled into a meaningless drivel. The deformed creatures didn't survive for long, of course. Shortly afterwards, the West Pacific Mer started developing cancers. The Mer had never before experienced cancer. Finally, the currents have stirred the unprecedented levels of radiation into the entire ocean. Undeniably, it's in the food we eat. But in lesser doses."

I search his face, stunned.

He's looking back out at the undulating white steam, and his voice is eerily even, as if he is talking about the weather, "Humans are fully aware of the damage, of course."

I don't know how he's holding it together. The burden of the ocean's fate rests on him, Poseidon, and he isn't appearing to panic. I don't know whether to feel awe at his collectedness, to hug the hidden parts of him that are surely terrified, or to shake him into waking up.

Once again, his addendum statement in attempt to discourage me has failed. This knowledge just adds more urgency to my campaign. At the very least, humans have to care about their food supply becoming radioactive, right?

There has to be some way to convince Poi of a Reveal. I just need to be extremely tactful. I look to Laude, the queen of tact. The ghostly pale, centuries old Mer, stares into the swirling mist with scarlet eyes. In this silent, heavy moment, filled with steam and unspoken fear, I decide to ask Laude to honor the dead Queen's final wish.

# CHAPTER 29

STELLA

The wind whips tendrils of my hair into my face, and lifts my skirt dangerously. Waves gulp and pop against the darkened rocks. The light has left the atmosphere, and the brightest stars are appearing in the deep sapphire sky.

Poi's hood rests upon his tousled dark hair as he gazes down at me. I realize he's not walking any further. My heart twists. His dark amber eyes reflect in the twilight. His palms gently grasp my upper arms. He leans in, and his intangibly sweet musk wafts towards me as his lips touch my forehead. My heartbeat is ragged, and I want so badly for him to stay.

He pulls back and stares into my eyes for long moment before whispering, "Good night, Stella." He turns down the pathway to the Ridge, his black cloak billowing behind him.

He disappears amongst the disarray of shadowy rocks, and I replay, once again, him on the doorstep, looking into my eyes, and kissing my forehead. I sigh into the empty air.

I turn in the doorframe and walk into the cottage. Guiltily, I wonder how long it will take him to go back to his quarters. I kneel beside the bed. Up to my armpit,

I separate the mattress and box spring. Finding Laude's letter, I stash it in the inner pocket of my emerald cloak.

Once night has truly fallen, and the sky shines with the scraps of diamonds, I return to the halls of the Ridge. Earlier today, I discreetly asked Kiara the location of Laude's quarters. I wind down many staircases to the sea-level floor, feeling a slight discomfort in my lungs and heart beat which compounds with my nerves. I look for the most undecorated, bare door frame which is in stark contrast to those adorned with eye-popping shell collections. The ebony doorframe is entirely unmarked. I knock with confidence I don't feel.

She swings open the door, and her small mouth drops open in surprise, revealing her set of razor-sharp teeth. I suppress an instinctual shiver. "Hey Laude… do you have a second?"

Her eyes narrow with suspicion. "Sure. I have a minute or two."

I walk into the room, and she slowly closes the door.

The room is small, the bed low to the ground and neatly made. The walls are sparsely decorated with ancient spears and weapons. I could never sleep in this room.

"So?" Her voice is sharp, defensive.

I turn. I decide to skip all pretenses. "I found this."

Gripping the note so hard it crinkles, I hand it to her.

She swipes it from my fingers quickly, extracting and unfolds the traitorous yellowed note.

Her protuberant eyes bulge impossibly wide. She regards it like it's dusted with arsenic. "How did you find this?" She whispers, her eyes flicking to mine with a hue of fear.

I shrug, not wanting to relinquish the useful hiding spot.

She stares at me closely, as if calculating. She blinks once, delicate pale brows crammed together, and speaks without her usual composure. "This is seriously dangerous for me Stella. Poi, he keeps it together, but he is still not over the death of his Queen. And if he links me to it in any way… I don't know what he'd do, but I bet it would include dry land." Then she swallows, and adds, "I did it for the Queen, but I wasn't in any way involved with her death. That was a complete accident."

It's hard for me to believe this, considering the Mer's resistance to Reveal. But I tread carefully. "How do you know it was an accident?"

She rubs her pale forehead. "The Queen was very beloved. And, it was clear that her death was caused by humans. I really shouldn't tell you more, Poi will be infuriated enough when he finds out what you know."

"Right." I look at my feet. I had wanted to let go of the Queen, for Poi's sake. Bringing her up really upsets him. I'm sure there's an impossible amount of pain and fear broiling around inside him. But I want to help, and the Queen's plan is an unavoidable part of that equation.

After seeing his eerily composed demeanor this evening, when he explained how incalculable amounts radioactive waste are poisoning the food supply… I just can't let him keep ignoring all of it. It's too much for him to handle on his own, and he needs help.

I ground my stance, and hold her unsettling blood-red stare. "Look." I cobble together my swirling thoughts and emotions, "Poi was telling me about Fukushima today. When he was explaining radioactive waste being stirred into the ocean, killing off life, and deforming what remained… his face was… detached. Almost like he's keeping all these human-imposed threats in separate, clean containers, and not recognizing the accumulating apocalypse."

Her arms are folded over her slender, tall frame. Her scarlet gaze is hard, unreadable.

I continue, "There was a point where he could handle it on his own, and we've passed it. He won't ask for help. But we need to guide him to that point. I can't watch him go through all this alone, only to fail."

Her fingers tap against her crossed arms. Her eyes dart around the room, as if following a trapped bird. She breathes in as she shakes her head, "I can't, Stella. I hear your point, but I can't go behind his back now, when he's already weakened and stretched-thin."

I deflate. "Exactly, he's exhausted, and…" I whisper torturously, "I wonder if he's even making a dent into the human catastrophe."

She shakes her head again and stiffly backs up, "We just have to trust him…"

Her words strike me as an insult. I do trust him. I don't want to go behind his back when he's weak. But he doesn't know best! He's scared and frozen. Wishing Laude would just understand this, anger builds in my chest like a hornet's nest. "He's not thinking clearly!! Don't you see that? He's scared!"

She glares at me, and her bared teeth make the hair raise on my neck, "Don't you think we're all scared? Humans are destructive and careless and will have our deaths on their hands. Even if they knew we existed, they wouldn't think twice. Do you know how many species they've killed off already? People are calling it the sixth extinction. Poi is mitigating a future that is unavoidable."

I glare at her, affronted. She's right about humans, but she's not leaving any breathing room for optimism. She's so incredibly closed that I can't imagine what the Queen could have said to her nearly thirty years ago.

I back towards the door, and she watches me with the note gripped tightly between her hands. The room is chilly and silent. My voice sounds stronger than my own, "You're wrong."

She shakes her head stiffly, arms still crossed. Her tight lips whisper, "I wish I were."

The last few weeks, Poi has met me at the cottage every morning, bringing breakfast before he scampers off to cover his responsibilities. He often asks me to come along, and despite my being human, he listens to my opinions and often asks for my advice before I can offer it. I am absolutely swooning over him.

We chat in the early morning chilly air as we look out at the sunrise. We're finding a flow, and with difficulty, I've accepted the physical distance he keeps. Now that I'm nearly accustomed to the insane magnetism between us, it's actually easier to talk to him. I can appreciate that he's really trying to get to know me, for me. And it makes me like him more, because he truly is interested in my mind, and all of me, which is what I really wanted all along.

We've talked about my grandmother's obsession with St. Patrick's Day, what I saw when I looked at the single picture of my parents, my favorite novels, and how teaching dance to five year olds is a contagious sugar high. He's told me about the compressed dark silence of the Mariana Trench, how he loved living in the Caribbean coral reefs when they were still bursting with life, how much he loves the fruit smoothies in Thailand, his surfing expeditions on one hundred foot waves off the coast of Hawaii, and how his most violent death was at the jaws of a swarm of belligerently angry hammerhead sharks. He has endless stories, and I want to hear all of them.

I lean back against him, looking out at the tangerine hues bursting through gray. He's warm against my back, his slow deep breaths are calming. His arms wrap lazily around my knees, and his chin rests on my head.

It feels perfect. I don't even feel the need to talk. We just quietly stare out together, watching the waves wake up, and begin to pitch against the shore below.

But thoughts bark at me like an unruly neighbor's dog, disrupting the perfection of this moment. And I'm so mad at myself for not being able to just block it all out. I just want to be here. I just want to be seeing the sunrise catch fire, in the arms of this amazing, kind, wise, sexy… god. What is wrong with me? Why can't I just see the beauty, feel it, and be in it?

My perfect moment caves to the incessant fears that cling to me like lice. I can't look at the beauty without knowing how incredibly delicate it is. I see the cocktail of radioactive waste, toxic debris, and hot acidity that it is. I know the graveyard of corals that span below this surface, I know the lonely empty spaces where there should be life. And I wonder how anyone can block all this out.

I know Poi isn't blocking it out. He's fighting it with a steadfast ardor that just tears me apart. I admire his commitment, but I just am so at a loss as to how to convince him to get help. I sigh without making a sound.

He kisses the top of my head. "What's up."

I feel deflated. I have no new way to talk to him about the Reveal, and I don't want to ruin this moment with it. I rake through the dark recesses of my mind for something else to ask him. Remembering our conversation in the library, ages ago, I ask him, "So you told me that you reincarnate eternally. But what happens if this Earth is in such rough shape that no more life can survive? What happens to you?"

I realize how dark this is after I say it. It's not far at all from the nagging thoughts I was trying to avoid.

He clicks his tongue with surprise, and is quiet a moment. I feel his sigh string out like his slow pulse. After a while, I think he's not going to answer. When he speaks, his voice is a contemplative murmur, "I've thought about that. I think I would become a formless specter, waiting for life to return."

His words span out towards the horizon as I mull them over with horror.

He calmly muses about his death-like limbo, "If life as we know it does end on this Earth, if human societies crumble and take all other life with them, it might take a long time for life to return. I don't think it would look anything like it has… but it will return in some form, and I will tend to it then."

The sun is peeling up past the darkness, and pouring golden light over the waters, creating a molten path straight towards us. It's so bright it's hard to look at. The clouds are flaming pink like valentine hearts, taunting us with a joy that I cannot feel.

Sadness grips at my every rib, tugging them inwards, impaling my lungs. "I can't let you become a ghost." Closing my eyes, I lean my head against his arm, and silent tears fall. I rasp, "This is all wrong."

He pulls me tighter, and he hums deep in his chest, which rumbles through my spine. But he doesn't say anything, because maybe there is nothing to say. Maybe it is all wrong.

Poi is doing everything he can to save the seas and all the life within them, but I recognize with fresh anguish, that some part of him has accepted the fate of becoming a time-biding ghost. I cannot let him turn to dust. With fumbling fingers and sweaty hands, I grip Hades' note tight like a shield. My legs move as if I'm trying to run, but are on a slow-motion tape.

Like waiting on death's row, I sit on the pale driftwood benches of the dining hall. My heart whines with fear of what Poi might do if I completed the Reveal without him. He might leave me. But I focus every fiber of my being. I love the fact that he exists more than it's fair to need him in my short, human life.

The moments drag, and I think of the Queen's plans. The documentary will be first. I will ask Hades to be the star. It might take some convincing, but there's no way he wouldn't be a natural on-screen.

Hades strolls into the brightly-lit aqua hall, and it's easy to picture him in a Hollywood film. His lithe demeanor makes for possibly the most confident stroll I have ever known. Our eyes meet, and my gut clenches. I've avoided him since his lie, and cruel assessment of my remaining lifespan.

He skips the line and saunters over. I'm gritting my teeth, scrambling to think of any way that Poi wouldn't be mad at me for doing a Reveal without his permission. I can't think of any. But I keep picturing Poi's ghost, and I can't live with it haunting me.

Hades beams effusively at me as he approaches. He doesn't sit, he just puts a leg up on the bench across from me and cocks his head, "Is this real? I'm not invisible?"

I press my lips together, "May I remind you that you were the one who heartlessly calculated my life expectancy?" I don't mention the other part. I'm still too angry.

He raises a brow, "It doesn't have to be that way. I gave you an alternative."

I inwardly groan. I don't want to do this again. "Look, I'm sorry things got weird between us, but I need a favor."

He smirks, "Go on…"

I look around the hall, with its bustling lunch crowd. I gaze back at him in his ostentatious Captain Morgan's pose, "I was actually hoping we could be discreet."

His eyes flash. "This favor just got more interesting." He glances around the crowded hall with regal countenance, "May I suggest the armory? No one will be in there now."

The armory is dim, the lanterns extinguished, light filtering from the far, sea-facing wall. The hundreds of long spears and knives lining the walls are more disturbing in the darkness- setting the spooky ambiance of a haunted house. White chalk lines are traced along the floor, as if to practice sports plays.

He locks the door with a clang of the long metal bar. His pale eyes seem to glow in the shadows. "So, my little sneak, why are we here?"

Nerves rope around me, I still don't know if this is the right thing to do, but I can't do nothing. My voice sounds out of tune, "I think I want to do the Reveal without Poi."

His walk towards me stumbles as he raises his eyebrows, "Really?"

Guilt crowds against me, but I can't handle the idea of Poi turning to dust. Or of giving up on the world. It feels like the same thing. "Yeah."

Hades crosses his arms and leans a forefinger against his chin. "So what's your plan?"

I slip the letter into my cloak, deciding not to drop so low as to use blackmail. My bare toes scuff a chalk line as I talk, "I was thinking of going forward with a video…" I look up at his bemused expression, "I'd need your help. It's pretty damn traitorous, I understand if you don't want to do it to your brother."

As if deciding, Hades is so still I can't see him breathing. His crystalline stare could force me back a few steps. His voice is grave, "I'd do it for you."

I pause a beat. "You should know I'm doing this for Poi."

He blinks and looks away. He gazes back at me and takes one step to close the distance between us. "Look. Stella. I know you think Poi is better for you, but... I understand you, and I'm not asking you to change your views on anything. You won't have to change for me." His expression shrinks the air between us.

My lips purse, "I'm not changing."

His head tilts, "But you're going behind his back. If you chose me, you wouldn't have to hide part of yourself."

His words sink through me like stones. Hiding is no better than changing. Hiding is the first stage of cutting away a part of myself. I breathe in, unsure of what to say.

He takes a step closer, so that he's just an arm's length away. He stares down at me seriously, deep voice knowing, "You don't hide with me."

My breathing falters. He's right. And it's wrong. I should be this open with Poi. I should keep trying to convince him in the open- not go behind his back. Even if it's to save him- Poi deserves my honesty.

Hades searches my face, lips tightening. His eyes hold mine like a fortune teller, "It's the Reveal now, but what is it later...? You'll just keep hiding if you stay with him. You won't want to, but- you'll change."

I breathe in unsteadily. This is not what I wanted to hear. But it's true. And I can't allow it. I have to come clean. I have to give us a chance to be whole together.

"It doesn't have to be so complicated Stella." He reaches out and pulls a hand through my loose hair, traces down the back of my arm, and holds my hand. There is so much want in his eyes that it breaks my heart.

I have to make him stop trying. I have to tell him the truth, too. My voice comes out breathy, "I'm in love with Poi."

His expression contorts with pain. He steps back, drops his hand from mine, and disappears. Into thin air. Like a television screen shutting off- he is totally gone.

My eyes bulge. I swing my arms through the air where he was and feel nothing. "WHAT?!" I frantically gaze around the room, seeing nothing but dusty spears set into shelves against the shadowy walls. Hades is gone. Apparently, some Greek Mythology was spot-on. I only wish I was warned of Hades' actual ability to become invisible.

"Hades, come back! I didn't mean to hurt your feelings! I just didn't want you to hope-"

The door latch lifts, the door swings open, and slams shut.

Heart wrenched, I stare at the door, haunted by the last glimpse of Hades' tortured expression. But his words haunt me more, clawing at me viciously. I begin pacing. The darkening room weighs in on me, as if shadows could be measured in pounds.

Everything he said was right. I'm hiding from Poi, which is no better than changing for him. How can we have a healthy connection if I'm not showing him all of me? And I won't give up on myself.

I'm not giving up on saving Poi from becoming a stupid ghost, or the world from crumbling beneath humanity's refuse, but I'm going to need to find an honest way to do it. A way that doesn't require first backpacking across the treacherous lands of betrayal.

I grit my teeth. I don't know how to do that. I don't have a plan for that. I will just have to tell Poi how I feel- and really lay down all my cards. I've done that time and time again, but if I tell him I was thinking of betrayal, maybe he'll understand how serious I am. Maybe he'll see how I need some sort of compromise, because I can't stand around in these damp halls and do nothing for the world.

# CHAPTER 30

STELLA

Hall windows reveal pitch black sea, but I don't want to wait until tomorrow. Hades held a light up to reveal my shadows. I'm done hiding. I have to come clean with Poi. I'll scrap my plan for something we build together.

Placing my hand against the silken robes, I nervously check my pocket. I've replaced Hades' letter for Adrian's. The thick paper crinkles behind the silk.

My heart hitches before the scalloped engravings on Poi's mahogany door. I've never been in his room before. Seconds after knocking, the door opens. The light is on above his desk, a book with a shiny new binding lying on the clean surface. A crowded bookshelf squats beside it. The four-poster mahogany bed dominates the room, covered in red satin. Two large wardrobes stand side-by-side on the left wall. A black woven rug spans the floor, and a skylight dome stretches above the room like a bubble.

Poi's face shifts to worry as he sees me, "Are you okay? Is something wrong?"

I squint as I think about the proper answer. "Yes, I'm fine. But we need to talk."

His expression softens to concern. "Okay, just hold on a moment." He gestures for me to wait at the door, as he shuts off his lamp, closes the door, and joins me in the hall. "Can we talk in the library?"

"Sure." I hold back a smirk. If he thinks that place is less tempting than his bedroom, he's forgetting that's where we shared our first kiss. But he has nothing to worry about— I doubt he'll feel like kissing me after I fess up to what I had been planning.

Foreboding weight drops in me like an anchor. I'll feel better once I come clean. He said he expected me to keep trying to convince him. But I don't think he expected me to be so sneaky, to hide my plans, and work my way towards betraying his trust and his rule…

Compiling with that, he did ask for me to leave the Queen's history alone. Bringing her into it feels low—a reminder of his pain, who he has lost, and it's weird talking about such a daunting "ex."

We approach, and the black stone library fireplace roars alive with blue flames licking upwards, then dies down to a calming low crackle. I notice the thick species population ledgers stacked into deeply carved shelves. My mind flickers with anger, thinking of the human-caused, spiraling sixth mass extinction. My drive is cemented.

He gestures for me to sit in a lime green armchair beside the fire, and drops into its pair beside me. His knees span far past the seat's cushion, and he leans an elbow onto the armrest, facing me.

His hand drops down to find mine. Poi's thumb slowly rubs the back of my hand. Guilt erupts in me, at what I have been hiding, how I have been planning to betray his trust.

My eyes trail up to his.

His knowing eyes are soft, and his lips pull down into a lop-sided pity frown. He sighs. "I think I know what this is about."

I raise my eyebrows, highly doubting it. My voice is tight, "Maybe… it's about the Reveal." Nerves spike in my gut.

He blinks, as if that wasn't what he expected me to say. "Okay…" His voice is guarded. He pulls back his hand as he straightens his back, rests his forearms across the armrests, and laces his fingers together. He regards me stiffly.

My heart starts galloping wildly in my chest. Do I really have to be totally honest? Could I just say part of the truth? I think of Hades words: You don't hide with me.

"I was planning a Reveal without you."

Poi's eyebrows twitch together, a deep line forming between them. His deep voice drags, "How…?"

My heart ricochets violently in my chest. All my muscles are tight with anticipation. Please understand, I silently beg his tight eyes. Then I decide to preface my response, to cushion the truth with why I did it. "Well, first, let me just say, the way I heard you talking about becoming a…" the words yank from me, "roaming ghost… it tortured me. I can't allow it to happen. I just can't let you give up…" Heat surges behind my eyes.

Leather groans as he leans forward and grasps my hands in his, catching me with his fervent gaze, "I haven't given up. We're still fighting."

My heart wrenches, "But you expect to lose."

He keeps staring at me, and I know I've spoken the truth.

"I can't let us lose everything. I can't let you become a lonely speck of nothing. That isn't okay with me, Poi." Angry tears threaten hot at the corners of my eyes.

He tightens his hands around mine, maintaining his ardent gaze as he listens.

"I don't agree with your vision because it doesn't have a happy ending. I know we can do this, Poi."

His gaze is pained, and pitying. The pity kicks my rebellious heart awake.

I glare at him, "The Queen wanted to do a Reveal too, did you know that? Maybe it's not such a bad idea after all."

His eyes widen to saucers and he impulsively leans back. Low blow… I shouldn't have said it that way…

His eyes search mine with a fervor, his voice is urgent, "How did you know that?"

I breathe uneasily, "I found her letters."

His eyes roam quickly across me, "What letters?" There is an edge of panic in his voice.

I breathe in slowly, trying to calm the situation. "She wrote letters… setting up meetings with world leaders, and an independent film crew, to Reveal the existence of the Mer to humanity—to ask them to take responsibility for their actions."

He looks at me as if he's being impaled by an airplane. He shoots up to stand, breathing heavily, dragging a hand through his dark wavy hair, and looking around the room without seeing. I stay perched, unsure of how to react, but certain this was not the reaction I was expecting from him.

Jaw clenching, he towers dangerously before me. His voice is rushed, "Do you have the letters?"

My mind goes to my pocket. "One."

He inclines his head, polite even at this time. "May I see it?"

"Yes." I pull the long envelope out of my cloak pocket, and hand it to him uncertainly, suddenly feeling like I'm in the middle of crossfire, and I don't want my leg to get blown off by a mine.

He strides two paces away, and faces me again. He quickly unfolds the yellowed letter, holding the envelope between his knuckles as his eyes scan the lines quickly. As he reads, he inclines his head as if farsighted, brows contracting and eyes bulging with horror. His eyes stop, and he slowly leans away from the page. His eyes find mine, and he stares in rancid disbelief, as if I've turned into his dead Queen. Like it's my fault that she betrayed him so thoroughly.

My chest pangs. I hate that she did this to him. I hate that I almost did.

"And you were going to go through with this? Follow her plans?" His voice is both hostile and disbelieving.

Suddenly I don't like how this is going... I don't like that I'm somehow this complicit in her guilt... I push up from the seat with shaking arms, and cross the distance between us, barely breathing, heartbeat rapid.

His eyes tighten as I approach, he takes a step back, and my gut drops. His voice is nearly a growl, "Answer..."

My eyebrows twitch together and my blood zips through too-tight veins, "Yes, I was—"

His face hardens at my confirmation, and he lowers the letter to his side.

"—but I changed my mind. I know it was wrong to even think about going behind your back—I just didn't want you to lose everything."

His amber gaze is searing, "What does it matter if there is no trust?"

His caustic words singe the air from my lungs.

His almond eyes take me in as if for the first time. Panicking, I study the lines of his face—the way his black wavy hair brushes just above his brow, the slight arch to his brows, his high cheekbones, his straight nose with tightly curled nostrils, his carved burgundy lips and square chin, his cut jawline, and his pained amber eyes that won't let me in.

Something between us is breaking. I can feel it. Panic like a high-pitched tea kettle screams in my mind. My voice shakes, "I came forward, Poi. I'm not breaking your trust."

His eyes twinge with pain, and his lips tighten. His voice is final, "You already have."

Agony twists in me, I'm spinning with fear. "This can't be happening—"

He shakes his head, eyes me like I killed someone, and backs away towards the door.

Horror thumps against me like a wall. My heart restarts. I run to close the distance between us, grasping his arm. "Please, Poi, this is crazy. I didn't actually do anything."

His gaze is hard, "Yet."

Trust is a thing between us that has broken. I let him go. The door clicks closed behind him. I back up, as if able to get further from the horror that just transpired. The empty space of the room swallows me whole.

I'm sucking in air faster than it can take hold. Did Poi really just leave me? I grip a desk for balance, heart thudding at a scary rate. I try breathing slower. Looking around at the audience of inanimate objects, I murmur, "This can't be real."

My palms press harder against the wood, as if trying to keep reality from crushing me. He's just mad. He's just hurt at what his Queen did. I did nothing compared to her. He has to forgive me.

My heart is skittering unpredictably, as if I'm on the edge of a cliff, afraid to look down, afraid to move, afraid to fall, and one wrong heartbeat could jerk me off balance.

This doesn't make sense. He can't leave me for just considering betrayal, can he? Guilt and dizziness wash over me as if I'm looking at the world from too high up. I swallow, and try to get my bearings.

Poi never knew about the Queen's treacherous plans. He lost trust with his soul mate. He must feel like everything they had was a lie. I feel like a complete idiot for not seeing how her letter would tear him apart. I am horrified with myself for considering the same route of action. My only saving grace is that I didn't act. I can only hope that he eventually stops blaming me for what she did.

Thoughts wrap around me, constricting me like a snake. I can't stay here, but I can't go back to my room. I want someone to tell me I'm not crazy. I want someone to tell me that Poi will eventually forgive me, and that he's just mad at his Queen.

Shaking like it's too cold, I stand up on uneasy legs. Like a defendant going to trial, I march to Laude's quarters. Floating my fist above her door, I hesitate, it must be two am. I knock anyways. Seconds later, Laude whips open the door, vividly alert, gripping a lethal spear like a staff in her pale fist, and looking around the dark hall as if I was being chased. I would laugh at her middle-of-the-night battle-readiness if I weren't so wired myself. Her gaze drops to mine, "What's wrong?"

My forehead crumples above my puffy eyes. Agony twists in my ribcage. "I told Poi about the Queen's plans, and now he's somehow labeled me complicit. He left me in a rage."

She backs up, I walk in, she shuts the door.

We stand unceremoniously, speaking near the door. Her tight voice holds all the urgency I feel, "What did you tell him?"

"I just showed him the letter about the documentary. I didn't mention you or Hades."

She inhales and holds her breath, then nods. "Thank you."

She gestures for me to follow her. To the right, her lounge is arranged behind their door- a collection of large bean bag-like chairs of tightly woven seaweed. I plop down, sucked in by the stretching, foamy mass. From this vantage point, I can see that beyond her bed, most of her space is set up to practice with her weapons. The lines drawn on her floor are similar to those in the Armory.

The lounge corner is decorated with close-ups of massive calla lilies, signed in all caps by her partner Petrika. They soften the harsh metallic vibe from all the weaponry hanging on the walls everywhere else.

Laude brings me a conch shell filled with freshwater. I cradle it, then set it on the floor, not really wanting to drink. "Thanks."

Like a spider pedaling a bicycle, she sits awkwardly with her spindly limbs, as if unaccustomed to bean bag chairs. Her voice strikes order into the confusion, "So what's going on."

My mind spins like a coin trying to find the right side for gravity to pull. Everything feels wrong. This whole thing was to avoid hurting him. But that's been the only result. I gaze at Laude's red eyes miserably, "He just looked at me—like it was all my fault. Like he hated me."

Laude narrows her eyes, diamond-shaped face pointed with concern, "He doesn't hate you."

Torment rips at me like shotgun shards. "He might. That letter hurt him so bad. And I said I was going to carry out her wishes. He'll never trust me again."

She purses her lips, then shifts her weight, the woven seat rustling like wicker as she faces me head-on. She leans over, elbows on knees, voice grave, "This is big news for him. It's going to take him a while."

I remember what he asked me after we first kissed: Can you, as well, respect my mind despite the fact that my opinions are different from yours? The conversation flipped my whole world- I thought he was being too controlling for us to be together, but it was me. To answer, I told him I would try to respect his opinions, but I haven't. I feel like I've broken a treaty. I have- I've broken his trust. Fear percolates through my veins like a noxious gas. Reality snaps her jaws down on me, and I gasp, "I think he just broke up with me…"

My heart swindles all my energy, beating hard, and I can't breathe again.

She begins to shake her head, "I don't think—"

A knock resounds through her apartment. I freeze. She opens the door, and I hear his voice greet her. The lounge is blocked behind the door- Laude's holding the doorknob, facing him, and Poi is standing in the threshold, out of my eyesight.

Poi's voice yanks violently at my heart. "I'm leaving."

A bucket of icy adrenaline splashes over me. I tense, like a sprinter ready for the gun.

He speaks briskly, "I need you to be in charge while I'm gone."

"For how long?" Laude asks firmly.

"I don't know." His deep voice is tight.

Panic spins around me like a spider's fly. What does this mean? He's not even going to talk to me about it? Maybe he's so mad that we really are done. The thought constricts the air from my lungs. This is too far. We aren't breaking up over this. Fear casting me forward, I silently stride to the door.

He flinches back when he sees me.

Anger wraps my heart in prickly thorns. "You're just going to leave without saying goodbye?"

His lips tighten, and his expression becomes stony.

The injustice of it bursts out of me like angry rockets firing, "I came clean! Sure, I seriously considered carrying out your Queen's plans, and that was wrong, but I didn't actually do anything! I know you're upset, and I get that. But don't blame me for your Queen's actions. I am *not* your Queen."

The handsome features of his face pinch, contorting with pain. His eyes fire accusations again. He rips his eyes away from me like I'm some sort of car wreck, and he begins striding down the darkened hall.

I pause, unsure. Desperate, I switch tactics. I race after him, calling, "Poi, please—just wait."

Laude's door shuts as I grasp his stiff arm. He turns partially, clearly unwilling to fully face me. His dark eyes are stony as he looks down at me, and away. He's frozen, waiting for me to speak, to be released from me.

Panic, like a wildcat, crawls up my sternum, scratching and shredding my throat, "Please, Poi, don't leave—this doesn't make any sense! I was trying to be honest with you! Why are you this mad at me?"

He stares down past his high cheekbones, jaw lifted, face angled away, the stony face of an angel devoid of all warmth.

Tears start spilling down my face, and he doesn't stop them.

"Why are you leaving?" I demand.

"Because I cannot stand to be here." He won't even look at me.

My mouth drops, and suddenly I can't catch air in my lungs. His words are an iron cannon ball that's ripped a jagged hole through my core.

He walks away.

Shuddering disbelief gives way to waves of agony, threatening to suffocate me. My knees slam against the hard ground. Face in hands, my head falls. A cry rips from my lungs. Hiccupping, violent cries gush through me like vomit.

Poi is gone... My lungs struggle to grip air. I try breathing harder, but my lungs have shriveled to deflated balloons. I quake as my fingernails scratch the stone beneath me, clawing for some release from this loss.

I fumble for oxygen as a thought descends on me: The Queen loved Poi too—she created her whole treacherous plan with the same final goal: saving him. I'm just like her. The truth washes against me, overtaking me. He's done with both of us. Black splotches crowd my vision.

Fingers curl into my sides. "Stella, you have to breathe," Laude demands, lifting my stomach so I'm balancing on all fours.

I wheeze wildly, "No— I need— to be— alone—"

"No. You need to breathe." She demands. Her hand is on my belly, "Breathe into my hand Stella."

I cough through the tears, "I can't—"

But eventually, I do breathe. And the tears stop. And then there's just nothing. Poi is gone.

# CHAPTER 31

STELLA

I sit on Kiara's bed, and move my pawn forward two. Laude skips her black knight over my pawn and takes my white bishop. She's been patient company. My whole world has been ripped apart, because Poi was the center. It's like navigating without gravity.

Now I sleep here. I can't go back to the island yet. It's imprinted with too many memories- a reality that I don't fit into any more. Kiara's lent me her room. She's been spending all her time with the octopus-decorated, sandy-haired Levi.

Her room is tidy and well decorated. She has old sea glass bottles which sit on the ledge below her wobbling, arch window, and reflect light in the day. A dirigible of an antique sewing machine is tucked between a pair of handsome oak wardrobes. Her massive wooden xylophone, steel drums, and several other percussive instruments are lined along the farthest corner, near her tall wardrobe. I've already been politely told not to touch them. Although Kiara did offer to give me a lesson at some point in the indefinite future.

Despite the cleanliness of the room, dampness clings to the walls, and circulates in my lungs. I have been trying to convince myself that it's logical that Poi and I will be okay. He's just temporarily mad. I admitted to what I was planning, and didn't actually go through with it- he could come back. This is the hundredth time I've had to tell myself this within the last hour of five whole days without him.

There's a knock on the door, and my nerves spasm with hope.

Hades walks in. I sit frozen on the bed, my fingers wrapped around a rook. I stare at him in shock. I haven't seen him either.

He purses his lips and crosses the room. Folding his arms, he evaluates the chess board. He snaps his fingers, leans forward, and takes out Laude's queen with my knight.

She cries out, "How could I miss that?"

Hades grins winningly, sets her Queen beside the three pawns I managed to take, before bowing to me, "You're welcome…"

I find my mouth stretching outwards in a strange sham of a smile, "Pretty good." I replace the rook on its black square.

He leans against the sturdy bedside table. "Your move Laude."

She squints at the board, fingers hovering over her bishop with a clear path to my rook, but within striking range of my queen.

"No…" Hades leans in over her shoulder, "Look at your pawns…"

Her eyes light up. "Ah!"

She slides her pawn diagonally and takes my knight, safe from retribution.

"Hey—" I whine up at Hades, "I thought you were on my side—"

He shrugs his shoulders lazily. "No. I just wanted to show you both that you suck at chess."

I chuckle and look back at the board. "Success."

He stays a little while, increasing the speed of the game. And it's just normal again. No, it's different than normal. Things have cooled between us. He must have taken me seriously when I said I was in love with Poi. Too bad that doesn't seem to matter.

We don't talk about Poi, because no one has seen him. No one has news. But it doesn't take my mind off him. It just exaggerates his absence. I really didn't think he would be gone this long.

It's been more than two weeks, and I still haven't seen Poi. What we had has died, but was never given a proper burial. I no longer half-expect to see him stroll into the dining hall. Our mornings, days, and brief evenings are gone. He hasn't even returned for the council meetings. He's missing entirely. It feels like he's died.

I have given up on the Reveal. It hurts just to think about the subject. I have accepted the impending reality that everyone else -both Mer and Humans- seem to have accepted long ago: The world will likely implode due to the environmental atrocities humans commit, all life will die, and Poi will become a roaming ghost. There is no stopping it.

I have returned to the cottage on the sea. I can't handle being around people because I can't be normal. I can't even talk. The salty air fills my lungs as I gaze out at the stone cottage. It feels haunted with love and when things were right. The open door and empty windows stare at me like the gaping orifices of a skull. Wetness slowly seeps down my cheeks. I can't go in.

Numbly, I stumble over the rocks to find a place I haven't sat before. I face North, because there have been too many sunrises and sunsets here with Poi. The sea churns dangerously, pronouncing the world as an unforgivingly dangerous place. Waves slap the rocks violently, repetitively. Thick clouds swarm around the cold sun, casting more shadows than light on the endless slate sea. It is still beautiful, even in its tremendous monotony. As I sit, it feels like the eternal, wide-open plane of sea and sky swallows me whole.

## POI

My hiking shoes grind into the grit of hot sands. The landscape is scattered with leaf-like prickly pear and picturesque saguaros with their arms reaching toward the pale blue sky. With the bold clear sunlight, and barren red earth, it seems secrets cannot hide here.

Everything I knew before was wrong. How can you love when truth is absent? I don't know anything anymore. Her love is what I knew- it was my compass forward.

I step over coyote scat as the trail leads up a moderate hillside. Hiking is strange- I feel like I should be able to just glide up to the top. If this were underwater, this would be far faster to mount. But I want my hot feet to pound the dusty earth.

Sweating despite the dry air, I swig water from my canteen. My chest heaves with the strange altitude. In this last month, my heart has started to beat like a human's. Years ticking off my long life. It doesn't matter so much anymore.

I stare out at the wide-open earth, a large golden expanse bowing upwards with distant red-clay mountains. It's strange to think this land is on the same planet as the dark blue sea I call home. I look out for hundreds of miles through the clear atmosphere, reveling in the enormity. But my heart can't beat as free as the sky here.

No matter the landscape, I cannot forget her. And I cannot stop loving her.

## STELLA

It's been another two weeks. The memory of Poi becomes a shadow I cling to. But things have lost their meaning. I breathe like I'm lying at the ocean's floor.

I've found a forgotten, narrow lounge where a length of wall gives way to window, exposing the deep aqua sea. I have spent days here. I sit still in a wide, knit hammock seat. Glancing out the shimmering window, I don't feel a need to get out and do anything. I just sit here and let my heart batter strange and confused against my ribcage.

I stare out for what seems an age, watching occasional schools of flitting fish, coasting sting rays, and even a serenely floating plastic bag. The green-blue of the sea deepens as the light drains from the sky above.

"Hiding from me?" Poi's voice electrocutes the air. My heart blares like an alarm. My bones singe as if burnt by lightning.

Ten feet away, he's leaning against the stone wall, in shadows, staring at me.

My heart constricts. It's been so long, I don't know what to say to him. I can't even speak.

His voice, just as I expect it to be, is distant and cold, "I've been ignoring you, and I should have explained."

Here it is. The belated burial. A deep hole has already been dug through my core. I feel the sides aching. I try to keep breathing as I look at him.

His arms are crossed against the broad, cloaked chest that I used to cuddle up to. That gorgeous, stony face used to be open.

He speaks from the shadows, voice even: "The news you gave me- through the Queen's letter- shook the bedrock of my reality. I never knew she had the intention of Revealing without me, and behind my back."

I sit still, waiting for the wave.

His voice is detached, "I thought we trusted each other, I thought we were a team, but I was wrong." He stares at me from beneath his shadowy brows for a long time, as if the words would take an eon to reach me. I can't tell if he's talking about me, or his Queen.

Because I considered her plan, maybe I'm just as bad as the Queen. But I didn't go through with it. I chose honesty. I don't deserve all this blame. I find my voice, and I can barely keep it even, "I'm not her."

He looks away, and leans against the wall quietly, propped with one foot against it, knee jutting out.

I guess I haven't fully given up on him, because I'm gripped with the hopeless need to get him back. "I told you about all my plans, and I stopped trying." My voice cracks, "I am not going to do it without you. I don't want to hurt you."

He tilts his head just enough to look at me, and his whisper carries, "I know."

I'm silent. I don't know how else to convince him, and it's clear he's here to end things. I can't handle the dragging seconds any longer. It's like slowly getting impaled by a knife. I just want it to be quick. My heart doesn't stay in my chest as I rasp, "Please- just end it quickly."

His silence is like a sledgehammer. My body is rioting as I try to hold everything in. He stares into the darkness as if he belongs to it.

I feel like I'm tumbling down a staircase that won't end.

Finally, he turns his head to face me again, and his expression betrays churning emotions. He speaks haltingly, "I'm mad at you. But I'm not leaving you."

The words spin and spin in my mind and I can't seem to catch them. "What?" I blink through my tears, incredibly confused. "But you already have."

"No." He stares at me plainly, the distance between us gapes like a hole. "I've just been angry."

For some reason, this makes me cry more. I pull up my knees, and hiding my face, fall apart.

The hammock seat jolts me up as he sits beside me. I look up at him, through the blur, with shock. After all these weeks of feeling like he was dead, he's right here. His same insanely beautiful visage of dark features and deep amber eyes, his same slow-beating heart, as before everything went wrong.

I feel inside-out and raw. I whimper, "If you're so mad at me, why aren't you breaking up with me?"

His breath is slow, and he takes his time to speak, "Because I… have faith in us. I can't forget you, cuddlefish. I know… we have differing opinions for what's best in the world. When you get an idea, you are full steam ahead, nothing's stopping you. Sometimes when we have such strong visions, we're blind to the casualties."

It takes me a few seconds to digest his forgiving words. Hesitantly, my heart flickers with hope. He hasn't broken his gaze. Electricity seems to kindle, and hover, in the air between us. My mind is a re-run of his words. Certain ones in particular seem worthy of repeating, "You have faith in us?"

"Yes..." He remains still, like a stray cat just out of reach that doesn't want to be touched.

"I am sorry I even thought about doing it without you. I just couldn't handle the idea of you being a dead ghost, and the world becoming a lifeless, noxious nothing."

"I know."

He's still incredibly guarded. His eyes are downcast, dark brows are pulled together in pain. The edges of his carved, tightly set lips are minutely downturned. My chest aches for him. "I'm sorry she hurt you so badly."

Not meeting my gaze, he shrugs his big shoulders weakly.

"You can talk to me," I whisper.

His brows are peaked, and his eyes roam across the floor, the hammock, but can't seem to look at me. They rest on the intricate weave of the backrest. His voice is a rumbling whisper, "I had trusted her, with all of my heart."

Like the wind collects leaves, my heart pulls with the grief of his. "I'm so sorry," I whisper, hating to see him hurt like this.

He shrugs again, still not making eye contact. A tear threatens below his dark lashes, spills over, and runs down his cheek.

Tentatively, I float my hand out and rub his rounded shoulder. I feel the spark of him beneath my palm, but he doesn't pull away. Gruffly, I pull my arm around his shoulders, and he lets me pull his back down and against my chest. He's crooked and large against my small frame, but I hold him tightly, my arms around his broad shoulders and warm chest, as he faces the dark sea, shaking with silent sobs.

# CHAPTER 32

STELLA

Very slowly, awkwardly, we resume the old patterns of breakfasts by the sea with morning chats, my support during the day, and his distant goodnight pecks on the forehead. It's like he's a stray cat I've tried to adopt, and is learning to trust me again. It's frustrating that he has apparently looped my guilt in with the Queen's, but I also can't imagine the hurting he is going through. I'm just relieved he was strong enough to be vulnerable and work through it with me. Every time I think I have an all-encompassing view of how amazing he is, I just have to expand it out more. And I literally cannot contain how much I love him. I am bursting to tell him, but petrified.

After dinner, instead of leading me back to Kiara's room, we walk towards the Ridge's main entrance. Poi had been upbeat all dinner, and now there is an urgency in his voice, "There's something I want you to see." His eyes burn with more excitement than I've seen in a month.

I have to laugh at his sudden, childlike enthusiasm, "What?"

He raises an eyebrow with a tauntingly playful expression. "Surprises, are more fun."

I smirk. He has a point.

Hand in mine, he pulls me to the wobbling barrier against the darkened sea. Fear ripples through my veins. I've only been in the night sea once; the time he brought me here. The flat blackness is more daunting than the woods at night. I look at him uncertainly, "Do we have to go in?"

His eyes twinkle in his somber face, "I don't know... I have a terrible fear of the dark, and the ocean is swarming with hungry sharks."

My eyes bulge, and I shove him playfully, "Don't freak me out!"

Laughing, he pulls me in to him. He tucks a strand of my hair behind my ear, "I'll keep you safe."

But now I'm imagining sharks in the pitch-black ocean.

"Sharks don't want to hurt you. They know you're not food." His expression is so earnest, his eyes so serene, that I start to loosen up again. And it's entirely impossible to be unhappy with his arms around me.

My brain refocuses on his words. "Wait, but they're still swarming?"

He shrugs casually, "They do feed at night."

I stiffen and involuntarily grip my fingers into his thick biceps. I stare at the blackness in panic. My voice pitches, "I'm not going in that!"

He chuckles, and his voice is soothing, "Sharks navigate through electromagnetic fields. So do I. I can sense their pulse- their electrical field. I would sense them coming. It also helps, that I can see in the dark."

The idea of him being the only thing protecting me from an ocean of hungry sharks is pretty damn scary... but his warm amber eyes are reflecting ridiculous amounts of light in the shadowy hall, and begging me to be adventurous. I swallow my considerable fear, and say seriously, "Please don't let me die."

His grin stretches across his face, brightening his eyes to an impossible luminosity, "I'll see what I can do."

Fear surges through me as we break through the midnight barrier, and blackness barricades my eyes. Panic encircles me for a terrible instant of crushing, icy pressure. Swiftly, his warm lips are against mine, breathing air into my lungs. His lips linger, and I open my eyes to see the wide rings of his golden irises reflecting within darkness. He's so otherworldly, a thrill runs through me.

We swim for miles through thick, slippery blackness. It feels like a float-tank in an anxiety-producing way. There are no sounds. There is nothing to see. There is no space around me. There is only the feeling of his large hands gripping beneath my shoulders, the silken black sea pulling past, and air recirculating in my lungs. I think of night-prowling sharks, and try to keep my breathing even.

After a long time, the water drags down on us as we swim upwards. The crushing darkness relents. We near the surface, and starlight warps through translucent water. Suddenly, neon green lights are sparking around us like microscopic mines exploding. I internally gasp as my fingertips drag through the black, igniting light. I twist in Poi's hands to see him swimming above me; in a halo of tiny, dancing neon lights. Glowing, he smiles down at me. He's breathtaking.

We breach the surface, fresh air floods my lungs, and the tiny green lights curl around us. Laughing, I look up at him, as the green light twinkles and fades from his dripping hair. Our bodies are setting off swirls of liquid light which dance and dim into the black abyss.

Our eyes lock. He's even more beautiful in the starlight. Shadows carve around the lines of his face, and his eyes practically emit light. Grinning, he looks up. The stars are so clear I remember we're in space. The milky way is a mind-bendingly immense, colorful plume which raises from the dark horizon and stretches up into the sky like a magnificent flame.

His hand gently cradles the back of my neck, and his other lifts my tailbone to the surface. His voice is hushed, "Here, it's better like this…" He lays me out on the sea as lights spark around my body like celestial dust. He spreads out beside me.

Floating, I am free of gravity. The universe looms close. It's exhilarating. I am on the edge of infinity. It's utterly scary, but I have never felt so liberated in my life. We stare up into the universe for a very long time, speechless.

"Did you know," he muses, "Seals navigate by the stars."

I smirk, "Really?"

He rumbles, "If you ever get lost, find a seal. They'll bring you home."

I laugh, and collapsing from my float, splash him. It sparkles like a firework. "You're messing with me."

Of course the water doesn't faze him. He stares straight up into the abyss, his voice distant "I'm serious. They have maps of the skies in their souls."

I return to my float. My eyes scour the scattered celestial light, pausing on the brightest stars, wondering how a seal could use this infinity as a map. The faint memory of the puppy-eyed, captive seal returns to me like a whimper. In another life, I imagine her roaming the open sea, gazing across the galaxies to find her way home. This reality is so much more divinely beautiful than I ever let myself imagine. My heart swells to fill the infinity before me, and I am gone, and I am home.

The silence is full with our heart's study.

A faint light glows in the air like moonlight, but the moon has already set. Dropping from my float, I tread water, mouth gaping. Only this could make me break my gaze at the stars. A haze of white is burning across the sea all the way to the surrounding horizons. Around us, the dark ocean is transforming into fine silver light.

Eyes huge, I slowly turn my head to Poi, my voice hushed, "What's… happening…?"

His dark visage is ghostly in the white light. He grins wide. His eyes twinkle, voice velvet, "This, is the surprise. It's bioluminescence."

"But it's… everywhere…" I whisper in reverence.

I spin- every direction burns white. The expansive sea is teeming and twinkling with mysterious life, shining with more intensity than magnified moonlight. I have never seen such beauty.

Awed, I know I could never forget this moment, even in another lifetime.

He watches with the reverence of a grandmother holding a grandchild. "The sailors used to call it; "The Milky Seas." The last one was probably fifty years ago."

I raise my arms, which are ghostly with light, and look at him; smirking and doing the same. Silhouetted with light, I feel made of magic.

And then he kisses me. A world explodes between us as his lips meld and trace mine. Heart like a meteorite, I melt into him. His touch skitters fire throughout my racing blood. His long fingers thread beneath my braid, he expands my lungs with a gust of air, and drags me under.

We drop into the lightning seas. We twist with desperation, insatiably trying to touch every part of the other. Fireworks explode in my chest. I've missed this closeness with him.

His muscular arms hold me close to his rippled body, and suddenly, he shifts. With a shock, I feel his heavy, undulating tail against my legs. My mind riots against the surreal sensation of his scales against me, while his velvet lips pursue mine. Experimentally, my hands slip across the strange, rough leather of his hips. He sways with a force that stirs the sea round me like winds. I trail up to trace the indentations and swells of his muscular form, lightly grazing along the sides of his ribcage, embedded with feathery gills. Gripping his bulky shoulders, my tongue yields to his.

He swings me into his arms, and twirls me around him, surrounding us in a whirlpool of green fireflies. He slows to a pause like the end of a waltz. The lights flicker around us like dying fireworks. His incandescent, probing gaze holds mine. He reaches his empty hand into the open sea, and trailing light, he writes, "I love you."

My heart swells through my ribcage. Lightning rattles my bones. He has stopped breathing. His eyes are tight, waiting.

I drag my hand out to where his letters have turned to darkness. In messy cursive, I scrawl, "I loved you first."

His chuckle shakes through my chest. I meet his gaze. He's beaming in a way that makes me melt and blaze at once. He shakes his head and raises an eyebrow, as if to say, "No way."

I wind my fingers in his locks and pull his head towards mine. Green embers burn around us as we are lost in each other. We tumble through darkness, gripping each other, never close enough.

Water molds around me and gives way to air. My lungs swell with fresh briny oxygen, and the chill of the sea becomes invigorating. As we scrabble over the rough rocks, dripping water, he's smiling at me with his eyes. It's a sexy, loving, knowing smile that makes my legs wobble and heart jitter.

He takes my hand firmly in his, and I follow his long stride up to the cottage. He shuts the door and locks it. My stomach flips. In the dim, pre-dawn hint of light, the shadow of him walks to me.

He shudders. He lifts his face from my neck. His wavy black hair disheveled, lips swollen, and his cheeks rosy perked up with a grin. His gaze inspects mine with only room to breathe between us. His dilated amber eyes are reflecting the light of a coming dawn. He rumbles, "Do you love me?"

My heart flutters, my throat constricts, and my eyes water, "I really do."

My heart beats hard as his reflective eyes search mine fervently. Then his face softens, his dark brows peak sweetly, and his eyes become watery. There's so much joy on his face that I feel it reflected in me. He cups my head in both hands, kneeling over me with muscles flexing, as if I were the most precious thing on earth. His amber eyes alight, his voice is thick with emotion, "I love you."

Heart swelling wildly with hearing the spoken words, tears brim as my lips stretch wide. He takes my mouth with his again, kissing me sweetly, wearing away all doubt, all worries, and like a fresh spring rain, leaving only promise.

And finally, we get as close as possible.

Smiling, I'm catching my breath, and the air makes me high. Every atom in my nebulous form is singing. He pulls me against him in a languorous embrace. I reach my mouth to his, and press my lips against his softly. He pulls me against his body tighter, molding to me.

Separating my lips from his is difficult, because he keeps holding me to him. Smirking, I whisper up at him, "You looove me."

He grins back at me. "I do." And his expression is totally open, like he's not hiding anything anymore.

# CHAPTER 33

STELLA

I feel him against me before I open my eyes. His stomach contours warmly around my back. He fits so naturally around me. He loves me. Poi, loves all of me. It's utterly, flabbergastingly miraculous. I'm swirling in it. I didn't ever expect my life to get so good.

I blink my eyes open to the brightness of the sun bouncing off open seas and through the cottage windows. The cottage has come to feel like home, and I run my eyes over the familiar lines of the window frame. I can't tell if Poi's still asleep, so I roll around gently to face him. He's up on one elbow, his thick shoulders and muscular chest bare, his sun-kissed skin remarkably smooth. His dark eyes hold tension and worry.

Sleepily, I try to work out what could be wrong. I come up empty-handed. Everything in the world feels exactly, deliciously, right. Last night was the most glorious of my life- not only was it mind-blowingly beautiful, insanely romantic, and ridiculously orgasmic- but Poi loves me.

His stare is unnerving. He seems too still. Purple shadows linger around his dark gold eyes. Suddenly, I wonder if he's slept at all.

"How do you feel?" He says it slowly, but his eyes burn with the question.

I sigh happily, impulsively smiling, "Heavenly." I lean towards him, and wind my hand behind his neck. He stiffens further.

I freeze, then recoil. He's not really breathing.

His eyes are so intense that his red veins are showing. His voice is strained, "You don't feel… strange? You feel completely… the same?"

I quickly take toll, and aside from feeling totally sore muscles from our romp in the water and in the bed, I'm fine. "Yeah, I'm goood." I stretch out the word, because "good" doesn't do us justice.

His eyes catch between mine with a fierce urgency. "No…" His voice cracks.

"Hey, what's wrong?" I want to reach out and stroke him, but I get the feeling he might bite me.

He sits up quickly, and breath has come back to him, fast and hard. His bulky shoulders are shaking, and he seems like he can't speak. His chest is raising with fast, shallow breaths he can't seem to control.

I reach a hand out to his shoulder, but he's already out of the bed, his back flexing as he roughly pulls the cloak over himself.

"Wait, why are you leaving?" Fear rumbles through me like thunder on the horizon.

He's buttoning his shorts with fumbling hands, his voice shaking, "I shouldn't have done that. I shouldn't have done that." I realize he's talking to himself, totally ignoring me. "I shouldn't have done that. FUCK!!" He belligerently hollers, slamming the wall with his forearm.

I leap out of the bed, and step in front of him to catch his eye. "What's going on with you?"

I try to reach out to hold his shoulders, but anger contorts his face, and he pulls away before I can touch him. He swears in Merglossa, voice tremulous.

I've never seen him act this way before, and I am completely flummoxed at his change from pronouncing his love to me. "What the hell is happening? Last night you said you loved me, and now you regret it?"

He's striding, almost running, towards the door, not looking back. "Don't follow me." He demands roughly.

He leaps over the rocks, and I stand in the silent room, stunned and watching. My mind grapples to catch up with the moment as an icy fear licks up my ankles, seethes in my blood, and sews seeds in my thudding heart.

POI

"NO!" I release from my whole chest. It echoes around the cavern and fills my ears, and I have to shout it again. And again.

Heart beating chaotically, I bleed my fists against the rock walls, echoing my torments until they become meaningless.

She is gone, really gone. Gone forever.

Despite my efforts, this is my fault. The prophesy warned of "Fate's perilous game" of "a lover's vigil," and I failed.

I rake my mind for the words: "Heart memory rekindled, unity forged, guise shattered" equals "power resurrected." In short: love found and consummated, returns her memory and immortality. While "consummation before love" "decimates Hope, power forever lost."

Cursing, I slam my worn palm against the unforgiving rock wall. If I had been able to discern her lust from love, I could have waited, and she would have come back. I caved. She didn't truly love me. She's gone forever. There is nothing to be done. She won't come back.

Hating Fate, and wishing to rip my lungs out, I scream. I scream with every molecule of my being.

Weight crushes against me from all sides.

Slumping against the wall, holding my wet face in my hands, I let the emotions rack through me. Until there is nothing left of me.

## STELLA

The thunderstorm on the horizon has rolled in, and static lightning forks angrily in the thick atmosphere. I watch through the window, from my bed, alone with my thoughts. I can't let myself keep asking questions, keep looking for him, so I'm at the cottage, waiting again.

My eyes stare out of my head at the threatening, low-hanging clouds, and I can't seem to blink.

He's nowhere. I try to understand logically. I can't. The last time he ignored me, was because he was mad. This time he told me he loved me, then clearly regretted it. Impossibly, this reaction is worse than before. And I have no idea what I did.

But the panic doesn't care. My heart is a hummingbird's wings that won't rest. My brain feels like it might be cracking. I mechanically replay the events: Hovering between the silken worlds of sea and sky, his glowing words, his probing eyes, his laughter when I told him I loved him first. Giving in to each other, feeling his love all around me. Then, abruptly, his shuddering breaths, his fist against the wall, his lamentations of regret, his demand that I not follow.

Distant thunder growls threateningly, jarring my thoughts. The air is flammable. The sky is black. Lightning waits for its next strike.

I fumble for meaning in the darkness. How can I fix things without knowing what to apologize for? Without him here? He has to let me apologize. I cannot consider any other outcome.

Lightning flashes and the world is white. Immediately, thunder cracks my skull and rattles my bed.

## POI

I haven't been able to think. I've just been in a daze, diving through darkness, not really sure where I am. But vaguely, I realize I must be hurting her. This is the thought that pulls me back. I don't ever want to hurt her. The thought of it makes my heart ache deeper, which I didn't think was possible.

My insides are scalded with the recognition that her full self is lost forever. The water pulls against my raw skin and scales, demanding me to not let go.

I am in love with this strange human version of her. But humans die.

The blackness drags on as the pressure decreases. I hadn't realized just how deep I had swum.

I will drag myself through this, for her. She's not gone yet. I can love her for her human life. Maybe another 75 years, if I'm lucky. The rest of eternity without her.

The darkness is crushing.

## STELLA

I don't know how long he has been gone for. He is gone. The thought echoes and scrapes around my marrowless bones.

I don't really remember the walk here, I just remember getting really cold when I left the blankets. Kiara pulled me up from her abandoned bed this morning, saying "C'mon. You need sunshine."

It's low tide. We are far along the southern end of the Ridge. A single staircase and rock outcropping led to this white sand beach. It's surrounded by gentle, low-tide seas. A nearly invisible, temporal island. I don't register any surprise at this.

The sun is shining but won't soak into my skin. It must be beautiful here. The sand is very fine. The ocean is a blue color. We walk along where calm tide meets grit.

I have accepted that this will succumb to the ocean again, just as humanity and all life will pass. Destruction, just as creation, is inevitable. Relationships pass. People pass. Things end. It's okay. It's normal. I don't have any feelings about it. Why would I get attached, when it's all going away?

One feeling is tapping lightly at me like the tepid water around my ankles: I have lost something. I shiver against the cutting breeze. It slips around me, and the ineffable something is gone again.

Kiara is silent as she tugs my elbow, and leads me along the flat beach. She drops to pick up things. Maybe shells.

Maybe she's acting like I've lost something, too. Maybe she knows something has gone terribly wrong. It reminds me of when my uncle died. I didn't know him well, but my grandmother loved him very much. I didn't understand my grandmother's grief, but I knew I should just be with her.

# CHAPTER 34

STELLA

A cacophony of Merglossa resounds off the arching walls of the dining hall. A dense line crowds before the shells of piping hot seafood. I wait.

When it's my turn, I decide to be adventurous. I have had seaweed toast for two weeks straight now. Baked, opaque, jellyfish holds up to its namesake, wobbling as I carry it to the table with Laude, Kiara, and Levi. I sit.

It's like eating undercooked gristle from a pork chop, without the bacon flavor. But I don't mind. It suits me.

I don't really listen to them talk, and I don't think they expect me to. Time passes. Light fades from above, telling me it's time to sleep and begin the cycle again. Predictability, even when harsh, is a comfort. It's good to just know what will be.

I make my way out of the hall through teeming, colorful Mer.

Poi walks into the hall and locks eyes with me.

I thought it might be hibernating, but sickeningly, my heart slides to my feet. I realized I've stopped.

He strides over to me, through the merry crowd. His black silken cloak sways around his bulky shoulders and tall form as he slips a small leather volume into its inner pocket. He looks paler than usual. He stops before me, and the din of the hall seems to hush. He meaningfully tilts his head back towards the hall's gilt entrance. I follow.

In the passageway, he turns. I faintly realize we're in the same place where he pressed me against the wall, months ago. He's standing three feet away. My heart beats hollowly.

His face is shadowy and drawn. His eyes scan my face. "You don't look, normal…"

His voice grates against my skin. I feel fine. I shrug.

His palm drags through his unkempt hair, and his fingers rub at the purple around his eyes. His voice is thin, "I want to apologize." His eyes are calm, but not quite alive. His body seems to be sagging with exhaustion. "I'm sorry I left you abruptly, and without explanation, again."

I haven't directly thought about that moment, for a while. The memory tugs at me weakly. I look at him, and then remember he's waiting for a response. "That's okay." My voice sounds distant, I realize. I haven't used it very much.

His eyes squint at me, voice suddenly rough, "Whoah. You're really not okay…" He steps closer, just a foot.

For some reason, I back up. It was an impulse.

His eyes widen.

"Sorry," I mumble, feeling confused.

His eyes flick quickly between mine, but I can't keep up. I look at his chest. His white shirt is wrinkled.

He heaves an expulsive sigh, "I'm an idiot."

I look at him, not really having an opinion on that label.

He tenses, and his voice becomes suddenly animated, "No. Not this too. I won't lose you."

I watch him come towards me, but I don't feel frozen. I don't really feel.

He gets closer, and I blink a lot. His face just holds so many memories. Memories that are distant and different from what we will be now.

His palms are warm at my shoulders. He towers over me, and smelling him stirs something in me. His dark amber eyes are gazing into mine with intensity. I want to tell him I'm fine, but I don't think he would care. I don't really know why he's talking to me. He's actually made it really clear we're over. A flicker of anger burns in my chest, then dies out. It doesn't matter. Ends are inevitable.

He leans down, and face is really close to mine. My brow knits and I drop my face down, mumbling in confusion, "What are you doing? I thought we were over."

His voice is furious, "We are not over."

His fingertips tug my chin upwards, so he can fix me with his unnerving glare. His voice urgently ardent, "I love you."

I blink hard as his words attempt to congeal in my brain. I squint up at his shadowy face filled with runaway stubble. My voice sounds weak, "But you left—"

He sucks in a breath like he's hiking a mountain. His words gush out roughly, "Fate has not been my friend. I was running from Fate, more than I was running from you."

My mind spins with the concept I have never been able to pin down. I gaze up at him, "What does that mean?"

Suddenly, his eyes are nearly luminous again, "It means I'm sorry… and I promise," He squeezes my shoulders, "…that I'll never leave you again."

I am afraid to contemplate these words. I am afraid to drop what I have built to keep me sane. I look up at him through the invisible walls, "I can't go through this. I can't do this."

His hands slip up to cradle my head, fingers weaving into my ponytail. He tilts my head up to him, his dark gaze scorching, voice rough, "I'm sorry I hurt you, and I'll work to make it better. But you can't live numb. It's not living. And I need you."

I knit my brows again, but my heart whispers like rustling leaves.

He collapses the distance between us, and his warm lips knead against mine until I thaw. My heart rate increases. I find my hands pulling against his back, bringing him into me. The kiss is wet with tears, and I'm not sure who they belong to.

Our lips separate, and electricity fizzes across my raw lips. His hand gently pulls my head against the concave of his chest. I want to be here, but I'm petrified now.

With cold stone beneath me, I face south, and the whole world opens up. The dome of wrinkling royal blue is calm, and low tide barely whispers a wave on this small expanse of gritty beach exposed to the barren sun.

I come back to this place because being here was the closest I've come to remembering, whatever it was I've lost. It's more than something nameless between Poi and I. It's like there is some part of me that is inaccessible and numb.

No gulls fly in the empty sky, and no bird or fish crosses between the worlds of water and air. I'm very alone here. I wonder if this is what it will feel like when the oceans have been suffocated, when life has fallen. The sun will still shine, gravity will still hold the seas. It will feel like this.

At this rate, I shouldn't worry so much about being human. Poi might not live much longer than me. But he will still exist here. Alone in this beautiful, primordial nothing, waiting for eons of evolution, for life to take some near-intelligent form again.

I wonder how long this exposed bar will last, and how long I have until I have to return to the Ridge. Thin, translucent waters creep and crisscross into the sand. Maybe thirty minutes.

Poi emerges from beneath the hidden stairwell, his tall form passing just a foot below my dangling feet. He walks out along the shrinking expanse of sand, looks around, sighs, and pulls his long fingers through his black locks.

When he turns, he sees me, and stops. His smile is easy, and heart-melting. He calls, "Good hideout."

I mirror his smile.

He grabs my toes, and looks up into my face with his caramel-flecked eyes, "I have a bone to pick with you…"

I raise an eyebrow, "Oh yeah?"

He climbs up and sits beside me, wrapping his arm around my back, and protecting me from the lifting wind. He leans down and rests his forehead against mine, murmuring, "What makes you think humans would care enough to fix what they've done to the Earth?"

My eyes go wide. A wind whips through my veins. He's thinking about a Reveal. I feel that spot deep in my chest where I know there's truth. I breathe in the briny air and feel more alive.

I grasp his stubble-lined jaw, and fix him with a penetrating gaze, "Because we are the Earth. We are made from it, and our bodies return to it. Without the earth, we are nothing. Humans just need a reminder."

His dark burning gaze holds mine. "You really think, letting them know about the existence of the Mer, would be a sufficient reminder?"

My heart leaps, electricity riots in me, and I try not to beam. He hasn't agreed yet. I try to keep my voice level, calm. "I do."

Wind tugs at my sun-bleached hair, and he tenderly gathers it behind my ear. His voice is diplomatic, "And why is that?"

"Because the Mer do live in harmony with nature. Humans just need to see it can be done, and see how beautiful it is to be connected to the Earth. Materialism and willful ignorance are empty, they just need to be reminded of that."

He takes a deep breath, not breaking our gaze. His voice is deep and tremulous, "This is a big risk, Stella."

Ohmygodohmygodohmygod!!!! I am running up and down inside, doing cartwheels and jumping-jacks and high-fiving myself while doing a victory dance. HUZZAH!! But, with a straight face, and very casually, I state, "I know."

He takes a deep breath and expands his chest as he looks out at the empty sea. "Damnit. Fine." He looks into my eyes with the most serious, challenging expression he's ever worn, "We'll do it your way."

I squeal so dolphin-like that he cringes. I hug him so hard I send us falling off the rock as he curses in Mer, and we splash into the shallow sea.

The water is icy around us as I kiss every surface of his face, "You're the best!!!" I insist repetitively.

He laughs and hoists me out of the water, "I'm glad you're back."

I stare down, grabbing his biceps for support, and dripping seawater on him, "If only I knew it would only take a little pouting to convince you. I would have done it ages ago."

His laugh is deep and rumbles out of his chest as he pulls me back against him, "I've missed you." His mouth sends warm flutters to my stomach as we tumble back into the sea.

I stretch against him as the sun peeps across the horizon. I just smile happily at his handsome face. Now, everything is right. We can pull this off together. I know it.

He raises an eyebrow before opening a single dark-lashed eye. His voice is hoarse, "You staring at me?"

I grin wider. "Maaybe."

I just feel so bubbly. I can't help it.

Eyes shut, his burgundy bottom lip pouts. He wraps his steel arm around my waist and pulls me in against his expulsive heat, "Go back to sleep."

I feel jittery in his arms. I feel good about this day. I can't stay horizontal.

I nestle my head against his neck, murmuring "What do you want to do today?"

"Sleep." He croaks.

I kiss his throat. I get up on my knees and straddle his side-sleeper position. I lick his ear, and he smirks, moaning, "Nooo."

"Yes!" I pipe, and then begin tugging on his ear with my teeth.

"Oh my god what has gotten into you." He laughs and turns over, holding my hips on him.

I shrug, "I'm just happy. I have you, and the world isn't going to end! Life is good!"

He smirks, and his palms rub my thighs, "I'm glad you have so much confidence."

I wink at him, "I'll make up for yours."

He glares at me through lashes.

I beam at him. "So. What are we doing today?"

His expression is butterfly-making in its mischief, "Well, now that I'm awake…"

He grabs my hands in his and pulls me against his chest. I laugh, loving that he broke my spell of numbness with his open heart.

His voice is velvet against my neck, making me shiver, "I can think of several things I'd like to do with you today…"

He bites my neck, and I yelp. He chuckles. He sucks my ear, and goosebumps shiver across my skin like a breeze. I realize I'm starting to get woozy. Starting to lose my momentum, and gain a different one.

I push my hands into the pillows next to his head, hovering above him. I glare through my grin, "Troublemaker. Anyway. Are there any day trips going out today? Any scouting? I know you're not ready for the Reveal yet, but I feel like I need to do something today!"

His hands grip my head and he gently brings me to him, his mouth etching playfully against mine. A burning, deep wanting grips me, and I mold myself to him, yielding against his searching kiss.

I feel him against me, and every fiber of me wants to be against his silken skin. But it's like there is an itch in the back of my brain. I extract myself from him, my golden hair hanging around his handsome face. Breathlessly, I ask, "Is anyone going out to the reefs today? I think…. I think I want to go see reefs today."

He grins crookedly, shakes his head slowly, and groans gutturally. His voice is rough, "You are incorrigible." His fingertips softly stroke my sternum, his voice gentle, "Just stay here with me."

"I'm too hyper to stay inside. I need to get OUT!"

He laughs, his voice irresistible "I like you hyper…"

I smirk through a don't mess with me stare.

His sun-kissed chest heaves, "Oh fine… Yes… there's a troupe headed to the corals in…" He raises his head out of the pillows just enough to see the position of the sun, then falls back into the pillows, "Oh, they've probably left already…"

I whip my leg off from him, and spin towards the edge of the bed, hopping off before he can so much as blink. "We gotta hurry then!"

He sighs loudly, his voice almost weak, "I'm not going to convince you out of this, am I?"

Whipping off my night shirt, I pose sassily for him, "Nope."

He laughs and rolls out of bed.

We peel through darkness as cold pulls against our skin. A jittery hope beats in my chest. A certainty rings in me. Plans of the perfect Reveal spider out in my mind. How the right shots, the right words, the right stories, will create swells of people changing: meeting the Mer, finding the sacred in nature again. My heart beats strong against the chill of the waters. I feel electricity circuiting my veins, and I know in my heart that we can fix this.

With a sudden blinding brightness, sapphire light from Poi's palm illuminates the view for my human eyes. Little skeleton bits of white lay haphazardly in the muddy landscape. Shadowy trains of Mer tails lilt ahead. We follow the spattering of broken coral debris.

With his arm firmly holding me to his chest, Poi sways outside of the group, and I see. The entire ocean floor is not mud. Just in the tracks. Outside of the highway-sized track is a delicate, alien landscape. We're flying over a miniature forest: overgrown antler moss, bolts of orange branches, and feather-quills stretch into the mid-day night. Pale silver-gold fish scatter as we swim close.

Poi pulls us back into the track. It's a graveyard, a clear-cut forest, a dead zone. For dozens of miles, we swim above the scarred seafloor. I don't blink as we pass the shards of centuries-old life. My eyes trace the dragging shadows of ocean trawlers which ripped pain into the solitude of darkness. The decimation pokes at the fear which hides beneath my sternum: It's starting to appear that the Earth's delicate beauty is created, just to be crushed. It makes me ask: what's the point of life if there's so much suffering?

Poi steers us away from the troupe of Mer tracking humanity's destruction. We coast above the line of life and destruction. On my right, my eyes dance across the medley of stubborn life: menorahs of flowers, aqua hair-dos, and sunset-colored cacti, all tracing veins of life into a dark abyss. Around me, life innocently blooms forth into pain and suffering.

Poi firmly holds me against his chest as we coast up the side of a mountain, and further away from the muddy decimation. Aqua light filters down, and bursts of colorful life burgeon and crowd towards it. We glide over blooming mounds of fuchsia floral arrangements which flutter in the current. Colonies of fish scatter like leaves in a gust of wind. We coast over stacked plates of bubbling color, wind between bushels of tightly-packed rubbery stars, and trace along mazes of gargantuan petals. Life is so riotously joyful that it seems to be growing for the sake of it. It grows like suffering doesn't define it. And I know, it wants to survive.

A strange, alien trilling calls through the seas, and goosebumps erupt along my spine. I see no source of the sound. My blood zips around nervously. It draws nearer, sounding like a game of laser tag- frenetic shooting beams, then chugging booms. Incredible variance. I am half expecting to see a submarine light show in a moment.

A pack of dark silver seals crest the florescent ledges, uttering machine-like trilling and chirping. Their sleek forms dart around the corals, chewing on leafy orange seaweed, and chasing small fish.

Poi calls to them with eerie similarity that shakes through my ribcage.

A seal paddles her fins towards us. She has dense, dog-like fur and clever Labrador Retriever eyes. She's teething a pale-yellow starfish by the end of one lethargic leg. Poi slows. With a jerk of her jaw, she throws the starfish at me. Shocked, I don't grab it in time, and it spins slowly towards the jelly corals. She darts down and fetches it between her teeth, then swims to my face again. Her eyes are light, and her black pupils fixate on me. Nodding her head, she releases the massive spiny starfish, and before it's out of reach, I grab it. Trilling, she spins her body upside down. She circles us like an excited pup.

My smile is stretched so wide I nearly swallow seawater. I'm struck by the playful innocence of life, the lust for existence, the determination to just be. This seal might get jostled by the seasons, be weathered by pain, hunger and loss, but she's more than her suffering. She's beautiful. And I think that's the whole point: life is so incredibly beautiful in its existing. This what the Reveal is about; Life is worth saving, because life is worth living. Can humanity honor that?

Poi begins swimming again, and the seals follow us. They weave and play, and spin upside down, until they eventually grow tired, and return to feeding on the fish weaving between corals. I'm still tenderly holding the starfish, feeling like the luckiest human on earth, when another sound seems to approach from a distance like a missile through the water.

An explosive blast ricochets off the mountains and into my skull. Suddenly the world is black. My brain is pounding with excruciating pain. My ears are bleeding. I'm gripping my head trying to not fall apart, and I feel Poi drop me. I'm dropping down, down. I hear whales calling to me. They're dying, and there's nothing I can do to save them. It's my fault. My lungs have popped. Then I feel hands holding me up, and I squeeze open my eyes to see light, and the world is normal for an instant.

Poi's face is full of concern. I'm paralyzed with stabbing pain. The blackness grips me again, I'm spinning and spinning in a tumultuous whirlpool.

A sonic boom. Crushing pain. Spinning and spinning. Ringing. Silence. Nothing.

A sonic boom. Immeasurable pain. Blackness swirling and silence. Whales writhing. Lights dancing on dark water, I'm in a boat. I'm human. Hear nothing, gone.

A sonic boom. My organs implode with searing pain. Hearing nothing, I'm spinning uncontrollably in the black seas. The whales are dying. The seas are writhing in their agony. Our lungs punctured with the force of explosion, my gills bloom blood and I taste it on my tongue. Blunt force: blackness. Blinking twilight: I'm in a boat. I see my bare legs. Men's mouths mouthing. I hear nothing. I am gone.

A sonic boom shatters my brain. My insides scald fiery agony. Ricocheting ringing decrescendos into silence. The dark seas are twisting with enormous flailing bodies. The pod is dying. A tail compresses and cracks my chest. I am numb and free falling sideways. I blink my eyes open and see a lobstering boat approach. I close my eyes, weak. Limp, a man holds me in the water. With the last of my energy, I Shift. I'm in a boat. I see them talking, but close my eyes, and I am gone.

Water pulls cold against my skin, as if the very essence of the sea wishes to hold me back from spilling its secrets. But I have to. Enough catastrophe has mounted. We can't manage this anymore- we have to ask humans to get their act together Poi will eventually forgive me. I have to believe that his love for me is stronger than any other conviction he holds.

The space before me is unnervingly empty. My heartbeats reverberate and are lost to nothingness. Time drags on slowly, willing me to lose my nerve. My gills are pulling in lead. I keep swimming forward.

Just as much as Poi, I fear the humans and their predictably violent nature. Unlike Poi, I know we can't compete with the refuse of their technology. I am pursuing our only option towards survival.

Focusing on the immediate plan allows my gills to loosen and drag in water. In moments, I'll meet the two American indie film producers- and Adrian and Ned. I like them, based on the letter communications. They seem share my vision- to inspire humanity to clean up the "Ocean Wasteland" they are creating. However, I'm a little unnerved about my contribution to their film… what will they do when they realize my cute, "folkloric," and "fairytale" "art project" is actually the existence of a hidden, ancient, and pre-human species? I don't have Poi's water-controlling abilities to protect me. I am wholly relying on my gut here, because aside from shifting to any animal, and the normal Merikoi magic, my only gift is that of communication. And as I am going alone, I am going to rely on that heavily.

My lungs become impossibly heavy as I near the deep cove. Passing over the graveyard of rotting shipwrecks, I rub my gills gently, massaging out the nerves. This is the only way.

The baleful call of humpbacks feeding reaches my ears, and their tremulous croons cocoon me. This far out, the water stirs in nearly undetectable ripples. I careen forward.

Through the shadowy waters of dusk, I pause, watching their leading lady. Alone, she dives into the black. She chases a swarming cloud of silver-bellied mackerel, and her eight companions fall into trailing formation. Bubbles spout from each massive whale, knitting together in a curtain of glitter. The skittish mackerel are trapped within a column of air pockets which wobble, dance, and sparkle in the remaining light. Continuously painting air, the whales spiral downwards until the lady bellows a tremulous call. Mouths open, the whales rocket to the surface. Seconds later, they thunder back into the sea, long mouths stretched with water and fish.

I am grateful to be reminded of the Humpback's way. Grateful to witness this lesson. In order to obtain a slippery goal, there must be unity. Unity is not on my side. However, a lady needs to start things first. I have to believe that Poi and the Mer will follow.

Shifting into human form, the ocean chill cuts through my skin. I breach the surface, and wonder about human time. They have built so many constructs to fit more into their stress-filled short lives. Fortunately, these two filmmakers were not so bound by the exactitude of a clock, and were willing to meet just past sunset.

The sun flames red as it kisses the gold horizon, dousing the clouds with brilliant magenta. Gulls swarm madly above the fishing boats, calling raucously, and I remember why I don't often visit land. The cove is built up like a small city, overflowing from Portland. Halogen lights bleach out the coming darkness. Just beyond the outlet, a long, slender naval ship sulks just miles from its shipbuilding home. Its communication tower is painted pink in the sideways light.

Shivering, I swim towards the rickety old dock where Laude stashed human clothes. Squinting around at the industrial lights, I see the sign for "McGreggories." Stacked on old masonry, the tavern leans precariously over the lapping sea. I wonder if the filmmakers are already sitting inside. The glass windows reflect the orange sunset. I am always dazzled when I surface and see light unencumbered by water.

Suddenly, my human legs are walloped with screaming pain. A fifty-thousand-pound humpback is now rolling at the surface before me, roughly pushing me towards the open sea. I can't Shift without breaking my focus, and the sheer force of this whale is deadly to my frail human form. Panicking, I try swimming around its massive barnacled back, and nearly lose my breath as it's flipper forcefully cuts me off, and guides me in the direction of the harbor entrance.

What is this whale up to? It couldn't possibly know of my plans. I suddenly wonder if this not a humpback at all, but a Mer. Is it Poi? I thought I had been far more careful than this...

Grunting against its stubborn weight, I hold my arms back and try to catch my breath, thinking as it coasts me away from the shabby dock.

I decide there's no way Poi would find out. If he did, he would just Shift and not risk my life. If he wanted the silent treatment forever, he could just carry me back screaming. No other Mer would risk my life, or go against my wishes.

The whale must be a whale- trying to tell me something. It's still rallying me towards the open waters as I try to protect my fragile human stomach. With immense effort, I pull myself onto her slick back, slipping back over her into the water and away from her momentum. With enough distance, I focus and shift back into Mer form. I dive under the surface. The dark waters are crawling with humpbacks, given up on their feast, and pacing around me. They careen with oar-like flippers, their bumpy under-bites jutting into the sea.

Frustrated, I tell myself it's been a long time since whales have gathered around me like this. I remember they don't waste their attention on meaningless pursuits. I stare into their noble eyes, as they repeat: "dangerous ship, leave now..." in slow, ominous tones.

My heart beats faster. This has nothing to do with my Reveal plans. Maybe I am in real danger. I listen harder. Beyond the guttural moan of whales and gritting chug of old fishing boat motors, a resonant chinking and buzzing makes my hair rise. Quickly pulling water past myself and flicking my tail, I swim towards the surface. Past the small fishing boats, the naval ship has entered in the harbor, and hovers only fifty feet away. Towering into the dulling sky, it's an Egyptian pyramid of steel. My heart stops when I see it lowering a missile into the water. I drop my head below the surf to see a mechanical arm adjusting the two weapons, aiming the long torpedoes out towards the sea. My blood freezes in my veins. My heart kicks out of my chest. The sound will be enough to kill us all. In Merglossa, I cry out to the swarming whales, asking them to leave.

Panicking, I resurface. How long until they release the weapons test? I glance to shore, calculating the distance, and whether I would have time to make it. Staring back at the looming ship, my eyes jerk at the single figure hanging over the stern and staring in my direction. I near impulsively with a wild hope that they might be convinced to stop.

As I near, I see it's not a figure at all. The form is a mess of wires and metal boxes. Not a human being is to be seen- only a large metal grate spanning the back of the barge like an empty face. Lifeless, earless, sightless, dominating a domain that is not its own.

The bilge pump ejects a gush of water from the back of the boat, smelling of iron and reminding me of blood. I desperately cut through the water towards the distant bow, looking up for any sign of the humans manning the ship. But they all remain locked inside, unaffected by the dazzling red light of sunset.

Fear constricts around my throat, at any moment the missiles could go off, shattering the eardrums and imploding the organs of all life in the cove. My voice becomes raspy with calling out to the uncaring metal machine. The ship sits heavy in the water.

Maybe I could make it to the shore. I rip through choppy water. My tail whacks jutting rocks as I near the shore. Mournful whale song keels in my ears. My heart drops. They are waiting for me to leave the cove by water.

I turn. There is a chance we can all get out. I tear through seawater towards their chant of "danger, leave now." I reach them, and the water is thick with fear. They seem to understand from my speed that I am taking them seriously, turn quickly, and flank my sides. I guide them low as we head towards open waters, praying to the Great Ocean Spirit itself that we survive this Naval missile test.

# CHAPTER 35

STELLA

I am paralyzed with lifetimes upon lifetimes. Memories barrel in like hurricane waves, battering my mind, rushing back and forth over it, seeping in. I remember who I am. Goddess and Queen Guardian of the Sea.

My human experience is a day of eternity. I am back at the beginning again, and I am all of time. Suddenly my responsibilities weigh like the pressure of the ocean, but I am strong as the sea floor. My heart swells against my body's frozen state. This is what I was meant to do.

My heart flutters around all the resurfaced memories of Poi. All the memories I can't believe I was capable of forgetting. My mind reels with Poi. My skin fizzles with all his kisses, his every touch. My heart warms the memory of his deep vulnerable love, his childlike fun, his mind-stretching wisdom. In a timeless flash, I savor us like fine wine, sniffing and smelling and remembering again. My soul mate.

My eyes pop open. I'm in my cottage bedroom. I rip up from my bed, throwing blankets aside violently. I dart past the walls and the furniture laden with memories and the feeling of home. I want my true home. I must find him.

I squint against the bright light of day, my head heavy with the weight of memories. I fight down the rocks, the ache to see Poi overwhelming all else. I leap lithely into the hidden staircase and I throw myself down the stairwell.

My heart is consumed with a need for Poi. His face, with all the love I've always known, and could never replace.

Hitting the bottom, I break into a run. Sprinting down the hallways, I'm assaulted with all the old memories of life here. But all I care about is getting to him. When I reach his door, I swing it open and stumble in.

He looks up from his small desk, eyes with dark sleepless circles, a small leather book suspended in his palms. And I recognize it, my diary. I am touched. This is how much this man missed my mind. My eyes well up with tears as my heart thuds out of my chest. I have so much to say but it seems to be all getting caught in my throat.

He begins to stand as he asks, "Hey, what's going on?"

Tears are now streaming down my face, "You're reading my diary," I choke out.

His dark eyes widen, his whole body seems to be hit with a wave of recognition. "Oh my god," His voice cracks.

He rushes forward. He roughly hugs me to his chest. I feel his heart thudding fast and hard.

Electricity prickles and pops between us. I smell his seductive, musky skin that feels like home. He gently holds my head in his large palms, staring me down and I finally know what he was looking for.

His gorgeous face leans towards mine, making my heart pump desperately. His warm lips push against mine hungrily. Live wires are dancing across my skin as I feel his familiar body against mine. I realize I'm pulling him closer, grabbing him tightly like I'm afraid we might part again.

He unlocks his mouth from mine, and grazes his lips softly against mine, whispering, "I've missed you."

"I'm sorr—" I attempt to speak, but his lips are pressing against mine, his body engulfing me again.

After a moment, he leans his forehead against mine, his dark amber eyes just as deep as ever. "I love you." He pauses seriously. "All of you. As a human. As my Queen. As my soul mate."

My eyes are swollen with tears. "I love you too" I whisper back roughly. I grab his face in my hands. His stubble is rough against my palms, his hair soft in my fingertips. I look into his dark eyes, still stricken with pain. "I am sorry I hurt you. And risked us. I'll never do that again."

"If you had died as a human—" his eyes are tight with emotion, and he can't finish the sentence.

I know there is nothing I can say to this. My ribs rub painfully at my insides.

Then I whisper, "But we found each other again."

"Barely," he rasps, pulling my waist tighter against him. "You have no idea how much I searched for you. I thought I'd never find you." Anguish, unhidden, fills his face.

I reach through the tufts of his silky dark hair, gently massaging his scalp, and his eyes soften like a cat's. "But you did. You found me." I realize I'm still crying. "Sorry I was absolutely no fucking help."

A smile twitches at his lips, but it's quickly replaced with a frown. "I had the terrible feeling you would figure out your secret before we could consummate true love. And it turns out, after all that, I got the prophesy all wrong. You were here all along. Just deep in the depths." He strokes my cheekbone gingerly.

"Wait, what do you mean? I have no idea what happened. Did I die?"

His brow knits in concern. "No. I mean," he grasps for words, "You didn't die. But you didn't come back after we had sex. Because of the prophesy, I thought falling in love and consummating that would make you come back. When you didn't…" His voice drops to a whisper, "I thought I didn't give you enough time to fall in love with me."

I gasp with indignation. He puts his long finger against my lips.

"I thought I had ruined our chances…" His eyes gaze off, expression anguished.

I tighten around him, "But I'm back. I remember you."

His eyes shine brightly as he emanates love. "You're back."

He just holds my face in his hands, and I relish this feeling of knowing between us.

I smile with disbelief, "How is this happening right now?"

He raises his brows and shoulders, "I really must have got the prophesy wrong."

He squints, "It said: 'Heart memory rekindled, unity forged, guise shattered' means 'power resurrected.' Because of all the lover's warnings, I had interpreted that as: love found and consummated, returns your memory and immortality."

He rolls his eyes, "And 'unity forged' I just assumed it meant sex…" He smirks, "but I guess that wasn't literally stated. 'Unity forged' could mean our vision. My agreeing to the Reveal, that was certainly a unity forged… wow… I got it so wrong…" He shakes his head, but can't stop grinning at me, "Fate could have made it a little easier for us…"

"So you think… I was here… this whole time… how—" I stumble on my words, "Why did I never change- never figure it out?"

The back of his fingers brush my cheekbone before he tucks my hair behind my ear. His eyes are full of a pain that tugs at me. His voice is gentle, "I think your soul was deeply traumatized by the naval weapons test. When you reincarnated, your spirit had a block against returning to your Immortal Mer form. Your cross-lifetime memory and immortality were at the mercy of Fate's game."

Fear throbs in my chest. It's so surreal. I almost lost everything. I almost lost him. I curl my arms around his tight torso and hug him close. I nestle my head against him, feeling overwhelming love and gratitude, and guilt for putting him through this. I just say, "Thanks."

He rubs my back slowly and sighs a deep hum into my hair. We just stand for a while, and I feel totally encompassed by his warm love.

After a while I lean back and gaze up at him, asking, "So what triggered me to come back? If it wasn't sex, and it wasn't unifying our beliefs, what was it?"

He's the picture of astonishment, "Well actually, I think it was all of it. I played my cards right, we unified our beliefs, then just a few days ago, when we were out tracking the trawling-"

"Days ago!!?"

He nods, "Nearly a week."

My eyes widen with shock.

"The sound you heard- it was just oil exploration, but it definitely was the final step to 'shatter your guise' and trigger your old memories to resurface. You had to face your full self. And here you are. You broke through." His smile is like the sun over the horizon, a dazzling, brilliant, sunrise. A new day.

The reality of it all can't quite sink in. But standing here, looking at him, and really remembering, is all I need.

I wake up holding his scruffy face in the crook of my arm and against my heart. His expression is peaceful, his long lashes closed with sleep, his breaths long. I love the way his messy hair falls around his head. Happiness has settled into my skin, and I feel like I'm shining from the inside out. Waking up next to this man, for the rest of my lifetimes, is all I ever want.

Life is perfect. But a lurking shadow forces itself to the front of my mind. I dragged him through so much pain by sneaking around behind his back, recklessly dying, and then showing up and betraying him all over again. I could have saved him from all that if we had only worked out a plan together. If I could convince him of the Reveal as a human, I certainly could have convinced him as his Queen. I'm ashamed with all the pain I caused him, and he's still right here, in my arms. I feel like I'm not worthy of his love.

As if sensing my distress, Poi's arm tightens around hips, and he nuzzles closer to me, making my heart squeeze. I run my hand through his disheveled black hair, scratching his head.

His amber eye peeks up at me through dark lashes. "Morning, you." His voice scratches through his sleepy grin.

I try grinning back, stroking his hair back from his eye. "Morning."

His eyes narrow, "What's wrong?"

Damn. He misses nothing. I wish we could just be in this sunlit bubble, but I think I've already popped it.

He raises his head from me, causing a chill to wash in. He leans up on his forearm, fixing me with his serious gaze, patient. His angelic features make me woozy for him.

I grasp his warm fingertips in mine, and curl his hand against my chest, wanting to keep him, but for the first time, not certain I deserve him. My heart batters against my ribcage, not wanting to speak these words, "I betrayed you. How can you still be here with me?"

Pain constricts his brows, "Because I love you." He says it like it's simple.

My heart aches like it's been put on the wrong side of my chest. "Poi. I can barely live with the pain I caused you. How can it not change us?"

He sets me with a serious stare, and I shiver. "Because our love is bigger than anything that happens in this world, bigger than anything you or I do. It's just a constant, always there. Like the waves in seawater, or the light of the sun. I'm not going to stop loving you. I tried—it didn't work." He grins playfully.

My chest buzzes warmly. How did I get so damn lucky. "Thank you…" My words are breathy, "…for loving me so deeply, for not giving up."

He pulls me in, leaning over me, dark hair hanging around his face, his palm stroking my face. "Of course, cuddlefish. I will never give up."

My heart flutters free. "I love you."

His dark amber eyes gaze into mine with relief. He smiles sweetly, big shoulders raising as he sighs gently, "It's good to hear that again."

My heart stabs for all the years I wasn't here, telling him that. Tears stream as the words bubble out of me, "I'm sorry I hurt you. I'm sorry for leaving you alone for so long… I swear I'll never—"

Furrowing his brow, he leans down and kneads his lips fervently against mine, cradling me against him. His muscled, silken skin expels an addictive heat. He bites and drags my bottom lip, grinning. He lifts his carved lips from mine, and his dark brows peak, his amber eyes incredibly clear, "Leave all that behind. You're here with me now."

My heart opens, and again I'm awash with his greatness. I reach for him- and he comes willingly.

The lofty molecules of ultramarine atmosphere radiate light. Wisps of violet flames paint the wind in currents. The water broils and churns orchid, teal and sapphire. Waves suck, pop and squelch across the jagged black rocks.

"You know what I just can't get over?" He looks out across the expanse of technicolor sea.

"Huh?" I say, nestled in and warm against his chest.

"Even as a human, you wanted the exact same thing as when you were Mer. Not just to help the oceans, not only to help the Mer, but to ask humans to take responsibility for their destructive wake. It's really uncanny."

I smile out as the clouds catch fire, burning magenta. "I guess I have a one-track heart."

He pauses, gently squeezing his arms around me. "The freaky thing is, you wanted to do the Reveal in the exact same way. Even before you found your old letters." He sighs, "It makes me wonder… if it had been me, if I had become human, lost my memory… would I have been so strong? Would I have remembered in my soul what was important? Would I have gotten distracted by human luxuries, or would I have somehow found a way back to you, and a way back to saving the ocean?"

There's no doubt in my mind. "Certainly. You devote so much of yourself to saving the oceans, it's written in your soul."

He kisses my hair, and whispers, "Thank you." He pauses a minute as we look out at hot pink glow in the east, a still image of the crashing waves in heaven. All around us, the sky is burning down.

His voice is gravelly, "Can you believe, after all this time, you convinced me in your human state?" He chuckles into my hair.

"It was all part of the plan," I smirk, but I'm struck with the memory of my last death. The leading lady, and her determined dive through darkness.

Pensively, we look out to turquoise skies painted scarlet with abstract angel's wings. Rabid sea spray sparks and glints as the sea simmers ruby and indigo.

Poi muses in his rumbling voice, "Despite losing your memory, the knowing in your heart came through. A heart cannot only be flesh, veins and blood. It must hold a link to an eternal, wordless truth that cannot be lost."

"You told me you didn't want to change for someone— you haven't. Nothing could change this part of you. Even when you couldn't remember to hope, the truth was always written in your heart, guiding you home."

Spread Love

# ACKNOWLEDGMENTS

Thanks to my husband David, who encouraged me to actually get my work out into the world and believing in my dreams more than me at points. Thanks to Alexis, for being my writing buddy at certain stages. Thanks to Lizzy, for looking over my book with professional eyes giving me my first words of encouragement. Thanks to Heather, for her round of edits. Thanks to Ashley, for making a beautiful cover and design. Thanks to author Susan Casey, for her book *Voices in the Ocean*, which gave me insight into the consciousness of cetaceans. Thanks to my mom and my family, for being so supportive and generous. Thanks to my Aunt Marnie, who always encourages me with my projects. Thanks to my Aunt Leigh, who always told me I could be a writer. Thanks to my Grandma, for all the time at the beach house and introducing me to the ocean for the first time. Thanks again to all my family for instilling and sharing a reverence for nature. Thanks to all the awesome musicians who inspire me as I write. Thanks to the Ocean, for your eternal beauty.

Wannabe Movie Soundtrack :)

listen here:

https://open.spotify.com/playlist/5TxlMSP3T3oMnUqJm
HTF05?si=Nxbz4Dj5SumSjIdN5SY9KQ&pi=AQ4PWvtMTkSFl